T

Nothing in the Middle East danger ~~~ ~~~ ~~~ ~~lone what it seems, and much of it is potentially lethal...

The strength of Roger Radford's headline topical thriller, THE WINDS OF KEDEM, is that its race-against-time plot doubles as a manual on ancestral hatreds and vendettas reaching from old-time Arabia to modern Israel. Sedawi, a Lebanese-based extremist, plants a nuclear device beneath the Syrian desert, counting on seasonal winds to make Israel uninhabitable.

Only David Katri, fugitive Syrian Jew brought up on a kibbutz and Army veteran turned Mossad agent who can pass as an Arab, may be able to stop him.

A former Reuter man, like ex-correspondent Frederick Forsyth before him, Radford knows the people, the places and the inside stuff. So standard tension is nourished by authoritative, fascinating details and insights.

SHAUN USHER, Daily Mail

THE WINDS OF KEDEM

For my wife, Yael, *eshet chayil*. A woman of excellence.
And my children, Max, Karen and Dan

ROGER RADFORD

The Winds of Kedem

PANDORA BOOKS

A Pandora Books Paperback

THE WINDS OF KEDEM

First published by Pandora Books 1992
Reprinted 1993

© Roger Radford 1992

ISBN 0 951 8998 0 5

Printed and bound in Great Britain
by Cox & Wyman Ltd, Reading, Berkshire

ROGER RADFORD was born in London in 1946 and for most of his career has been a journalist. He spent almost ten years based in Tel Aviv working for various news organisations including the Associated Press and the Jerusalem Post. He also worked for the Press Association and Reuters. He covered the 1973 Yom Kippur War as a freelance and accompanied Israeli troops across the Suez Canal and also up the Golan Heights.

The author wishes to thank Major (res.) Aharon Shochat, Israel Air Force, Michael Gold and Artset Graphics for their assistance.

And it came to pass, when the sun did arise, that God prepared a vehement east wind; and the sun beat upon the head of Jonah, that he fainted, and wished in himself to die, and said, It is better for me to die than to live.   (JONAH 8:4)

Therefore will I bring forth a fire from the midst of thee, it shall devour thee, and I will bring you to ashes upon the earth in sight of all them that behold thee.   (EZEKIEL 28: 18)

PROLOGUE

Hamed knew not at first how long he had lain unconscious. He screwed his eyes at the fiery orb in the sky and guessed it must have been at least two hours.

The hamsah had attacked them as the sun was nearing its zenith. ''Aullad 'al k'lab,'' he spat. They were truly sons of dogs.

Still lying on his back, Hamed turned his face from the furnace in the sky. He felt the dried blood caked to his cheek and peeled it off, realising slowly that the bullet which had creased his temple had saved his life. He propped himself gingerly onto his left elbow and, as his eyes readjusted to light, surveyed the scene of carnage around him. His brother, Salim, was spreadeagled to the right as if the Nasrani himself, a bullet hole plum in his forehead. God blacken their faces, he sneered, the boy had been circumcised only two seasons ago. A curse upon all the Beni Sadr. May their mothers' milk poison them all.

To his left lay his uncle Ahmed. There were no outward signs of injury, but the glazed eyes spoke their message eloquently enough. The old man's loincloth lay askew, exposing his member. Hamed crawled the short distance between them and restored his uncle's dignity. He lowered the eyelids of the man he had loved as a father. For old uncle Ahmed had taught him the lore of the desert. He was truly blessed by God and a giant among the Bedu. The old man had instructed him on how to discern members of his own or of other tribes by the tracks of their camels. How, from droppings, it was possible to deduce where a camel had been grazing or even where it had last watered. Most of all, he recalled how they had loved to go

1

falconing together. The spirit of the hunt was in their blood and, oh, how excited they were when their falcons swooped to kill the hubara. The ungainly bustards had been no match for the cunning of both man and hawk.

Lying at right angles to his uncle lay one of the accursed Beni Sadr, the hilt of a knife protruding from his bare chest. Hamsah. Five. There had been five of them. Hamed turned and saw two other Beni Sadr lying crumpled together, their hair matted with blood. A fourth lay a short distance away, still as the desert air before the shurqiya. The fifth must have fled for he saw some camel tracks leading over a dune nearby. The bedouin sat upon his heels and contemplated his predicament. Allah, it was not good. It was at least three days' camel ride to the nearest well and the fifth Beni Sadr had ridden off with all the camels and the waterskins. His throat was already parched and he realised his position was hopeless.

Just then he heard a sound. It was only a murmur, but in the stillness of the desert it was as the thunder of the Great Rains. Hamed arose, gripping the hilt of his curved knife until his knuckles blanched. He crept stealthily in the direction of the sound, his body as taut as a cat sensing danger. The Beni Sadr were renowned for their treachery and he must take no chances.

It was the Beni Sadr lying adjacent to his uncle. God blacken his face. His eyes, glistening yellow, were pleading. But were they imploring mercy or craving an end to pain and misery? The wounded man's gaze quickly turned to that of recognition and, finally, of resignation.

Hamed's eyes, piercing as a falcon's, narrowed in contempt. There was no doubt in his mind. "God blacken your faces, Beni Sadr," he spat, and knelt beside the stricken man. There was no question of torture. It was not the way of the Bedu. He quickly pulled his knife from its scabbard and slit the throat as he had done many times before, both of men and of animals.

The Beni Sadr's pulse must have been weak, for there was

2

not the usual gushing of blood. Hamed's movement was swift and he was already springing back as the knife ended its arc. He wiped the blade on the sand and sat down to wait, aware that the fifth Beni Sadr would return with other jackals of his tribe to bury their dead. Theirs had been a long-standing feud and no quarter was shown by either side. His uncle, the finest Dahm who ever lived, had often recounted to him the legend of the feud. He said it had begun long ago during the reign of the Great Turk. It had all started over the theft of a camel, a huge black bull. But this was no ordinary beast. It was truly Ata Allah. God's gift. There was always a gleam in uncle Ahmed's eyes and a smile would crease his mouth as he spoke of the sexual exploits of that bull. "Allah be praised," he would say, "if only I had the strength of that bull, I would rob the Sultan of his harem." With this, the old man would break into a hearty laugh. It was a comic sight to see the wrinkled craggy face with that single front tooth wobbling as he spoke.

But Hamed had always laughed with his uncle and not at him. His respect was too great and affection too deep to mock such a man. The giant black bull had served the females so well that the Dahm became rich in camels. Word spread quickly throughout the desert and there were those whose envy could not be tempered. The Dahm had always to be on their guard, especially against the Beni Sadr, who were renowned for their covetousness.

Inevitably, the guard was one day lowered. A ghazu, a Beni Sadr raiding party, rode out of the sun and lifted five females and the black bull. They had also shot and killed two Dahm, one of them the revered Sheikh Musallem.

It was the beginning of a feud that had lasted many seasons and it would last forever, thought Hamed. Shuddering with the chill of the evening air, he summoned what little spittle he had and spat into the sand. In a short while the sun would set, casting a great shroud over the earth. He was safe until dawn. Then they would come for him and he would kill as many of them as he could.

He was envisioning his final battle when he heard another sound. It was a sound more familiar to him than his mother's voice. It was a sound that meant life. "Ata Allah," he mumbled. For there before him stood truly God's gift. The camel was an old hazmia, a female long past its prime. It obviously belonged to the Beni Sadr and must have wandered away from their encampment to search for grazing. The long drought had left it thin and he noticed that it hobbled slightly. Her udders were dry and it was clear she would not last long. Hamed prayed that she would get him to the well. He would travel by night, using the stars for guidance as was the way of his forefathers. He gripped the old camel's tether and sank to his knees. It was sunset. He bent forward, his forehead touching the cool surface of the sand, and twice intoned the prayer of the believer.

"God is Great.

There is no god but God.

And Mohammed is the Prophet of God."

Hamed kept his forehead touching the cool sand for a few moments longer. He then rose to inspect the old hazmia. She was indeed in a sorry state. The Beni Sadr had ridden her hard recently for there were ulcers on her hump and withers. Hamed again drew his knife, but this time not in anger. He cut the suppurating and noxious flesh away, knowing that the camel would feel no pain. She, like him, was more concerned with another kind of suffering. The more insistent and more intolerant pain of thirst.

The bedouin's thoughts returned to the well. He knew that without the old camel he was doomed. He would reach the well even if he had to pull her part of the way. He noticed an empty waterskin tied with palmetto and attached to her saddle. If only the waterskin had been full, he thought, and for a brief moment could taste the nectar swilling luxuriously in his mouth, but the reality of his furred tongue and dry spittle soon returned. His thirst was truly ferocious and could only worsen. Hamed lowered the hazmia's head and put his right foot on her neck. In one graceful movement, she raised her head and he slipped into the saddle. He would have to treat her gently for her soft soles were worn. Man and beast had but one aim: to find water. The drought had been severe for seven seasons and the few wells scattered throughout the great sands were the lifeblood of the tribes. In normal times, he thought, the wells would be their joint property, as it was with the al-Saq and the Mujarrah. But a Beni Sadr would never allow a Dahm near a well he was using and vice versa.

He did not question the ways of the Howeytat, the great bedouin nation, for everything in life was ordained by Allah. He would organise a sulha. The feast of reconciliation, if it came, would be one of the grandest in the history of the tribes. "Insh'a'Allah," he rasped. It would indeed need God's help.

Hamed kicked the hazmia and, guided by the northern star, man and beast moved slowly through the silent dunes. The lights of the firmament were as the grains of sand upon which he rode. He had always wondered whether it was true, as uncle Ahmed had told him, that each star was a human being in the Garden of Paradise. If uncle Ahmed had said it, he counselled, then it must be true, for he was the wisest of men.

After several hours, Hamed decided to couch the hazmia and try to get some sleep himself before the furnace of the day returned. What little clothing he wore provided scant warmth in the cold emptiness. His sleep was fitful as it always was in the winter months. But he was so hardened by the conditions of his daily life that the discomfort troubled him little.

When he awoke at dawn, the old camel was already on her feet. Hunger and thirst must be tormenting her, too, he thought, as they rode off in a northerly direction, the sun's rays greeting them with a warmth that would remain pleasant for only a few

5

moments. Sunrise and sunset were short-lived affairs in the desert, but they were the best times of all.

After three hours of slow progress, Hamed sensed he would soon be reaching the region of the High Dunes. They would provide the biggest challenge to the hazmia and he prayed she would survive them. He would have to call upon all his skills to negotiate the inclines. He knew the leeside was unscalable because the sand was too soft. But there were ridges that would provide firmer footing for his mount and he would have to choose them carefully. It was a question of judging the steepness of the slopes for there were some the beast would never be able to overcome. Hamed coaxed the animal up and over the first great dune. There would be many more and each would further exhaust the hazmia and himself. He prayed that she would carry him through, for her death would be his also.

Each great dune produced its own torment. The downslopes provided a little relief, but there always seemed to be more and more inclines to negotiate. After three hours or more, both man and beast were totally spent. Hamed slumped to the ground, his body wracked and his throat as parched as day-old dung. He decided to rest until sunset, couching the old camel and lying down in her shadow. The burning disc in the sky would soon reach its zenith and he would be further tortured.

The bedouin wrapped himself in his rags and waited until an hour before sunset, stirring himself only to pray. By his reckoning, there should be only a few more high dunes to overcome before they would reach the great plain leading to the well. They would probably reach it by mid-afternoon on the third day.

But by the evening of the third day Hamed was still far from the well and the hazmia could no longer bear his weight. He knew he would have to walk the rest of the way and that each stride would sap the little strength he had left. He attempted to curse the Beni Sadr but all that resulted was a rasping whisper that frightened him.

With each tortuous step, he slipped further and further away from reality, the hallucinations becoming more and more colourful, more and more fantastic. He imagined himself at the oasis of Wadi Lawi, sipping the cool milk of the coconuts and munching the succulent dates that grew there in such abundance. This is where God will place me when I die, he envisioned. The oasis was now nirvana. He was not alone, for he could see old uncle Ahmed grinning at him, first to his right and then to his left. Uncle Ahmed was everywhere, the single tooth gleaming like a beacon in that mischievous mouth.

By sunrise, Hamed was no longer aware of his terrible thirst and it was thus that he neared the well. He was only a few paces from the life-giving hole when he returned to his senses. Suddenly he became aware that he was walking alone, for the old hazmia had given up the unequal struggle some time ago. It had simply sunk to its knees and died from sheer exhaustion.

The bedouin gripped the coping at the top of the well. He recalled that it was sturdily built with stone stayning and that there were foot and hand holds in the masonry to allow a man to descend. The fact that someone had thought to paint the rim of the well a bright green aroused in him only faint curiosity. The ways of the desert and its dwellers were myriad in their mystery and, anyway, his mind was preoccupied with the imminent salving of his thirst.

Hamed had just hoisted one leg over the parapet when instinct halted him abruptly. Every nerve tingled in his pain-wracked body. He narrowed his eyes and peered westward. There, discernible on the horizon, were two dots. Two men. The bedu crouched by the coping. He was sure they had not seen him for the sun was in their eyes. As they neared, he could tell by their gait that they were Beni Sadr. They must have encamped nearby for they were on foot. They were probably scouting the well to make sure it was unoccupied by enemies.

Hamed crept towards the coping furthest away from the direction in which the men were approaching. He knew his sole advantage would be surprise. He thrust the ache in his limbs and the rage of his thirst into his subconscious. They were supplanted by an emotion far stronger than pain or discomfort: the will to survive. He lay prone and still for what seemed an eternity as the two Beni Sadr neared the well. He heard them talking. They were discussing a raid, a raid against the Dahm. They spoke haughtily of the number of his tribesmen they had killed and the number of camels they had lifted. Well, Hamed of the Dahm would avenge his brothers this day, he swore. As he lay motionless, he heard a goatskin being lowered into the well, the palmetto scraping against the rim of the coping. Sensing that one of the Beni Sadr was leaning over the parapet, Hamed crawled slowly, silently, towards the man. Then, in a single swift movement, he lunged forward and lifted the Beni Sadr by his ankles. There was a sharp cry as the man plummeted headlong into the blackness.

Before the other Beni Sadr could react, Hamed was already upon him, knife drawn and lunging towards his breast. But the second Beni Sadr was quick and he stepped nimbly to one side, although surprise forced him to drop his rifle. Hamed gasped as he hit the ground. Now pure animal instinct guided him and he rolled over as the Beni Sadr, his gold teeth glinting in the orange sunlight, aimed his own blade. Both men were quickly on their feet. They circled each other warily, like a pair of scorpions, right arms extended and knives poised to strike. The Beni Sadr made the first move, the blade swishing towards Hamed's midriff. The Dahm pulled in his stomach and felt the point tear the top of his loin-cloth. Sensing that the Beni Sadr was off balance and summoning the little strength he still possessed, he hurtled forward and knocked his bitter enemy to the ground. He could smell his opponent's stale breath as he lay upon him. He saw the man's eyes open wide in surprise as he thrust the knife into the heart from beneath the breastbone. The

Beni Sadr groaned and died.

For a few moments Hamed lay upon his victim, too exhausted to move. Then the torment of his thirst returned. Water, once again, became of paramount concern. He rolled off the corpse and stumbled towards the awning. The goatskin and rope had disappeared over the side with the first Beni Sadr. Hamed felt gingerly for the foot and hand holds in the corners of the interior masonry and descended slowly. At the bottom, his foot brushed against the body of the first Beni Sadr. It was already cold. In the darkness, Hamed felt around the corpse. His heart sank. The floor of the well was bone dry. He scraped the earth with his fingers and then used his knife to dig for some tell-tale moisture beneath the surface. But each handful of earth was dry and crumbly.

Suddenly there was a clanging sound as the blade struck metal. He could feel the object was curved. It must be an old cooking pot, he thought. Whatever it was, it was of no use to him now.

He slumped next to the body and the blackness seemed to give him comfort from the reality of the flaming sphere above and the knowledge that his situation was hopeless. Without the hazmia, he had no chance of reaching the next well, a further three days' ride. His choice would be in the fashion of his death. He could either wander into the vast emptiness beyond to die of thirst, a slow tortuous death, or await the swift justice of the Beni Sadr who would shortly come searching for their brothers. Hamed climbed the well wearily. He sat with his back resting against the coping furthest from the sun and waited. After what seemed an eternity, he felt a subtle change of climate brush his desiccated skin. Then a bitter chill began to permeate his bones. A bedouin always knew when the Shurqiya was about to strike. The jinns, the spirits of the desert, were already stirring.

The merciless wind from the east would hasten his end. Insh'a'Allah.

BOOK ONE

CHAPTER ONE

David Katri fought to control his emotions. The welling tears were likely to prompt a concerned inquiry from other members of the family grouped round the Passover table. Questions would demand answers and a little knowledge was a dangerous thing for the Jews of Damascus.

David listened to his little brother Naftali recite the ancient formula: "Why is this night different from all other nights? Why on all other nights may we eat bread or matza but on this night only matza? Why on all other nights may we eat any kinds of herbs, but on this night only bitter herbs? Why on all other nights we do not dip one food into another even once while on this night twice? Why on all other nights may we eat sitting up or leaning, but on this night we all lean?"

Little Naftali smiled sheepishly at his older brother whom he worshipped. Answers to the questions could be found in the Bible, thought David, but who would provide the answers to Naftali when he would ask: "Why did my brother leave me?" Who would explain in terms that a nine-year-old could understand that he might never see his brother again? Would he feel forsaken? Would he bear a resentment as strong as that of David's against the country of his birth and its leaders?

David sighed, the sound and gesture lost in the general hubbub of prayer and recitation. He looked at his father, an old man deeply engrossed in the wonder of the Passover legend. His father, gaunt and bent from his work as a coppersmith, was so frail. But beneath the weary frame was a determination and will that was his legacy to his eldest son.

Mordechai Katri would understand. He would guess the truth

10

almost immediately. Other children had escaped and the heartbreak of separation would be softened by the knowledge that a loved one had tasted freedom.

David had first understood what it meant to be a Jew in Damascus at an early age. The taunts of his Moslem peers were merciless. *Yahud rud.* Jew monkey. *Falastin biladna wal Yahud klabna.* Palestine is ours and the Jew is our dog. The tiny, treeless Jewish quarter was both a refuge and a target. Then, two months after his barmitzvah, the Six-day War erupted and with it the fury of the Arab masses. The violent rhetoric on the radio was frightening. 'Arab brothers arise and push the Zionist enemy into the sea. Drink the blood of their children. Kill all the Jews'. The Jews of the ghetto cowered in fear, but not Mordechai Katri. "We must pray for an Israeli victory, my son," he had counselled. "The Arab respects strength and we will not be harmed as long as Israel is strong. If, God forbid, Israel is defeated, we will all be slaughtered within minutes."

Their prayers were indeed answered. The irony was that the Mukhabbarat, the secret police, had been despatched to the ghetto to protect the Jews from incensed Palestinians.

Life, however, became even more restrictive for the Jews of Damascus following the war. David was now at an age when he could appreciate that there was a world outside the confines of the ghetto that needed to be investigated. The dream of freedom tormented him for no Jew was allowed to travel more than four kilometres from his home. The Mukhabbarat would later issue special passes, but only to adults.

The list of restrictions seemed endless. Jews were completely forbidden from emigrating and this applied even to those who held foreign passports. A ten o'clock evening curfew was imposed. His uncle Solomon had been caught on the streets of the ghetto one night and severely beaten.

Jews were barred from jobs in the public service and in banks and government, and military personnel were forbidden to purchase from Jewish shops. Jews were also banned from owning radios or telephones or maintaining postal contact with the outside world. Their isolation became almost total, although some found a way to circumvent the new laws, despite the risks. But Mordechai Katri found hardest to accept the decree stating that possessions of deceased Jews were to be confiscated by the Government and that their heirs must then pay for use of the property. If they could not, then it was handed over to the Palestinians living in Damascus.

"I am working for nothing if I cannot provide for my children when I am gone," he would lament.

A Muslim director was appointed to David's school, the Talmud Torah, one of only two Jewish schools permitted to operate in Damascus. Any mention of Israel, except in a biblical context, was strictly forbidden.

David recalled with bitterness how he had been treated when he and three school friends had dared to visit the Sariani swimming pool near the beautiful picnic spot of Arabweh to the west of the city.

How thrilled they had been to see trees, to feel the sublime pleasure of cool water enveloping their hot, dry bodies. There were many children at Sariani that day but none was happier than the four friends from the ghetto.

The taste of freedom, however, had had its price. The Mukhabbarat had been informed of the escapade and the four had received "invitations" to attend the Rowda interrogation centre. There they were beaten and their heads shaved to deter other Jewish youngsters. As in most cases of adversity, the victims turned to humour to alleviate their plight. Everyone joked that it would be his turn next to receive an invitation. Sometimes "invitations" would be received for the most absurd reasons. David recalled how his cousin Avner had raised chickens on the roof of his home. The Mukhabbarat accused him of using this as a pretext to signal to Israeli planes. Avner's hobby had cost him a beating at the Talet el Hajarah interrogation centre. The chickens, protesting loudly, were quickly transferred to ground level.

"Le'Haim, David. Le'Haim, David."

David, lost in his reminiscences, suddenly became aware that the prayers had concluded. Everyone was standing around the table with raised glasses. He rose slowly and raised his. "Le'Haim," he toasted. "To life," he repeated in Arabic. He smiled at all of them in turn, his father, his mother, his sister Rachel, and little Naftali. This would probably be the last time he would take wine with them. "To the best family in the whole wide world," he said, the nectar causing an instantaneous feeling of well-being, a temporary respite from his dejection.

The following morning, the first day of the Passover holiday, David rose early. The sun was just beginning its daily ritual and he knew he should have to be quick to avoid a confrontation with his father who would soon be rising to attend services at the al-Raki synagogue.

It pained him that he could not wish them all farewell. It was better that they did not know where he was headed for the Mukhabbarat would not treat them gently under interrogation, especially if they had something to hide. A slip of the tongue and David might not succeed in reaching the border. He knew he would have to travel with no more than the clothes he wore. A suitcase would arouse suspicion. He had saved about twenty pounds over the last few months and this he now removed from the small chest beside his bed. Washed and dressed, he knelt gently by the bed of Naftali. His brother's face was so beautiful in repose. David kissed him gently on the forehead and then crossed the room to Rachel. Gently, he stroked her long ebony hair. She stirred slightly as he kissed her. "You will one day break a few hearts, my dearest sister," he whispered.

Upon entering the kitchen, the centre of every Jewish home, David luxuriated in the familiar aroma of coffee and cardamom.

For a fleeting moment he envisioned his mother there preparing the sabbath meal. Her presence was almost tangible. Swallowing hard, he opened the refrigerator and withdrew two yabrack, courgettes stuffed with beans, meat and rice. He hoped it would be enough to sustain him on the journey to Beirut. Finally, he entered the courtyard, his favourite place in all the ghetto. The intoxicating fragrance of jasmine combined with the dull light to rock his senses. Soon the incandescence of the day would beat upon this refuge where the vine and the pomegranate trees provided such welcoming shade. This scene and this moment would be forever locked in his memory.

David slipped quietly through the front door, not daring to enter his parents' room lest he wake them. Once outside, he made his way quickly along Zukak al-Madaar, through Suk al-Jumu'a and past the al-Raki synagogue. All was quiet now, but soon the synagogue would be humming with prayer and ablaze with colour as his people celebrated the holiday of deliverance. David gritted his teeth. For one Damascus Jew at least, it would be 'Next Year in Jerusalem'.

Unfettered by the fear that would gnaw at an adult, David strode confidently out of the ghetto. How different everything was. The streets were already alive as traders made their way to the market places to erect their stalls. Vehicular traffic, so rare in the narrow streets of the Jewish Quarter, was beginning to stir as David made his way to the taxi stand at the central bus station. He believed his chances of crossing the border safely would be better in a taxi. Only the poor travelled by bus and they were more likely to be victimised. He had inserted ten lira into his identity card and hoped this would be enough to bribe the border guard.

David noticed the look of scepticism as he approached the taxi driver.

"Do you have room for one more to Beirut?" he asked, trying to appear confident.

The taxi driver sported a large handlebar moustache and was probably a Druze. The man eyed him suspiciously. "What's a young lad like you doing travelling to Beirut? Why aren't you at school?"

David knew that his swarthy complexion and facial contours made him appear more Arab than Jew. He was relieved that the driver believed he should be in class with his Moslem peers rather than in a synagogue.

"My money's good, so why should that concern you?" he answered boldly. David was quite tall and well built for his fifteen years, taller in fact than the average adult Damascene.

The Druze shrugged at his brash passenger and then smiled. "Show me the colour of your money and you can take the last place."

"Will five lira be enough?"

The Druze's paunch joggled as he chuckled. "Of course, my Lord Feisal, pray enter." And with this he opened the rear door of an old Mercedes, seemingly held together with chicken wire and optimism, and bowed with a flourish. Even David was forced to smile at the cameo.

The journey to the border proved uneventful, although David's heart beat wildly every time they approached a security checkpoint on the Damascus-Beirut highway. Fortunately, the guards seemed to recognise the Druze and waved them through with only a cursory glance at the passengers. The fresh air of the countryside intoxicated David and did much to abate the odour of garlic emanating from the man alongside him.

After what seemed like an eternity he could see the scenery changing in the distance. The reddish ochre that was Syria was about to be transformed into the lush verdant landscape of the Lebanon. He had read much of its beauty and now the photographs of its hills and cool mountains were about to become reality. David was so mesmerised by the change in scenery that he hardly noticed the Mercedes pulling to a halt.

The Druze turned to the passengers in the rear. "Get your identity cards and exit visas ready, please."

It took a few seconds for David to come to his senses. As he fumbled in his pocket for his identity card a face appeared at the open window. The countenance of the stooping Syrian border policeman did not inspire confidence. It was pockmarked and menacing. He held his palm open.

David, his heart beating wildly, thrust his security card into the man's hand. Most of these men, he had been told, were illiterate and he prayed the officer would not recognise Mussawi, the word for Jew, printed in small letters. The border guard stood upright and David was left staring at his dust-coloured tunic, grubby with food stains. The wait seemed interminable, each passing second carrying with it the threat of arrest and incarceration.

The man's face did not appear again. Instead, a seemingly disembodied hand was thrust through the open window. It contained his identity card. A wave of relief engulfed David as he took it. He put it straight into the back pocket of his jeans. No longer did it accompany a few grubby banknotes. All that he possessed now was some loose change.

The disembodied hand flicked disdainfully. "Yallah, imshi!"

As if she needed no second invitation, the Mercedes belched black smoke and roared across the border to freedom.

For an hour David enjoyed the scenery and smell of a free land before the old taxi croaked to a halt in downtown Beirut.

"Okay, Feisal, out you get. And don't get up to any monkey business in Beirut. They say the whores are rougher than a camel's arse."

David joined in the Druze's hearty merriment. The sensation of freedom was as intoxicating as kiddush wine. David Katri, a young Jew from Damascus, was alive and well in the most vibrant city in the Arab world.

Upon reaching Hamra Street, he gazed in awe at the shop

windows. Anything and everything could be bought here, he thought. Beirut's most famous street was bustling with life. The rich mixed with poor, Sunni with Shi'ite, Druze with Maronite. Almost penniless, David allowed himself the luxury of window shopping before pangs of hunger and thirst began to demand more serious action. He had already decided that his best course was to make his way to the International Red Cross. He felt so free that he surprised even himself at his bravado in asking a policeman for directions.

Tired but elated, David entered the white stucco building. Flying proudly from the flagpole atop the portal was the symbol that meant so much to the poor and downtrodden of the world. Rumours in the ghetto had it that the organisation would help Jewish refugees from Syria, but he was tense with trepidation nevertheless.

The receptionist, a rather weedy man wearing a pence-nez, cast a disparaging look at the dishevelled youth standing before him. Waifs abounded in the city and if this was another one searching for a free meal ticket, he would soon send him on his way.

"How can I help you, boy?" he asked, his eyes narrowing in suspicion.

David decided instantly. He was penniless and there was no other course open to him. "I am a Jew who has escaped from Damascus and I wish to go to Israel."

To his surprise, the receptionist betrayed not a flicker of emotion. It was as if this sort of thing happened every day. "Wait here," the man said, disappearing through a door at the rear of his desk.

After a few minutes he returned. Monsieur Legrand will see you now. Please follow me."

David was led into a high-ceilinged room. In front of him stood a large oak desk. The Moorish windows were redolent with stained glass mosaics and a large fan whirred overhead, bringing a welcoming respite from the stuffiness of the entrance lobby. Behind the desk sat a handsome, blond man engaged in trying to write something.

"Mon Dieu," he cursed. "Why can't they bring me pens that work." He shook the pen as a cat would a rat and smiled at his visitor.

David did not know why, but something in that smile inspired confidence. The man before him had kindly grey eyes, eyes that encouraged trust.

"Please, sit down," he motioned, "and let me see your identity card."

After a few moments, the man in the white suit stood up and extended his hand. "Well, David, my name is Armand Legrand and I'm what you might call the boss around here."

David half rose. He was rather nonplussed by the warm welcome from this stranger who spoke flawless Arabic, albeit with a French accent.

Legrand sat down, placed his elbows on his desk and clenched his hands beneath his chin. Handsome kid, he thought. Had plenty of guts, that was for sure.

He smiled again at his visitor. "You know, you're the twenty-third Jew so far this year to come to us for help. I don't suppose you've got any money and I suppose you hope to reach Israel."

It was more of a statement than a question and David could only lower his eyes in acknowledgement.

"You know, you're lucky, David," Legrand continued. "A year ago it would have been impossible to help you. There was still a lot of anger about following the Six-day War and our hands were tied. But since then the authorities have relaxed to such an extent that I believe they wouldn't arrest you even if you were Moshe Dayan himself."

David smiled at the mention of Israel's hero. He also felt intense relief that the man appeared ready to help him reach the

Promised Land.

Legrand went on. "We have what you might term 'an arrangement' with the Israelis. We help them as long as they keep it a secret. Of course, with all the people involved it's rather an open secret. Nevertheless, I want you to swear to me that you will never reveal how you reached Israel to either a third person or the media."

"I promise, Monsieur Legrand, and I want to thank you sincerely for what you are doing." David was surprised at the adult way he had voiced his appreciation. His actions had always been mature for his years, but now he felt he had truly come of age.

Legrand smiled self-consciously and cleared his throat. The Frenchman was blushing.

"Thank you, David. Now I want you to take this money and buy yourself a decent meal at the restaurant on the corner. After you return, Albert in reception will take you to a nearby youth hostel. You will sleep there this evening. Tomorrow evening you will be taken to Jounieh where you will be given some fisherman's clothes to wear. Don't worry, the fishermen are being paid well by your people and they're born smugglers anyway."

David's heart skipped a beat. Was this really about to happen to him?

Legrand was obviously warming to his subject. He loved to see the thrill of expectancy tinged with apprehension in the eyes of these refugees. Sometimes he wished he could be more involved in the action rather than simply acting as a go-between.

"David, you will be taken by the fishermen to a rendezvous off the coast with an Israeli patrol boat and then our work is complete." With this, Legrand lifted his telephone receiver and pressed a button. "Albert, please come in and take Mr Katri. You know what to do."

Legrand rose and again shook the bewildered youth's hand.

"Good luck, David. And remember, don't breathe a word of this to anyone."

The following night, David Katri from Damascus was hauled aboard an Israeli patrol boat off the shores of Lebanon. Yet another refugee was about to enter a land of refugees. He was going home at last. The sight of the flag of the Star of David fluttering in the night breeze awakened in him a sense of pride in his Jewishness that he had been forced to repress throughout his childhood. He was surrounded by bronzed strong-looking sailors, most of whom were probably the sons of immigrants. They were unfettered by the insecurity of a repressed minority. He wondered whether he would ever feel as confident as they. It was so much better to be arrogant than to be subservient.

David spent the hours before dawn chatting with the Israeli crew. He was surprised at his own grasp of Hebrew, although some of their colloquialisms baffled him. Mostly it was he who spoke. How beautiful was Israel? Was it really the Land of Milk and Honey? Did you fight in the Six-day War? His questions were endless and the sailors did not disenchant him.

As dawn broke, the patrol boat came within sight of Haifa, Israel's principal port. The sun's rays glared from the whitewashed walls of the apartments stacked on Mount Carmel. It was like a giant wedding cake, thought David, the boy in him gaining the ascendency. Every nerve in his body tingled with excitement.

As he hopped from the side of the boat onto the quay, he saw a lone figure standing a few metres away. The man, wearing an open-necked shirt and grey trousers and carrying a briefcase, approached him slowly. David noticed that he had a slight limp. The man smoothed his hair before offering his hand.

"Welcome to Israel, Mr Katri."

The greeting was perfunctory. It was evident to him that this strange man had more important matters to discuss. A small scar above the man's upper lip added to the severity of his appearance.

The man beckoned David to follow him and they entered a disused warehouse. Packing crates made makeshift chairs and a table. The building must have been used for storing spices for the aroma of cardamom still laced the air. David, reminded of his kitchen at home, suddenly realised that this was the first time he had thought about his family. He blew his nose in an effort to hide the emotion welling inside him. "It's a bit dusty in here," he said rather tamely.

The man, paying no heed, withdrew a sheaf of papers from his briefcase and a pen from his shirt pocket and placed them on one of the crates. He looked David firmly in the eye.

"Have you heard of the Mossad?"

David vaguely recalled mention of the word in the Syrian press but its meaning evaded him.

The man, noticing David's pensiveness, continued without waiting for an answer. "It is the name of our secret service. We didn't expect that you would have heard of it. We try to keep a low profile as far as our operations in Syria are concerned."

The man withdrew a packet of cigarettes from his briefcase and lit one. David stared at the packet. He could make out the word "Royal" in Hebrew on the red and white box.

"We've had reports that you're quite an intelligent lad," the man went on, dragging deeply on the cigarette. "The fact is that one day we might like you to help us. You speak fluent Arabic with a Syrian dialect and that's a rare quality for a Jew nowadays. Of course, you're a bit young yet but when, and if, the time comes perhaps you will repay us for helping you to escape."

David was dumbstruck. The stranger, as if recognising that the young man before him was confused, deftly changed course. He pushed the pen into David's hand.

"Write a few words to your family. Add the name and address

and I will make sure they get it without arousing any suspicion."

David scribbled a few words of greeting and concluded by saying he was happy and well. His senses were still reeling as he handed the pen back to the man.

"Keep it and sign this," the stranger said, thrusting forward another piece of paper.

"What is it?" asked David hesitantly.

"As far as you are concerned lad, this conversation never took place. This is a copy of the Official Secrets Act and should you divulge any details of our little talk to a third person or the media, you will be prosecuted. Get it."

David, his mind confused, nodded meekly and signed the paper. With this the man gathered the documents and limped towards the warehouse door. David could just make out a shadowy figure as the sun streamed through the awning. The man's voice, seemingly disembodied, spoke once more. "By the way, a guy from the Jewish Agency will be here shortly. You'll be going to a kibbutz or something. Shalom and good luck."

CHAPTER TWO

Arik Ben-Ami had decided the previous day. Nehama, his favourite cow, was due to give birth and there was absolutely no way he was going to attend high school in Afula. As one of the new generation of native-born Israeli youngsters, his firm declaration of intent was accepted with equanimity by his Polish-born parents. They knew better than to argue with their strong-willed offspring. Arik thought the kibbutz education commit-tee might raise a stink, but he had nurtured Nehama thus far and he wanted to deliver her calf personally.

The dormitory was empty. Arik vaguely recalled the other children rising for school, but his vigil in the cowshed for most of the night had exhausted him. Nehama had stubbornly refus-ed to go into labour. Arik glanced at his watch. "Elohim," he gasped. God, it was already eight-thirty. He rose quickly and showered. Opening the wardrobe, he withdrew a fresh set of grey trico underwear and the ubiquitous blue work overalls worn by kibbutzniks throughout Israel. He was just donning his boots when a voice called urgently from the path outside the dor-mitory. It was Avner Wilder.

"Arik, come quickly. Her contractions are quickening."

"Beseder, Avner. Okay. You go ahead. I'll just be a couple of minutes," he replied, hastily tying the interminable laces on his army regulation boots. Arik dashed past the line of eucalyp-tus trees lining the path to the cowshed. The air was already shimmering. A khamsin, the hot wind that blasted Israel from Egypt and North Africa, would soon reach its full force, transforming the Jezreel Valley into an oven which would melt the resistance of both man and beast. The ethos of labour, so revered by the kibbutzniks, faced its biggest test on such days. Only those working in the air-conditioned offices and laundry room were spared the torment.

Arik reached the cowshed in time to see a pair of hooves protruding from Nehama's vulva. The cow snorted. She was obviously in pain.

"Okay, Avner, you take one of its legs and I'll take the other...now heave gently. Don't tug whatever you do."

As they exerted pressure, the water bag enveloping the calf's legs burst and they were drenched by steaming liquid and mucous. "L'azazel," cursed Arik. Bloody hell, what a mess.

After what seemed ages, the head began to appear. Arik, bathed in sweat, forced his fingers into the swollen vulva and slowly prised it out. He unclipped the brown leather protective cover on his watch. They had been straining for a full forty minutes. After an hour, as if sensing that it was now her turn, Nehama gave a concerted effort, huffing and snorting in a paroxysm of pain. Suddenly the calf's shoulders cleared to be quickly followed by the haunches and hoofs.

To Arik there seemed a joy in Nehama's languid eyes as she slowly turned her head and began licking her offspring with maternal gentleness.

The young kibbutznik turned to his older comrade. "Okay, Avner, let's go I'll come back later on to make sure the afterbirth is out."

Arik trudged wearily along the path leading to the main complex of the kibbutz. Hunger pangs made him suddenly aware that he had not eaten breakfast. A cursory glance at his watch told him it was too late to head for the communal dining hall. They would already be preparing lunch for two hundred and fifty people and he did not want the gossip-mongers grilling him over the reason he had not gone to school. He turned down the path leading away from the dining hall and towards his parents' cottage. He could always find a few goodies there.

As he approached the line of cottages he could see his mother standing in the front garden and pointing in his direction. With her was another person whom he did not recognise.

"Arik, Arik, come quickly," she beckoned, her thick Polish-accented Hebrew grating on his ears. "Arik, we have a special guest. This is David. He has just arrived in Israel after escaping from Syria. The committee held an emergency meeting this morning and your father and I agreed to adopt him."

Arik examined the stranger. They were so different. The boy was tall and swarthy with a slightly hooked nose and large brown eyes, while he was stocky with blond hair, freckles and piercing blue eyes, so piercing that some said they made them feel uncomfortable. He thought the youth looked more Arab than Jew and hoped he could speak Hebrew for he himself knew hardly a word of Arabic other than the usual swear-words used by everybody. His mother, sensing the silence was becoming a little too pregnant, placed her arms around the visitor's shoulders. "I've just been showing him round the kibbutz. Would you believe that he's never seen a farm before?"

Arik, sensing David was embarrassed by this fact, shook the newcomer's hand warmly. "How would you like to see a new-born calf?" he asked, smiling broadly.

The two youths quickly discovered they had much in common despite their disparate features and backgrounds. They complemented one another. Arik, unlike the typical only child, was brash and forceful, thanks mainly to the kibbutz policy of raising the children in communal dormitories. If there was any spoiling, it was done collectively. The children of the kibbutz were often wild and unruly but beneath their rough exteriors lay qualities that produced the nation's leaders and generals.

David was the more thoughtful and taciturn of the two, which was just as well. If their natures had been similar, they might never have developed the love and comradeship that was to blossom in the months ahead. To their mutual surprise, they discovered that their birthdays were only a week apart. "I'm the Scorpio with the sting in the tail," Arik once joked.

Like his friend, David, too, became passionately involved in the welfare of the milk cows. They would often work the early shift on Saturdays and this became a full-time job once the two had completed their matriculation.

The young Syrian Jew integrated successfully into kibbutz society and quickly became one of the hevreh, the lads. He was almost delirious in his happiness. The odours of the farm and scent of the breezes wafting lazily through the leaves of the eucalyptus trees intoxicated him. He could not foresee himself ever returning to live in a city, even Jerusalem which entranced him with every visit. He was now a country boy and that was the way he intended to stay.

Arik, however, was restless. The two had often discussed the opportunities open to them following their three years' compulsory national service.

"David, I just can't see myself working in the cowshed for the rest of my life, as much as I love it," Arik had told his friend, a note of desperation in his voice. "I love the kibbutz, but sometimes I find it so restrictive. Everybody knows everyone else's business."

"Yes, it's a bit like our ghetto in Damascus," said David comfortingly, "except here you have trees and you can travel wherever you like."

Arik smiled at his friend and sighed, "I suppose I crave a bit of excitement in my life. It can get a bit dull around here. In the old days the place used to come under attack from Arab marauders, but now it's all rather tame."

"Maybe you ought to join the Mossad after the army."

David regretted the words as soon as he had finished saying them. It was a stupid comment on a subject he could discuss only in general terms. He had told Arik the story of his

26

escape but had been careful to omit any mention of the Mossad's role in the affair.

Arik's eyes lit up. "Yeh, can you imagine it. Me as James Bond." He winked at his friend and added, "You can be Eli Cohen."

The mention of Eli Cohen's name revived a flood of memories in David. Every Israeli knew the story of Eli Cohen, but only a handful had lived through those traumatic days in Damascus after Cohen had been found out by Syrian Intelligence. The press had regaled in an orgy of vituperation. Cohen was villified as a Jew and a Zionist and the infamous day in nineteen sixty-five when Cohen was publicly hanged in Martyr's Square was etched into the collective psyche of the tiny, frightened Jewish community. It was only later that David was old enough to comprehend fully the tremendous courage of the Egyptian-born Israeli who had succeeded in penetrating circles close to the Syrian Government and High Command. With the aid of a transmitter in his flat opposite military headquarters, Cohen had managed to pass priceless information to Israel, information which helped his country capture the Golan Heights in the Six-day War.

"Talking about the army," said David, changing the subject, "what are we going into? For me, it's a choice between the paratroopers and tanks."

Arik scratched the crown of his tousled blond head. The paratroopers had always carried more mystique. He envisaged a pair of the distinctive red boots in the porch outside his front door. The red beret would go well with his hair, he mused. But, on the other hand, armour was playing an increasingly important role in Tzahal, the Israel Defence Forces, and the thought of commanding twenty tons of metal appealed to him.

"How would you like to run up Massada, David?"

"What do you mean?"

"Well, you remember the Jewish zealots of Massada committed suicide rather than become slaves of the Romans…''

David envisaged the mountain fortress of Massada by the Dead Sea. He had read the story and seen photographs and had always wanted to visit the place.

Arik continued, ''Well, in the Armoured Corps you run up that damned rock and swear allegiance that Massada shall not fall again.''

As he finished speaking a flight of three F-4 Phantoms screamed overhead on their way from the Ramat David airbase nearby to attack Palestinian bases in Fatahland, the area in southern Lebanon controlled by Yasser Arafat's Palestinian Liberation Organisation.

''I'll go where you go Arik,'' David shouted above the din.

Unknown to the two friends, those same Phantom jets were to provide the catalyst which would later bring them into conflict with a man dedicated to the destruction of their people.

Rashid Sedawi was tending the tobacco crop on his father's farm land when the three Israeli jets screeched low overhead, forcing him to dive to the ground. A fraction of a second later he heard a series of explosions rip through the air. He rose gingerly and looked eastwards. The billowing black smoke hanging lazily over Kfar Chouba confirmed his worst fears. As he broke into a run, Rashid prayed that his parents and three younger brothers were safe. The palpitations in his heart grew stronger as he neared the village for he realised that today was Friday, the sabbath, and that they would all be at home.

''Ya Rashid, Ya Rashid!''

It was his friend, Mustafa Allam, running to meet him. There was the urgency of catastrophe in his eyes as well as in his voice.

''Rashid, come quickly, they have hit your father's house,'' he beseeched, his manner becoming more and more frantic. ''Allah have mercy, Allah have mercy.''

Rashid quickened his pace, his bare feet pounding on the well-trodden path from the fields to the village. A thousands fears flashed before his eyes.

A crowd of villagers and Palestinian fighters blocked his way. Some just stood by while others attempted to clear the rubble with their bare hands. A fire had started and this, too, hampered rescue work.

"Babba! Mama!" he screamed, pushing aside the onlookers.

Suddenly, there before him was a scene of utter devastation. The home of the Sedawi family had taken a direct hit. Rashid, tears running down his face, sank to his knees and prayed to Allah, his sobs drowned in the general commotion around him.

By the following morning, the bodies of Rashid's parents and his little brothers had been recovered. He had taken little part in the search, innate fatalism having already convinced him that his family had perished and that he could now look forward to meeting them again only in the Garden of Paradise.

All that was salvaged was his father's gold watch and chain, part of which had melted in the heat. The inscription on the inside of the watch cover was English. It had been apparently a gift to a British soldier from his father at the time of the war against the Turks. Rashid turned the timepiece through his fingers. If this could speak, he asked himself, how much would it reveal of the bestiality of the infidel? The Christians, like the Jews, were dhimmi, second-class people worthy only of contempt. Even if they assumed the garb of lions, they hid within them the fear of jackals.

His father, of blessed memory, had worked hard and long to provide his eldest son with an education and Rashid was determined now to put this to use for the glory of Islam and the defeat of its enemies.

The Sunni Moslems and Christians of the north had been less than generous when it came to buying their meagre tobacco crop via the Regie in Nabatiyeh. His father had often railed against the state monopoly.

Rashid had good cause to be bitter. The Shi'a of southern Lebanon were amongst the country's poorest citizens, neglected by the government in hedonistic Beirut. The authorities provided scant protection for the villagers against Israeli ground and air attacks. He also cursed the Palestinians and their leader, Yasser Arafat. They had swaggered into his village in order to carry out operations against the Zionist enemy. But it was never the Palestinians who suffered the reprisals. Their casualties were minimal compared to those of the villagers. Their quarters, either by luck or design, seemed to escape retribution.

The Palestinians were Sunnis and the Sunnis were heretics, Rashid believed. It was probably true that they were in league with the Israelis in a bid to usurp the land of the ordinary fellah. The Arkoub was thick with Arafat's men and Kfar Chouba, the perfect artillery target, was the sacrificial lamb.

"What will you do, Ya Rashid?"

It was Mustafa. Rashid felt his friend's hand upon his shoulder as he crouched beside him and surveyed the scene of destruction in the early morning light.

"The village is dying, Mustafa," he replied sadly. "Soon there will be none of us left. The Palestinians are taking over and the Israelis will retaliate again and again until not a single building will be left standing." He spat into the rubble. "A curse on both their houses."

"Perhaps we should join the Lebanese Army," Mustafa suggested half-heartedly. "At least we'll be assured of food and clothing."

Rashid laughed sardonically, his front left tooth, solid gold, glinting in the sunlight. "The Lebanese Army is as potent as a eunuch in a harem. They look good in uniform but they cannot perform when it really matters. They have sealed off all the roads to Kfar Chouba and are sending the villagers to emergency relief centres. We can trust no-one, ya Mustafa, least of all our own army.''

''My family is going to Beirut, Rashid, and I will go with them. We have relations there.'' Mustafa took his friend's hand and peered adoringly into his eyes. How he loved those dark curls and small nose. They had lain together as was customary in puberty and he could not imagine a woman giving him as much pleasure. The hope that Rashid would accompany him to the capital burned within him.

But Rashid Sedawi had other plans. Tormented by the belief that Allah had visited upon him a great catastrophe because he had desecrated the sabbath, he would now seek salvation only in revenge. He would fight his family's killers to the death, but not alongside the heretic Palestinians.

''Mustafa, we are but a few kilometres from the Syrian border. The Syrians will never leave Israel in peace. They have a mighty army and one day it will crush the Zionist dogs and fling them into the sea.''

Mustafa, already fearing that he would never see his friend again, squeezed Rashid's hand anxiously, ''What do you mean, my brother?''

''I mean that the Palestinians for all their bluster have succeeded only in bringing death and destruction to us. They will never have enough power to be anything other than nuisance value against Israel.''

Rashid turned his head away from the pile of rubble that had been his home and stared directly into his friend's eyes. Mustafa was at once entranced and frightened by the iron will that those small brown eyes portrayed.

''Ya Mustafa,'' the eyes began to narrow in determination, ''I am twenty years old and I am willing to die a martyr in order to defeat the infidel. I will cross the border tomorrow and volunteer for the Syrian Army.''

CHAPTER THREE

October 6 1973 GOLAN HEIGHTS

David Katri stood in the turret of his Centurion and re-checked that the belt of .3 machine gun ammunition was ready for firing. Everyone was nervous. His brigade, the Barak, had been on alert for a few days although nobody seemed sure if a Syrian attack was imminent. Now it was Yom Kippur and brigade commanders had confirmed that the Syrians were indeed planning to strike although the precise hour was not revealed.

David, honed and burnished by four years of freedom and the sweet air of the countryside, turned and waved to the tank commander to his left. Arik Ben-Ami, blond fringe protruding from his helmet, grinned back. Arik was always smiling, thought David. Even now his buoyant optimism helped relieve the tension of impending battle that seemed to hang thickly in the air. How strange that only a few weeks ago they had voiced regret that their first year of compulsory service was coming to an end without them having seen any real action. David had longed to be able to train his 105mm cannon on his sworn enemy. Most of his comrades despised the Syrians' inhumanity but few, if any, could feel the bitterness and hate that came with having been persecuted by them.

Thoughts of home tormented David. He worried for the safety of his family. The Syrian Government was sure to crack down on the Jewish Quarter and they might encourage hooligan elements to attack his people. He knew they would be suffering the same anxieties as in nineteen sixty-seven. They were totally at the mercy of the authorities.

David prised open his flak jacket and withdrew a dog-eared scrap of paper. He had carried the letter everywhere with him since receiving it two months earlier while on leave. He did not ask questions but it had been obvious that through the Mossad he was able to correspond with his family. On average, he had received about four letters a year.

David cherished each and every word his sister Rachel had written.

Dear David,

We all miss you so very much especially now that you will be unable to attend my wedding. Yes, David, your little sister is actually getting married. You remember Fardos, my best friend from Talmud Torah? Well, she has an older brother. Selim is his name. I knew that he always took a fancy to me, but I must say I was more than a little surprised when his father approached Babba and asked for my hand on behalf of Selim. I was pleased for I had always liked him. He is kind and gentle. He works as a tanner and is very good at his job. I know he is only nineteen and that I am sixteen but I think we are both mature enough to make a success of our marriage. By the way, it is planned for early October. I know you can't be with us but you are always in our thoughts. God willing, we will all be together one day. Naftali is doing very well at school and we are all looking forward to his barmitzvah next year. Uncle Zvulun will be teaching him his Haftorah and we're sure he'll give a good account of himself in the synagogue.

Babba and Mama are well and everyone sends you their love. Please do not worry about us. We are born survivors.

Your loving sister Rachel

David felt the tears welling. Would he ever see them again? What would happen were he to be killed? He could not bear the thought of the pain and suffering it would bring them. "I must stay alive," he muttered.

"What's that, David?"

It was his gunner, Rami.

"Nothing, Rami. I was just telling myself what a wonderful crew I've got."

"Well, let's all hear it loud and clear. You haven't been too lavish with any praise lately. We've got this ship into the best possible shape and all for you," the gunner laughed. Rami Bernstein from Tel Aviv had spent the whole morning boresighting his cannon and the Syrians had better beware.

David had just folded away Rachel's letter and was refastening his flak jacket when the scream of low-flying aircraft forced him to duck. A fraction of a second later the bombs dropped by the three MiG fighters exploded among the battalion's tanks further up the line.

David recognised his battalion commander's urgent voice over the net. He was using the codeword for all tank commanders under his aegis.

"All firemen stations, this is the battalion commander! Start engines! Prepare to move! Massed Syrian tanks reported three kilometres due east and moving towards us. Prepare to engage. Over and out!"

David instinctively turned to Arik. They waved to each other simultaneously, Arik adding a thumbs up sign. The blond warrior was not smiling now. His features portrayed neither fear nor incaution. Simply grim determination.

David gripped the hilt of the machine-gun with one hand and the lip of the turret cupola with the other as his Centurion lurched forward, the Continental V-12 diesel engine roaring with indignation as if it, too, was angry that the Syrians had had the audacity to attack.

David hoped the Syrians had not changed their tactics since the Six-day War. He knew that the only real advantage Israel had was in the quality of its manpower. Israelis were generally a brash lot and most soldiers feared letting their friends down more than the threat of death. In other countries it may be called machismo, but in Israel it was more than that. It was the knowledge that one defeat would spell the end of the whole Jewish Nation. David was comforted by the fact that should he fall in battle, he could rely even on the lowliest private to perform heroics, take the initiative and possibly turn the tide. How different we are from the Arab armies, he thought. They had rigid segregation of officers and men in the Soviet style, while in the Israeli army everyone used first names and your boss at work could be your driver in uniform. The Arabs were hidebound by their strict order of command and the ''Insh'a'Allah'' syndrome was often their undoing. Every setback could be accounted for in that one phrase. It was the classic cop-out, stunting imagination and initiative.

David, caught in a moment of meditation in the lull before the storm, recalled Yael Dayan's account of the Six-day War. The daughter of Israel's most famous general had been amazed when an Egyptian jeep had strayed into Israeli lines by mistake. In front were two scruffy and dirty enlisted men while in the rear sat two career officers reeking of eau-de-Cologne. Even their fingernails had been spotlessly manicured. David smiled as he recalled the story. Suddenly, a voice on the brigade net barked orders sharply. ''Green company move to protect forward position Charlie on the Kuneitra-Damascus Road. Constant enemy movement towards the frontier.''

David signalled his company to peel off from the main battalion. He could hear the repetitive crump of artillery as the seven tanks crossed fields pitted with craters where shells had fallen only minutes earlier. It was obvious the Syrians had not yet succeeded in getting their range. David prayed that they would not be forced into fighting in Kuneitra itself. The town had been derelict since the conflict six years earlier and his tanks would be vulnerable to bazooka squads and snipers. He knew that in city combat only one tank at a time could fight effectively and that, should the lead tank be crippled, the whole unit would be brought to a halt.

The company had advanced about two kilometres when the Syrian artillery found its range. Chunks of basalt rained down on them and each tank commander ducked instinctively inside his turret. David felt his tank shudder but Amnon, his driver, was still driving the machine forward and they appeared to be unscathed. After what seemed an eternity, the shelling ceased. David was the first to stand erect in his turret. He noted that Manny's tank had fallen behind. He switched to the internal net. "Manny, can you receive me? Report your damage."

"Nothing to worry about, boss." The reply was calmness itself. "Seems we've shed a track. Can you ask battalion to get us a tow? I don't think it was a shell. This damn terrain is playing havoc with us."

"Okay. Don't be too long in getting back to us, will you." It was more an order than a question. David now had only six tanks in operation and a glance towards the skyline told him he would need every one of them. He could see the pillars of dust to the east. He estimated that hundreds of Syrian tanks were moving against them.

Before he could relay Manny's plight over the net, the battalion commander's voice pounded his ears.

"Green company, this is Chief Fireman. Charlie has fallen. I repeat, Charlie has fallen. Find high ground and hold. Israel is counting on you. Over."

"I read you, Chief. One of our firemen has shed a track. Please arrange a tow. Over."

"Will do as soon as towing vehicle available. Meanwhile, tell him to sit tight. Over and out."

David relayed the instruction to Manny, whom he knew was feeling rotten about missing the action.

"Don't worry, boss. I'll be joining you before you reach

Damascus, you can count on that."

David waved to Manny in acknowledgement and turned to the matter in hand. The high ground would give him an advantage in spotting the enemy, although this would be counteracted by the nullification of the Centurion's inherent low-shoot capability over the Soviet-built T-55.

"Prepare armour-piercing and hollow charge shells." David knew the armour-piercing variety would stand a better chance of scoring hits because of its high velocity. The hollow charged shells would cause havoc should any infantry or armoured personnel trucks accompany the Syrian onslaught.

It was already three in the afternoon. The sun was at its most ferocious and the air inside the tank was fetid. Lieutenant David Katri knew his crew were suffering but he wondered how many of them would change places with him. Israeli tanks commanders traditionally stood in their turrets, exposing themselves to withering enemy fire and shrapnel. Nothing would be gained from staying down below as did the Arab commanders. That was simply a recipe for defeat.

"Boss, I can see the enemy dead ahead. Request permission to fire."

It was Arik. David turned to his left and saw his dearest friend peering through binoculars. He followed suit. "Yes, I see them, Arik. The range looks just about right. Okay, commanders. Remember, the fire must be rapid, at the discretion of each of you." David paused a second before uttering the words that marked their entry into the war. "Fire at will!"

The Centurions shuddered and the smell of cordite was almost overpowering as the 105mm cannons roared their defiance at the enemy. David judged there were about one hundred and ninety Syrian tanks before them. It was impossible to miss.

"They don't seem to realise they're being shot at, boss." It was Gidon's voice in the tank furthest to his right. "I think I've already scored five direct hits."

"That may be so, but they're still moving forward," retorted David. The last thing he wanted was over-confidence. The odds were still stacked against them. Unless the Syrians halted their advance, Green Company was doomed.

David switched to the battalion net. "Chief Fireman, Chief Fireman. This is Green Chief, do you read me? Over."

"Reading you loud and clear, Green Chief. What is your situation? Over."

"We are facing an estimated enemy tank force of nearly two hundred. Cannot hold for long. Urgently request reinforcements. Am pulling back from Jeba ridge."

"Okay, Green Chief. Retreat and hold new line half a kilometre to the rear. Try to tie them down until dark. Can't send you any reinforcements until morning earliest."

"L'azazel!" David swore. Hell, where was the damned airforce? In the past they were always there when you needed them.

The battalion commander was also unsure. "I think they're having trouble with the SAMs. I hope they won't take too long in learning how to overcome them. Over and out."

Until now David had seen only MiGs in the Golan skies although even their attacks were few and far between. Maybe they were also wary of their own umbrella of Surface-to-Air Missiles. The Syrians had shot down their own planes with missiles often enough in the past. The Russian technology must have been too much for them.

David ordered his company to retreat. Once the Syrians had advanced to a point where the angle of depression atop the ridge was too acute for his cannon, there was no more advantage to be had in holding the high ground.

The Syrian force appeared to split into two with one half turning north and the other proceeding towards them. The odds were still horrendous enough and David could only hope he could contain them until nightfall.

But as dusk approached the Syrians opened up with a

devastating barrage accompanied by accurate artillery fire.

"We're hit! We're hit!" It was Yossi on the left flank. David saw the Centurion almost leave the ground as a second shell slammed into the cupola. The tank erupted in a ball of flame. The crew had no chance. David was stunned momentarily. Yossi, the bright-eyed Yemenite from Tel Aviv's Shabazi quarter, had been with him since he had been given his first company command.

"Arik, Yossi's bought it. Move further to your left to cover the gap." David tried to control the fear in his voice. He saw Arik's Centurion swing a further fifteen metres to the left.

"Now listen carefully, Green Company. If your tank is disabled but you and your crew are okay, then try to make it back to Manny's tank in the rear. There's a good chance help will arrive there soon."

No sooner had David finished speaking than the three Centurions on his right flank took hits almost in unison.

"Boss, this is Boaz. Our cannon's out of shape. We're all okay and we're abandoning ship. We'll try to make it back to Manny. Over."

"Okay Boaz. God be with you."

The other two Centurions were burning fiercely. David called the commanders on the internal net but there was no answer. My God, he thought, they were being roasted alive and there was nothing he could do.

Darkness had fallen and David could see Arik's tank illuminated by the blaze. They were both sitting targets. "Arik," he gasped, the smoke and cordite in the air choking him, "pull back with me. Darkness is our only hope."

Arik pulled up a few metres from David's Centurion.

"Arik, don't use your infrared headlamps. Cut engines and maintain radio silence. It's our only hope. Maybe they'll lose us in the dark."

"Will do, David. Just remember that I love you, so don't

go doing anything foolish."

David heard his friend chuckle. Even in this desperate state of events Arik still exuded optimism. He wished he could share in it.

The following hours seemed endless. David imagined he was a blind diver in a sea of barracuda. He could hear the clanking of the Syrian armour around him. At times he felt he could actually reach out and touch them. Occasionally he heard voices in Arabic calling in the blackness. But towards morning the sounds had ceased and an eerie silence enveloped them.

The tension of constantly peering into the darkness had warded off any craving for sleep that David might have entertained. His crew, however, had taken the opportunity to get some shut-eye. It was amazing, he thought, how some men could just doze off even in situations such as this.

As the sun cast its first light over the battlefield he could make out the shapes of his comrades' Centurions. Two of them were still smouldering.

Suddenly he heard Arik's voice urgently breaking radio silence.

"David! Dead ahead fifty metres there's a Syrian T-55 with a shed track!"

"Yes, I see it, Arik. It looks as though it's been abandoned but take its range anyway to be on the safe ..."

The words had hardly left David's lips than he felt his tank buck. There was a tremendous explosion followed by the screams of his crew as a fire broke out below. David felt his body collapse. He could not stand up and he could not understand why. Something had taken away the power of his legs and he could feel the heat beginning to sear his flesh as he slumped into the well of the cupola.

"Arik, Arik! We're on fire! Everybody's screaming and I can't move. Arik, save me!"

Arik Ben-Ami had already ordered his gunner to fire at the

T-55 and then acted immediately on seeing David's tank take the direct hit. In one swift movement he leapt from his tank and raced across to the second Centurion. David was screaming in agony as he lifted him free of the burning cupola. Arik dragged his friend clear of the searing twisted leviathan as two more explosions rent the air. Both his Centurion and the T-55 had scored simultaneous direct hits. His own tank was ablaze and he felt utterly powerless.

Arik was torn between caring for David and trying to rescue his own crew. But within seconds there was a further tremendous explosion as the Centurion's turret was blown clean off. In that instance he knew he would never again see the men with whom he had shared the formative years of manhood.

The T-55 was also ablaze and its commander, uniform in flames, was rolling on the earth.

Arik knelt down by his friend and cradled David's head in his arms. "David, please don't die. You mustn't die. Not now. Not after all this."

David saw the familiar face above him. He felt himself slipping into unconsciousness. Everything was becoming a blur. He thanked God he no longer had any sensation of pain. Suddenly another face appeared behind Arik's. It was filled with hate. It must be the Devil incarnate, thought David, for it even had a golden fang. In one gasp of effort, David managed to alert his friend.

"Arik, behind you!"

The blond Israeli turned instinctively as the Syrian fell upon him with a bloodcurdling curse in Arabic. The two men, both almost spent by the rigours of battle, grappled in the barren earth.

David, only vaguely aware of another tremendous explosion to his left, saw a procession of faces, his father, his mother, Rachel and little Naftali, before slipping into oblivion.

Tel Hashomer Hospital, a hotch-potch of semi-circular Nissen-huts left over from the British Mandate, was more renowned for the expertise of its doctors than the aestheticism of its architecture.

Lying just east of Tel Aviv, the hospital and its adjoining army base had become the central point both for soldiers on their way to battle and those who had already made their personal sacrifice. For some the sacrifice had been ultimate.

For David Katri the war was over. Only vaguely aware of entering the operating theatre, he came to in a crowded ward full of the sick and the dying. Still groggy from the anaesthetic, the full circumstances of his predicament were not immediately apparent.

He had a peculiar sensation of lying on his back in the shade of a tank with his legs propped on one of the upper tracks.

"Good morning, David."

The voice was pretty and the face that went with it even more so. David's eyes flickered open. He could smell the starch of her uniform as she delicately dabbed at his brow.

"What happened? Where am I?"

"Don't worry. You're in Tel Hashomer and you're going to be all right."

David stared at the pretty Yemenite nurse, her reddish olive skin almost iridescent in the haze of his returning consciousness. He tried to move but to no avail. As the nurse stood back he saw what appeared to be two strange white objects suspended before him. It took him a few seconds to realise they were his legs.

The nurse noticed the concern in his eyes and pre-empted his question.

"I'm afraid you're going to be with us for quite a while. You really are a lucky man. You suffered only superficial burns, two broken legs and a fractured pelvis.''

"You call that lucky.''

"Yes. There are some hevreh here who will never walk again.''

David realised she was right. He admired her forthrightness and the honesty in her large almond eyes. She really was extraordinarily pretty.

"What's your name?''

"Yael. And you better get used to taking orders from me over the next couple of months if you want to get better.''

"It'll be a pleasure, sir.'' David tried a mock salute but the very movement made him wince. The pain brought back memories of his final battle on the Golan.

"Where's Arik? Where are my hevreh? How did I get here? Are they all right?'' David shuddered at the panic in his voice.

The nurse stroked his forehead once again.

"All I can tell you is that you arrived here by helicopter from the north and that you've been out like a light for three days. You have some visitors from your kibbutz. Perhaps they can tell you more.''

David was at once filled with both eagerness and trepidation. He knew Arik's parents were outside and yet what if they were to inform him that Arik was dead? He did not think he could bare it.

"Please send them in,'' he said weakly.

Sara and Mordechai Ben-Ami shuffled into the ward. David could see the look of concern on their kindly faces, but he dreaded that this was more to do with the loss of a son than his own troubles.

"How are you, lad?'' smiled Mordechai wanly, his shock of white hair sticking straight out from all sides a la Ben-Gurion. Sara Ben-Ami gave David a peck on the forehead and busily began arranging the flowers she had bought.

"I'm fine. I'll soon be back milking the cows, Motti.'' David used the diminutive of Mordechai. The man really had become a substitute father for him in the last few years.

Mordechai Ben-Ami could see the question in David's eyes. There was no need to prolong the formalities.

"David, Arik is all right as far as we know." He paused as the young man sighed with relief. "We received a message from him via an officer in the 77th battalion who had a phone link. Apparently he's managed to commandeer a tank with the 77th. They've all but repulsed the Syrian attack."

Neither men noticed that Yael had returned to the bed. Over her arm was a tattered army shirt.

"I was just about to throw this away, David. It's yours, you know." She produced a slip of paper from the top pocket and handed it to him. "This was in the top pocket."

David took the note. There was no mistaking Arik's handwriting although it was hardly legible. "The doc says you'll pull through. I'll let you know all about it when I get home. Get well soon. Arik."

David handed the note to Mordechai Ben-Ami. "Here, you take this, Motti. If Arik says he'll be home, you can bet on it. The very fact that he survived to join the 77th is enough for me. Your son's a born survivor."

Mordechai Ben-Ami smiled. He was reassured.

"When I fought in the War of Independence and the Sinai Campaign I prayed that my children would see no war. Unfortunately that was not to be. But with young men like you and Arik, Israel is in safe hands. We are all survivors in one way or another, David."

It was not until one week after the end of the war that Arik made good his promise. By that time David had already heard from Mordechai that Arik was fine but could not get leave because of mopping up operations.

It was raining the day Arik turned up at Tel Hashomer, the sort of rain that every Israeli looks forward to after a hot, dry summer.

The patter of raindrops on the corrugated roof of the Nissen hut had already lulled David into a half-sleep. He was still strung up like a chicken and welcomed any respite from the discomfort.

He thought he could hear a familiar folk song being sung in the background. "Here is what is pleasant and good. All the brothers sit together in peace."

David opened his eyes slowly. Before him stood Arik, dishevelled and wet, his blond locks plastered as if with hair cream. He was grinning.

David could not speak. They both felt that special emotion shared by soldiers and comrades who had survived battle. There was so much to ask, so much to know, yet the words would not come. It was Arik who broke the silence.

"You didn't think I was going to get myself killed after going through all that effort to save you, did you?" The blue eyes sparkled and the nostrils of his snub nose broadened as his grin exploded into a guffaw.

David laughed with him despite the pain.

"When I read that note you stuffed into my shirt, I knew you were going to get through it, Arik."

The blond soldier beamed. "The idea of that note came to me as they were taking you off the helicopter. The doctor gave me a pen and a scrap of paper. It was a rush job as you could see by the handwriting."

"I'm afraid I don't remember much, Arik. The last thing I recall is seeing this gold-fanged monster standing behind you with his arms uplifted."

"As it happens, you didn't miss much. I had the bastard on the ground when there was this tremendous explosion. When I came to, I was lying next to you and the Arab had disappeared. He must have thought we were both dead."

David listened intently as Arik described how he dragged him clear of the burning tanks, took off his webbed belt and made a splint for the broken legs.

"There was nothing to do but wait and pray that we would be rescued. You were still out cold. I checked your pulse and it seemed strong enough. I reckoned you were just using the opportunity to get some shut-eye."

David grinned. He knew that Arik was making light of the incident now. At the time he was probably close to panic. His friend was more than a little headstrong and this was probably the reason he had been passed over for command of a company.

Arik saw David's expression turn to one of anxiety and concern. He knew what was coming next.

"What about the hevreh, Arik? How are my crew?"

Arik lowered his eyes and gripped his friend's hand. "They're all dead, David. If that Syrian hadn't jumped me I might have been able to rescue at least another one of them."

The realisation that both crews had died the worst death imaginable in that inferno made David feel guilty.

Arik read his thoughts. "Dear friend, we must not allow ourselves the luxury of wallowing in guilt and self-pity for surviving. However much they try to get rid of us, there'll always be Jews."

"It's just so damn hard sometimes that..."

Arik was interrupted by the appearance of Yael. Motioning him to stand aside, she felt David's pulse, checked his temperature and adjusted the saline drip alongside the bed.

David noticed his friend appraising the girl in white. There was little doubt those piercing blue eyes were undressing her. After she had gone, Arik, thankful for the opportunity to lighten the situation, whistled through his teeth.

"Wow, who's the looker?"

"I'm glad you're impressed, Arik. Her name's Yael Hazan and she's going to be my wife."

"Only she doesn't know it yet," Arik interjected.

"True. But then that's a mere formality. You know how

determined I am.''

Arik knew his friend was the type who succeeded at most things he undertook. If David decided to make the army his career he'd make it to general.

"You're only twenty, David. There are a lot more girls out there to play around with before you settle down.''

"Yes, Arik, but you know how it is with us Sephardim. We like to get married early so we can have ten or eleven kids.''

Arik laughed. He loved the warmth of the Sephardim. There was no doubting they were different in mentality to the Jews of European extract. The Oriental Jews possessed a vitality, a love of life, and close family ties that were missing in many Ashkenazi homes.

He noticed Yael busily tending a patient further down the ward. Yes, he thought, they would make a handsome couple. David, tall and lean, the slight hook to his nose giving his face such a powerful strength of character. Yael, of medium build, but with delicate facial contours which made her so intensely attractive, the sort of looks which would never fade and die. He was already looking forward to being best man.

As David had predicted, Yael not only nursed him back to health but the two fell in love. They were a fine match and, although the pretty Yemenite found the collective life difficult to take at first, she settled quickly once the kibbutz directorate decided to appoint her the settlement's official nurse.

David, meanwhile, immersed himself in the task of making the production of milk as sophisticated an operation as possible. The yield improved threefold and he was always eager to incorporate the latest technology despite grumblings from the finance committee.

Arik remained an extra three years in the army, reaching the rank of captain. True to his word, he left the kibbutz to join a small company involved ostensibly in the export of agricultural equipment and know-how to both Europe and the Third World.

Arik rented a flat in Haifa but regularly visited his parents and the Katri family at weekends. Boaz and Shoshana Katri eagerly awaited his visits, for uncle Arik always brought them presents from the big city.

But after four years of being spoiled thoroughly by their favourite uncle, Arik's visits became more sporadic. It was explained to them that he had been promoted and that this meant lengthier spells abroad as a sales executive for his company. David wished his friend would settle down and raise a family as he had done. But he never pressed the matter during Arik's infrequent visits to the kibbutz. Instead, he luxuriated in his friend's tales of far-off lands. David felt no pang of envy. He was idyllically happy, his only regret being that his family in Damascus could not join him.

A further ten years were to pass before a disaster high over the Mediterranean and a telephone call were to change all their lives irrevocably.

BOOK TWO

CHAPTER ONE

It had been a bad day at Leopardstown for Patrick McQuinn.
One after the other, the four-legged beasts had let him down.
Even the Irish horses, begorrah. McQuinn knew he was in trouble. He was now in debt to Joe Quade to the tune of five thousand pounds. Joe Quade had been good to him, but he knew there was a limit to the big man's patience when his clients' debts reached unmanageable proportions. And when Joe Quade turned nasty, a debtor would be well advised to emigrate.

The last race run and nightfall fast approaching, McQuinn prepared to slink out of Quade's betting shop, his thin gangling frame stooped as if in submission to this final humiliation.

"No winners again today, Paddy?"

McQuinn could not decide whether the voice of one of his cronies was sympathetic or condescending. He averted his eyes and slipped quickly into Camden High Street, the sudden coldness of London's February air causing him to gasp for breath.

The ginger-haired Irishman would normally have taken a bus home. But today Patrick McQuinn was broke and it was still two weeks to pay day. Darkness had enveloped his tiny Victorian terraced home by the time he had completed his lonely trek up Kentish Town Road.

McQuinn rubbed his hands together vigorously. He could hardly feel his fingers in the bitter cold. He fumbled in his coat pocket for the key and let himself in. The hallway was almost as cold as outside and he decided it would be wiser to keep his coat on and light a fire in the lounge before anything else. He entered the lounge and switched on the light.

"Mother of Jesus!" he gasped.

"Good evening, Paddy," one of his unwanted guests sneered. The man, seated in the armchair facing the door, motioned him to sit in a chair placed purposely in the centre of the room. A second man, just as big and just as menacing, stood behind the door.

"We'd like to discuss a little matter with you, Paddy."

The steam of the man's breath reminded him of a horse at the end of a steeplechase. Only the horse was better looking, he thought. Patrick McQuinn found himself smiling, somewhat incongruously given his predicament.

The first man continued. "Joe Quade is a decent man as you know, Paddy." He paused to wait for McQuinn's affirmative nod. "But there comes a time when even he loses patience. And that time has come with you, my son."

The Cockney voice grew more threatening.

"You've got two days to cough up the dough, mate. And just to show you that we mean business, Jimmy here is going to give you a little taster of what you can expect if it aint forthcoming."

McQuinn instinctively sprang up and lunged towards the door. The second man, in one swift movement, closed it and grabbed the Irishman by the lapels of his overcoat. McQuinn grimaced at the smell of garlic on the man's breath.

Noticing his prey's discomfort, the man breathed heavily and slowly into the Irishman's face. "Doner kebab," he said laconically, at the same time bringing his knee swiftly into McQuinn's groin.

The Irishman groaned and collapsed in agony on the floor. He gasped, the pain almost exquisite in its intensity. So much so that he was hardly aware of the boot that rammed into his cheek. Barely conscious, McQuinn rolled over, his mouth oozing broken teeth and blood.

"Two days, McQuinn." It was the first man's voice. "We know you Micks aint got a lot up top, so whatever grey cells are up there, you'd better start using 'em quick, mate.''

The Irishman, his grey cells scrambled, vaguely heard the front door slam.

Nobody paid particular attention to the T-registered Ford Cortina parked in a north London side-street. The car, pitted with rust, matched the drabness of its surroundings. If anyone had bothered to take notice on such a cold and misty night, they would have seen a swarthy man sitting at the wheel, his gaze fixed firmly on a house about fifteen metres away on the opposite side of the road. To all intents and purposes, he was another of London's immigrants from the far-flung reaches of the Commonwealth.

The man shivered with the cold. God had cursed these infidels by imposing upon them cold and darkness for such long periods of the year. He longed for the life-giving warmth of the Middle Eastern sun. He had suffered the bleakness of this metropolis for long enough.

But now, after six months of meticulous preparation, his efforts were about to bear fruit. He had employed a private investigator to follow the Irishman's every move. He had needed to know the very psyche of the man who was about to play such an important part in the Islamic Jihad, the holy war which would culminate in the triumph of Islam over the Infidel.

The man in the car knew that, as a foreigner, any questions he might ask would arouse suspicion. But people were always more co-operative with their own kind. The private detective had done an excellent job and had been well rewarded. That he would have little time to enjoy the fruits of his labours was of little consequence. The onlooker was well versed in the vicissitudes of life. War had dominated his life. It had brought about the loss of his family, it had mutilated both his body and his soul. Allah had demanded of him that he fight in His cause. Each time he had been called upon to serve Him, whether against the accursed Israelis in nineteen seventy-three or nineteen eighty-two or against the equally vituperous Falangists during the last ten years, he had been ready to die a martyr's death. It seemed, however, that Allah was sparing him for a greater purpose, one which, in the fullness of time, would be forever inscribed as the greatest tribute to His name. His present task would be a precursor to that great event, a sort of hors d'ourvre. It would convince his leader that he was a man who could accomplish great things, a man whom Allah, in his wisdom, had blessed with ingenuity and cunning.

The figure in the Ford Cortina shivered once again. But this time not with the cold, rather with the thrill of expectation of great feats to come.

It was then that he saw the two big men leave the house he had been watching. If the private detective had been correct then his quarry should be in an amenable frame of mind. He waited a few minutes after the men had driven away before crossing the road and ringing the doorbell.

Patrick McQuinn was in two minds as to whether to answer the front door. He felt he needed help from whichever quarter but, on the other hand, it might be Quade's two heavies again. The Irishman, his jaw aching, decided that his adversaries would not need to ring the doorbell to let themselves in and made his way gingerly along the hall before opening the door.

"Who are you?" he mumbled, aware that he must have presented a pretty sore sight to the stranger.

"A friend. Someone who can help you out of your present difficulty."

The man had a foreign accent and McQuinn was almost mesmerised by the reflection of the hall light on the stranger's golden front tooth.

"I suppose you'd better come in," he said, wondering how

much this man knew about him. "I'll get cleaned up and light a fire." It was a further five minutes before either man spoke again. The stranger was the first to break the silence.

"My friend," he smiled warmly, "how would you like to earn ten thousand pounds?"

McQuinn was flabbergasted. "Mother of Jesus!" he muttered, still holding his painful right cheek. The first thing he envisioned was handing over the money he owed Joe Quade. He could just imagine the bookie's look of surprise.

The stranger noticed the Irishman's far-away gaze. The Christians were all alike, he thought. They would do anything for money.

As if reading his mind, the ginger-haired man answered. "What do I have to do?"

The swarthy stranger withdrew a brown packet from his inside pocket and placed in on the table between them.

"In here are five thousand pounds. You will receive a further five thousand pounds once the task is completed."

McQuinn fingered the brown envelope. Whatever he would be asked to do could not be worth more than the freedom from Quade's henchmen that the money represented. And he would also have a further five thousand to boot.

The stranger continued. "We know that you are a loader at Heathrow and my friends wish to smuggle a suitcase into the hold of an airliner bound for Tel Aviv tomorrow." He noted the Irishman's quizzical look and cut short his question. "All you need know is that the suitcase contains contraband, counterfeit dollars. Inflation is rife in Israel and everyone is purchasing dollars to hedge against it."

"What flight is it?"

"Flight LY 314, departing sixteen hundred hours."

The Irishman scratched his ginger hair, his apprehension tempered somewhat by the sight of the brown envelope in front of him.

"Security's pretty tight. We're checked before we enter the loading area. How am I supposed to smuggle the thing in?"

The stranger smiled. It was absurdly simple.

"It is true that you are checked when you enter the loading bay. But your vehicle is not. You will simply place the suitcase, it is only a small one, in the well beneath your seat. You will then drive the loader from the depot and deposit the case with the other luggage on the conveyer belt."

"I might be watched by your security people," McQuinn answered in the mistaken belief that the strange little man before him was an Israeli.

"They are used to seeing you by now. I'm sure you will find a way to avoid their prying eyes."

McQuinn fingered the brown packet. "What if I refuse?" He regretted the question as soon as he had asked it. The stranger's eyes contained a menace that made Quade's two goons resemble kindly maiden aunts.

"I think, Mr McQuinn, that your present employers do not know that you have served time for robbery," said Sedawi slowly through pursed lips. "I think that a clean record is, how you say, a prerequisite for the job."

McQuinn lowered his eyes in submission and once again fingered the package. The Jew knew a lot about him, it seemed. Well, what did he care if they wanted to screw each other with counterfeit money while he was getting the real stuff.

"Flight LY 314, departing sixteen hundred hours, you say," the Irishman stroked his chin. "I'll just be finishing my shift around then."

"I know."

"When will I get the rest of my money?"

"As soon as you get home tomorrow, either myself or a colleague will deliver the remainder."

The temptation proved too great for Patrick McQuinn. "Okay, I'll do it," he said, rising to shake the stranger's hand.

It was a reddish purple. Funny that he had not noticed it before. The guy must have been pretty badly burned.

Patrick McQuinn knocked off work the following day at sixteen-thirty hours, his task accomplished. He was looking forward to clearing his debt with Joe Quade before the betting office would close. He might even lay a few quid on the dogs for the night meeting at Walthamstow.

It took the Irishman nearly an hour-and-a-half to get home. He entered the lounge and removed his coat. He then went straight to the middle drawer of a dilapidated chest next to the television and withdrew a brown packet. He had been worried about it while at work but it was still there. He just hoped the stranger would come with rest of the money so that he could nip round to Quade's betting shop before it closed.

McQuinn turned on the television. He might as well watch the news while he was waiting.

Suddenly, the doorbell rang. Good, he thought, this will be the biggest payday of my life.

It was indeed the stranger from the previous night. "Well, hello there, will yer please come in an' make yerself at home," McQuinn enthused in his best Irish bonhomie.

The dapper guest followed him into the lounge, withdrawing a brown envelope from under his raincoat. The Irishman's incredible naivety was matched only by his greed, the stranger thought.

"As you can see, Mr McQuinn, we keep our side of the bargain if you keep yours. Please accept this further token of our appreciation."

The Irishman smiled in anticipation as he stretched out his right arm to take the packet. But the expression turned to one of pained surprise as he received instead a hammer blow to the ribs. He was not immediately aware that the blow was anything other than one perpetrated with a fist. But as Patrick McQuinn sank slowly to the floor, he could feel a warm sticky liquid oozing between the fingers that were clutching an area just above his stomach.

The Irishman was already entering oblivion as he felt a sharp object enter the side of his neck. He was spared the indignity of knowing that the precious brown package in his inside jacket pocket had rejoined its previous owner.

Patrick McQuinn's guest turned away from his lifeless body as the BBC newscaster introduced the six o'clock news. He listened intently, the blood still dripping from his knife.

"We are receiving reports that an El Al Jumbo Jet has crashed into the Mediterranean near Rhodes. There are believed to be three hundred and fifty-three passengers and crew aboard. Eyewitnesses report seeing the airliner explode in mid-air..."

Rashid Sedawi switched off the television and gave thanks to Allah. Jibril the Palestinian had been responsible for Lockerbie, even if he was working on behalf of the Iranians. This time it was no action by proxy. He sank to his knees and recited the ninth Sura of the holy book that he knew by heart.

"Fight against such of those who have been given the Scripture as believe not in Allah nor the Last Day, and forbid that which Allah has forbidden by His Messenger, and follow not the religion of truth, until they pay the tribute readily, being brought low."

So long as Jews and Christians did not submit, the Jihad against them would continue, Rashid vowed silently.

CHAPTER TWO

Yariv Cohen waited impatiently for his advisers to seat themselves round the boardroom table at Mossad's headquarters in the Hadar Dafna building on King Saul Boulevard, not far from the Kirya, the sprawling military complex in north Tel Aviv. Cohen's normally stern face, accentuated by the thin scar above his right upper lip, was distorted in its severity. The features of the men around him reflected not only the pain that was felt all over Israel, but the humiliation at the security lapse which had led to the disaster.

The chief of the Mossad was reminded of the fiasco of Lillehammer in July, nineteen seventy-three. He had been on home leave when news came through that his fellow operatives had botched the task of assassinating Ali Hassan Salameh. To their eternal shame they had killed instead a harmless Moroccan waiter named Ahmed Bouchiki. The farce in Norway had left its mark on all of them. Salameh had been the architect of the Munich Olympics massacre and he was due to be the last of the Palestinian terrorists involved to be disposed of. The Lillehammer affair culminated in the *mehdal*, the disaster, of the Yom Kippur War which was a nadir for both the Mossad and Aman, the Army intelligence service.

Secretly, he wished he had been in charge of the Norwegian operation. But his future as a member of the Mossad's hit squad had been determined during the elimination of Black September's agent in Rome a few months earlier. The stupid stairwell on the third floor of that Roman apartment must have been constructed from balsa. As Cohen recalled the incident, he instinctively gripped his shattered right knee. His quarry was already dead with three .22 bullets in various parts of his anatomy when the accident happened. He recalled Mohammed Houri's death mask and how it had sported a cynical smile. It was as if the PLO terrorist was having the last laugh when the elite of Israel's Secret Service slipped and fell. It was a good thing his partner was there to extricate him.

It was assumed in Tel Aviv that Yariv Cohen had been wounded in action and he certainly did nothing to disabuse this view. If a busted knee was all that was necessary to create a climate for promotion within the organisation, then it was a small price to pay.

His progress within Mossad had been steady and sure. He had been in control now for nearly six years. They had been six years of success save for a few hiccups involving pseudo spies in America. His network of informants in Lebanon was second to none. Some of them, however, were coming close to being exposed and this would endanger his own men. They might need to be withdrawn.

The insignificant click of a match being struck was enough to rouse Yariv Cohen from his musings. He examined the faces of his officers. They bore pain and resentment and not a little frustration. He had to be firm yet not insensitive.

"Gentlemen," he said slowly, "today Israel is in shock, tomorrow it will be in mourning and the day after tomorrow it will demand revenge."

Cohen, in his usual uniform of white open-necked shirt and grey flannel trousers, withdrew a packet of Royal from his breast pocket. He dragged deeply on a cigarette before continuing.

"I will obviously need a full report from our London operatives on how the bomb was smuggled on board. It may have been an inside job and we cannot rely solely upon the efficiency of Scotland Yard to put the pieces together."

The Mossad chief's beady grey eyes fixed on Moshe Weinberg, the head of European Central, the organisation's headquarters in the Hague. Weinberg squirmed in his chair. He prayed this would not be the beginning of a witch-hunt.

"Moshe, I need not emphasise to you enough the necessity of tightening up security all round. Ours is a small country. Probably ninety per cent of the population knew someone aboard that plane. We cannot afford the luxury of such a loss. It must never happen again."

Cohen's eyes passed from Weinberg to the other members of the Mossad's higher echelons. They rested upon Rahamim Ben-Yaacov, the only Sephardi in the group of six. Although he himself was a Sabra, a native-born Israeli, his parents had immigrated to Israel from the British protectorate of Aden in nineteen twenty-one. Rahamim, small and wiry, was born ten years later. The family had settled in Petah Tikva, east of Tel Aviv, and Shmuel and Leah Ben-Yaacov eventually raised eleven children. Rahamim, with twenty-five years of service both as an agent and home-based operative, had been chosen by Cohen to head the Mossad's Arab Affairs Section. In five years he had efficiently organised the infiltration of some of the leading Palestinian terror groups.

"I believe Rahamim has some latest information for us," said Cohen. The Polish-born head of Israel's Secret Service drew heavily on his cigarette and nodded to the man with the crinkly grey hair.

Ben-Yaacov withdrew a piece of paper from a file in front of him. The whine of the air-conditioning system seemed deafening in the silence before he spoke. Despite being a Sabra, his Hebrew accent bore the familiar guttural intonations of Jews from the Yemen. It was said that this accent was the same as that used by the ancient Hebrews. Perhaps one of the things that endeared these people to Ashkenazi Israelis was their ability to intonate the Hebrew letters *ayin* and *het,* which had become indistinguishable from *aleph* and *chaf* as pronounced by those of European stock.

The Oriental Jew cleared his throat. "I have here," he said, holding the paper up for all to see, "a bulletin from Reuters in Beirut which has a group calling itself the Islamic Jihad Fundamentalist Cell as claiming responsibility for the bombing."

"Is anything known?" Cohen asked, more for the benefit of the others as he himself was already certain.

"I'm afraid that this group is entirely unknown to us. If no other terrorist group claims responsibility, then we will have to assume that they really do exist."

Reuven Weiss, another of the East European cadre in the organisation and head of the evaluation department, withdrew his pipe from his mouth and raised it to interject. He had already seen the report. His section was responsible for analysing information from all sources, whether they be Mossad agents in the field, foreign agencies or the media.

"The only help we have is in their name. I think Rahamim will agree that the words 'Islamic Jihad Fundamentalist' implies they are Shi'ite and the word 'Cell' gives the impression they are a small group."

Ben-Yaacov, nodding in concurrence, took up the reins. "I also think it's fairly safe to say that they are based in Beirut, although I think their recruitment may come from the Bekaa Valley."

All in the room were aware that the Bekaa had become the hotbed of Shi'ite fanaticism with its guiding lights being the mullahs of Iran. There was no shortage in the area of martyrs for the cause and Israel was increasingly suffering suicide attacks against its troops in southern Lebanon.

The Sephardi Jew continued. "If their base is indeed Beirut, then I think we're in with a chance of infiltrating them. The city may be a kaleidoscope of warring factions, but this can work to our advantage. Intrigue is rife and tongues wag. I haven't met an Arab yet who could keep a secret." The men around the table smiled. A crack was even discernible in the otherwise stoic features of Yariv Cohen. He knew their main problem would be sifting the truth from the lies, a task that was so much an important part of espionage. "Who have we got on the ground, Rahamim?"

The head of Arab Affairs section looked perplexed. "To be quite honest, boss, I don't think I'd risk one of our own men already there. From the feedback I've been getting, I'd say all of them are in danger of being exposed. Also, they've been acting as Sunnis or Palestinians and are well known as such. They can't become Shi'ites overnight."

"Then what do you suggest?" Yariv Cohen was becoming impatient at the negativity expressed.

"I would like to train someone especially for the task. It may take upwards of six months, but I believe it will work. He would, of course, have to be someone whose native tongue is Arabic, yet is young enough to withstand the rigours of the job and old enough to be taken seriously."

Yariv Cohen was already formulating in his mind who that someone should be. Syrian Jews in their mid-thirties were at a premium. Most of those who had been approached had either turned him down, which was their prerogative, or had been of insufficient intelligence or psychological aptitude for the task.

Cohen cast his mind back to the September morning in 1969 when his first real task in the organisation, albeit a mundane one, had been to welcome a young Syrian refugee to the Promised Land. He rubbed his chin pensively. Now what was the lad's name?

The room had fallen silent, save for the incessant heavy breathing of the air conditioners. The Mossad officers waited for their boss to take the lead.

"Katri!" he exploded suddenly. Six pairs of raised eyebrows waited for an explanation.

Cohen turned to Weiss. "Reuven, I want all you've got on a Syrian refugee by the name of David Katri. He escaped from

Damascus in September, nineteen sixty-nine. I know because I got him to sign the Official Secrets Act.''

The Mossad chief then turned to Rahamim Ben-Yaacov. ''Rahamim, I know that these matters are usually your domain, but on this occasion I'd like to interview the man first. It's a personal thing.''

''Tfadal.'' Ben-Yaacov's use of the Arabic for 'if you please' brought a smile to everyone's lips. But it seemed strange to the Yemenite that a man who conferred regularly with the Prime Minister should be bothering himself over such a trifling matter as recruitment.

David Katri was just finishing breakfast in the communal dining hall when Yossi Brenner called out that he had a telephone call in the offices of the secretariat.

''Can't they put it through here, Yossi?'' he asked irritably.

''Sorry, it's come through on the outside line.''

David rose, pushing aside the plate of leben, omelette, tomatoes and myriad other vegetables that made the kibbutz breakfast probably the best anywhere. But today David Katri was in no mood for breakfast, however good. He surveyed the glum faces around him. Everyone was in shock. Normally the hader ochel was bubbling with noise as members caught up with some of the gossip they may have missed the day before. But today the kibbutzniks of Ramat Shlomo were bowed. The news of the air disaster would have affected them deeply anyway, but the fact that one of their own members had been aboard cast a pall of gloom over the settlement.

David wondered whether Arik, wherever he was, had heard of his friend's death. He knew that Avner Wilder was almost as close to Arik as he was. David had taken over duties in the cowshed after Avner had decided to transfer to the factory.

He had been returning from a successful trip to Europe selling the water valves the kibbutz produced so well. David felt a lump in his throat. The settlement had lost some of its members in Israel's wars, but this was different. In a war, you knew there was a chance you could die. But to be blown up in mid-air with no warning was such a horrific way to die that he could not get the vision of his friend's death out of his mind.

David felt especially for Nehama Wilder and her three sons. It would scar them forever. He prayed that Avner's body would be washed up on some Mediterranean coast. It would enable them to hold a funeral and it would also enable the rabbis to declare Nehama a widow.

Despite the fact that the kibbutz belonged to a secular movement, it was, like everything else in Israel, subject to certain rules imposed by the religious minority. According to the constitution, Israel was a Jewish State and the religious authorities made great capital from this, both political and theological.

David despised the way the religious parties had conspired to force their will on the government. The trouble was that any government in Israel, whether left wing or right, needed the support of those parties in order to survive.

He knew Nehama would not be allowed to re-marry unless Avner's body were found or only after the rabbis were satisfied that he had indeed been aboard the plane. He recalled reading a story about a pilot who had crashed over northern Galilee. It was the job of the rabbis of a branch of the Civil Guard called Zihu'i Hallalim, Identification of Souls, to carry out the harrowing task of searching for what was left of the airman's body. They had combed the area in vain for three days until one of them found part of an ear hanging from the branch of a tree. The rabbis gave thanks to God. The piece of ear was all that was buried, but it had been enough to enable the wife of the pilot to re-marry if she so chose.

Should Avner's body not be found, thought David, it might

take many months before the Chief Rabbinate would grant Nehama the right to wed again. It seemed to him that basic humanity was being sacrificed in order to safeguard the traditions of religion.

Immersed in morbidity, David entered the secretariat's office. He was hardly aware of Ruth, the telephone operator, speaking to him.

"They've rung off, David. But I've got a message for you... David, are you listening?"

"Oh, excuse me, Ruth. Yes, what was the message?"

"Well, you know you're supposed to be going to Tel Aviv now for a meeting with the Milk Marketing Board..." Ruth Stein did not wait for an affirmative. She had a crossword puzzle to finish. "Well, they said the meeting had been transferred to Derekh Petah Tikva number fifty-two. You're to go up to the third floor and it's the door marked 'Dairymaid Import-Export Company'."

David took the note and thanked her. As soon as he had left the office, he made his way to the car park. He was glad the Citroen was available. It might not be a fast ride to Tel Aviv, he thought, but at least it would be comfortable.

David was ambivalent about Tel Aviv. It was a noisy, bustling metropolis, the most Levantine of Israel's cities. He welcomed the change from the quiet seclusion of the kibbutz, but not for long. A few hours of traffic, fumes and people were more than enough for him.

As he drove along Derekh Haifa and headed south, David thought even the leaves of the palm trees in the central reservation were more bowed than usual. The traffic was its usual choking self, but there seemed to be something missing. It took a few minutes for him to realise the conspicuous lack of hooting of car horns so characteristic of Tel Aviv. At each traffic light he was surrounded by a sea of glum faces which he knew mirrored his own.

David parked the Citroen in a side street and entered the rather nondescript edifice at number fifty-two Derekh Petah Tikva. He thought how boring was most of the architecture in the nation's largest city although he had to concede most of it had been built in a hurry to accommodate the vast influx of new immigrants. The only sections of town that appealed to him were the bustling shopping thoroughfare of Dizengoff Street and the old quarters of Balfour and Neve Tsedek.

There was no sign to the effect of 'Dairymaid Import-Export Company' in the lobby and he found this rather strange. The lift was out of order, although this was hardly an unusual occurrence in Israel. The whole building was run-down and David was beginning to think he had been given the wrong address.

He ascended the stairs to the third floor. To his relief, one of the offices bore the title of the company. The letters were written in script on a piece of card which had been fastened to the door with drawing pins. As he rang the bell, he thought it strange that the company had not even bothered to affix a proper metal nameplate.

"Please come in. The door's open," came a gravelly voice. David twisted the doorknob and entered the lobby of a small flat. He stared in surprise. The lobby was totally empty. There was not a stick of furniture in sight.

"I'm in here, David. Straight ahead and first right," the gruff voice called again.

David entered the room, his feelings a mixture of trepidation and curiosity. Before him seated behind an old table sat a smallish balding man in his mid-fifties. David noted the man's beady eyes and the thin scar above the lip. There was something familiar about that face but he could not place it. David was momentarily mesmerised by the man's stern features. The situation was totally incongruous. The sole contents of the apartment were himself, this stranger, two chairs and a rickety table.

Yariv Cohen allowed himself the briefest of smiles. The man

65

before him still possessed the swarthy good looks that had impressed him in their first meeting many years earlier. The slightly hooked nose gave Katri a classic profile. He was unusually tall for a Jew from an Arab country and this gave him a somewhat distinguished bearing.

Cohen motioned David to take a seat. He wondered whether his guest had recognised him. No matter, he thought, all would be revealed within a few seconds.

"Please excuse the rather sparse furnishings. It's the best we could arrange under the circumstances." Cohen could see the Sephardi was still bemused. "Tell me, David," he continued, "does the name Yariv Cohen mean anything to you?"

David shrugged and shook his head. The only Yariv Cohen he knew was an old army buddy and he thought it wise to remain silent until this strange man made his purpose clear.

He did not have to wait long.

"My name is Yariv Cohen and I am the head of the Institute for Intelligence and Special Operations, better known as the Mossad."

David's heart skipped a beat at the mention of the name of Israel's Secret Service. In an instant he recognised the man as the Mossad agent who had welcomed him to Israel. He was older, greyer and balder but the scar above the lip and the beady eyes were the same. He wondered whether the man still limped.

"I...I remember you now. You were at the quay in Haifa when I first arrived in Israel. You scared me a little then, I can tell you."

Cohen smiled fleetingly. "My bark's worse than my bite, David," he said, "except where Israel's security is concerned."

The older man withdrew a packet of Royal from the breast pocket of his shirt and lit a cigarette. He dragged deeply before continuing. He did not offer David one because he knew the younger man did not smoke.

"You may be wondering why the head of the Mossad

66

is bothering to sit face to face with a kibbutz dairy manager."
Cohen did not pause for David's affirmative nod.

"I need not tell you how we all feel about yesterday's events.
Perhaps we feel stronger than the general public. In a way, we
are responsible for the safety of every one of our citizens abroad
and we need slip up only once for a catastrophe to occur. The
war against terrorism is never ending. Most times we succeed,
but we are human beings, David, and the occasional failure,
however bitter, is inevitable."

David was already thinking ahead of the Mossad chief. He
knew that he owed the organisation a debt and that the time
had arrived for him to repay it.

"What do you want me to do, Mr Cohen?"

The head of Israel's security noted the question was uttered
in total sincerity. By its nuance it was already clear the man
before him was prepared to accept whatever responsibility would
be thrust upon him.

"I am obliged to say, David, that you have every right to
decline to join the organisation. We do not press gang our
citizens, and as you have already signed your compliance with
the Official Secrets Act, you can walk out of this room at the
end of this meeting and never be bothered again."

Before continuing, Cohen stubbed out his cigarette in a cheap
tin ashtray, the table's sole ornament.

"I know that this does not really apply in your case, David,
but all the same I'd like to paraphrase a description by Isser
Harel, a former head of the Service, of the way in which
we select our agents. We will never accept any adventurer
of the James Bond type. We don't want that sort of hero
in our Service, and we don't want any of the volunteers who
so often approach us. As a rule it is we who suggest to a man
that he might work with us. If he accepts the idea, we allow
him to volunteer. The first question we ask ourselves is

why the prospective agent is out for adventure. We want our operatives to be honest, loyal and devoted patriots but, above all, modest. Anonymity and total secrecy are essential if the agent is to succeed. Those with loose tongues are ejected as quickly as possible."

Cohen paused to let the words of his former boss sink in, although he was as certain as he could be that David Katri possessed more of the qualities of Eli Cohen than those of James Bond.

"Please tell me what you want me to do?" David repeated, his face taut with apprehension.

"Okay, now I'll get to the point. The group claiming responsibility for the blowing up of our airliner is unknown to us. It will be a long job. It may take more than a year, but we want to train you and infiltrate you into that group. We reckon they are Shi'ite and that they are based in Beirut, with connections to pro-Iran fundamentalists in the Bekaa. We have already instigated a thorough investigation of how the disaster occurred and our men in the Arab world are attempting to get more information on the so-called Islamic Jihad Fundamentalist Cell."

David's mind raced. How would he learn to be a Shi'ite? What would he tell the kibbutz? What, most important of all, would he tell his wife and children?

Cohen saw Katri's forehead furrow in concern. Although David had not uttered a word, the small man held up the palm of his hand.

"If you agree to join us, you will be meeting our Arab Affairs director shortly. He will be your point of contact. Look upon him as your Godfather. He will be your mentor, a man you can and must trust implicitly. Meanwhile, I suggest you inform the kibbutz that you have decided to leave to take up a position as director of an American-based dairy equipment import-export agency in Tel Aviv. The job will require extensive travel. We will set up the front for you and I can assure you your office will have more that just a table and two chairs.''

David smiled. "I hope it will have a proper metal name-plate on the front door as well." He hesitated as the older man grinned, the scar adding a distortion to the features, reminding David of a friend who suffered from Bell's palsy.

"What about my wife and children, Mr Cohen?" David had never kept any secrets from Yael and she knew him better than he knew himself.

"Your wife and children must be unaware of your true activities. And that, I am afraid, is a prerequisite for joining us."

"My wife, Mr Cohen, is not only the most tactful of people I have ever known, she is also the most perceptive. I think she will guess fairly quickly what I am doing. Only last week, I told her how much I loved my work and that the kibbutz was the only life for me. Although I must admit she would welcome a return to the big city."

"David, if your wife is as tactful as you say, she will not do anything to jeopardise your position. Nevertheless, you will be duty bound not to divulge any information which may confirm her suspicions."

"I understand." For a fleeting moment David envisioned his wife. How sweet and kind she was. It was true she would welcome a return to Tel Aviv. She could get her old job back at Tel Hashomer and practise the sort of real nursing she so sorely missed on the kibbutz. But he knew she would be surprised by his decision.

"Good," said Cohen, rising and extending his hand. "Welcome to the Mossad. Our motto is 'by deception thou shalt do war'. You will be contacted in a couple of days by Rahamim Ben-Yaacov. He's one of our best men. You can trust him with your life."

David shook the hand as Cohen added a rider.

"You may have to."

As Yariv Cohen watched the handsome Syrian Jew leave the

room, he felt Katri was the right man for the job. Owing to the urgency of the situation, David would be put through a punishing routine in half the time it usually took to train a Mossad agent. Cohen felt confident Katri would cope with the pressure. But he also knew that there was no Secret Service anywhere that could prevent its agents revealing secrets to their wives in moments of intimacy. In warning Katri, Cohen had complied with the bounds of duty. Nevertheless he had ordered a check on Yael Katri and the report indicated that she had a character as flawless as her husband's.

In another land, in another world, Rashid Sedawi entered the shell-pocked apartment building in West Beirut by the rear entrance. Some would have said the construction was uninhabitable, which was just as well. Members of the Higher Council of the Islamic Jihad Fundamentalist Cell had been careful in choosing the site for their headquarters. Here there would be no prying neighbours to gossip about strange happenings at number six on the third floor. Almost the whole street was derelict, a fitting tribute to the internecine war which had brought Lebanon to its knees.

But Rashid Sedawi was unconcerned at the plight of his country. This torn, tragic land had never really been his. It belonged to the land barons and the financiers, the drug runners and the pimps of Hamra Street. Lebanon would die as it had lived and the world would shed barely a tear. Rather it would smile as enigmatically as the Mona Lisa. He chided himself for recalling the great Christian work of art. He had tried to dismiss all the Western culture he had absorbed prior to delivering himself to the embrace of Allah. As he climbed the stairs, he consciously wiped clear the painting by da Vinci. The Renaissance of Islam would dwarf anything the Infidel had given civilisation.

There were no guards at the front or rear of the building; they would simply attract attention. The third floor landing, too, was devoid of human form. The familiar musty smell of the hallway intoxicated him. He stood for a moment opposite the door of number six, luxuriating in a sudden surge of elation at the great deed he had accomplished and the acknowledgement for it that he was about to receive.

Rashid Sedawi gave the pre-arranged signal: two sharp knocks followed by two longer, heavier blows. After a few seconds he heard a bolt being drawn.

The man who opened the door was dressed in priestly garb.

"Allahu Akhbar!" The grey-bearded mullah raised his arms and enveloped Rashid, kissing him on both cheeks. Rashid felt momentary discomfort as the wiry beard scraped his cheeks. But the warmth of his mentor's welcome suffused him with a glow he had last enjoyed watching the news of the El Al crash on the Irishman's television.

"I am but the reed to the wind," he said, gripping the old man's arms in warm embrace. "I bend to the will of Allah and His commands."

Mehdi Laham smiled. Rashid was truly righteous in the house of Allah. He had proved beyond doubt that he was a worthy member of their group. Great things could be expected from this man, so small in stature yet with an intelligence as sharp as a bedouin knife.

The mullah beckoned Rashid into an adjoining room. The visitor could smell the delicious aroma of Lebanese food emanating from the kitchen. He caught a glimpse of a woman dressed in a chador. He knew it was Fatima Fadas, the only female present and therefore a centre of sexual attraction. But the mullah guarded her dignity diligently and no member of the group dared make the slightest advance. It was said that she was his niece, but no-one sought to verify this. Rashid suspected her almond eyes betrayed a lack of innocence, but women concerned him little. They were chattels to be used and discarded at will. And, anyway, they could never replace the ecstasy of ravishing a young boy.

Rashid followed the mullah into the room. It was as he remembered it, sparsely furnished with a nargillah in the far corner, although the bubble pipe was mainly for show and only rarely smoked. Seated on the floor around a low table were the other members of the Higher Council, Hassan Hilbawi, Fuad Kerekeh and Ali Al-Majid Saleh. The men broke into applause, and Rashid revelled in their approbation.

"Shukkran, my brothers, it is good to see you again," he said quietly and moved towards the wash basin in the corner. He prayed as he washed his hands and then sat quietly at the table, surveying the mezze before him. It included all his favourites, from the Yemenite helba, ground fenugreek seeds whipped to a froth, to tabbouleh salad and dolma. The sight of the stuffed vine leaves made his mouth water.

The four men waited for the mullah to take his seat. Their leader then took a pitta in his right hand and began the meal with thanks to Allah, the provider.

"Bismillah..."

After the short prayer he offered pieces of bread to the four men. The first morsel was presented to Rashid. He realised that this was in honour of his deeds and that he was now a fully accepted member of the Cell. Rashid accepted the bread and uttered the prayer for food under his breath. Now he would feast. They would have plenty of time to discuss his plans after lunch. Although this particular safe house was still miraculously linked to the national grid, it was never used at night. Any light emanating from the derelict building might arouse unwanted attention.

The meal was eaten in total silence. Fatima Fadas entered occasionally to refill empty dishes. Only the tinkling of crockery in the kitchen disturbed the earnestness of their eating. It was only after they had drunk piping hot Turkish coffee and intoned further prayers that the mullah turned his attention to the deeds of Rashid Sedawi.

"Our Brother Rashid," he said, deliberately looking the younger man in the eye with stern conviction, "we are indebted to you for the great work you have perpetrated against the Zionist enemy. We have shaken the world in the name of Allah, the Compassionate and the Merciful. And the world now knows of our existence. However, we must be vigilant. Our name and what we stand for must be the only things it knows about us. What mighty armies have failed to achieve, we will achieve, Insh'a'Allah, but only by stealth. I know that our brother Rashid has many thoughts which he wishes to impart to us and he has earned the right to so do."

Rashid accepted the mullah's permission to speak but waited a few seconds as a matter of courtesy. He had researched the speech he was about to make a dozen times. He had studied the works of Abdallah Tal, Al-Akkad and others and it was important for him to deliver his preamble in fiery oratory before reaching the kernel of his plan to shake the world.

The Lebanese farmer's son took a deep breath. The eyes around the table were fixed upon him. They betrayed little emotion although he thought they mirrored a new respect for him. "My brothers," Rashid began slowly, "Islam calls for adhesion to the chivalry of generosity, pride, courage, zeal and energy, for the defence of the weak, the stranger and the convert. As you know, the Jews have nothing of all these qualities. Islam calls for faith in another world, hell and paradise, while the Jews' only aim in life is materialist effort which will give them complete enjoyment and fulfil their degraded aspirations and their vile purposes in this world. Islam honours woman and protects her honour and nobility. The Jews despise woman, employing her as a servant and as cheap merchandise with which to earn money to achieve their aims. Islam forbids the shedding of blood except by law, forbids robbery and immorality, while the Jews permit the shedding of the blood of a non-Jew, the stealing of his money and the defilement of his wife's honour.''

Rashid paused. He could sense the hate that was mirroring his own. Rhetoric came naturally to him and he felt himself growing stronger in his conviction.

"The clash between Jew and Moslem," he continued, "is the clash between good and evil. Either Israel disappears to the place from which it came or the Arab and Persian nation will be left as prey to Israel, which will devour their flesh and blood and stand in the way of their progress. Israel's disappearance to the place from which it came is an easier and more reasonable result. It is the inevitable result of the reality of Zion's fate. Israel is the cancer, the malignant wound, in the body of Islam, for which there is no cure but eradication.''

Warming to his task, Rashid turned his attention to Israel's links with imperialism and spat out the word 'rabiba'. He recalled that 'fosterchild' had been a great favourite in Nasser's repertoire.

"Israel is a fosterchild of imperialism and, until now, we have been unable to teach that child a lesson.''

Rashid could see that the mullah was preparing to interject. In deference to his mentor he halted his speech.

"Ya Rashid," the old man smiled, stroking his long beard, "what further lesson had you in mind?"

The younger man realised that he was rapidly approaching the moment when he must reveal his master plan to them. It was still basically in its formative stages but he had to convince these men, and especially the mullah, that it was practical. Long term, but practical.

"My brothers, Israel is supported so completely by the United States and the other imperialist lackeys of the West, that it would appear to me futile to continue our struggle in a conventional manner. I fought for the liberation of the Golan Heights and Kuneitra in nineteen seventy-three. The Syrian army, as replete as it was with weapons and manpower, did not possess the necessary will to press home its early advantage. Assad and his Alawites are paper tigers. The glory of Allah and of Islam lies with us and us alone.''

As is the Arab custom, Rashid did not answer the mullah's question directly. Further rhetoric was necessary before he would reveal the essence of his plan.

"The cancer that is Israel will not be removed by the blowing up of civilian airliners. Not one and not a hundred. The Jews breed like flies upon a sheep's carcass. We can remove the cancer only by the use or the threat of a weapon so destructive that the Jews will cower like dogs before it.''

The men in the room were entranced by Rashid's oratory. Each had secretly harboured the dream of destroying Israel in a mushroom cloud. But such a task needed not only a fanatical desire but a man who was willing, and able, to convert that desire to practicality. They shared a feeling that before them sat a man capable of anything. It was at once both exhilarating and frightening.

Mehdi Laham's hazel eyes, watery in old age yet nonetheless threatening, pierced Rashid's. As a guardian of Islam, he would not allow the destruction of the holy places of Jerusalem, the al-Aksa and Omar mosques.

"Ya Rashid,'' he said firmly, "I care little for the Sunnis of Jerusalem but I cannot allow the destruction of our holy places. Once a mosque is built it is sacrosanct. No mosque, not even one that is crumbling with the ravages of time, must be demolished or destroyed by the hand of a true believer. It would presage the end of Islam.''

Rashid was as well versed as the mullah in the intricasies of Islamic theology and tradition. He believed he had taken into account most eventualities of this kind.

"The mosques will be untouched, my master."

"How can you promise that? Everyone knows that nuclear bombs destroy everything." It was Hassan Hilbawi, a small, wiry man with a jet black handlebar moustache. Rashid thought he looked more Druze than Shi'ite and he did not trust him.

"That is true, Hassan my friend, but everything depends on the size of the bomb and its siting. During my many months in London, I had time to study this matter thoroughly. I spent many hours in the library of the Institute of Strategic Studies. I read every book about nuclear weapons that I could lay my hands upon."

Rashid paused to withdraw a Marlboro from an open packet someone had left on the table. It amazed him that they had already skipped to the destructive power of a bomb without considering the task of its procurement. But then few around the table possessed his intelligence. He would martyr himself if the mullah so wished, but the old man, too, was not well informed on the subject they were discussing. The stooped figure before him appeared to be losing the powers that once made him as wise and as cunning as a desert jackal.

He smiled at the mullah before continuing, his gold tooth glinting as a ray of the afternoon sun streamed through the balcony window.

"My brothers, we will get to the finer points of the technical details later. Suffice it to say at this juncture that the procurement of thermonuclear weapons such as a one megaton bomb or even a neutron bomb, which as you know kills people but leaves buildings standing, is completely out of the question. It is not within the bounds of practicality to steal such weapons which, I might add, are to be found only in the arsenals of the great powers. Moreover we do not need such huge explosive force to achieve our goal. It is far easier to steal a relatively small small amount of enriched uranium metal, say thirty kilograms. This would be enough to produce a fifteen kiloton bomb. It could be packed into a gun type metal case measuring less than a cubic metre.''

Rashid could sense that he was holding his audience in thrall. The room was silent. No sound emanated from the kitchen either. It appeared Fatima Fadas had completed her dishwashing.

Fuad Kerekeh, who shared a similar background to Rashid's in that he originated from a small Shi'ite village in South Lebanon, broke the silence with the inevitable question.

"Ya Rashid, what is a fifteen kiloton bomb?"

Rashid looked kindly at the man. Fuad was fat with effeminate features. But he was dependable and the only member of the group with whom he felt a close bond, so close that it had enjoyed expression in mutual sexual gratification.

"Fuad, my brother," he said without condescension, "it is almost the same as the amount dropped by the Americans on Hiroshima.''

"But that destroyed a city. It did not lead to a mass exodus of the Japanese from their land," interjected Hassan, at the same time reaching for a cigarette.

"That is true. But the bomb that destroyed Hiroshima was exploded about five hundred metres above ground. This caused the maximum amount of blast damage and that is why most of the buildings were destroyed. My plan would not involve the destruction of a single building. It would not necessarily mean an immediate loss of life. The Jews and the Palestinians who have chosen to remain in submission will die slowly, whether they choose to remain or to flee.''

"How is that possible, ya Rashid," the cleric questioned, his right hand still stroking the fulsome beard as an aid to concentration.

"In a word, fall-out. The amount of radiation released into the atmosphere will be of unimaginable proportions. The Holy

Land will be uninhabitable. If we cannot live there, then no-one will live there. Our sacred mosques will stand in silent tribute to Allah for the next thousand years.''

Hassan Hilbawi had been listening intently to the strange man opposite him. The plan was bold and imaginative but there were still many questions to be answered.

''You have still not said how such a relatively small bomb will force the abomination of Israel to submit.''

Rashid glared at Hilbawi. His eyes, black pools of venom, transmitted their displeasure momentarily, then softened into a smile.

''My dear brother, Hassan, it is not the size of the bomb that is important, it is where it is placed.'' Rashid took a puff from the Marlboro before continuing. The room was already laced by cigarette smoke.

''A bomb placed beneath the earth's surface, say in a desert, will produce a huge mushroom cloud of millions of tons of sand. Each grain will be irradiated. Each grain will bear the slow death of radiation sickness to our enemies.''

''Surely that will depend on which way the wind blows,'' Hassan interjected.

''Of course. Of course,'' Sedawi enthused. ''And that is the beauty of my plan. I shall explode the bomb on the day of a shurqiya. The wind blows from east to west. Only this time it will carry with it the seeds of destruction to our enemies.''

The mullah stroked his grey beard pensively. Sedawi was a zealot, possessed as they all were by a consuming hatred for the Zionist abomination. But too much zealotry carried with it an inherent blindness to other possibilities.

''Ya Rashid,'' he said slowly, his ancient eyes reflecting both understanding and wisdom, ''you are talking as if this plan of yours should be carried out come what may. I believe we should give the Israelis at least an option to leave Palestine of their own volition. Our threats may be enough to persuade them.''

Rashid realised his mistake. He had spoken of the exploding of the bomb as a fait accompli. He should have included in the description of his plan what the Americans termed a soft option. "Of course, my master," he smiled in deference. "The Israelis will be made aware of the validity of our threat, but I believe they would rather commit mass suicide than give up the land they have usurped."

"Nevertheless, Rashid, they should be given a chance to atone for their sins. Islam is a forgiving religion as long as recompense is made for injustice. And, besides, the Israelis will never have been faced by such a threat to their existence."

Hassan Hilbawi, tiring of this discussion of ethics, twirled the end of his moustache irritably. He waited for Sedawi's eyes to register concurrence with the mullah's viewpoint. Salient or not, Hilbawi was more concerned with the details of this madman's plan. Somehow, he must be stopped.

"And from where are we supposed to procure this threat?" he asked, adding sarcastically, "It is not an item you usually find on sale in the local suk."

Sedawi ignored the barb but made a mental note to keep a close watch on Hilbawi. There was no room for doubters. The will of Allah demanded total and unquestioning support.

"You are quite right, ya Hassan. But we are fortunate that a friendly nation has recently acquired the capability of making a nuclear bomb. In fact, it already has manufactured three. And I propose to relieve it of one of them."

Rashid noted with amusement the puzzled looks of the men around him. "My brothers," he smiled, "I am speaking of Pakistan. An Islamic nation, my friends. And where there are Moslems there will be help for our cause. I intend to fly out to Karachi next week. I may be gone for at least two months, maybe more. Fuad Kerekeh will accompany me."

"It will be an honour, ya Rashid," chirped Kerekeh, his pudgy fingers twiddling a set of mahogany worry beads. He could hardly contain his excitement. The fat man's devotion to Sedawi transcended the purely physical lust of their lovemaking.

Rashid directed his eyes at the mullah. He had been bold, maybe too bold, in his approach. He needed reassurance from the cleric. He saw no glimmer of reprimand in the pallid eyes.

"What is the time span for this plan of yours?" asked Hassan Hilbawi, the question tinged with scepticism.

"I believe we can be ready with our threat in a year or two from now, depending on the will of Allah. Around the time of the Jewish passover. Only this time the Angel of Death will not pass over their homes."

Sedawi waited for the laughter to subside before assuring his audience that they would learn more of his plan at a later date. Irritatingly, Hassan Hilbawi brought up the question of finance. "Many palms may need to be greased, let alone the cost of your travelling expenses, ya Rashid," he said, the scepticism now as piercing as a thorn.

Betraying no emotion, Sedawi scooped the last few sunflower seeds from the bowl before him and began splitting one in the groove between his two front teeth. He spat out the husk before answering.

"We shall increase our levy on the farmers of the Bekaa. The harvest has been good this year. Also, I will request from Abu Mussa a loan."

"Phhh! We should never ask a favour of that idolator," spat Hilbawi. He voiced the consternation of them all. Abu Mussa was a necessary evil, but this did not mean that they should demean Islam by being in debt to a Christian, a dealer in drugs and other commodities whose only interest was profit. The man should be treated as a pariah.

"It is but a means to an end, ya Hassan. Abu Mussa needs the hemp. If we threaten the farmers, he doesn't get it."

Hilbawi was not convinced. "But the other freedom groups

would not welcome such unrest," he said, his voice cracking in agitation.

"You worry too much, Hassan," Sedawi smiled, the gold tooth glinting menacingly.

Mehdi Laham, deciding it was time to exert his authority, put an end to the argument with an aphorism that was as apt as it was trite.

"My brothers," the mullah said, raising his hands and turning his palms towards them in a gesture that called for restraint, "it is sometimes necessary to deal with the Devil in order to destroy him."

Rashid Sedawi judged by the mullah's tone that the meeting was now at a close. He knew Mehdi Laham would demand more details from him in private.

But those details would not contain certain important elements. Rashid Sedawi alone would know the exact location of the bomb. Rashid Sedawi alone would decide the fate of Palestine.

As the men around him broke into excited conversation, he heard a rustle behind him. The right arm of Fatima Fadas brushed his ear as she filled two empty bowls with sunflower and pumpkin seeds.

CHAPTER THREE

The tall thin man wearing a red check shirt and beige trousers entered a sidewalk cafe. He sat down and called the waiter. "Black coffee, and make it quick!" he barked.

David Katri, seated at a table nearby, delved into his morning paper. He was grateful for the parasol which protected him from the burning sun.

The waiter had still to approach David for his order than the thin man rose, slapped some coins on the table and proceeded at a brisk pace northwards along the busy thoroughfare. David waited a few seconds before slipping away from his table, noting from the corner of his eye the look of consternation that waiters have when they have allowed a customer to get away.

David trailed his quarry at a discreet distance. After walking about a hundred metres, the thin man broke into a run. David could see he was making for a number twelve bus which had just pulled up outside the Shalom Tower. Thankfully, there was a long queue which should at least delay the man enough for him to catch up. By the time David had pushed his way aboard, he was separated from the man by a sea of bodies. The combination of body odour and diesel exhaust fumes almost overcame him. The fact that both men were taller than the other passengers meant that the two were as visible to one another as coconuts at a shy. Katri averted his eyes. He could not afford to give his quarry the slightest inkling that he was being followed.

The packed bus lurched from side to side as the driver negotiated corners at breakneck speed. At the third stop the man disappeared from view. David felt the insidious encroachment of panic as he realised he was hemmed in.

"Slikha, Slikha!" he cried. "Excuse me, I must get off here."

He began pushing his way to the nearest awning, at the front of the bus.

"Here, you!" the driver blurted. "You can't get off at the front. Don't you know it's only for boarding passengers."

By this time David was in no mood to comply with Dan Bus Company regulations. He pushed his way past the boarders, some of whom began cursing in the foulest language.

His heart skipped a beat as he realised he may have lost his quarry. Feeling a growing sense of helplessness, he screwed his eyes against the glaring sun and peered in every direction. He was about to give up when he glimpsed a red check shirt disappear into a sidestreet about fifty metres away.

He ran the fastest fifty metres of his life before stopping at the corner abruptly in order to catch his breath. Peering round the edge of the building he was just in time to see the thin man enter a shop doorway.

David entered an alley opposite the shop and waited, making a mental note of the name and address of the premises.

The time passed slowly and he felt himself drifting into reflections on how his life had changed so radically since his meeting with Yariv Cohen barely six weeks earlier. His fellow kibbutzniks had tried hard to persuade him not to move to the city. They had found it incomprehensible that he should want to leave a community in which he had appeared to be so happy. It would affect the children, they had said, and it was true that Boaz and Shoshana were rebelling against their new school, although he was certain that within a few weeks they would settle down. Kids were very adaptable.

Despite Yariv Cohen's admonition not to confide in his wife the reason for his sudden change of heart, David realised it would prove impossible to maintain a charade for very long. Yael knew the story of his escape from Syria and they had joked that one day he would probably have to repay his debt.

The move to Tel Aviv was so out of character that Yael had come to the conclusion almost immediately. They had been lying in bed after a particularly exquisite session of lovemaking. His beautiful Yemenite was resting her head in the comforting well between his chest and arm. As was her wont at such times, she had begun twisting the hairs on his chest into delicate spirals. He was intoxicated by the perfume of her ebony hair and all was bliss until she uttered those two simple words.

"I know," she had said quietly.

David's mind had raced. What if she would demand to know every detail of his mission? He had felt the needlepoint of a pricking conscience as Yael, displaying once again the extraordinary telepathy between them, sought to put his mind at rest.

"David, I never want you to tell me anything of what you are doing. It will be enough for me that you return to me safely." He bathed in the glow of her warmth and understanding. He knew he was a lucky man.

"David, David…"

Katri felt a hand tugging his shoulder. His heart raced as he wheeled round. It was Rahamim Ben-Yaacov.

"David, my friend. Did you not know I have been following you all the time? Also, Amnon - the tall thin man - said he realised you were tracking him from the very moment you sat down in the cafe. I am afraid we'll have to do it all over again."

Katri felt foolish. Not only had he been caught daydreaming but he realised he had committed the cardinal error of trying to hide behind a newspaper while keeping an eye on his target. He had been told that that was strictly the stuff of movies.

During the next few weeks, David Katri followed the path taken by countless agents before him. Some, like Eli Cohen, had become legends. But most would remain faceless for eternity, never reaping recognition individually from a nation that was nevertheless proud and grateful for their selfless dedication.

Like those before him, David Katri was made to traverse the streets of Tel Aviv, attempting to identify and unmask those shadowing him or, conversely, tracking a target without giving himself away. At first he failed miserably. But before long, David began to recognise the tell-tale signs that give away both pursuer and pursued. He did not know it, but his masters were becoming increasingly impressed with his ability to grasp the essentials of each task.

David was especially adept during the exhaustive memory training course. He had never really appreciated that he had something approaching a photographic memory. It was an asset he had generally taken for granted. However, time and again his instructors were astounded by his ability to remember objects crowded together on a table and uncovered for only a few seconds.

More arduous for David was the course on judo and self-defence. As with most Israelis, he had acquired a paunch soon after leaving the regular army.

"You look like a reservist, David," Rahamim Ben-Yaacov had quipped. "It's all that home cooking and too much bread."

In a surprisingly short time, even Yael had enthused over her husband's new leanness. His stomach muscles had become as hard as iron.

Coupled with his physical training came exhaustive instruction in firearms, mainly Soviet. Chief among these was the AK-47, the Automat Kalashnikova, the pivot of the Soviet small arms family. David learned to strip and reassemble the 7.62 mm gas recoil weapon. At six hundred rounds per minute and with a range of four hundred metres, it was a good match for the more familiar Israeli Galil which, out of respect for its Russian counterpart, employed the same rotating bolt locking system.

Pistols represented more of a problem. Terrorists of all ilks could be expected to be familiar with a wide range, from Berettas to the Walther PBK with silencer. David learnt the intricacies of a broad selection, although in line with the cover which had been mapped out for him, he concentrated on the Syrian army issue 9 mm Automatitscheski Pistolet Stetschkin.

Israel was fortunate in that it had captured so many Soviet weapons during the numerous conflagrations with its Arab adversaries. Pride of place went to the T-62s captured during the nineteen seventy-three war.

Rahamim Ben-Yaacov took control of David Katri, body and soul. It was the wiry Yemenite who constructed David's new personality. It was he who decided to put the new agent's experiences in the Yom Kippur war to good effect.

"Only this time, David, you will learn what it was like to be a Syrian gunner in a T-62 facing your own battalion. It makes the job easier that you are conversant with the terrain and the general scenario."

"Why a gunner and not a commander?" David had countered. After all, he had himself been a commander, albeit of a Centurion.

"The amount of information you would have to know as a tank commander in the Syrian army would be infinite compared to that of a gunner. It gives you a lower and less checkable profile."

Ben-Yaacov's answer made sense and David spent the following two weeks studying the idiosyncrasies of a captured T-62 kept in excellent condition by mechanics at the Sarafand army base. He cursed the amount of information he had to absorb. From the names of Soviet-built helicopters to a complete run-through of Syrian combat dress and regimental badges. His only comfort was the knowledge that as a Syrian of his age he would have had to have been conscripted into the army prior to the Yom Kippur War, a conflagration of which he had had first-hand experience. Most fascinating of all were the confessions and statements of Syrian officers captured after his battered

Barak brigade had fought back to repel the invaders following the initial debacle. "Read these," Ben-Yaacov had said. "They'll give you a few useful names, from company commanders even down to some lower echelons."

David marvelled at the thoroughness of both the army and the Mossad. Did they throw nothing away?

Neither David Katri nor Rahamim Ben-Yaacov were to know that this thoroughness was to face its greatest test before a man whose knowledge of Syria's battle for the Golan Heights was second to none.

A few hundred kilometres to the north, a large distinguished looking man was pacing back and forth. Abu Mussa was nervous. The man he was about to meet was obviously mad, more so than the usual selection of fanatics with whom he was forced to deal in a country which bred them like flies.

The big man kept his eyes to the floor, avoiding the looks of apprehension from his two henchmen guarding the front door. He had recoiled at the thought of holding discussions in such a place. A shell-pocked apartment in the warren of crumbling concrete between Christian East and Moslem West Beirut might be neutral but it was definitely not his style. He thanked God that he could always return to his palatial refuge high in the mountains. The Shi'ites could keep their slums and their bomb sites.

How different it had been before the civil war. Then he had dealt only with his own kind. How odd it seemed that now he was becoming increasingly embroiled with people who regarded him as their sworn enemy. Taking into account the record of butchery on all sides, the paradox was almost obscene.

The Maronite crossed to the window and peered down at the street below, if street it could be called. There was rubble as far as the eye could see. There had just been enough room for him to manoeuvre his blue Mercedes. He could have bought a Rolls Royce but it did not pay to be ostentatious in Beirut these days. A man could show his true worth only amongst his own kind. Revolutionaries were not impressed by the trappings of wealth. Reputation and power were usually enough, and Abu Mussa had plenty of both. As a smuggler of infinite versatility, precious metals, drugs and even tanker loads of oil had passed through his hands leaving their residue of profit.

In the old days his dealings had been enlivened by the slave trade in nubile girls, with selected blondes being processed by him on their way to becoming the concubines of sheikhs. Some were naive tourists who had been kidnapped and it had pained him knowing that they hardly deserved the fate awaiting them. Nevertheless, the profit margin had been enormous.

The Christian stepped away from the window and entered the bathroom. It was hot and the apartment was stifling even though there were no panes in the window frames. Thankfully, there was still running water. It was something of a miracle considering the utter dereliction of the place.

He splashed some of the lukewarm water on his face and balding pate. Drying himself with a handkerchief, he gazed at his reflection in the mirror. A diagonal crack in the glass fragmented his features cruelly. The heavy jowls revealed his age, although his body still looked surprisingly lean considering the large frame now supported more than one hundred kilograms. But the face, despite its pampering, reflected the excesses of his sixty-five years. The ravages of time had not been influenced by deposits in Swiss banks.

Hearing the screech of tyres outside, Abu Mussa quickly folded his handkerchief and thrust it into the right pocket of his white suit. He reached the balcony in time to see three men enter the building. Outside there remained three others, heavily armed and leaning against a white Peugeot 504.

The Christian hurriedly assembled his thoughts. He knew he was in no position to deny his visitor. The Shi'ite had no idea that he knew the reason for the meeting and it was imperative that he maintain this front. What he had been told had seemed too preposterous to be true and there was no certainty these fanatics were capable of carrying out their plan. Bomb or no bomb, he craved the chance to recover his money.

Abu Mussa stiffened as three resounding knocks shook the front door. His two bodyguards moved sideways instinctively, at the same time withdrawing pistols from their shoulder holsters.

Their boss motioned them to relax. "Open the door, Georges. Our guests have arrived."

Rashid Sedawi entered flanked by two men, one of them carrying the ubiquitous Kalashnikov and the other a machine pistol of dubious origin. The fact that he was apparently unarmed told Abu Mussa that the man in the middle was the one about whom he had heard so much. The man was smaller and more swarthy than he had imagined but the gold front tooth lived up to its description. It certainly was conspicuous.

The two men did not shake hands but their eyes registered a recognition of sorts.

Abu Mussa decided to take the initiative. "I think we can dispense with our entourages, Mr Sedawi," he said, nodding at his own men.

Sedawi dismissed his men with a flick of the wrists. His bodyguards left the room immediately, followed quickly by their Christian counterparts, their eyes burning with contempt.

Abu Mussa continued the niceties as he had arrived first and was therefore in a way the host of this strange meeting in an empty room in a building that was no more than a shell.

"I hope my friend Mehdi Laham is well. It is a long time since we have met."

"He is well and sends you his regards," Sedawi lied.

"I am glad. Please pass to him my best wishes. He is a true leader of his people."

The mutual well-wishing was totally insincere. Both men knew this but both were products of their culture which, however the Christian might protest, was Arab. And Arab etiquette demanded preamble, whether sincere or not.

"We live in a troubled land, my friend," the Christians sighed, "but with goodwill there is room here for us all. Cooperation is so much better than conflagration." The statement was flat, Abu Mussa stopping short of any intonation which might imply that the fanatic before him should concur with such an aphorism.

Rashid Sedawi said nothing. He despised the man before him. He despised his decadence, he despised his flaunting of wealth and, above all, he despised his idolatrous religion. For too long the Maronite papists and the heretic Sunnis had held sway in Lebanon. Their hegemony had to be ended.

The Christian could feel the hate in Sedawi's eyes cleave him as a bedouin khanjar through ghee. He cleared his throat. "I know times are hard, but in what way can I be of assistance to your people?" he asked obsequiously.

Sedawi moved towards the balcony. He saw his men below standing by the Peugeot, about twenty metres away from the front of the building where Abu Mussa's men stood guard.

"Times are hard, but they can always get harder," the Shi'ite said, still facing away from the big man.

"I do not understand, my friend," said Abu Mussa, feigning ignorance. Rashid Sedawi turned slowly away from the awning to face the man with whom he was forced to do business but who was nevertheless his bitter foe.

"As you know, Abu Mussa, your success in smuggling hashish to Egypt is due in no small measure to what you might term our protection of the farmers in the Bekaa. We think it is about time our efforts in this respect were, you might say, more rewarding.''

The big man knew what was coming next but continued the charade.

"I'm afraid I do not understand you," he said, shrugging his shoulders. "Up till now the arrangement we have had has worked well for all concerned. You levy the farmers and I market their produce. My prices are fair as everyone knows.''

Rashid Sedawi knew this to be true. But he also knew that the profits his group made from the arrangement were infinitesimal compared to those accrued by the Nasrani. The Shi'ite knew he held a trump card but he also did not want to kill the golden goose.

"That may be so," he said, "but for you to be happy, the farmers must be happy." He paused before adding, ''And the farmers will not be happy unless we are happy. Of that I assure you.''

Abu Mussa realised it was now time for straight talk. He knew the Shi'ite wanted money but he did not know how much.

"What would be the extent of my helping to keep the farmers happy?'' he asked, the first pangs of apprehension striking deep within him.

Rashid Sedawi announced the figure laconically. "One million dollars.''

The Christian's palms broke into a cold sweat. The sum was huge, far more than he had envisaged. "B-but that is an enormous amount of money,'' he stammered.

"Yes, you are right, Abu Mussa. But we are just men and the money will be in the form of a loan. You will be given a letter of credit to our bank convertible two years from May fifth next. You will note that the sum to be repaid includes interest at eight per cent. We are not robbers.''

Should there have been a chair in the room, Abu Mussa would have leaned on it for support. The sum demanded was extortionate but he knew also that there was nothing he could do.

"The fifth is only four days away," he said tamely. "That does not give me much time."

Rashid Sedawi knew that the manicured and sweet-smelling Christian had much more than one million dollars at his fingertips. This abhorent creature was one of the richest middle men in the Middle East and he was getting off lightly. At least for the moment.

"You know our bank," he said, ignoring the bigger man's plea. "Meet me there at ten o'clock on that date with the cheque." With this, he walked across to the open balcony. "Ahmed! Mustapha!" he called to the men below. "It's over. I am coming down."

The small man strode to the front door of the apartment and paused before descending the stairs. The Christian's perfume permeated the whole room and made him feel nauseous. It was almost feminine. "Until we meet again, Abu Mussa," he said half turning, the golden tooth seeming to glow a warning.

The Maronite returned to the balcony and watched the white Peugeot screech away in a haze of blue smoke. He had met many undesirable characters in more than three decades of drug smuggling, huge arms deals and the trading of secrets, but he had never felt as apprehensive as he did in the presence of Rashid Sedawi. The man was evil and dangerous.

Abu Mussa felt his tension unwind only when a pair of tender hands began to slide around his waist. He had not noticed her enter the salon from what once had been the main bedroom.

"He is truly evil, my darling," she said, placing her head gently between the huge man's shoulder blades.

Without turning, the Maronite gripped her long delicate fingers. "I fear for you, hilwati," he said, his voice quivering with emotion. "Diri balek."

"I will be careful, my darling, but they suspect nothing," she said, trying to reassure him.

He turned to face this exquisitely beautiful woman who had

given so much happiness to him, a man forty-five years her senior. He ran his fingers through her ebony hair and gently kissed the almonds that were her eyes.

"I must safeguard my investment with them," he said, "but I intend to take out an insurance policy."

"What do you mean?"

"If that madman succeeds in stealing the atom bomb from Pakistan, I am sure there are those who would be willing to pay handsomely for information."

"You mean the Israelis?"

"It would not be the first time."

"But they are also our enemies."

"Yes, eyooni. But Sedawi is more of an enemy. And in this case, our enemy's enemy is our friend."

Abu Mussa took his beautiful maiden in his arms and gently placed her head upon his chest. "If Sedawi succeeds, it will not only be Israel that is harmed. We, too, shall be destroyed."

"I know," said Fatima Fadas quietly. "That evil man seems even to have my uncle totally within his power."

She snuggled closer to the older man with whom she felt so safe and secure. It was a love born of kindness, understanding, fidelity. And desperation.

CHAPTER FOUR

Imran Ikbal alighted from the special green bus which plied its way six days a week to and from Pakistan's nuclear plant at Kahuta. The half-hour trip seemed to have taken much longer this day. His colleagues had found him uncommunicative and sullen and had left him to his troubled thoughts.

Imran had always impressed them as an ascetic type. Taciturn almost to the point of muteness, he nevertheless handled his task as a centrifuge technician at the plant with grim expertise. The fact that their slight, fine-boned colleague was the only Shi'ite among them may have been the source of his reluctance to be more open with them. But they were too intelligent to regard his reticence as being a direct affront.

The small man felt a sense of relief as he stepped onto the burning pavement. It had been hard for him to remain stoical after a day of humiliation in which he had once again been passed over for promotion.

God would bless Dr Abdel Qadar Khan as the father of the Islamic Bomb, he mused, but which Islam? It always seemed to be the Sunnites who made the decisions, who had the money, who reaped the rewards.

Feeling the first pangs of evening hunger, he decided to walk through the Old City before making his way to his small apartment in the Saddar area. The locals inns, the muzzaffar khanas, may have disappeared, but there still remained other traditional eating places with kitchens out front on the pavements and hunks of chicken and meat hanging from smoke-blackened ceilings. The small man's features were sallower than most of his fellow citizens, a fact no doubt due to the long hours he spent in the air-conditioned sterility of the laboratory. Imran grimaced as he narrowly avoided a horse drawn tonga weaving its way through Bazaar's congested alleys.

He passed market stalls laden with striped watermelons, sweet melons, pomegranates and citrus fruits and proceeded at a pace towards his favourite eating place deep in the Bhabra bazaar. As luck would have it, the restaurant was practically empty save for a rather rotund gentleman with a camera seated at the far left. He was dark skinned but the features were not those of a native of the sub-continent. Probably a tourist, he thought.

Imran took a table about four metres from the tourist and ordered sajji. They did a wonderful whole roasted leg of lamb and there was no doubting that he was hungry enough to devour it all. But before he would eat, he must drink. The fresh limes of nimbu pani were his favourite and, without being asked, Assif the waiter began pressing the fruit for his regular client. The nuclear technician had just taken his first sip when the sound of the muezzin calling the faithful to prayer reverberated through the bazaar. Almost as one, the restaurant's two customers rose from their chairs and sank to their knees. The fat man took his lead from the native for he was not altogether sure of the direction of Mecca.

Imran noted the tourist's strange accent and guessed that he was an Arab. As he finished praying he noticed the man was having difficulty in rising.

"Excuse me, my friend," the fat man said in English. "I wonder whether you could help me. My knee sometimes locks and I find it difficult to rise."

"Of course, of course." Imran moved quickly to his right and placed his arm around the man, straining to bring him to an upright position. He was indeed very heavy.

The tourist grunted and rubbed his knee as he slowly stood upright.

"There," he said with apparent relief, "it's gone back again.

Shukkran, shukkran. I'll be all right now."

The Pakistani was always much more comfortable in the presence of strangers and this man presented him with an opportunity to improve his English.

"Please, won't you join me at my table. I always eat here and I can recommend some wonderful local delicacies."

"Why thank you, my friend. It would be an honour."

Fuad Kerekeh, relieved that initial contact had been made, followed the Pakistani to his table and sat down.

"It's a Canon," he said, lifting the camera strap from his shoulder and placing the apparatus carefully on the table.

"Yes. They are very good cameras. You must have taken some wonderful pictures during your visit to Pakistan."

"You have a very beautiful country, my friend."

Imran felt himself warming to the fat stranger. He felt it was time he introduced himself and held out his hand. "My name's Imran Ikbal. How do you do."

"Fuad Khalifa. Pleased to make your acquaintance."

"I must say that you speak very good English. Yet I also noticed you used some words in Arabic."

"Yes, my friend. I am an Arab from Beirut in the Lebanon."

Imran wondered whether the fat man was a Sunnite or even a Palestinian. He hoped he was a Shi'ite like himself, but he knew it would be too disrespectful to ask bluntly.

"I am so sorry that your country is facing such difficulties," he said with honest concern.

Fuad, seeing an opportunity to win the man's confidence, leaned towards his host. "For too many years, our country has been ruled by other than true believers."

He paused before adding the sentence which he knew would hook his companion. "The Sunnis, the Druze, the Christians and the Palestinians have conspired to deprive us of our rights."

Imran's mind raced through the other options. He had always been keenly interested in events in the Middle East and was intensely pro the late Khomeini. The Shi'ites of Lebanon had been downtrodden for too long.

"Then you are a follower of Ali." It was a statement rather than a question.

"Yes, my friend."

Imran took Fuad's hand and shook it warmly. "So am I. So am I. Ahalan wa'sahalan. Welcome, my friend, welcome."

For the next hour the two men devoured leg of lamb and talked about one another's countries. Never once did Fuad inquire after his companion's occupation. The Arab, however, declared that he was involved in the carpet trade and that he had found those made in Pakistan to be almost as good as the Persian variety. Imran Iqbal spoke briefly about the arts and crafts of the Punjab and then held forth at greater length about how he felt the fact that he was Shi'ite had made him subject to discrimination. Fuad Kerekeh truly sympathised with the Pakistani. Iqbal's outbursts had been heard in this and other restaurants by another man, a man who had been quick to note the Pakistani's usefulness to his sworn cause. Imran Iqbal was a talkative fellow away from the confines of his work. He had been followed and observed for more than two months, his every move monitored. It would shortly be time to test his dedication to the Shi'a cause. Upon presentation of their bills, the Pakistani insisted on paying. Fuad knew that he must reciprocate his generosity. He smiled warmly at his companion.

"Imran, my friend, you must allow me to extend thanks from my heart for your hospitality. Will you kindly allow me also to invite you to share a meal with me at my hotel, the Intercontinental?"

"I should be deeply honoured, Fuad."

"Shall we say Wednesday at six?" Fuad Kerekeh said, shaking his companion's hand. "There's someone I'd like you to meet."

STOCKHOLM

The goulash was excellent, but then it was supposed to be the capital's finest Hungarian restaurant. Not that he frequented the place often for it was unwise for an Israeli agent to allow himself to become too set in his ways. Nevertheless, he always enjoyed a stroll along the Skeppsbron and through the quaint narrow streets of the Old Town. They made a welcome change from the more frenetic area around his apartment near the Humlegarden.

The handsome, stocky man glanced at his watch. He hated eating alone but his contact was late and, anyway, an empty stomach invariably made him irascible. He took another sip of Bull's Blood and thought about the Swede. The Scandinavian was usually punctual. And, besides, he had sounded as if the information he had was urgent.

The Israeli loosened his tie. How he hated the things. In his country they were about as rare as a Jewish building labourer. He chuckled at the analogy. The English had their Irish and the Israelis had the Arabs from the West Bank and Gaza. Murphy and Mustapha Limited. Absolutely indispensable.

"Sorry I'm late, Jonathan."

The Israeli turned to see the familiar face of the tall Swede beaming at him.

"The traffic was terrible uptown," the Scandinavian said, clapping his companion on the back and crossing to the chair opposite. He seated himself with the minimum of fuss.

"How's the goulash?"

"Delicious, Bjorn you should try it."

The tall blond Swede complied, at the same time requesting

the waiter to bring a further bottle of wine.

"Hold on, Bjorn, you'll get pissed."

Both men laughed. Bjorn Lundqvist took great pride in his knowledge of English colloquialisms. Like most Swedes, he spoke the language fluently, but not well enough to discern the accent in another man's English.

This was just as well. For the Israeli could never disguise his gutturals well enough to convince an Anglo-Saxon. But as far as the Swede was concerned, Jonathan Webley was as English as Tottenham Hotspur.

The Israeli filled the Swede's glass. The man had been worth cultivating during the preceding two years. A leading official at the Swedish Institute for Peace Research, there was little Bjorn Lundqvist did not know about nuclear proliferation. Through his own highly coveted contacts he had become privy to much classified information, knowledge that could prove extremely useful to competitors in both industry and government. Any industry. Any government.

Bjorn Lundqvist did not need to know more than that which the muscular man before him had volunteered. Whether or not he was a representative of British government interests was of little consequence. Confirmation of a deposit in his Swiss bank account was enough. It was a lucrative business, especially if you could sell the same information to an assortment of interested parties. One simply had to give the impression to the buyer that he was the sole recipient.

The Swede leaned forward conspiratorially. "I have some information which may interest you, Jonathan."

"I gathered that, Bjorn. How much?"

"My usual."

"Consider it done." The Israeli was not about to quibble. The Swede's track record was hitherto unblemished and, anyway, he liked the man.

Lundqvist relaxed. He never had qualms about selling information, but he hated having to barter. He liked doing business with the Englishman. Fair play and all that. The Arabs were different. But then with them he always started with a higher figure and allowed them to bate him down. The end result was the same.

"You may or may not know, Jonathan," the Scandinavian continued, "but in Sweden we have developed a flash X-ray machine which can take high-speed photographs of a hollow ball of concentrated explosive blasting inwards on either highly enriched uranium or weapons grade plutonium. This is what we call imploding. The X-ray enables scientists to see the shock wave set up by the implosion. If this is not symmetrical, the nuclear explosion will probably not take place."

"In other words, Bjorn…"

"In other words, it helps you perfect the detonators necessary to trigger a nuclear explosion."

The Israeli felt the muscles tighten on the nape of his neck. "Who's got hold of one, Bjorn?"

"Well, normally controls are extremely stringent. Companies or authorities wishing to purchase one are subjected to thorough investigation."

"Who is it, Bjorn?" The Israeli was becoming impatient.

"We are ninety-nine per cent sure it's the Pakistanis."

The revelation did not surprise him. Dr Abdel Qader Khan had always been frank about his nation possessing the bomb even if the country's leaders had denied it. This was just another piece in the jigsaw. He recalled the jailing of three Pakistanis in nineteen eighty-five for smuggling nuclear weapons parts out of the U.S. They had procured about fifty krytons, small high-speed switches made by an electro-optics company in Massachusetts. The krytons resembled tiny light bulbs but were used in intricate triggers of nuclear bombs. Lundqvist paused as the waiter gently placed a plate of goulash, rice and peppers before him. He took a mouthful, chewing and swallowing the meat quickly before continuing.

"They've used shell companies to disguise the real purchaser. It's been the same with other parts used in manufacturing the bomb. Like America and other Western countries, we've put an embargo on such small things as magnets and maraging steel used in centrifuges. But somehow they've been slipping through."

"Where do you think that puts the Pakistanis now, Bjorn?" the Israeli asked, wiping the corners of his mouth with a napkin.

The Swede took another forkful of goulash and washed it down with wine. There was nothing he liked better than explaining the intricacies of nuclear physics.

"It all depends on the number of ultra centrifuges Khan has. These machines whirl the $U-235$ and $U-238$ atoms at eighty thousand to one hundred thousand revolutions a minute, splitting the atoms and increasing the percentage of weapons grade $U-235$. He'll probably need thousands of these centrifuges in cascade to get a good degree of uranium enrichment."

The Israeli preferred to believe a worst case scenario: that the father of the so-called Islamic Bomb had his centrifuges and consequently already had at least one nuclear device. The implications for Israel were frightening. If the bomb got into the wrong hands, not only his country but the whole world would be threatened.

The two men finished their meal more or less in silence. Lundqvist sensed that the implications weighed heavily upon his companion. It puzzled him, for the consequences were more terrifying for the countries of Asia than of Europe. But then he remembered that Great Britain still had a hang-up about the Indian sub-continent and felt responsible for everything that went on there. Such was the legacy of empire.

The Israeli paid the bill and the two left the restaurant. The evening was fine with a slight chill. The days were getting longer and the sense of renewal was almost tangible as spring clawed aside the icy tentacles of the long Scandinavian winter.

"Let's go for a walk down the Skeppsbron," the Israeli suggested. "It will give the goulash a chance to settle."

"Fine by me, Jonathan. I love strolling through the Old Town as much as you do."

The two men, one so obviously Nordic and the other of more indefinable heritage, confined their conversation mainly to the merits of English football and how most of Sweden's best players played for clubs outside the country. Engrossed in conversation, they walked slowly along Storkyrkobrinken turning right along Trangsund and past the Storkyrkan.

Unhurried, the companions strolled through the narrow streets delighting in the spectacle as the miniature shops greeted dusk with a kaleidoscope of light.

Neither man paid particular attention to the headlamp and noise of a motor scooter in the distance. As it neared, the Israeli noticed that the rider was wearing a balaclava, not uncommon in winter but somewhat of an exaggeration in late spring. He saw the rider pull something from the inside of his jacket. Instinct coiled his nerve-ends and then released them in an explosion of kinetic energy. He tried to drag the big Swede down as he flung himself to the ground. Vaguely aware of two popping sounds and the shattering of glass, he looked up to see the tall man stagger slightly before crumpling in a heap. The Swede's throat rattled and his legs began to jerk in a desperate final link with life. In one swift movement the Israeli rose to his feet and darted towards a nearby alley. He could not afford to be linked with his friend. He did not pause to consider whether or not he was the intended target. He just knew he must get to Arlanda airport that night and leave Sweden for ever.

The body of the man he left behind lay at an obscene angle, like an off-duty marionette. Lundqvist's empty gaze was directed at the window of Per Petersson's arts and crafts shop. The big man would never know that the second bullet from his assassin's gun had shattered Petersson's window, reducing to kindling the shopkeeper's pride, a six-foot model of a sailing boat from Aland. The sight would have pained Bjorn Lundqvist also for, like most Swedes, he loved the sea.

CHAPTER FIVE

The sign on the door of the administration block at Kahuta could hardly have been more explicit. In three languages, Urdu, Punjabi and English, the words 'Entrance Strictly Forbidden to Unauthorised Personnel' were emblazoned in red letters ten centimetres high.

The small sallow man had often passed the door, but it was not until the fateful meeting with the Lebanese that what lay behind it became of consummate interest to him. He had earlier noted the name Farley Electronics inscribed on the brass plate surrounding the locking device. Since his initial meeting with Rashid Sedawi it had taken two months for a sample to be obtained from the American manufacturer.

Imran Iqbal had studied the device for weeks. He had practised disassembly and assembly until his fingers ached. An engineer by choice and by nature, the little man had succeeded eventually in reducing to thirty seconds the time it took for him to open the device, cross certain wires to release the locking mechanism and put the whole thing together again.

There was an alarm system outside the door although it was comparatively rudimentary. It was of the photo-electric type whereby a current was created when a strong light was projected onto a lead sulphide photocell. This current activated an electric relay and as long as the light shone, the relay was kept open. Once the light beam was interrupted, it triggered the alarm. Imran had been surprised by Sedawi's knowledge of bugging and security devices but he did not need to be told that a powerful flashlight would be enough to avoid triggering the alarms. He simply had to shine it directly at the electric eye as he prepared to step through and break the normal current.

Now the time had arrived for the Pakistani to put his ability to good use. It had been easy enough to transfer to the night shift. He had also practised dummy runs along the corridor, noting that the guard always took a fifteen minute break at three a.m. Routine was always security's worst enemy, he thought, as he waited for the soldier to leave his post. The muffled clump of the man's boots receding down the corridor was the signal for Imran to leave the cranny in which he was hiding and, shoes in hand, traverse the twenty metres to Khan's office with the minimum of sound. He shone the torch directly into the electric eye and bypassed its stunted beam. Withdrawing a simple Philips screwdriver, he stooped slightly to undo the brass plate covering the locking device. Within thirty seconds, Imran Iqbal had replaced it and had gained access to the most important room in the whole complex.

Closing the door silently behind him, the small man noted that there were three smaller rooms leading from the entrance hall. Turning left, he saw the words 'The Office of the Chief Scientist' on a black name-plate on the door of the first room. He tried the handle. It was open. Imran Iqbal entered the Holy of Holies, the office of Pakistan's most famous man after its president, not knowing what he would find or even where to look. His first inclination was to inspect the stack of files on Dr Khan's desk. With the aid of a flashlight, he went through each folder, scrupulously careful to return each sheet to its correct order. There was little but worthless scientific data in the first four files.

Imran glanced nervously at his watch. He had already spent ten minutes fruitlessly. Although not beyond the bounds of feasibility, he would hate to have to make a further visit. The air-conditioning had been switched off and he felt himself beginning to gag on the fetid air in the room. Resigning himself to having to attempt to go through the whole process again another night, he suddenly noticed a plain beige file near the bottom of the pile. The words 'TOP SECRET' printed diagonally in the top right corner made his heart race. The Shi'ite felt his legs weaken as he scanned the contents of the file. It was beyond his wildest dreams. Khan's plan of action was all there down to the minutest detail.

By three-fifteen in the morning, Imran Iqbal had photographed his country's most confidential secret and had slipped away into another part of the maze that was Kahuta.

Back in Tel Aviv, David Katri was beginning to find his training a strain. After six months, the romance the task held at first was dissipated by dull routine and long periods of monotony. Many times he had travelled the length and breadth of Israel, changing buses and taxis according to a complex itinerary to which he was obliged to comply. But worst of all were the bogus missions during which he had to stand at street corners waiting for contacts who never showed up.

His frustration was finding its outlet at home and David regretted that arguments with Yael were becoming more frequent. They were invariably petty and there was no question of their mutual deep love and affection being undermined. Nevertheless, tension ran high, especially when the children misbehaved. David was still wrapped up in his personal problems as Rahamim Ben-Yaacov entered his office. He had some important information for the Syrian Jew. At last things were beginning to move.

"What's up, David?" the olive-skinned Yemenite asked kindly.

"Oh, nothing much, Rahamim. Just a stupid argument at home over me buying the wrong type of bread from the bakery in the morning. Yael prefers Slepak and I like Aviv."

Ben-Yaacov knew his ward was under some strain. Nevertheless, David Katri had to be taught to disguise his feelings. He made a mental note to get the psychology department to give Katri a few pointers on how to hide his emotions. The Yemenite drew up a chair and straddled it, the back facing Katri. The problems of marital dispute would soon be over, at least for a couple of months.

"David," he said gently, "next week you'll be going to live in the village of Jebel Shams in our part of Southern Lebanon. You'll be the guest of Kamran Abdullah Khan, the village's spiritual leader."

David's heart skipped a beat. "How long will I be away?"

"About two months. You'll inform your wife that you have to make a business trip to Europe. We'll provide you with a convincing cover."

"Does this Khan know my true identity?"

"No. As far as he is concerned, you want to convert. He's done it before for several Jews and Christians. His missionary zeal will stand you in good stead."

David wondered what South Lebanon was like. He had never been outside Israel since his flight from Syria. He had not been called up for Operation Peace for Galilee. In a way he was glad, because it had not been his kind of war. It was not a war of *ain brera*, no alternative. David had not given much thought to any reason for his reserve unit not being called up. He had regarded it as the luck of the draw. But since his induction into the Mossad, he had felt an occasional doubt, although he had never raised the issue.

"Rahamim," he said, rubbing his chin pensively, "you know I never fought in Lebanon in eighty-two."

"I know, David." Rahamim Ben-Yaacov anticipated what was coming next and decided the time was right for an explanation. "We keep a list of potential candidates. Sometimes it's possible just to prevent an individual from being mobilised. On other occasions we have to pull the plug on a whole unit. It depends on the operation. We have no say when it comes to a defensive war like Yom Kippur, but Lebanon was different. It wouldn't have been responsible to have you wasted in that sort of operation. Casualties among tank commanders were relatively light, but the risk was there nevertheless."

Rahamim knew from David's nod that the younger man had understood and that the matter was now closed. It was time to move on to the task in hand.

"Tell me, David, what do you know about Shi'ism?"

"Not a lot really," he said, grateful that Ben-Yaacov had changed the subject. "I know that Assad's Alawites are a sub-sect of the Shi'a and, of course, that the Shi'ites have risen to prominence in Lebanon since Peace for Galilee."

Ben-Yaacov could see that his ward's knowledge was rudimentary. "You'll be briefed in detail over the next few days but, meanwhile, I'll give you a potted explanation, although Khan will be your best teacher."

The Yemenite had studied Islam at the Hebrew University of Jerusalem and there was little he did not know about the subject. He cleared his throat before continuing.

"As you probably know, the word Shi'a means partisan and the Shi'ites reject the first three caliphs who succeeded Mohammed. They are, in fact, partisans or followers of Ali, Mohammed's cousin and son-in-law, whom, they believe, was designated by the Prophet as his successor."

David listened intently. He knew that he would soon be required to think and act like a Shi'ite Muslim.

"The Shi'ite world claims that Ali was endowed by divine will," Ben-Yaacov continued slowly. "They say that the correct line of succession was through the descendants of Ali and the Prophet's daughter Fatima. Ali claimed the caliphate but was rejected three times before finally making it on the death of Uthman in six hundred and fifty-five. He was outmanoeuvred by his enemies four years later and assassinated.''

"And that's the root cause of the split between Shi'ite and Sunni," David interjected, recalling something he had learned long ago.

"That's right," said Ben-Yaacov, glad that his student was grasping the fundamentals quickly. "Shi'ites believe that it was Ali who compiled the Koran and codified Arab grammar. They maintain that he was not the fourth in line of the caliphs, but the first in line of divinely guided imams. This imamate is a basic precept of Shi'ism and the one that most distinguishes it from Sunnism. Shi'ism rejects the Sunni belief that the divine law bestows upon the people themselves the authority to choose the ruler of an Islamic society.''

"And that's why the Shi'ites feel compelled to overthrow Sunni regimes and install clerics in their place," David said confidently.

"Precisely. In Sunni societies all adherents are said to be equal before God, but the Shi'ite clergy, with the ayatollahs at their head, possess an elevated spiritual status. Even prior to the revolution in Iran, the network of mullahs and ayatollahs not only conducted the country's religious affairs but also controlled immense wealth, owned huge estates and nurtured a nationwide political organisation with independent finance without parallel in Sunni countries.''

Rahamim Ben-Yaacov went on to explain that about fifteen per cent of all Muslims were Shi'ites and that they formed the greater part of the population of Iran and Lebanon, about half in Iraq and a sixth of Pakistanis.

But the part that fascinated David Katri was the fact that the violent deaths of Ali and his son Hussein had instilled in the Shi'ites an admiration and even a desire for martyrdom. This was seen in the readiness of some of them to blow themselves up in car bombs directed at Israeli and other opponents. They also indulged in self-flagellation in exhibitions of spiritual devotion.

Ben-Yaacov ended his discourse by pointing out that for Western policy-makers, the most important difference between the Sunnis and the Shi'ites was political rather than religious. "But never forget, David, while Shi'ism is revolutionary and anti-western, it is rigid in its religious precepts. You must learn to conform to these so that they become second nature. Not only your survival is at stake but maybe that of the State of Israel. We are the front line, David."

With Rahamim Ben-Yaacov's words ringing in his ears, the Syrian Jew drove his Subaru the short distance to his home in north Tel Aviv. It had been a long day but a rewarding one. He hoped he would be able to assimilate all the information he was receiving.

As he took the lift to his fourth-floor apartment, he felt uneasy. He would hate having to leave Yael and the children for such a long period but they both knew that the time for an even longer separation was drawing closer.

Yael opened the door as David slid his key into the lock. She was beaming radiantly. "Guess who's here, darling. Oh, it's wonderful."

She pulled him firmly by the arm into the lounge. There, sitting on the black leather setee, was a man he had not seen for more than two years. "Arik!"

The stocky figure with the tousled blond hair rose to greet him. The two men hugged one another. Their embrace was long and emotional, as if neither man wished to be parted from the other ever again.

"My God, Arik Ben-Ami," exclaimed David, holding his friend's hands and moving his arms outwards. "You've put on some weight."

"It's all the foreign food, David. Sometimes I feel desperate for some of Yael's cooking, or my mother's for that matter."

"Have you seen your parents yet?" David asked, his conscience pricked by the knowledge that he himself had not seen his kibbutz family for more than six months.

"Yes," replied Arik, "although until recently you tended to see them much more than I. The trouble is that my work takes me away for such long periods. I hope you got my postcards."

"Yes, you've certainly been around. Which country did you like best?"

"Oh, Brazil, I suppose. The girls were the sort of stunning mixture you get here," said Arik, winking at Yael in acknowledgement of her beauty.

"Arik, you know that none of them matches we Israeli girls," Yael laughed confidently. "And we can cook, too. Now I'll leave you two to do some catching up. I'll prepare the spare room for you. The kids'll be home from school shortly. They'll go crazy."

David looked on approvingly as Yael gave his dearest friend a hug and planted a warm kiss on his forehead before hurrying to the kitchen.

"I know I always say it, but that's some wife you've got there."

David nodded and smiled. "She's coped better with the transition to the big city than I have."

"Yes, I must say the whole thing was a bit of a surprise when my parents told me. Why did you do it?"

"Oh, I just felt like a change and this position came up," David replied, hoping his friend would not be too inquisitive. "It will also involve a bit of foreign travel but I suppose we'll probably end up back at the kibbutz before too long."

Arik shook his head. "All this travelling about is not for the family man, David. It gets a bit tedious at times."

"Well, I hope you'll be able to spend some time with us before you go off globetrotting again." David hated himself for his insincerity. He felt a desperate need for Arik's companionship.

Arik, too, felt a sudden yearning to spend at least a few weeks with the man he loved as a brother. But the lifestyle he had chosen precluded the establishment and reinforcement of relationships other than in the context of his work, and those were of necessity superficial.

"I'm afraid I can only stay for shabbat, David," he said quietly. "My company is a pretty hard taskmaster."

David felt a strange mixture of relief and disappointment. "Where to next?" he asked tamely.

"Central Europe somewhere. Apparently there's some big trade deal brewing, with the Iranians of all people. Anyway, the East Europeans will be involved in it somewhere along the line and I have to be near the centre of all the action."

"I just don't know how we can trade with those people, Arik. They're real fanatics."

"Who?"

"The Iranians. And, anyway, do they ever cough up the money for the goods they buy?"

Arik laughed. His friend was very naive about international trade. "They promise a lot, although if I ever hear an Iranian say 'on my mother's honour' or 'on the memories of my ancestors' I know a hard task lies ahead and that he'll try to cheat. But, as it says in the Koran, 'do not think that God is unmindful of those who act unjustly'."

"I didn't know you studied the Koran," David said, genuinely surprised at Arik's knowledge. "That's all I remember from school," the blond man laughed. "My Arabic has practically all gone. Anyway, my German is much better."

Engrossed in their conversation, neither man noticed that Yael had re-entered the salon. "Talking about German, Arik," she interrupted. "I've made you your favourite, sausage and Sauerkraut."

The three of them laughed heartedly, although their eyes betrayed a sadness born of undisclosed confidences.

CHAPTER SIX

The fat man sat watching as the twenty-thousand-ton Panama-nian registered cargo ship Stella Aqua berthed, at once attrac-ting Karachi's shore derricks like praying mantises and dock workers like ants. How different, he thought, was this hive of activity compared to the laissez-faire attitude of Arab dockers and the redundancy of parts of Europe.

Fuad Kerekeh was confident. The ship had already spent three weeks plying the Mediterranean, including the Syrian port of Latakia, before cutting through the Suez Canal on its way to the sub-continent. He could afford to wait patiently for it to be unloaded.

His was a container just like any other. He would present his bill of lading as was required. He would also present a bribe as was the custom. That the bribe was enormous by Pakistani standards would ensure that the description of the goods as agricultural machinery was accepted at face value. Five hun-dred dollars was a year's wages for most of these people.

Fuad Kerekeh had every reason to feel confident. Soon he would be driving his rented truck almost the length of the coun-try. It bothered him little that he was transporting enough arms and explosives to equip a small army.

Almost fifteen hundred kilometres to the north, Rashid Sedawi sat patiently on a bench in the Japanese garden of Rawalpindi's Ayub National Park. He breathed in the delicate fragrances that had made the garden his favourite place for meditation and observed the gardener carefully tending the water lilies in one of the ponds. The man seemed to caress the plants as one would a lover.

The Shi'ite from southern Lebanon had done some careful cultivation of his own over the previous six months. Imran Iqbal had proved a worthwhile investment. The sallow little man had kept them abreast of events at Kahuta. It was true he was being well paid, but he seemed genuinely to support their cause.

Rashid felt the late afternoon sun penetrate him with its comforting rays. He had a feeling that all his efforts were about to bear fruit. Something had to happen soon for Fuad Kerekeh was already complaining about expenses. Although he did not like leaving financial arrangements in the hands of his obese lover, the man with the golden tooth was more concerned about the logistics involved in the pursuit of his grand strategy. Thirty members of the Cell were awaiting his command to enter Pakistan by various routes. Each man would book into a small hotel in the main cities, from Karachi and Hyderabad to Lahore and Peshawar, and each would await a telephone call that would bring him to a derelict house in a deserted little side-street in west Rawalpindi. The house was of less importance than the lock-up at its rear.

Rashid Sedawi suddenly felt a surge of impatience. Allah, something must happen soon. Kahuta, surrounded as it was by tanks and all manner of rockets, was well-nigh impregnable. He just hoped that Imran Iqbal was not playing games with him. As if the mere thought of the Pakistani were enough, Rashid made out the figure of the man proceeding at a hurried pace towards him from the garden entrance.

Imran Iqbal could hardly contain his excitement as he greeted the Arab. His sallow face creased into a broad smile. "Allahu Akbar, ya Rashid. I have some truly wonderful news."

"Try to be more contained, Imran my friend. We do not want to draw attention to ourselves."

"Yes, yes, of course."

"Now take things slowly and give me all the facts," said Rashid. He did not want the Pakistani overlooking details in his exuberence.

"One of our three bombs is being moved," the Pakistani enthused.

"Where to?"

"To an F-16 air base somewhere in the south. It's the only plane we have that can realistically be used to deliver the weapon to its target."

"When?"

"If everything goes according to schedule, it should be two months from today."

Rashid rubbed his chin. Wherever it went, the bomb was bound to be massively protected. It would take all his ingenuity to devise a plan to steal it and it would have to be done quickly.

Imran Iqbal noticed that the Arab was lost in thought. How he admired the man. Islam could achieve its former glory only through a man such as this.

"Rashid, my friend, there is more."

Sedawi was only vaguely aware of the Pakistani tugging at his arm. "Go ahead," he mumbled.

"The bomb is fifteen kilotons. That's the equivalent of fifteen thousands tons of TNT, just a little more than at Hiroshima. It only weighs about thirty kilograms."

"I know," said Rashid. It was just what he needed.

Imran Iqbal was saving the best news for last. "Ya Rashid," he said excitedly, "the fools are taking it by road first to Chaklala where it's to be put aboard a C-130 Hercules bound for the south."

Rashid Sedawi felt the adrenalin begin pumping into the very depths of his soul. Allah, they were using as a half-way house the very airport that served Rawalpindi and Islamabad. A plan was already formulating in his head. "You have done well, my friend," he said, gripping the Pakistani's arm. "Allah will bless you."

Imran Iqbal had never felt more worthy than at that moment. The man with the golden tooth was truly among the righteous. "There is just one more thing, ya Rashid," he said.

"What's that?"

"The bomb will not be carrying any detonators."

Sedawi smiled. "Do not worry, my friend," he said warmly, "we have already procured them."

Kamran Abdullah Khan, the mullah of Jebel Shams, vigorously keened the barber's razor on a leather strap. The blade had already made a hundred cuts this day, the tenth of muharram, and it would make a hundred more. But for the white-haired and aged mullah the most important cut was about to be made.

His student had shown an eagerness to learn the true faith. He had studied the tenets of Shi'ism from dawn until dusk. He had chanted in slow melodic phrases the one hundred and fourteen suras of the Koran. He had discussed some of the seven thousand hadiths, appearing to revel in the wisdom of the sayings and stories from the glorious past. The young Jew had adopted a Shi'ite name. From now on he would be called Anwar Hindawi. God was great. It was the will of Allah that all infidels should accept Islam and it was the will of Allah that he and other clerics should be the catalysts for conversion to the true path.

David watched apprehensively as the blade hovered over his head. He heard the mullah mumble a prayer in celebration of Hussein and then grip his head with his free left hand. The razor moved in a short downward thrust to a point just above his hairline. The incision felt like a stab with a needle. A thin trickle of scarlet began its slow descent. David Katri knew that by the end of the festival he would be soaked in his lifeblood.

Rahamim Ben-Yaacov had told him that it was important that he participate in the Ashura, the festival celebrating the birth of the Shi'a faith thirteen hundred years before and the break with mainstream Sunni Moslems. It was just possible that he would be tested on the holiest time of the Shi'ite calendar. It was also possible that someone might check to see if he had the tell-tale scar.

David had watched spellbound as villagers, dressed in their brightly coloured battle robes, circled each other upon a makeshift stage in the village square. Each man cut and thrust with real swords, although the movements were so slow and exaggerated as to make the likelihood of accidental injury unlikely.

For the actors, the re-enactment of the death in battle of Hussein was re-affirmation of their faith in a man who had given the Shi'a hope throughout the centuries of being the underdogs of the Moslem world. The grandson of the Prophet had died fighting against overwhelming odds, all his followers having deserted him. For more than a millennia he had provided an enduring symbol as a figure of martyrdom.

David joined the stream of chanting men, many of them much younger than he, in a stamping procession around the stage. The air was heavy with the stench of sweat and blood as their white death shrouds became completely stained. Some of the men around him had driven themselves into a state of frenzied ecstasy, their willingness to bleed and suffer proving that they were the living embodiment of the martyrdom of Hussein.

"Heida, Heida," the procession chanted in unison, each man slapping his wound with the palm of his hand, thus preventing the blood from coagulating until the end of the festival five hours later. For some, either the loss of blood or the disorientation caused by their mental state proved too much and they collapsed into unconsciousness. David almost tripped over a man in front of him who fell without warning. He turned to see the stretcher bearers drag him clear. He almost wished oblivion would free him, too, from the surrounding fanaticism.

The only thing that kept David Katri sane was the knowledge that he would soon be returning home.

Most of Kahuta's three thousand workers were in their homes when three regular army GMC trucks pulled to a halt outside the centrifuge block. The lights of the complex were still ablaze and the silhouettes of scores of soldiers could be made out on the perimeter wall. Appropriately, a crescent moon shone above as the Islamic Bomb prepared to make its first journey beyond the citadel that had been its cradle since inception.

An innocuous looking crate resting on a palette was delivered by a small forklift to the centre truck. Neither the drivers nor any of the soldiers on guard knew that the crate contained a cylinder of gun-type metal, the sort one might find on a navel gun barrel. Neither did they know that within the one-metre long cylinder were fifty kilograms of high explosive, a fire plug and, most deadly of all, thirty kilograms of enriched uranium metal. Convoys of this kind were not unusual when parts for the centrifuges and laboratories were being transported to and from the complex. The only difference this time was that, once outside the perimeter wall, the trucks would be joined by two M-48 tanks fore and two more aft. Also joining the convoy would be four M-113 Armoured Personnel Carriers, each with two crewmen and eleven highly-trained soldiers of the elite Special Services Group.

Lieutenant-colonel Abdul Azziz, too, did not know the contents of the crate he was transporting to Chaklala airport. Whatever it was and whatever its importance, it was his responsibility and he intended that everything should run smoothly. He knew the fifty kilometres to Chaklala as an old man his years. As a boy he had often picnicked by the ancient temples at Kahuta.

All that had ceased since Dr Khan had initiated his dream. Tanks now guarded all entrances and exits to the area. French Crotale surface-to-air missiles and anti-aircraft guns watched the skies, ready to pour venom on any intruder. During daylight hours the Pakistani air force flew combat patrols.

Lieutenant-colonel Abdul Azziz did not have cause to lack confidence as he climbed into his jeep, his driver firing the starter with one hand and thrusting the gearstick into first with the other before moving off in a cloud of dust towards the front of the convoy. The might of the Pakistan armed forces was based around Rawalpindi. As far as the colonel was concerned, this was just another manoeuvre.

In the night sky above Pakistan another man had no reason to be apprehensive. Captain James Tindle eased back on the throttle as the giant 747 settled into its regular flight path to Islamabad. British Airways flight two-two-three had proved as uneventful as it usually did. The stopover in Bahrain had taken its customary hour. The passenger manifesto recorded that thirty passengers had disembarked in the Gulf state and that twenty had taken their places. He was now responsible for three hundred and forty-six passengers and a crew of twelve. The plane was running perfectly smoothly and there was no reason why it should not reach its destination. There was also no reason why he should not be back in Pimlico within the week. He had promised his two sons a trip to the Safari Park at Woburn and, being away from home as much as he was, he did not aim to let them down.

What Captain Tindle could not know was that five of the passengers who boarded in Bahrain possessed an assortment of small arms and a number of hand grenades. Nor could he have been aware that each carried one and a half kilos of explosive in a pouch around his waist.

Outside the derelict house in west Rawalpindi stood a fleet of two black Ford Transit vans and three blue Volkswagen minibuses of more modern vintage. Each had been bought for cash. Each had been inspected and serviced. There could be no room for mechanical failure of any kind.

Rashid Sedawi peered through an open window, gazing upon his own convoy as a father would his sons. Imran Iqbal had done well. It would have been importune for a foreigner to buy the vehicles. The natives always new best and Iqbal had not aroused the slightest suspicion on his buying trips throughout the city. Rashid looked at his watch. The Pakistani had caught the Saudi Airlines flight an hour before. By the time the action was over, Imran Iqbal would be safely ensconced in the Cell's headquarters in southern Beirut. By the will of Allah, he prayed silently, Iqbal would help put the finishing touches to all their efforts and he, Rashid Sedawi, would possess the only weapon big enough to avenge the death of Imam Hussein.

The sun was just beginning its descent as Rashid entered the adjoining room. It was heavy with the sweat of men, an odour that never ceased to excite him. The sweat before battle was like that of sexual fervour.

Rashid moved across the room and faced his two lieutenants. Fuad Kerekeh and Hassan Hilbawi stood with legs apart and hands behind their backs. Before them sat thirty of their best fighters, men who had been bloodied in battle in Beirut and in actions against the Israeli army in southern Lebanon. He smiled at his men. It was almost sunset. The time for rhetoric was over, although he knew that he must once again instil in them their desire for death and martyrdom.

He began slowly, his voice containing that mystical depth and intonation that had attracted the faithful to prayer over more than a millennium. Not for Moslems the peel of infidel bells. Allah Himself had called upon the Prophet to encourage the use of the human voice itself to lure the pious.

"Allahu Akhbar!" Rashid cried. He paused while the assembly returned the affirmation that God was indeed Great. "My brothers," he continued, "we are gathered here in a strange land to restore honour to Islam and avenge the martyrdom of Hussein. Each of you knows he is going to die and each of you will welcome death. As it is written, what awaits you is Paradise. Its cool running waters and lush pastures will bathe you in permanent bliss. You shall be dwelling in the house of Allah and you shall be His honoured guest forever."

"Allahu Akhbar!" the men chanted in unison. "Allahu Akhbar wa'Mohammed Rasul Allah!"

Rashid crossed to a blackboard to his left. It was time to go over every detail once more. Each man knew his allotted task and each knew how to handle the weapons at his disposal. Their arsenal included ten TOW anti-tank rocket launchers with Starlights for night attack and ten eighty-one millimetre light mortars.

He had pointed out to them that the Afghanistani rebels bearing only light arms had kept the Russians pinned down for more than a decade. Recalling the debacle of the Syrian army's defeat by the Israelis, he had spat at the ground as a mark of ridicule. Rashid Sedawi knew that his power of oratory had entranced his followers. Each would don his belt of explosives and each would blow himself to eternity if wounded or captured. They had accepted their fate with equanimity. Only Islam had this power, he thought, clenching his right fist and punching his left palm. He, too, was prepared to enter the Abode of Peace, to recline on silken couches amid cascading waterfalls and clusters of date palms. But not yet. Rashid Sedawi did not wear the lethal cummerbund. He had no intention of bringing about his own death. He would gladly die upon completion of his mission but not beforehand.

Fuad Kerekeh and Hassan Hilbawi, as members of the Higher Council, would also not have to wear explosives around their midriffs. The former hung on his master's every word and would have been prepared to die not only with him but for him.

Hilbawi, too, had found himself mesmerised by Sedawi's eloquence. But Hassan Hilbawi was not prepared to die for anyone. He stared at the neck of the Lebanese farmer's son and the whites of his eyes contained the milk of venom.

The convoy from Kahuta moved slowly through the main gates of Chaklala's military airfield. Lieutenant-colonel Abdul Azziz sighed with relief as his jeep headed towards a hangar near number two runway. It was not that he was expecting trouble. His task was nearly over and now it was simply a question of transferring his secret cargo into an outbuilding. By the thin light of the moon he could just make out some shadowy figures in the distance. As his convoy neared the building, he noticed chinks of neon emanating from within. Over the net, he ordered the two leading tanks to take up their positions facing the runway.

The colonel jumped from his jeep before it had drawn to a halt and began directing the trucks into their allotted spaces. The middle vehicle turned half circle and began reversing towards the doors of the cargo shed. Suddenly, the chinks of light became a flood as the building's doors were flung open. A fork lift manoeuvred busily towards the truck's tailgate. Silhouettes could be seen scuttling to and fro as the fork lift carried the pallet and its precious cargo into the shed. There it would rest for two hours until higher authority would command it to be placed aboard the Hercules C-130 waiting in eerie darkness at the end of the runway. Cloud had increased and it was difficult to make out the stubby shape of the plane which was more than a hundred metres away.

Azziz ordered his men to relax their positions. The soldiers of the Special Services Group left the relative safety of the welded aluminium hull of their APCs and eagerly trotted down the power-operated ramp at the rear to stretch their legs. The 12.7 mm Brownings on the forward sections of the commander's cuppolas remained unattended as the throaty roars of the GMC Detroit diesels died almost in unison.

Azziz felt reasonably confident that he had performed his duties well. Everything had gone without a hitch thus far and his men would stand guard around the cargo shed until he ordered them to withdraw. Despite his rank, intelligent improvisation was not one of the colonel's strong points. He was the product of a culture that was rigid and an army that was even more so. Therefore, he would obey the orders of his superiors without question. Without his orders, Abdul Azziz was as efficient as a computer without software. Without him, his men were as organised as headless chickens.

A light breeze was blowing and the night air was cool and pleasant. He stared at the twinkling lights of the neighbouring civilian airport. How odd, he thought, that people there were going about their business blissfully ignorant of what was going on just a kilometre away.

But then Lieutenant-colonel Abdul Azziz was ignorant of many things also. He was unaware that he was being observed through high-powered Telstar night binoculars, that British Airways flight two-two-three was less than an hour's flying time from Chaklala and that he would not live to witness its spectacular arrival.

Captain James Tindle began carrying out the time-honoured procedures for landing. He was well acquainted with the idiosyncrasies of the 747 and, anyway, this particular flight had been as smooth as a pebble. He noted that although cloud cover was increasing, it was still pretty high. He figured they should break through it within the next couple of minutes. The jumbo's position was thirty miles southwest of Chaklala on a heading two-five-zero. The airliner was in ground radar contact.

"Calling Chaklala approach control," Tindle radioed, using the former name for the airport which served both the capital and Rawalpindi. Islamabad International Airport was a bit of a mouthful and, anyway, old habits died hard. "Chaklala approach control, this is British Airways two-two-three maintaining six thousand feet, heading two-five-zero."

The skipper heard the familiar cackle over the air waves. It was Mohsin Kamal himself. The Chief Air Traffic Controller was an old friend.

"BA two-two-three, this is Chaklala approach control. Runway two zero is clear for landing. You are now twenty-five miles southwest of the outer marker. Begin descent at your discretion. Start a right turn to heading two-six-zero. And James, meet me for coffee when you get in. Usual place."

Tindle smiled. The Pakistanis were such friendly chaps. Maybe it was a legacy of empire, but the more educated of them were on the same wavelength as himself.

The Boeing pilot was just about to comply with Kamal's instructions when he heard the startled cry of navigator Bill Hawkins. "Who the hell are you?"

Tindle and Stan Morton, the co-pilot, turned in their seats. Facing them was a swarthy man with a zapata moustache and burning eyes. In his right hand he held a pistol and in his left a grenade, its lever depressed and the pin missing. Around the man's waist appeared to be a bulky money-belt.

The man was coolness itself. "Gentlemen," he said slowly

in an accent that definitely was not Pakistani, "you will maintain radio silence from now on. But leave the radio open so that we can hear ground control."

Tindle could see his own fear reflected in the eyes of Morton and Hawkins. Like most air crew, they had attended seminars on the subject of hijacking. It had always provided a topic of conversation whenever such incidents were reported from around the world. But, like most people, Tindle and his crew took solace in the old adage 'it will never happen to me'.

Now it was happening and he felt as helpless as a trainee taking his first flying lesson.

The hijacker's eyes narrowed. They contained the contempt and self-righteousness of the religious fanatic. "You will not land at Islamabad International Airport but at the military airfield adjacent to it," he said firmly. "You have seen it many times from the air so it should present no problem to you." Ali Majid al Saleh had studied a diagram of the approach and he would recognise it once they were below cloud cover. "Just in case you try anything stupid, I can tell you that my comrades have taken control of the passenger decks. Any tricks and they will blow up the plane. It is as simple as that."

Tindle knew enough about hijacking to understand that the most vulnerable situation was while the plane was in the air. The Pakistanis would have to deal with the matter after he had landed. He wiped the sweat from his brow and altered course.

After a few seconds an urgent voice could be heard over the net. Mohsin Kamal sounded both agitated and surprised.

"BA two-two-three, you have veered from your landing approach. Return to heading two-six-zero. Please confirm. Over."

Ali Majid smiled thinly. "Maintain your present course, Captain Tindle," he ordered. The giant Boeing dipped further and suddenly the lights of Chaklala could be seen to the left, with the military airfield's runway dead ahead.

"BA Flight two-two-three, why do you not answer me?" The

consternation in Kamal's voice was reaching panic proportions. "James, can you hear me? You are on the wrong course. Can you hear me? Over."

Tindle felt sorry for his old friend. It must be harrowing to be faced with such a situation. But he knew he must now concentrate all his attention on the task in hand. He prayed that the military airfield's runway was long enough to accommodate a Jumbo. He did not fancy a roll in the grass.

What Tindle, Kamal and even Ali Majid al Saleh did not know was that a Hercules C-130 transport plane was parked at the end of the runway in an area bathed in darkness.

Among those who did know were General Ibrahim Shazli, director of covert operations, and three ground controllers in the military control tower. But they had hardly had time to warn their civilian counterparts. They had also not managed to ascertain the Jumbo's radio frequency. Disaster stared them in the face and they were as helpless as lambs at the end of Ramadan.

The Boeing zoomed over the edge of the airfield, its flaps at sixty degrees. Tindle flared out and levelled off. The jet thrum weakened as he closed all the throttles. He raised the wing spoilers and slammed open the thrust reverse levers. The runway still sped by at an alarming rate. The teeth-jarring sound of metal upon metal could be heard as he applied the toe brakes. Passengers and crew were spared the sickly smell of burning rubber as the giant plane's tyres screeched indignantly.

Lieutenant-Colonel Abdul Azziz watched the approach of the giant jet and its twinkling landing lights with undisturbed fascination. He was still entranced as the tyres of the 747 emitted the short screech of primary contact with the runway. The noise was so deafening that the colonel could be forgiven for not hearing the approach of his assassin. Even the dull sensation of the knife entering his heart was not retained long enough to form a memory.

Rashid Sedawi, his left arm encircling his victim's neck, felt the man's body go limp and swiftly withdrew the knife from below the rib cage. He allowed the corpse to drop to the ground before reverting his gaze to the onrushing airliner.

Within a fraction of a second a staccato of explosions ruptured the blackness. A casual observer might not have discerned the smaller blast which preceded the cataclysmic eruption as the 747 ploughed into the parked Hercules. But Rashid knew instantly that Ali Majid had had time to detonate his explosives in the flight cabin before the crash.

Further blasts followed along the length of the passenger compartments turning the whole plane into a fireball. As might be expected, the attention of onlookers was drawn towards the exploding leviathan, so much so that a smaller blast at the airfield's main gates was hardly noticed. Rashid smiled grimly. By the time he reached the cargo shed, his martyrs would be inside the compound, ready and willing to die for their cause.

The screams and shouts of horrified men could hardly be heard above the din. Before Pakistan's elite commandos could gather their wits, they were being slaughtered by fanatics wearing white headbands. The words daubed in blood on the kerchiefs were the same as those emanating from the throats of their attackers in such bloodcurdling fashion: "Allahu Akhbar!"

The desperate sound of starters straining to spark life into reluctant engines could be heard coming from the direction of the tanks facing the runway. The turrets rotated unconvincingly. It was impossible to know which of the figures illuminated by the fiery bursts of explosives was the enemy. Not that the tank commanders had long to ponder their predicament. Within seconds each of their dithering chariots of steel had been hit by a fusillade of TOW missiles and rocket propelled grenades.

The steady crump of mortars could be heard, followed by

a series of blinding flashes as their shells cascaded into the sleeping huts of regular army troops attached to the airbase. Most of the soldiers did not have time to dress or gather their weapons. Some died where they lay.

Rashid Sedawi reached the cargo shed in time to see Fuad Kerekeh pull up in one of the black Transits. Like its companions, it bore no licence plate and had had all identification marks removed. Kerekeh, his great weight precluding him from more strenuous participation, waved in recognition. Four would-be martyrs emerged from the back of the Transit and joined Sedawi as he entered the cargo shed.

A number of civilian technicians were seen cowering by the forklift. They were herded quickly to one side and more swiftly dispatched by a hail of 9mm Kalashnikov bullets, the sort that leave no chance for the wounded to even wish they were dead. One of the raiders, well-versed in the art of forklift driving, manoeuvred the deadly cargo to the rear of the Transit. A few jerks later and it was inside. Within a few seconds, Fuad Kerekeh had slammed the Ford into gear and was speeding towards the base's exit.

All the men inside were tight-lipped as they swerved to avoid a vehicle blazing fiercely by the side of the road. It was one of the blue Volkswagens.

"Let's go!" screamed Sedawi as they neared the gates. They had just turned the curve and were only fifty metres away when Kerekeh slammed on the brakes. There, dead ahead, were the two remaining tanks, apparently still operative. As the cannons swivelled ominously towards them, all six men jumped from the van. Two of those from the rear of the vehicle were immediately cut to pieces by withering machine-gun fire. The remaining two raced towards the tanks and leapt atop the turrets. They opened the hatches and disappeared inside. For what seemed an eternity all action seemed to be suspended. Suddenly, two massive explosions rent the air and bright orange flames leapt from the open turrets.

Rashid stood transfixed by the scene. It was only an animal sixth sense that told him his life was in immediate danger. He wheeled instinctively. Hassan Hilbawi, his shirt and trousers stained with blood, his left arm hanging by shreds, launched himself desperately at his leader. In his good right hand was a six-inch knife. Rashid felt the blade slash his neck as the two men collapsed in a heap.

Hilbawi knew immediately that he had failed to kill the mad-man. He felt the weight of Rashid's body crushing the life force from him. Weakened by loss of blood, he felt himself drifting into a state of semi-consciousness, powerless to offer any resistance as Sedawi forced open his mouth and stuffed it with something hard and metallic.

In almost one movement, Rashid removed the pin from the grenade and raced five metres before flinging himself to the ground. After the heat of the blast passed over him, he rose and made speedily for the black van where Fuad Kerekeh sat, ashen-faced.

As the van raced through the twisted gates of Chaklala air-base, Fuad Kerekeh noticed the cut on his lover's neck. The fat man pointed to something less tangible which was stuck to Rashid Sedawi's shirt above the right shoulder blade. The man with the golden tooth scraped off the matt of congealed flesh and blood and flung it out of the window. He thanked Allah it was not his own.

Mohsin Kamal watched the pyrotechnics in horror. The chief air traffic controller knew that his friend James Tindle could not have survived such an inferno. He could not begin to think what had possessed the Briton to overshoot the civilian airport he knew so well and land instead on the shorter military runway.

Tears trickled down Kamal's cheeks and he shuddered as he envisioned the terrible end of the crew and passengers of BA flight two-two-three.

One man less concerned with the flight of those aboard the stricken airliner was General Ibrahim Shazli. A career soldier, he had risen through the ranks to become deputy Chief of Staff. Awarded his country's highest decoration for valour in the Indo-Pakistan war, he was tipped by most to succeed his immediate superior.

The general wiped a brow pockmarked by a childhood attack of smallpox. The flickering of the thermal illuminations outside the control tower gave his face a devilish aura. Inside the tower, there was debris everywhere. A mortar shell had scored a direct hit, instantly causing a blackout and sending showers of splintered glass over the occupants.

Shazli, himself unhurt, disregarded the moans of the wounded. Unable to raise Abdul Azziz on his portable handset, he knew he must get to the cargo shed as quickly as possible. He made a conscious effort not to think the unthinkable. The general almost tripped over something soft lying on the floor. He heard a groan. It was too dark to make out the features of the victim. Climbing over the body, he made his way instinctively towards what was left of the door. He felt himself beginning to gag from the dust.

Fortunately, the stairs were still intact. Pistol in hand, the general descended them two at a time. Stumbling two or three times, he reached the exit as yet another fierce explosion ripped through the air.

Some men were rushing around in all directions. Others, imobilised by fear, could be seen cowering behind stationary vehicles. It was immediately obvious that the chain of command had collapsed. He headed straight for the cargo shed, where lights were still blazing and the building appeared to be undamaged.

Once inside, General Ibrahim Shazli could feel panic clamp his throat. Five technicians, their white coats stained deep red, lay on the floor entwined in deathly embrace. He ran to a number of crates and tea chests stacked to his right. None looked the right size and none bore the stamp of the secret code. In that instant, the general knew that at best his career was over and at worst he would face a firing squad. The president of Pakistan was an austere man, a man not wont to suffer humiliation. Scapegoats must and would be found. Blame would be apportioned. The Will of Allah was an unconvincing excuse.

"General Shazli! General Shazli!"

He wheeled round, every nerve taught as chickenwire. It was one of his young adjutants, an Urdu speaker from the south. The man's uniform was in tatters but he appeared unhurt.

"We have trapped one of them, sir."

"Where is he?"

"He is in amidst some oil drums in the fuel compound."

"Achah," the general replied in Urdu, "okay, let's go. But for the sake of Allah don't shoot him. We need every piece of information we can get."

The two men dashed the hundred or so metres to the fuel compound which, miraculously, was still intact. Neither was aware that their captive was the last of the attackers in the base left alive. Neither did they know that of the others only small unidentifiable pieces would be found.

A group of soldiers was positioned about twenty metres from a stack of oil drums. They were highly nervous. Each knew that a single shot would turn the whole area into an inferno. They looked at the general imploringly. Shazli cupped his hands and shouted towards the oil drums. "In the name of Allah, give yourself up and you will not be harmed."

The general had invoked God's name but he was not even sure whether the attacker was Moslem.

There was a long pause before Shazli reiterated his promise.

He was just about to call out a third time when a voice in halting English was heard from behind the drums.

"I will speak only with your commanding officer. He must to come here to speak. I will throw away my weapons."

With this, the vague shape of a rifle could be seen flying through the air. It landed with a clatter, the sound magnified because of a sudden lull in the shooting.

"I will go to him," Shazli said immediately.

"You must not, sir. He may still be armed. Let me go in your place."

The general could see that his adjutant was sincere. He was touched by his loyalty, but he knew that this might be his last chance to redeem some honour from a desperate situation.

"Thank you, Wasim," he said warmly. "But this is something I alone must do."

The onlookers watched with bated breath as the general walked slowly towards the oil drums. They could just make out a figure rise to greet him. What they could not see was the serenity of the man's smile as his right hand dropped to a toggle switch at his waist.

As Rashid Sedawi had calculated, the Pakistan army and police force were slow to react. The black Ford Transit traversed the five kilometres between the airfield and the outskirts of Rawalpindi in less than four minutes. What little traffic there was in the early hours came from the opposite direction, drawn by the flames in the night sky.

Fuad Kerekeh drove to the deserted street in the west of the city. He parked the vehicle in the lock-up. Both men were bathed in sweat by the time they had transferred the innocuous-looking crate to a secondhand chest freezer on their Toyota pick-up.

Despite his exhaustion, the exhileration of his success gave

Rashid Sedawi a sexual urge which could only be requited within the lush depths of his obese companion.

Fuad Kerekeh allowed himself to be violated in a variety of ways, ecstatic in the certain knowledge that his lover had been blessed by God. It was only after he, too, was spent that doubts began to gnaw at him.

"Ya Rashid," he said slowly caressing the thinner man's hair, "I am sure they will come looking for us."

"Fuad, my friend," Sedawi replied soothingly, "I have told you before to trust in me. This is a city of almost one million people. Tomorrow morning we will drive leisurely to our house on the better side of town. No-one will take much notice of the delivery of a chest freezer."

"But the authorities are bound to carry out a house-to-house search."

Rashid's voice was calm. "Let me tell you, ya Fuad, why I do not envy the president of Pakistan this day. Firstly he has an international incident in which a British aircraft has crashed killing all on board. Secondly, and, of course, most importantly of all, he has mislaid his little toy."

Kerekeh chuckled, the kind of giggle of which only fat men seem capable.

"Now, our friend the president has a problem," Sedawi continued. "He has always denied the existence of the Islamic Bomb so how can he complain now that it has been stolen?"

Kerekeh's giggle turned into a guffaw.

"No, do not worry, my fat friend. If the president instigates a country-wide search, he'll have to have a pretty good reason. The last thing he wants is exposure so I believe he'll just cover the whole thing up."

Sedawi felt the fat man snuggle closer to him. He had already decided that he and Fuad would stay six more months in Rawalpindi until the slim likelihood of a concerted search had receded. He would then transport the freezer to Karachi before shipping it to Akaba and the next leg of his grand strategy.

Neither man had mentioned the treachery of Hassan Hilbawi or the comrades who had died in more heroic fashion. Rashid Sedawi had already decided that at the first opportunity he would give thanks to Allah for his deliverance at the shrine of Bari Imam, set at the foot of the Marghalla hills east of Islamabad. Festooned with black Shi'ite flags, it seethed constantly to the beating of drums and the heady aroma of hashish.

CHAPTER SEVEN

When Yael Katri next saw her husband, it was as if a different man had entered her life. Gone were the flowing locks of jet-black hair, in their place a fine fleece shaven almost to the bone. She noticed the fresh scar upon his forehead.

"My God, David, what have they done to you?"

Katri put his arms around her and kissed her full lips with a passion born of prolonged abstinence. "Are the children asleep?" he asked quietly.

"Yes, about half an hour ago."

David entered the children's bedroom. A purple night light glowed comfortingly. Boaz, whose resemblance to himself people said was striking, was lying at a tangent across his bed, one arm dropped over the edge. It was one of those nights when heat and humidity made living in Tel Aviv a bane. The bedclothes were lying half on the floor.

Gently, David lifted the child and placed his arm by his side. Boaz groaned slightly as he replaced the topsheet. Kissing his son softly on the forehead, David felt himself re-living the scene so many years earlier when he had bade farewell to his brother Naftali in the same manner. A lump formed in his throat as he realised he had not seen Naftali since. He shuddered. Was this the last time he would see his son, too?

David rose wearily and crossed the room to Shoshana's bed. How like her mother she is, he thought, but in a way like his sister Rachel too. He stroked her long ebony hair the way she liked it, from the roots to the ends. Shoshana stirred but made no noise.

Yael Katri watched her husband's kneeling figure from the

doorway. Instinct told her David would not be able to stay the whole night. She touched him gently on the arm.

"Come, David, let us go to the kitchen." It was their favourite venue for discussion. "Tell me what happened."

"Yaelli," he began quietly, using his pet diminutive for her, "I am not supposed to be here. If the organisation found out, I'd be in great trouble." He gripped her by both arms before continuing. "I just had to see you. I still have three weeks of instruction left."

"Why didn't you stay, darling. We could have survived another three weeks."

David felt a heaviness in his breast. The pit of his stomach tightened. He sighed wearily, the words refusing to come.

"Please, my darling, tell me everything," Yael said soothingly. "I can cope with knowledge. It is the unknown which frightens me."

The Syrian Jew gazed lovingly into his pretty Yemenite's almond eyes. He took her right hand and held the palm against his cheek, luxuriating in her touch. He had missed her delicate softness so much.

"Yael," he said, almost whispering, "you know that officially I am supposed to be somewhere in Europe on business and that I was due to come home in three weeks' time."

The colour drained from Yael's cheeks. The words 'was due' sent warning signals to her brain, but she did not speak.

David could see the hurt registered in his wife's eyes. "I have been ordered to go to Beirut directly on completion of my education," he said gently. "My name is now Anwar Hindawi and to all intents and purposes I am a Shi'ite who was orphaned when Israel took Kuneitra in nineteen sixty-seven."

Yael felt herself go cold. The Amcor refrigerator seemed to hum like a swarm of angry bees and the room began to swim.

David moved quickly to his left to support her as she slumped against him. Gently lifting her out of the chair, he carried her to the bedroom. He placed his arms around her waist and let the top half of her body slump forward. The sudden rush of blood to the head brought her round and she groped uneasily for the edge of the bed.

Katri found the pain of guilt almost unbearable. They hugged one another in silence for almost ten minutes before he gently removed her silk dressing gown and negligee.

Yael gasped as he entered her. She fought back the tears as their lovemaking reached its climax with almost the same intensity as she had experienced when their mutual aim had been conception. Then life itself had been the outcome. Now, a vision of tragedy was her constant companion.

For a few fleeting moments she bathed in the warming throbs of orgasm, her body convulsing with pleasure. She felt her husband stiffen and took delight in his grunts as his seed spurted into her very soul.

In that instant, Yael Katri prayed that she would bear her husband a child for the third time. In the same instant she feared she would never feel the warmth of his embrace again.

It was the Friday following the theft of the Islamic Bomb that Rashid Sedawi and Fuad Kerekeh decided to visit the shrine of Bari Imam to give thanks to Allah for their salvation.

A Moslem sabbath like any other, the mosques lining the roads leading from the capital were packed with worshippers, albeit most of them Sunnis.

The newspapers and other media had been full of the jumbo jet disaster and of how pieces of burning debris had set off a series of explosions at nearby fuel and ammunition dumps. But, as Rashid had forecast, there was no mention of a catastrophe of far greater significance. It was an eerie sensation for both of them. They felt as if they had been members of a World Cup winning team only to find that the rest of creation was totally unaware of their achievement.

"Do not worry, Fuad, my friend," said the man with the golden tooth, "in our particular case the less publicity the better. Allah knows what we have accomplished in His name and that is enough."

The fat man nodded as the Toyota picked up speed on the road leading to the shrine. Fuad Kerekeh liked to drive fast, but on this occasion he would adhere strictly to the speed limit. It was not unknown for a simple speeding offence to lead to the capture of fugitives.

As the vehicle neared the holy site, hundreds of pilgrims, malangs and fakirs dressed in green and white shrouds, could be seen filing in silent procession along the roadside verges. A general hubbub could be heard as they approached the main entrance, where hundreds more whirled as dervishes to the frenzied rhythm of the tabbles. A stiff breeze descended from the rolling marghalla hills causing the black Shi'ite flags to flutter and billow. The sickly sweet smell of marijuana hung heavy in the air.

Dressed in white shrouds, Rashid Sedawi and Fuad Kerekeh joined the throng of worshippers as the voice of the muezzin repeated its familiar petition to the faithful. How much more attractive was the resonance of the human voice than the peel of infidel bells, thought Rashid.

Both men washed their hands and feet before joining the rows of supplicants preparing to touch their foreheads to the earth in time-honoured homage to Allah and His Prophet. The muezzin repeated his shahahda: "God is Great. I testify that there is no god but God. I testify that Mohammed delivered God's message. Come to prayer. Come to prosperity..."

In unison the columns of worshippers bent to place their hands on their knees. Then, in a jerking movement, they knelt with palms on thighs before brushing the ground with their foreheads.

The midday sun, merciless in its intensity, did not deter the faithful from prayer, the second of the five pillars of the Moslem faith.

Rashid and Fuad were bowing for the third time when they heard a staccato of car horns and the wailing of sirens. Most of the worshippers were too immersed in prayer to comprehend immediately what was happening.

Within seconds the police were everywhere, wielding their truncheons in an unnecessary show of force against victims who were too dazed either by hashish or shock to offer any resistance. They had never known such a thing to happen before.

Sedawi cursed vilely as he grabbed Fuad by the scruff of his shroud and hauled the fat man towards a thickly wooded area nearby. How could he have been such a fool. Imran Iqbal had gone missing from Kahuta and Imran Iqbal was a Shi'ite. They had probably searched his flat by now and discovered that his neighbours had not seen him around for a few days.

The Lebanese knew that as foreigners they were conspicuous. Their Mediterranean features might arouse suspicion although there was nothing to link them directly with the incident at Chaklala. Nevertheless, they could not afford to be captured.

Rashid fingered the Beretta nervously beneath his shroud. He had made a stupid error in visiting the shrine so soon and now he was afraid that he would pay the ultimate price for it. He was prepared to shoot himself or Fuad should there be any risk of capture. They had discussed this option many times and death held no fear for them. But Rashid Sedawi, on God's mission, was convinced that the martyr Hussein himself was his guardian.

Fuad was perspiring profusely as they ran deeper into the woods. "I cannot go on, my brother," he gasped. "I need to rest." The shrieking of whistles and the barking of dogs told both men that it would not be long before the police were upon them.

"We can rest only for a moment Fuad, my brother," Rashid

said kindly, realising that the fat man was in no fit state to continue. The straining of his breathing seemed to dwarf the sounds made by their pursuers.

They had paused for only a few seconds when a shot rang out.

Rashid threw himself to the ground and peered through the undergrowth in the direction from which it came. "Come, Fuad, we must flee," he urged and turned his head towards his companion.

A red stain had begun spreading on Fuad's shroud. The fat man, his eyes wild with surprise, groaned and sank to his knees before collapsing full length.

Rashid cradled his obese lover's head and looked sadly into the misting orbs. The fat man's mouth quivered but no words came. The eyes, however, delivered a message that was as clear as the waters of paradise.

The small man, his eyes glistening, gently propped against a rock the only man outside his family who had ever meant anything to him. He carefully placed the barrel of the Beretta into his lover's mouth. Fuad Kerekeh's eyes reflected both understanding and love as his brains were blown away.

Rashid rose from the bloody corpse and then stiffened as the symphony produced by the dogs and whistles seemed to reach a crescendo. He fired three more shots into the remains of Fuad's head. It was necessary to obliterate any facet which might lead to identification.

Realising that his shroud stood out like a beacon to his pursuers, Rashid ripped the garment away, remaining only in underpants. Gritting his teeth, he fled deeper into the wood.

Before long it was clear that there was very little hope of avoiding capture. The police and their dogs were gaining on him. He was just resigning himself to having to share Fuad's fate when he noticed a lone policeman cutting his way through the undergrowth. Rashid crouched, every fibre of his body taut as a violin string. He knew he must kill or be killed.

The policeman, a small man with a thin moustache, turned first this way and then that, muttering something in Punjabi. The machete swished through the air, slicing through branches with unequivocal finality. The man was only two metres from Rashid when he stopped suddenly. Dropping his machete, he wrestled with a prickly fern which had hooked itself onto his khaki shorts.

The Shi'ite saw his chance. Leaping from behind the tree he brought the full force of the Beretta down on the man's skull.

The policeman slumped to the ground dazed. Rashid pounced on his wounded prey. Lying on his back, he clamped the Pakistani's head with his powerful arms and heaved it into the pit of his stomach. He then wrapped his legs around the man's torso and rolled gently to his right. The policeman's body was still twisting in that direction when Rashid suddenly jerked the man's head the other way with vicious force. There was a loud crack and he felt the full weight of his victim's body as it went limp. The Shi'ite struggled out from beneath the corpse and then quickly relieved it of its uniform. Fearing that other policemen would recognise their dead colleague, he hacked at the lolling head with the man's own machete until the features were unrecognisable.

Rashid hastily donned the man's khaki shirt and shorts and made himself clearly visible to his pursuers. Circling to his right, he too appeared to be determined to catch the fugitives. But as the ring tightened, Rashid Sedawi moved gradually outwards until the frantic whistling and the frenzied barking became increasingly less threatening.

CHAPTER EIGHT

Fatima Fadas hated wearing the shapeless chador. It was to her a symbol of the religious fanaticism which had caused her so much hurt personally and was now threatening to hurtle the whole world into a maelstrom.

Her own people's preoccupation with fundamentalist principles had become more intense since the Iranian revolution and outright confrontation was inevitable.

Fatima inspected the garment to make sure it was spotless. She had to appear as a dutiful daughter of Islam whenever her uncle bade her attend his home. He was, after all, officially her benefactor although he did not know he was not the only one. Her uncle seemed to her a strange man in whom good and evil were locked in earnest combat. Many men in his position would have remarried after the death of a wife. However, unlike many of his contemporaries, the mullah had been monogamous and had refused to countenance a new partner following his wife's fatal stroke five years earlier.

Ironically, the tragedy had brought Mehdi Laham closer to her mother, although brother and sister met only rarely and any intelligent conversation was impossible.

As if by telepathy, Fatima's thoughts were interrupted by a gurgling sound downstairs. She slipped into her clothes quickly, adjusting the headcovering so that no hair showed, and descended the stairs.

Fatima prepared some egg salad and began slowly and carefully feeding her mother, whose glazed eyes registered the confusion so symptomatic of her illness. How childlike she was, thought Fatima, with a mixture of love, tenderness and frustration. Ever since the doctors had said her mother was suffering from a progressive brain disorder, her loyalty had been stretched to breaking point. Leila Fadas had been ostracized by her brother as a cretin. He provided a meagre allowance which barely allowed Fatima to care for her.

Leila Fadas had reared her only child alone since her husband had died from a stray bullet during the Civil War. Now it was Fatima's turn to reciprocate the love and selflessness which had been shown her. But leading a double life was causing her great strain, not least because of the ambivalent attitude adopted by her uncle. On the one hand he expected her to serve as his chattel whenever he desired while, on the other, he could ignore her for months on end. Mehdi Laham's disposition granted her freedom to practise duplicity but she knew that should he ever discover the deception, he would not hesitate to order her death.

A knock at the front door jolted her from her morbidity. It was probably the nurse. "Umma," she said kissing her mother softly on the forehead, "Fardos has arrived. She will look after you until I return from uncle Mehdi's."

The empty eyes of Leila Fadas watched her daughter leave. If she had been able to organise her thoughts, let alone express them, she would have praised Allah for blessing her with such a daughter.

Fatima Fadas took a taxi through the teeming streets of South Beirut to her uncle's home two kilometres distant. She had made the journey on countless occasions, each time with trepidation. She was not a natural spy and, however much she hated her uncle, her own duplicity frightened her. She knew that this time, too, she would be required to wait upon Mehdi Laham's guests and to maintain a strictly low profile.

Upon arriving at the apartment, she knocked three times. She could see movement beyond the peephole and knew she was being scrutinized. A moment later the bolt was drawn and the door opened. Fatima Fadas was not prepared for what met her eyes. Rashid Sedawi crooked his head to one side and smiled his enigmatic smile.

"Ahalan wa'sahalan, Fatima. Tfadali, please come in."

The palpitations of her heart felt like an express train. She hoped her face did not betray her emotion. She first lowered her eyes in deference and then raised them again, demurely, saying nothing.

She followed Sedawi into the salon where her uncle, alone, nodded a silent welcome. She knew without asking what needed to be done and entered the kitchen to make coffee, but not before noticing the map laid out upon the dining table. Fatima Fadas strained every fibre to catch the conversation of the two men. She heard Sedawi's voice first.

"....due to arrive at Akaba at the end of this month...will go north...ask local bedouin tribes...around here is the best place."

There was a pause before her uncle's gruff voice could be heard.

"You have done well, my brother...it is an excellent plan, but will you need more men?"

Then came Sedawi's reply. "I shall require four men initially...purchase block and tackle in Amman...other equipment."

She heard her uncle's voice again, only this time directed at her. "Fatima," he called sternly, "where is the coffee?"

"I am coming, uncle. Just a moment, please." She quickly poured the beverage and carried it into the salon on a copper tray. Alongside the small ceramic cups were assorted sweetmeats, her uncle's favourites.

"Fatima," the old man said, "you should prepare coffee for two more guests. They should be arriving at any moment."

No sooner had Mehdi Laham finished speaking than there were three sharp raps on the front door. She noted how the two men hurriedly folded away the map before motioning her to open the door. The look in their eyes was familiar to her. Conspiracy.

Fatima Fadas did not recognise either of the two who entered, although it was obvious by their manner that they were of some standing in the Cell. She set before them their coffee as her uncle began introducing them to Rashid Sedawi.

"Ya Rashid, I have hand-picked these men myself since the martyrdom of Ali Majid, Fuad and Hassan. They will do as you command at all times. They know nothing about our final goal and will not ask. They, too, are prepared for martyrdom."

She watched Sedawi kiss each man on both cheeks before it was made clear to her that her place was in the kitchen. But, this time, Fatima Fadas did not have to strain her ears. The talk was loud and clear.

"You will be chosen to accompany me on a journey of destiny in which the honour of Islam is at stake," Sedawi enthused.

The room was soon heavy with cigarette smoke and the sickly sweet fumes from her uncle's nargillah. The talk was of little consequence, concentrating generally on the political situation in the Middle East and how the Great Satan, America, was forever protecting its lackies, Israel, Saudia Arabia and the Gulf States.

The meeting was enlivened only by the arrival of a fifth man, small, sallow and obviously not Arab. She heard Rashid Sedawi introduce the man as Imran Iqbal, adding that he was a Shi'ite from Pakistan who had been of great service to their cause. The new man was mostly silent and obviously could not understand colloquial Arabic. From time to time she heard Sedawi translate for him into a foreign language which she did not understand but knew to be English. But what Fatima Fadas could not know was that the guests would achieve martyrdom in less than an heroic fashion and that the map references pointed out by Sedawi to her uncle earlier had been deliberately misleading. Only one man would know the true site of Armageddon.

Abu Mussa was tending his favourite house plants when his servant, Georges, announced the arrival of the only woman he had ever loved.

"Fatima, my darling," he said, pulling her towards him, "I have missed you so much. If only I could see you more often."

She hugged the big man tenderly. She always felt so safe in his presence. "You know that is impossible, my dearest."

The Maronite sighed. It was miserable for both of them that she should have to lead this double life. He longed to spend the whole night with her.

The Christian led her to the Queen Anne dining table. It was lavishly set for two. The solid gold cutlery, which he used only when they dined together, glinted as the sun's rays sliced through the verdant foliage of the house plants on the veranda. He could detect a latent excitement in her which he knew meant she had important news for him.

But it was only after they had finished the mezze that Fatima began to describe the extraordinary happenings of the previous day. She confirmed the Maronite's worst fears. His investment was not only lost but the Shi'ite madman had almost achieved his incredible aim.

"Are you sure, darling?"

"Yes. There can be no doubt. The arrival of that Pakistani confirmed it. The fanatic has the bomb."

Abu Mussa felt the palms of his hands dampen. "But there has been nothing of any significance in the news. Only an air disaster at Islamabad's main airport. I have kept the cuttings." He pressed the bell attached to the bottom of the table. Almost immediately, his trusted manservant was by his side.

"Georges, bring my scrapbook. It is the yellow one on the main shelf of the library."

"Naam, sayidi." Georges, a thin and humourless man, half bowed and took a few steps backwards before turning to leave the room. He was truly a master of Arab etiquette.

Within three minutes Abu Mussa was reading to Fatima the news items he had collected ever since she had informed him that Sedawi planned to steal the bomb from Pakistan.

"'Dateline Islamabad,'" he quoted slowly. "'A British Airways Jumbo Jet exploded in a ball of fire yesterday after colliding with a transport aircraft parked on the runway at the military airfield adjoining Islamabad International Airport. All three hundred and forty-six passengers and twelve crew members died when the plane, a Boeing 747 from London via Bahrain, apparently overshot the civilian airfield and touched down on the military runway. An airport spokesman said there was no clear reason why the plane's pilot, Captain James Tindle, landed at the military base. We can only believe the plane suffered some kind of technical fault, he said, adding that the British pilot was very experienced and had flown the route many times'."

Abu Mussa paused.

"Is there anything else," asked Fatima, her curiosity aroused. She vaguely recalled hearing about the accident on the radio at the time. For reasons of his own, Abu Mussa had not raised the matter then. Maybe he had not recognised its importance.

"Hmmm, let me see. Yes, it goes on to say that pieces of burning debris flew through the air and set fire to fuel and ammunition dumps about one hundred metres from the runway. The explosions could be seen and heard thirty kilometres away."

Fatima Fadas' natural intelligence told her that this secondary item of news was the most important. "That's it, my darling," she said excitedly. "Sedawi was involved in it. Maybe he had someone hijack the plane and crash it."

"But why?" Abu Mussa was perplexed by her reasoning. "Perhaps to create a diversion while they attacked the military airbase.''

The Maronite smiled lovingly at his beautiful Shi'ite. ''You have a very vivid imagination, my dear. What has all this got to do with the nuclear facility at Kahuta which is more than fifty kilometres away?''

''I do not know. But if you say that is the only item of importance to come out of Islamabad in many months then that evil man must have had something to do with it. He has the bomb. I am sure of it.''

Abu Mussa placed her delicate hands in his and kissed them gently. ''One should always trust a woman's intuition,'' he said softly.

''What will you do about it?'' she asked, lines of concern creasing her silken brow.

Abu Mussa paused before answering slowly. ''My enemy's enemy is my friend.''

''But why them?'' she countered, knowing that they had had many arguments before about his links with the Israelis.

The Christian smiled as he wiped the corner of his mouth with a napkin. ''I am but a pretty bourgeois, my darling. It takes fanaticism to fight fanatics. And the Israelis become fanatical when their security is threatened.''

The man with the thin scar about his lip frowned in displeasure. ''Damn these Yardeni locks,'' he grumbled, ''they never seem to work.''

Yariv Cohen was so wound up with trying to open the camlock on his desk drawer that he failed to notice his head of Arab affairs enter the office. Rahamim Ben-Yaacov waited until the balding head jutting just above the desk top had resumed its vertical position.

''Oh, Rahamim,'' said Cohen, startled. ''I was just trying

to get my drawer open again. Remind me to get supplies to change all the locks in this damned place."

The wiry Yemenite was agitated. Although the news he had was urgent, he knew better than to burst into Cohen's office like an excited schoolboy.

He cleared his throat before speaking. "Yariv, I think something important may have cropped up."

The head of the Mossad motioned the Yemenite to take a seat. "Okay, let's have it."

Ben-Yaacov produced the transcript of a coded message he had received from one of his Maronite informants. "Abu Mussa has let it be known that he has some information for us."

Yariv Cohen stood up and limped towards a map of Lebanon on the wall. It was almost like a pin cushion and he was wont to fiddle with the coloured flags while thinking deeply.

"He's an expensive man, Rahamim," he said slowly, moving a red flag from Sidon to Tyre and back again. "And sometimes he's not always been worth it."

Rahamim Ben-Yaacov did not much like talking to the leader's back but they had been friends for many years and he had come to accept his idiosyncrasies. "Our contact says the information is of the utmost urgency and that it requires a meeting in person with someone of the highest standing."

Cohen moved to the window and stared at the sky. Rain clouds were gathering. The yoreh was late this year. It was already late October and the first rains of autumn had not yet fallen. "How much?" he said at length.

"He has mentioned no price."

Cohen wheeled and returned to his chair. "Now that is interesting."

"Yes," the Yemenite concurred, "it's certainly out of character."

"What do you think, Rahamim?"

"Well, Abu Mussa may always have been expensive and

sometimes his information has been overpriced. But, on the other hand, he's never lied to us. If precedent is anything to go by, then I think we should trust him.''

Yariv Cohen stroked his chin. ''You know what the phrase 'someone of the highest standing' means Rahamim, don't you?''

''Yes. He used it the last time to give us some vital information before Operation Peace for Galilee.''

As Cohen played with his lip, his excitement began to grow. ''And it was me he saw.''

Ben-Yaacov could see that his boss was exhilarated at the thought of active duty again. He knew that, like most men who had tasted action, Yariv Cohen longed to give up his desk job for just one more bout in the field. The coach was always a player at heart.

''Do you want me to arrange a meeting, boss?''

''Yes , I think I do. Make it for the end of this week, Friday. It's the Moslem sabbath and things are usually quiet in the north.''

''Same place?''

''Yes. Make it about twelve noon. We'll have lunch and it will give him enough time to get back to Beirut before dark.''

Although he had never visited Israel beyond the military compound at the Good Fence, Abu Mussa nevertheless felt that peculiar thrill known only to those who have ever set foot on enemy soil.

As he drove his Mercedes through the gates of the border outpost, he felt like a naughty boy who had trespassed into his neighbour's garden to scrump apples. The flags of Lebanon and Israel could be seen flying alongside one another all over the base. But whom did the cedar on his country's flag represent? Only the mainly Christian militia of the south as far as Lebanon's relationship with its Jewish neighbour was concerned. The flags further reminded him of his country's torment. He, too, did not particularly care for the Israelis, finding them lacking in manners and etiquette. However, he was forced to concede that their money was good.

The big Maronite grimaced as he struggled to get out of his car seat. The journey from Jounieh had been long and tiring and his muscles ached. He stretched his limbs and waited for the guard to approach him.

"Mr Abu Mussa," the soldier said in English. "The Major-general sends his compliments and asks you to join him in the hut opposite."

The Christian appeared slightly amused. Israeli manners were improving. He followed the rather earnest looking private into what could only be termed a shack.

Yariv Cohen, dressed in his military reservist's uniform, stood up to greet his guest. The room was bare save for a large table and four chairs. The table was laid for three. The Maronite was appalled at the state of the army crockery but hid his feelings as etiquette demanded.

"Ahalan wa'sahalan Abu Mussa," Yariv Cohen beamed. "Welcome again to Israel. I hope your journey was not too difficult."

The Maronite shook Cohen's outstretched hand warmly. "It is always a pleasure to meet you, General. Let us hope that one day we shall be able to meet more freely."

Cohen motioned towards the plain wooden chair. "Please, sit down. I have taken the liberty of ordering lunch. We have some splendid cooks in our army. I have to apologise for the crockery, but let me assure you that you will not be disappointed by the meal."

As Abu Mussa took his seat he could not help thinking how extraordinarily perceptive were the Israelis.

The two men were joined by a third, small and dark-skinned.

As Rahamim Ben-Yaacov was introduced to him, the Christian thought the man could pass almost for an Arab. It was only after a few moments that he recalled that Ben-Yaacov had been present for a brief period at his previous meeting with Cohen in eighty-two.

The three men ate their meal, which the Maronite thought wholesome but rather bland, and exchanged the usual pleasantries about the weather and the beauty of their respective countries.

Once the plates had been removed, Yariv Cohen produced a packet of Royal and offered one to the Christian. "It is a local brand," he said, "but it has quite a mild taste."

Abu Mussa accepted the cigarette and used a solid gold Dunhill lighter to light it. The Maronite inhaled deeply before relating what he knew would be traumatic information for the Israelis.

"Gentlemen," he began slowly, hoping that his English was not too halting, "what I have to tell you will sound so utterly fantastic as to be almost beyond the bounds of comprehension."

Abu Mussa studied the expressions of the Israelis closely as he related all that Fatima Fadas had told him. He omitted to tell them that he had known of Sedawi's plans for many months but had believed the Shi'ite was simply suffering from a wild imagination. He also kept secret details of his own meeting with Sedawi and of the loan he had made the Shi'ites. To reveal all this was unnecessary and would confuse matters. A man who played an open deck in this particular game courted defeat from the outset.

Yariv Cohen's features were expressionless. Despite feeling as if he had been struck in the stomach by a sledgehammer, the Mossad chief was experienced enough to hide his emotions. He must appear sceptical and yet at the same time play the devil's advocate.

The whirring of the air conditioning seemed to engulf him

as he paused to re-adjust his thoughts after the Christian had finished speaking.

"That is really some story," he said finally. "There appear to be no independent witnesses to these incidents, only your source."

"She is impeccable. You have my word on that."

Until that moment Abu Mussa had always referred to his informant as 'the source'. The Maronite realised he may have given away too much too soon.

The identification of the sex of the Maronite's source was not lost on Yariv Cohen. "How close is she to the Cell?"

"Very close."

"Close enough for her to recommend the induction of another member into the group?"

Abu Mussa knew the question was coming. Sedawi could be stopped only from the inside and Fatima was powerless on her own. But he also knew that for his help he could demand any sum. "Yes, she may be able to accomplish that," he replied wistfully.

Experience told Yariv Cohen what was coming next. There was always a payoff somewhere along the line. He would try to double check the Maronite's story, but at this stage he was prepared to believe this horror story. Therefore, money became no object.

"How much?" he asked. An age-old game was about to be played out. The Maronite might deny he was an Arab, but he was a son of their culture and followed their rules in the sport of barter.

Abu Mussa opened his arms expansively. "The information I have given you, sayidi, can have no price."

Cohen continued the game. "But you must have incurred expenses in this matter," he said diplomatically.

"It is true, I have already incurred much expense and taken many risks," the Christian replied.

Cohen smiled. "And of course there are the risks to come."

Obviously enjoying the game, Abu Mussa sighed and threw up his arms. "Everything is so expensive these days," he said. "To cover every eventuality I would need, say, at least three million dollars."

Cohen was astounded by the demand but did not show it. His only possible ploy was to continue the game. The Maronite held all the cards.

"I think that figure is somewhat high. It is possibly three hundred times the highest amount that we have ever paid out," he said.

"Correct me if I am wrong, my friend," Abu Mussa rejoined confidently, "but you have never been subject to a threat as horrendous as this. It is, as the British would say, not cricket."

As head of his country's secret service, Cohen knew every detail of the covert operations necessary to have ensured the success of actions such as the stealing of the Cherbourg gunboats, Entebbe and the raid on Iraq's nuclear reactor. These were incidents which became media events, but there were also countless other actions which went unreported, especially the gathering of plans and parts necessary to construct atomic weapons at Israel's own nuclear plant at Dimona.

Cohen rubbed his chin and complained again that he believed the Israeli government would not sanction such a sum.

"Then I suggest that you come up with a figure which you believe they will countenance," the Christian replied. He had already made one-and-a-half million his bottom line. He would recoup his losses to Sedawi and make a handsome profit.

Cohen, too, had calculated that the Maronite would probably accept half his original demand. It was usually so in the Levant. "I think we may be able to stretch to one million," he said tentatively.

Abu Mussa looked towards the packet of Royal. "May I?"

How he enjoyed bartering. It was in his very soul. He lit the cigarette with great deliberation, aiming to give the impression that he was thinking deeply about the offer.

"I am afraid that will not be enough to cover my expenses, sayidi," he said apologetically. According to the rules of barter, he had made his original demand and he would not mention another figure during the transaction. This would be the responsibility of the other party.

The Israeli played by the rules which had been set him. He had no other choice. "I believe I may persuade them to settle for one-and-a-half."

"Is that your final offer?"

The Maronite had narrowed his eyes and for a fleeting moment Cohen thought the rules had been changed. Nevertheless, he decided to stand firm. "It is," he said in a tone of finality.

The big man drew deeply on his cigarette and smiled. "Then I accept, my friend," he said almost demurely and offered his hand.

With the matter of money dispensed with, the three men got down to the finer details of trying to accomplish what was at best a long shot at overcoming the greatest threat to the survival of them all.

Rahamim Ben-Yaacov produced a recent colour photograph of David Katri in which the Syrian Jew, his pate shaven and wearing a white kerchief around his head, looked more Shi'ite than Shi'ite. The Arabic words daubed in red on the kerchief read: 'Avenge Hussein'.

"A man named Anwar Hindawi will contact you," he told the Christian. "Here is a photograph so that you will recognise him. All that you need know is that you can trust him implicitly, just as he is trusting you with his life."

Abu Mussa looked at the photograph. The man was extremely handsome with a slight hook to his nose which made him all the more impressive.

"I accept that Anwar Hindawi is not his real name. But I will ask no questions."

"But what about your source?" Cohen asked, aware that not everyone's silence or co-operation could be bought with money.

"We are as one, sayidi," the Maronite replied.

At that moment Cohen realised that he was dealing with a man and his mistress and that he had no choice but to trust them both.

"So be it," said Abu Mussa rising, a signal that for him the meeting had come to an end.

Yariv Cohen accompanied the Maronite to his blue Mercedes and shook his hand.

The Christian climbed into his seat. "Do not delay, my friend," he said, looking up at the Israeli. "I fear we are acting too late already and I have a sense of failure."

"If we fail, I am afraid I cannot guarantee your money," the Israeli rejoined quietly, his eyebrow raised in mock concern.

Abu Mussa switched on his engine and smiled. "If you fail, sayidi, neither you nor I is likely to live to care about it."

Yariv Cohen watched the car head through the gates and disappear down the hill northwards. He turned as Ben-Yaacov joined him.

"Those were the most extraordinary things I have ever heard," said the Yemenite.

"Extraordinary or not, Rahamim, we now have an opportunity to infiltrate this terror group. At best they were responsible for the El Al air crash and at worst they are planning the greatest crime in history."

"I shall brief David right away."

"Yes, if the bomb really has been stolen, we must find out where they intend to plant it, if it hasn't been done already. The deserts of Arabia are not exactly the size of my back garden."

"Do you intend to inform the Prime Minister?"

"Not yet. I need some sort of confirmation from my own sources first. Tell Reuven Weiss to contact our agent in Vienna. See if our man can find out anything from his contact at the International Atomic Energy Authority. Maybe they know something and are covering it up."

The Ashkenazi Jew glared with fierce determination at the rolling hills of the troubled land which threatened the peace of the world. He turned to Ben-Yaacov and shook his head abjectly.

"You know what the supreme irony is about this whole thing, Rahamim. It is that I proposed that we bomb Kahuta last year, but the Prime Minister vetoed the idea because he believed it would antagonize world opinion. You didn't know that, did you?"

The Oriental Jew was silent, but his eyes reflected the regret he knew his master was suffering at that moment.

CHAPTER NINE

As his grey Range Rover entered Mafraq, the driver pulled up alongside a roadside coffee house. The journey northwards from Amman had taken almost an hour but he had not been in any particular hurry. He did not intend to be halted for speeding and thus had decided to drive the vehicle himself.

"Yallah, my brothers," said Rashid Sedawi, "let us get some refreshment in this Godforsaken place. Remember, no questions and do not fraternize with the locals."

The three passengers alighted from the vehicle and stretched their legs. Two of them, Ahmed Shukri and Fahd Ibrahim, were happy to remain oblivious of why they were there. The third, a foreigner, knew all there was to know and deemed it a great honour that he had been of such inestimable service to his leader.

Rashid Sedawi, feeling the need to be alone, crossed the road and sat under a palm. He watched his men drinking their coffee. Everything so far had gone exactly to plan. The chest freezer, suitably crated, had arrived at Akaba without mishap. A bribe in the right quarter had seen it released from customs with the minimum of fuss. A dockworker had even been kind enough to help him load the crate into the back of his vehicle, the sum needed to elicit this aid being of paltry proportion. How strange, he thought, that everyone had his price. That which a rich man regarded as nuisance money could prevent another man's family from starving for a month. Each had his respective place in the order of things and it was the will of Allah that this be so.

The man with the golden tooth had met his companions the previous evening at their hotel in Amman. Imran Iqbal, so vital

158

to the success of the project, had been quick to pick up Arabic and had deserved to be given responsibility for the group. Rashid withdrew a map from his jacket pocket. He calculated that it might take three to four hours of driving before he was likely to reach his destination somewhere in that part of the Syrian desert which encroached into Jordan. He knew he must drive far enough to get away from the wilderness of black basalt that stretched from the Jebel Druze in Syria through eastern Jordan and around Mafraq. He was looking for a place where only a four-wheel drive vehicle could go, and that at great difficulty. The site, wherever it was, would have to be inaccessible to all but the hardiest of nomads.

As Sheikh Ali El Haraj emerged from his black tent into the chill dawn air, the night began to lighten almost imperceptibly in the east. It was the moment when, as the Bedu say, 'a white thread can be distinguished from a black one'. The dark blue of the sky was gradually being replaced by a pinkish tint. Sheikh Ali stretched his limbs and cleared his nose and throat. Within less than a minute he was joined by his brother Majid and their two sons.

The men knelt in the sand to pray together, the sound of their devotion drowned by the bleating of the sheep and goats and the crowing of the cocks.

The women had kindled a brushwood fire, the column of smoke rising through an awning in the tent, a refuge from the utter desolation around them. And thus another day of harsh extremes began for the family of Ali El Haraj, much like the day before it. Soon the sun would be high enough to first warm their bones and then roast them. The colours of the desert, at first rich and vibrant in their hues of red and orange-yellow, would soon be burnished in a haze of pure white light.

Just as the giant orb reached its zenith, the excited voice of his wife caused Ali El Haraj to leave the refuge of his tent.

"What is wrong, woman? Mah Leesh?" he called out irritably as he lifted the flap.

"Shuf hunak!" she exclaimed pointing to a dust cloud in the distance. "Sayyara, sayyara!"

The sheikh peered towards the horizon. He had seen automobiles many times on their visits to the towns and villages but before this moment he had never seen one on his own territory. He stood dumbstruck as he watched the vehicle make painfully slow headway along the rocky surface of the wadi. It was fully ten minutes before the Range Rover finally pulled to a halt outside the black tent. The driver left his seat and approached the sheikh. He was smiling, a golden front tooth glinting in the midday sun.

"Salaam Aleikum," the stranger said, bowing deferentially. "A blessing on all your sons."

"Aleikum as Salaam, and may Allah the compassionate bless you," Sheikh Ali replied, his suspicions aroused yet ready to offer the traditional bedouin hospitality to surprise guests.

"My name is Saleh Moheiddin," said the stranger, "and my colleagues and I are carrying out a water resources survey for the National Geological Institute."

"Please," the sheikh interrupted, "you must first eat with us and then we can discuss your business." He did not know what the stranger was talking about but at least he was not of his enemies, the Beni Sadr.

As Rashid Sedawi and his men entered the tent they could see it was divided into three sections. Folded quilts and rugs were piled up against one of the woven wall partitions. Leather bags, probably full of water, yoghurt and coffee beans, were stacked on the other side.

Their host led them into the section for the men and their guests. At its entrance stood a coffee hearth which had been scooped in the sand. Various saucepans and roasting pots were hanging by the hearth. Spread on the ground were brightly coloured rugs and cushions. There were also a number of camel saddles against which they could recline.

Sheikh Ali motioned his guests to be seated and called to his wife. "Prepare food for our honoured guests and tell Majid and our sons to join us immediately."

Rashid heard shuffling behind the partition and within a few minutes they were being served sweet tea by a woman he presumed to be the sheikh's wife. Her face was covered by a mask of soft black material, her eyes the only visible part of her anatomy.

Sheikh Ali and his family would normally have enjoyed their main meal of the day in the evening, but the unexpected arrival of guests was reason enough to bring this forward. He ordered a sheep to be slaughtered, no small sacrifice for a man of his limited means.

The guests blessed their host and his sons and the sheikh reciprocated. They enthused about the wisdom of Allah and recited passages from the Koran. Host and guests may have spoken with different accents but their common bond was the Koran and the language of Arabic, its verbosity given full vent as they drank their after-meal coffee spiced with cardamom.

After the sheikh saw that his guests were sated, he decided the time was right to question them on their visit to his land. "Pray, my brothers, please tell me of what assistance I can be in the continuation of your journey," he said, adjusting the black cord on his red and white keffiyeh.

The man who was obviously the leader was the first to speak.

"We would much appreciate your assistance, ya Sheikh Ali, to help us in our work in checking water sources and dry areas in the desert," Rashid said. "With modern tools it is possible to find water where you would believe there was none."

"Ah, the wonders of the modern world," the sheikh replied,

shrugging his shoulders and opening his palms. "We still follow the ways of our forefathers. For us it is enough that wherever we are there is at least a little water."

"Do you have enough here in this wadi?" Sedawi asked, anxious to move on to the topic of arid areas.

"Naam. Allah be praised, we do."

"I noticed some high ridges towards the east," Rashid said, a note of caution in his voice. "What is beyond those ridges?"

The sheikh spat on the ground. "Beyond the ridges are the wells of the Beni Sadr. But they have been cursed by their mother's milk."

"In what way?" asked Rashid, his curiosity aroused by the man's contempt for his neighbours.

"Their wells are dry and have been for four seasons. They have been forced sometimes to raid us or the Dahm towards the east. May God blacken their faces."

"So beyond the ridges the wells are dry," Sedawi repeated.

"Yes," said the sheikh, "and we pray to Allah that the Beni Sadr will shrivel to dust before another season is gone."

"But what if they were to find water again on their land? Would it not mean that they would have no reason to raid the other tribes. Perhaps there could be a sulha."

Sheikh Ali scratched his hooked nose. "Insh'a'Allah. There has been enough bloodshed."

Rashid Sedawi finished sipping his coffee. As his host offered him more he held out the egg-shaped china cup in his right hand and shook it between thumb and forefinger thus indicating that he was sated.

The four guests thanked their host effusively, their leader saying that they would return later to wish him a final farewell, although it was regretted that they would not have time to experience once again the splendid bedouin hospitality.

Rashid Sedawi said nothing as he drove across the grey and beige stone plain to reach the forbidding ridges in the distance.

The Range Rover groaned as its four-wheeled drive took up the strain and the vehicle rose gradually up and over the escarpment. The crate in the rear shifted ominously but he knew the bomb was relatively safe and that it could be detonated only by a remote controlled signal.

Once over the ridge there was more rocky plain to negotiate. He drove a further ten kilometres, a journey which took more than half an hour. Every rock sent shudders through his spine. Suddenly, almost without warning, the terrain changed dramatically. Instead of hard stone there was soft sand. The travellers could see rolling dunes in the distance. Rashid Sedawi knew instinctively that they had reached the end of their journey. Four-wheel drive or no, he did not want to take a chance on the Range Rover becoming bogged down. He brought the vehicle to a halt by the first dune. As the motor died they heard a strange singing sound, almost deafening in the great emptiness.

"Allah be praised," croaked Imran Iqbal, "what is that?"

Rashid Sedawi knew the Pakistani had never experienced a real desert before. He led him to the edge of the dune. "There, my friend," he said pointing, "you see the grains slipping down the dune? That is what is causing the sounds. The bedouin believe the noise of the singing sands is the work of spirits called jinns. They are a very superstitious people."

Both men stood in awe of God's power over all things, their meditation disturbed suddenly by Ahmed's voice calling them urgently from the far side of the dune.

"Ya Rashid, come quickly!"

The three men circled the dune to see Ahmed standing proudly by the coping of a well.

"Allahu Akhbar!" Sedawi exclaimed. Here was the very landmark he needed. He prayed the well was dry.

"Fahd, bring the car and back it up to the edge of the well," he ordered. "Quickly!"

Rashid picked up a large stone chip from the coping and dropped it over the edge of the well. There was a pause of just over a second before he heard a dull thud. It was then that he noticed the hand and footholds in the inner wall. He hoisted himself over the coping and descended. It was as he had expected. The bottom of the well was bone dry.

By the time Rashid Sedawi had reached the top again, the Range Rover was already standing with its rear door open and facing him. "Yallah, Fahd, Ahmed, take out the pulleys!" he ordered. "Allah be praised, the well is dry."

The two men immediately began unloading the equipment needed to lower the contents of the crate into the well. Meanwhile, Rashid Sedawi took Imran Iqbal to one side. "Imran, my friend," he said quietly, although the excitement within him was growing rapidly, "are you sure you have fixed the detonators accurately and that they will work on a signal from up to two hundred metres away?"

The Pakistani flinched momentarily, unhappy that the man he worshipped should doubt his ability. "I am sure, my brother," he said firmly.

Rashid smiled. "Without you, my brother, we could not have succeeded. The Avengers of Hussein are in your debt."

"It is an honour for me to be counted as your friend, ya Rashid," the Pakistani replied, the hurt dissipated by the warmth of Sedawi's praise. "You are the leader who will rekindle the glory of Islam."

The mutual back-slapping over, the two men returned to the well in time to help Fahd and Ahmed lower the bomb into the well, the pulleys shrieking as if in protest at the evil of the load they were hauling.

Once the bomb was safely installed, Rashid removed four shovels from the Range Rover. "We must dig and pour enough sand into the well to cover it," he ordered, handing each man a tool.

The work took only little more than fifteen minutes but they were bathed in sweat by the time Rashid Sedawi called a halt. He then withdrew a can and brush from the vehicle and began painting the top of the well a luminescent green. The paint was of a special kind which was almost impossible to remove without special chemicals.

The man with the golden tooth saw Fahd and Ahmed looking at him quizzically, but they said nothing.

"Come, our task is over," he said finally. "We must pay another visit to our friend the sheikh." He climbed into the driving seat and marked something on a map before switching on the engine. Almost imperceptibly, a wind was getting up. Within an hour their tracks would be covered by the shifting sands.

None of the men spoke as the Range Rover made its way back towards the home of Sheikh Ali El Haraj. The wind was growing stronger and by the time they reached their destination the black tents were hardly visible in the swirling eddies of sand.

Rashid knew that the sheikh and his family were crouched within the safety of their home. He turned to Fahd and Ahmed. "You know what you must do," he said without emotion. "Use the Kalashnikovs but finish off each one with your pistols."

Rashid could see the consternation in Imran Iqbal's eyes. The Pakistani had no qualms about killing millions of people from a distance, but obviously had no stomach for the more real experience of slaughtering men, women and children with whom he had not long dined.

"Imran," he said as the rattle of machine guns punctured the incessant whistle of the swirling wind, "the life of no human being is worth more than our cause."

The man with the golden tooth chuckled maliciously. "Anyway, the Beni Sadr did it, did they not. God blacken their faces."

It was more than an hour later that the Range Rover finally came to a halt. Progress through the wadi had been painfully slow, made worse by the driving sand which seemed to slip through every nook and cranny in the vehicle. All the travellers were covered in a patina of white dust.

"We will stop here to rest," Rashid ordered. "There should be some cover to our right. I will brew some coffee."

The men covered their faces as each grain of sand struck home with the ferocity of a bullet. In twenty strides they had reached the lee of an overhanging cliff.

Within a few minutes each felt the reviving warmth of the coffee as it salved their dry palates. Five minutes later, and with the howling of the wind reaching a crescendo, three of the party slipped into a peaceful drug induced slumber. The fourth, shielding his face from the swirling sand, brought one of the Kalashnikovs from the rear of the Range Rover. Unemotionally, he fired several bursts into the faces of his sleeping companions and then crouched beside them to wait for the wind to abate.

Less than a few hours' drive from where Rashid Sedawi sat contemplating the success of his mission, the man whose task it was to bring about his downfall was awaiting an audience with one of Lebanon's wealthiest and most powerful men.

As David Katri sat waiting in the entrance hall of Abu Mussa's splendid palace high on Mount Lebanon, he mulled over the events that had brought him there, especially his final briefing with Cohen and Ben-Yaacov. He had recited his cover story perfectly, although they had pointed out that the speed of events often affected the best laid plans and that the speed of his wits might prove to be his strongest asset.

"Your success is more important to the State of Israel than anything in prior history," Cohen had said gravely. For so long David's task had been to infiltrate a terror group that blew up airliners. Now this same group apparently aimed to wipe out a whole people. His people. It was grotesque and terrifying. "Just remember, David," his boss had added, "there are no good people in Lebanon. Only bad. So trust no-one."

"Not even God?"

"Especially not God. He gave up on that mother of a country years ago."

David smiled as he recalled Cohen's words of admonition. But this soon turned to a frown as he remembered the Mossad chief's final missive. He knew how difficult it was for any Israeli to utter those words. It was against every precept of the security services and the armed forces.

"There is just one other thing, David," Yariv Cohen had said. "It is possible that this terror group may test you by sending you on a raid against our troops in southern Lebanon, or by giving you another terrorist task to perform. It is vital that you comply with them. The lives of even a hundred Israelis are not worth the millions who will probably die painfully and slowly should you fail."

David shuddered at the thought of what he might be asked to do. Visions of planes blowing up, ships sinking and whole army units being wiped out flashed through his mind. He forced himself to push them away and recall instead his arrival in Lebanon. Childhood memories had flooded him as the Israeli navy patrol boat rendezvoused with the Maronite fishing vessel off the port of Jounieh. He was returning to a world from which he came, a world in which to be Jewish brought with it the threat of kidnap and death from the very fanatics he was attempting to join. He thought of the rabbi and other Jewish leaders who had recently fallen victim to the burgeoning tide of Islamic fundamentalism simply because they were Jews.

Katri also thought of his family. The fact that he was less than two hours' drive away from them gnawed at his insides. He thought of the recent photographs he had received. His sister

Rachel was more beautiful than ever and the proud mother of three children. His brother Naftali, too, had married and the Syrian authorities had relaxed their grip enough to allow him to run a small leather business without too much bureaucratic hindrance. But the smiling faces in the photographs belied a hidden grief which he now shared with them. The portrait of his mother especially could not hide the sadness in her eyes. For missing from the collection sent him was a photograph of his beloved father who had worked so hard all his life for his children and had died heartbroken that he could never see his first born again. It had pained David greatly that he was not able to say kaddish at his father's grave.

The Israeli, enveloped in his own thoughts, was unaware of the presence of the small thin man to his left. He was startled by the sound of a throat being cleared.

"Abu Mussa will see you now, Mr Hindawi," the manservant said, his squeaky voice barely disguising the contempt that most Maronites felt for Shi'ites. Although his features were a less reliable guide to his ancestry, Katri's newly adopted name indicated the sect to which he belonged.

The painfully thin apparition beckoned his guest to follow and then ushered him into a large salon lavishly furnished in Georgian style. The walls were adorned with paintings of scriptural subjects in bright colours and precise detail.

"Pre-Raphaelite," said a voice in Arabic behind him. It had a distinctive Maronite lilt. "That one's by Dante Gabriel Rossetti."

David turned to face his host. The man was as tall as himself and possessed an aristocratic bearing. Yariv Cohen had told him the Maronite was sixty-five-years-old although, despite his heavy jowls, he looked younger. He looked exceedingly fit and healthy, as did most millionaires, yet his eyes betrayed the weariness of those who have everything and yet have nothing.

"Welcome to my humble abode," the Christian said, offering his hand and at the same time glancing towards his manservant. "That will be all, Georges."

David matched the iron of his host's grip and complied with the older man's direction to be seated on the single purple velvet armchair to his left. The Maronite sat opposite him on a two-seater setee of the same style.

Abu Mussa studied his guest. The man did not look like an oriental Jew, being tall and extremely handsome, even by Arab standards. The steely grip of his handshake showed that he was a man of strength and purpose. He would need to be.

After a further pause, Abu Mussa began to speak. "Firstly let me say, my friend, that I and another person whom you shall soon meet know that you are not who you purport to be. However, as I told our mutual friend, Monsieur Cohen, your true identity does not interest me. What interests me first and foremost is the safety of the person who is prepared to risk her life for you and your country. Please be assured that if I feel her security is being threatened in any way by your, let us say, mismanagement of the task, I shall have no hesitation in assuring her survival, even at the expense of your own."

David thought how right Yariv Cohen had been in assessing that the Maronite cherished this mistress of his above all else, even his life.

"I appreciate your candidness, sayidi," Katri said with sincerity. "I will do all in my power to safeguard this person's position while at the same time pursuing my mission, the success of which is so vital to all of us." David felt that the Maronite needed reassurance despite the fact that the fate of the mistress was already inextricably wound up with his own.

Abu Mussa smiled benignly. "Good," he said, "it is understood then. You will be my guest until we have succeeded in gaining you an audience with Mehdi Laham, the Cell's spiritual leader. My home has twenty bedrooms. Georges will take you later to yours. It is in the west wing."

"It is most kind of you, sayidi," replied David, nodding in deference.

The Maronite moved his right hand underneath the arm of the setee. David heard the sound of a bell ring twice in a room to his right. A few moments later he was aware of a woman's perfume permeating the salon.

"Come, my dear, please meet our guest," said Abu Mussa rising.

Fatima Fadas, dressed in a delicate shade of blue chiffon, moved gracefully from the doorway towards the two men.

Nothing had prepared David Katri for the effect this woman would have upon him. She was quite the most beautiful he had ever seen. The sheen of her long ebony hair, the alluring pools of hazel in the expanse of her almond shaped eyes and the delicate shade of red in her smooth olive skin combined to hold him in thrall.

"She is truly beautiful, my friend, don't you agree?"

The sound of Abu Mussa's voice made David aware that he was staring. He felt himself blushing.

"She has a beauty worthy only of a man such as yourself, Abu Mussa," he said, half rising.

The Christian, obviously pleased with the compliment, motioned him to be seated.

Fatima Fadas sat beside her master, her face betraying not the slightest emotion. Neither Abu Mussa nor David Katri were given the slightest inkling of the turmoil the presence of the Syrian Jew was causing within her.

The Maronite was the first to break what had become a pregnant silence and the words caused David to start.

"This is Fatima Fadas and you wish to be betrothed to her," the Christian said, a mischievous twinkle in his eye. He paused before adding a rider. "At least that is what her uncle will be told."

David's mind raced. What on earth was all this about? It seemed too incredible that Abu Mussa was arranging to marry him off to his mistress.

The Maronite, enjoying his guest's apparent consternation, held up his right hand. "Do not worry, my friend," he chuckled conspiratorially, "I shall explain everything very shortly."

CHAPTER TEN

The stocky, handsome man who entered a third floor apartment near the Alte Rathaus was none too happy with his lot in life. True, Vienna was a beautiful city, the least spoiled of the great old Western European capitals. But it was also the city from which sprang forth a moustacheoed little man who became the epitome of evil.

The Viennese were the product of cross-fertilization between mountain and plain, the volatile Balkans checked by the more stoic Teutons. The combination amounted to more latent antisemitism in the city than in Deutschland itself.

Despite their urge for self-mockery, the Viennese were wont to reserve the more purple of their Weinerisch dialect for outsiders. Vienna, the cradle of European culture, was not as boring to him as Stockholm, but he had felt more at ease in the Swedish capital. There were too many ghosts in Vienna. A Jew felt haunted wherever German was spoken, whatever the dialect. The only high spot in his present circumstances was Frau Inge Muller. He had tried various methods of approach towards more important female members of staff at the Vienna-based International Atomic Energy Authority, but had been unsuccessful. However, although the widow Muller may have been among the lower echelons of secretaries at number five Wagramerstrasse, there could have been no-one better in bed.

He flung his Herald Tribune onto an armchair in the lounge, threw off his clothes and entered the bathroom. Within seconds the drumming of the massage shower was reviving his spirits. Running his fingers through his sleek blond hair, he exalted in the fierce stinging of the spray.

He dried quickly and patted his body with Dunhill eau de Cologne, frowning disapprovingly at the paunch reflected in the mirror. He would have to cease conquering mountains of whipped cream at Demel's tea-room.

Still in his bathrobe, he wandered into the lounge and sat down to read the newspaper. Inge would arrive at any moment and she did not like unnecessary delays in the pursuit of sexual gratification. The only thing not conservative about Inge Muller was her lust. The death of her husband in a motor accident nine months before had apparently left a void which needed to be filled at regular intervals. He was relieved that she had never raised the notion of his joining her at her house in the suburbs. It was one thing moving in with a young widow, but quite another playing surrogate father to two small boys.

The Mossad's agent in Vienna found his new identity as Israeli businessman Ephraim Epstein less of a challenge than that of playing the Englishman Jonathan Webley in Stockholm. He was daydreaming about the Swedish capital when the doorbell rang. Three times. It had to be Inge.

Arik arose from his armchair and opened the door. It was Inge. Taller than he, the way he liked it, she smiled at him lasciviously.

"I see you are ready for me, liebling," she said, the red gloss of her lips as inviting as another, more veiled, part of her anatomy. The Weinerisch accent jarred him a little.

Without further ado, he took her hand and led her to the bedroom, the organ beneath his bathrobe already tumescent and throbbing in expectation. Inge Muller was an agent's delight. She neither sought to deepen their relationship nor did she ask too many questions. She believed he was involved simply in industrial espionage. However, if she had not asked too many questions, she had also not provided too many answers. The information she had managed to impart so far could have been matched anywhere. It was altogether scant and even recent access to slightly more confidential data had revealed little about the so-called Islamic Bomb. It was true that Tel Aviv had been less than specific in its brief, but its demands were clear. He was to file any and every sliver of information on the Pakistan connection as a matter of the utmost urgency.

True to form, the Mossad did not let its right hand know exactly what its left was doing. He was mainly on his own, unaware of the true identities of most of his fellow agents in Europe. In the past, the significance of any successes in the field often remained unclear until after the de-briefing in Tel Aviv. Even then, the full picture was usually denied him by those who guarded his country's secrets jealously. Life could be extremely lonely for a man in his position.

Meanwhile, at least he could luxuriate in the tender ministrations of his mistress. He nestled closer to her as she gently placed his stiffened sex into her ruby-rimmed mouth. Arik groaned as she began to suck, at first slowly and gently and then with increasing vigour. He felt perilously close to ejaculation when she ceased suddenly.

"Liebling," she moaned dreamily, "I have some information that may be of use to you."

The widow felt her lover quiver. "But only after we have made love, liebling," she added firmly.

Yariv Cohen waited impatiently to be received by the Prime Minister of Israel. It was late on a Friday afternoon and most Israelis had returned home from work to celebrate the Sabbath. The secular majority would probably visit or play host to friends while their older children would more often than not have a party to attend. Meanwhile, the religious minority would welcome the Sabbath Bride in the fashion of their forefathers. For them, too, Shabbat was a God-given joy. But it was a time for piety, also.

The head of the Mossad was not a religious man. He would accept the label 'agnostic' as more or less representative of his thoughts on the matter of whether or not God existed. He had seen the results of religious fanaticism cause too much pain and suffering to be persuaded that any faith had a monopoly on the Almighty.

For one thing Yariv Cohen was grateful. Israel's shaky Grand Coalition of the Likud, Labour and the religious factions had run its course. For the first time in more than a decade the Israeli electorate had shown enough maturity to settle heavily on one side of the political spectrum. The country had returned to the pre-Begin days and had voted solidly for a Socialist government. The meagre vote for the religious parties guaranteed them only two cabinet members and nothing stood between Labour and the pursuit of its policies. It made things easier for Cohen to know that the politicians and statesmen he was dealing with were likely to be still in power the following day. It had also given new impetus to the stalemated peace talks.

Cohen's musings on the political constitution of his government were suddenly interrupted by the voice of the Premier's usher, who had been instructed to leave for home once his task of introduction was complete.

"The Prime Minister will see you now, sir," the man said, the urgency in his voice and small knitted yarmulka on his head indicating his desire to be home before the first star heralded the sabbath.

Yariv Cohen rose, a sudden weariness overcoming him and making his limp even more pronounced. He followed the man into the private meeting room as he had done on many previous occasions. None, he ventured, would be as awesome in its implications as this.

"Shabbat Shalom, Yariv," the Prime Minister said, rising from behind his desk and extending his hand in greeting. Cohen shook the hand of Israel's leader and sat down in the chair opposite. As he had requested, the Minister of Defence was also present.

The two men acknowledged one another with a cursory nod. They had had their differences in the past. As a member of the previous coalition government and as head of the same ministry, the defence chief had recommended to the former prime minister not to attack Kahuta.

"Prime Minister, Minister of Security," Yariv Cohen began slowly, using the formal approach of the titles of the two men rather than their first names. He could see that this caused them some puzzlement, "what I have to relate to you now is a matter of the utmost gravity."

The looks of puzzlement became those of concern.

"We have just received a message from our agent in Vienna to the following effect." The head of Israel's Secret Service withdrew a slip of paper from his inside pocket and read aloud: "'Contact overheard highest source at IAEA say quote how long can we keep this thing under wraps? Those damn Pakistanis have a lot to answer for unquote'."

He paused before continuing.

"This, gentlemen, in itself makes little sense unless used in context with other information which I received a week ago. I hasten to add that I did not call a meeting with you then because we were not totally sure we were dealing in reliable evidence."

The Defence Minister, a man noted for his slowness of speech but quickness of mind, interjected. "And are you sure now, Yariv?"

"Yes, we are, sir."

"Go on," the Prime Minister said.

Cohen cleared his throat. The story sounded even too fantastic for him to comprehend. "You may remember that several months ago a British Airways Jumbo Jet crashed on the military runway after overshooting the main airport at Islamabad. At

176

the time it was reported that flying debris caused a series of explosions at fuel and ammunition dumps near the runway.''

Cohen paused again to give the two men time to recall the incident which had caused only minor interest in Israel.

"Sir," he said, looking directly into the grey-blue eyes of the Prime Minister, "we have reason to believe that those explosions were caused by a terrorist attack and that the plane was hijacked and sent to its destruction as a decoy for this attack."

The Defence Minister was already ahead of Yariv Cohen. He knew that any mention of Islamabad could relate only to one thing. "But Kahuta is many kilometres from Chaklala, Yariv," he said, grabbing at straws to deter what he knew was coming next.

"Sir, we have reason to believe that one of the bombs constructed at Kahuta was in the process of being transferred to a site somewhere else in the country, probably an air base close to the main border with India."

Yariv Cohen took scant comfort in the knowledge that the defence minister was clearly regretting his earlier recommendation to refrain from attacking Kahuta. The situation was now too grave for an 'I told you so'.

"Who are these terrorists?" the Prime Minister asked, the hackles on his back already beginning to rise.

"We understand they are Shi'ites based in the Bekaa and a southern suburb of Beirut. We understand they are the same group which sabotaged our El Al Jumbo, the Islamic Jihad Fundamentalist Cell."

Yariv Cohen swallowed hard before continuing. He had arrived at the moment he had dreaded ever since his meeting with Abu Mussa. Officially, he had had to wait for confirmation from another source, but privately he had believed the Maronite from the beginning.

"Mr Prime Minister," he said gravely, "it is my duty to inform you that these terrorists are about to instigate a threat of annihilation against the State of Israel. We have reason to believe that they may already have planted the bomb. Our source is impeccable and he says the terrorists planned to plant the bomb to the east of Israel, either in the Syrian desert or the An Nafud of Saudi Arabia.''

''But why there?'' the Prime Minister asked, the coolness of his voice masking a kaleidoscope of horrific images.

''Basically, the terrorists have done their homework,'' Cohen replied. ''The bomb is of the fission type and we believe it is slightly smaller than that dropped on Hiroshima. The difference is that while the explosions in Japan were air bursts, causing a maximum amount of damage to buildings and property, the terrorists intend to detonate their bomb on or just below the surface to cause the maximum amount of irradiation to the millions of tons of sand particles which will be hurled into the atmosphere.''

''But surely that would constitute a threat against Syria and Jordan, not to mention Saudi Arabia,'' the Prime Minister interjected.

''Sir, Jordan for sure will be sacrificed along with us. They plan to explode the bomb on the day of a shurqiya, when the winds blow across Israel from east to west. We call them the Winds of Kedem.''

'''And God prepared a vehement east wind...''' the Prime Minister began quoting from Jonah.

''Precisely,'' Cohen frowned.

''We all know our bible,'' the Defence Minister cut in. ''But tell us more about this wind.''

Cohen was not unduly disturbed by the minister's antipathy. He had done his homework at the meteorological institute and began his description of the wind slowly and deliberately. ''The winds of Kedem develop from anticyclones lying over old mother Russia, often as far away as Siberia. A ridge of high pressure sits in behind a cold front and the wind blows across the northern part of Israel from the east and northeast. The air is both cold and generally dry.''

"Does that mean it affects only the northern half of Israel?'' asked the Prime Minister, his concern growing with every sliver of information Cohen divulged.

"Not necessarily,'' replied Cohen, "although the topography of the north, from Lake Kinneret, the Beisan and Jezreel valleys up until Haifa Bay causes those areas to be first affected by the wind, which intensifies as it moves westwards.''

"A kind of funnel effect?''

"Yes.''

"So how would the rest of the country be affected?'' asked the Defence Minister, aware that any damage to the Haifa bay area would be bad enough. It contained the oil refineries and Israel's industrial infrastructure.

"In the past, the wind has often turned in on itself and returned later in the day to hit more southern parts of the country, including Tel Aviv.''

The Defence Minister felt the vitriol rising within him. "For God's sake man, how on earth do we know that this fantastic threat is real?''

Yariv Cohen looked directly into the minister's sceptical eyes. "Please, bear with me a while longer,'' he said.

It took the head of Israel's secret service the best part of an hour to describe his extraordinary meeting with Abu Mussa. He told them how David Katri had been chosen and trained, and how the Mossad planned to infiltrate the Islamic Jihad Fundamentalist Cell ever since the El Al disaster. He informed them of what was known of the terror group's leaders and that Israel was dealing with fanatics who held their own lives in disregard. Summing up, Yariv Cohen could not have sounded more pessimistic.

"I am afraid that at this stage, we have only begun to scratch the surface. Our man has yet to infiltrate the Cell. We do not know how many of its leaders are party to details of the bomb's location and, to be quite frank, we are looking for the proverbial needle in the haystack or, more precisely, a metre-long metal cylinder somewhere in thousands of square kilometres of desert.''

The Prime Minister ran his fingers through his greying hair. His sixty years seemed suddenly to weigh heavily upon him. As things stood, Israel's fate lay mainly in the hands of a younger man a few hundred miles to the north. Both he and that man shared a responsibility awesome in its implications. Should either fail the Jewish Nation, it would mean the end of five thousand years of heritage and achievement. The People of the Book would go the way of the Canaanites, the Moabites and the Phoenicians. Those not destroyed in the nuclear holocaust would disappear elsewhere through assimilation. What was happening had been the secret fear of every Israeli leader since the birth of the State. The possession by its enemies of a weapon powerful enough to destroy the old-young Jewish nation. Years earlier it had been Nasser and the fear of nerve gas. Then, before Gorbachev, the concern that the Soviets might act hastily in the defence of Syria. The difference now was that his adversaries were not nation-states. They could not be pressurized by the big powers to act one way or another. The difference now was that one religious fanatic and his carrier-bag bomb could hold the whole world to ransom.

The Prime Minister of Israel sighed heavily. He knew that both men were waiting for him to give the lead.

''Gentlemen,'' he said slowly, ''our prime aim must be to discover the location of this bomb. We must act before the terrorists make their demands public if, indeed, they intend doing so. I need not remind you of the danger of leaks. There will be mass panic in Israel if even a hint of this gets out. There is also absolutely no point in informing the Americans at this stage. It will only complicate matters."

The Defence Minister gave his characteristic cough, a sign that he wished to interject. "We might ask the Americans if they spotted anything untoward on their Awacs. We don't have to give them a reason," he said.

"It's a long shot that probably wouldn't be worth the risk at this stage," said Cohen, preferring to keep the Americans as far away from the Middle East as possible. "Their naivete in a situation such as this is likely to be extremely dangerous."

The Prime Minister nodded his concurrence. "I think you're right, Yariv. It's too early to call in outside help. We've still got nearly five months before the Shurqiya season." He paused before continuing. "Yariv, I want from you a list of options. I also want the fullest details of the effects on our population of the detonation of this type of bomb. Play the devil's advocate. I want a worst case scenario."

"Yes, sir."

The Prime Minister collated the notes on the desk before him, and rose. "Gentlemen, I think that will be all for the time being. I do not think any of us will be getting much sleep tonight, or for the next few months for that matter. I need not remind you not to divulge any of this to your wives, even in your sleep."

The first star of the sabbath had long since been joined by its myriad companions in the night sky by the time the three men entered their respective homes. Much had been said. But what had been left unsaid was that which was tacitly understood: that if Israel faced destruction, then its neighbours, too, would join it. Within a minute of confirmation of nuclear attack, Israeli Jericho II missiles would carry their deadly payloads to Beirut, Damascus, Baghdad and Teheran.

David Katri stared at the purple and magenta bracts of the bougainvilleas as he sat alone in the main garden of Abu Mussa's majestic palace. It had been three days since his first meeting with the Maronite and his mistress and he had spent those days alone save for the ministrations of the ubiquitous Georges. The Israeli found it impossible to erase the vision of Fatima Fadas from his mind. She had not said one word at either their first meeting or over the supper that followed, although somehow he felt sure that she was attracted to him. He was nearly twice her age, but this fact seemed of little consequence. Abu Mussa, like a prospective grandfather, had restricted the topics of conversation mainly to his business successes and the imminent onset of winter. No further mention had been made of the Christian's grand plan to infiltrate him into the Cell.

By early evening the couple had bade him farewell, promising that they would return within a few days. David took the opportunity to tour the Maronite's fortress high on Mount Lebanon. The palace was Christian architecture of impeccable masonry. The stonework was so accurate that in most places there was no need for mortar. Flat arches were stabilized with interlocking voussoirs and windows were fitted within pierced stone tracery. The Maronite's home even had its own basilica, which was roofed with heavy timber trusses in the Roman style. Its major domes were also framed in timber and mosaics covered not only the floors but also walls, vaults and facades. The pre-Raphaelite paintings may have been his host's pride but the carved friezes and painted frescos in other rooms were not shamed by comparison. Paradoxically, the gardens were long and rectangular with an Arab design. Situated in the main garden were a central pool and fountain, fed by streams which ran down the hillside. Around the garden were enclosing walls and two-storey pavilions at the north and south ends decorated in stucco. It was a pity that the aesthetics were marred by a group of radio and television antennae atop the northern pavilion.

Although the sun was nearing its zenith, the mountain air never lost its autumnal chill. David shuddered slightly as he inhaled its freshness. How tragic, he thought, that the beauty of this land could be so tainted by the intolerance of its inhabitants.

Sometimes he thought the Jews would have been better off had they taken up the idea of colonising Uganda rather than Palestine. Israel's neighbours seemed pathologically incapable of coming to terms with themselves, let alone with the People of the Book.

The sound of a car horn disturbed the stillness in the garden. It emanated from the front of the house and David knew instinctively that the Maronite had returned. He hoped fervently that Fatima Fadas was with him, at the same time feeling a twinge of conscience over his hitherto passive betrayal of Yael.

David had just reached the steps at the beginning of the main garden when he saw the imposing figure of Abu Mussa striding towards him. "Kif halak, sahbi?" the older man enthused. "How has Georges been looking after you?"

By the time David could answer, the Christian had placed an arm around his shoulder and began leading him through the basilica and into the house.

"Good news, my friend," the big man said excitedly. "The mullah Mehdi Laham has agreed to see you next week. I suggest that you return to your apartment in south Beirut in the meantime, but not before you have lunched with myself. And," he winked, "your bride to-be."

The Christian would not have chuckled had he been party to the thoughts racing through his guest's mind. The fact that he would shortly see Fatima Fadas again caused David to feel

183

unsteady.

"Are you unwell, my friend?" the Maronite asked with concern.

"It must be this mountain air, sayidi," David replied quickly. "It is truly God's elixir."

The Israeli followed his host into the dining room. The table was laid for three.

"Sit, my friend," bade Abu Mussa. "I will see how Georges is getting on with our lunch. My man possesses many talents."

David sat at the table. He could have sworn the cutlery was cast from solid gold. The wealth of his host compared with the dire poverty of most of his countrymen was almost obnoxious. After about five minutes of twiddling with a soup spoon, David was distracted by a movement to his right. Almost in one flowing movement, Fatima Fadas entered the room and sat down in the chair opposite him. The Israeli was entranced once again by her beauty. She allowed her large almond eyes to meet his only for one brief, tantalizing moment. Even after Abu Mussa had joined them, she continued to act demurely and never spoke.

"I think you will find the yoghurt soup delightful," the Maronite said as the spidery manservant placed the porcelain bowls before them. "It is Georges' speciality."

Another of Georges' specialities was the ability to maintain a poker face at all times. "Merci, patron," he said dully, once again retreating backwards from the table before sidling away towards the kitchen. The spider to his web.

The three finished their soup in silence before Abu Mussa spoke once again, this time in French.

"Le Liban, mon ami," he said directly to David, "le Liban il est formidable!" He sighed before adding, "mais deux negations ne font pas une nation."

"I am afraid I do not understand French, sayidi," David said apologetically.

"Oh, I am sorry, my friend, I always thought you people

were multilingual," the Maronite said disingenuously. "I was quoting a man called Georges Naccache who said as long ago as nineteen forty-nine that a state is not the sum of a double negative. He meant by this that Christianity and Islam had based their alliance in Lebanon on the joint rejection of both Westernization and Arabization. He asked what unity could be achieved from such a formula."

David listened intently. It was obvious Abu Mussa was speaking from the heart and it was important to understand what motivated the man besides money.

"It is easy to see what half the Lebanese do not want," the Maronite went on. "And it easy to see what the other half do not want. But what one cannot see is what the two halves actually do want. The supreme folly was elevating a compromise to the level of a state doctrine, to treating an historical accident as an element of stability, and in believing that two Noes can, in politics, produce a Yes."

"You mean the National Pact which provided that the president is always a Maronite, the prime minister a Sunni and the speaker of the assembly a Shi'a was unworkable form the start," said David, anxious to find common ground with his Catholic host.

"Good," Abu Mussa said expansively, "I see you have done your homework, my friend." He paused while the ever-faithful Georges collected the empty soup bowls. The thin man's obsequiousness annoyed David intensely.

"The fact is," Abu Mussa went on, "we regard ourselves as a separate people and we consider Lebanon to be our homeland to be defended against all intruders."

David looked keenly to see what effect this statement had on Fatima Fadas. He knew that the belief of the Maronites that the country belonged to them made them so intolerant of the ambitions of others, including Shi'ites. But if the stunning woman opposite him disagreed with her master, she did not show it.

Abu Mussa was now in full swing. While conducting business deals with outsiders and those he despised, he would always have to watch his words lest he offend them. However, in his own home and mountain village, he was a za'im, a benevolent Godfather, to all under his patronage and his word was Law. The local population relied on him to arbitrate in squabbles, to build schools and roads and to run public services.

"You know, my friend," the Maronite continued, "we have never compromised with anyone we perceive to threaten our freedom. In the past it was the Byzantines, the Mamelukes and the Turks. Now it is the Arabs. We emphasise individualism and self-suffering, rejection of Islam and the Arab world, identification with the West and insistence on the survival of Lebanon as a Christian and democratic heartland in the Middle East."

The Maronite was enraptured by his own diatribe, thought David. How sad it was that men like this had destroyed the confessional balance time and again to bring Lebanon to its knees. But he also knew that in his own home Abu Mussa was not open to obloquy.

The Christian paused to dip some pitta into a dip of babagannouj. He licked some of the grilled aubergines from his fingers before continuing his lecture.

"The cross will always be superior to the crescent," he went on. "Did you know that we are descended from the ancient Phoenicians, a proud and noble people?"

David knew better than to counter the man's fanciful explanation of his ancestry. He also knew that he must be careful never to call the man an Arab, however loosely.

As if reading his thoughts, his host began reciting the story of the Maronite priest in Beirut who delivered a sermon in which he advised his congregation to think of themselves as Arabs, for their own safety.

"One of his parishioners accosted the priest after the service and told him the story of the lunatic who thought he was a grain of wheat and therefore was afraid of the hens. He was treated by a psychiatrist and cured. That's fine, said the patient, so I am not a grain of wheat. But do the hens know that?"

With this, the Maronite burst into laughter. "You know, my friend," he chuckled, "the priest and the lunatic were both wrong. Bolt the granary door and you no longer have to worry about the hens."

David wanted to reply that after a while the wheat would spoil and decay would set in. Instead he decided to humour his host.

"I am sure the Land of the Cedars will return to its former glory under the leadership of men such as yourself, ya Abu Mussa," the Israeli said, at once hating the sycophancy in his words and tone but knowing also that Arabic lent itself to hyperbole. He was sure that the Christian was motivated more by self-interest, prestige, power and money than by any ideological goal.

"Yes, my friend, we are indeed a rose among thorns. But in the meantime I have to deal with all manner of devils—"

The Maronite was cut short by the return of his manservant. For once David was thankful for the presence of the spidery Georges.

"Ah, le tour de force. Merci, Georges," exclaimed Abu Mussa effusively. The manservant did his usual bowing and scraping and sidled away unimpressed.

"And now, sahbi, I think we shall stop our discussions for the time being and concentrate on the main course. I think it will be to your liking."

Despite the influence of the French language and culture on the Maronites, cuisine was one area that had failed to make much impact and it had remained almost exclusively Levantine. The diners were presented with a choice between shoulder of lamb with saffron and roast leg of lamb with yoghurt and lemon. As his gold-plated knife and fork sank deeply into the latter, David envisaged that it might be the last such meal he would savour for some time. His apartment was in a particularly seedy part of Beirut's Shi'ite sector and he had been advised to keep away from the bright lights of Hamra as much as possible.

The rest of their lunch was eaten in silence. Compared with his verbose behaviour earlier, Abu Mussa seemed content with the odd comment on the quality of the food. It was only after they had begun sipping piping hot Turkish coffee that he returned to the matter in hand.

"My friend," he said suddenly, "you may keep the name chosen for you. Anwar Hindawi is a fine Shi'ite name and common enough. I think, however, you should tell me your cover story."

David tensed. He was still not sure he should trust the Maronite although Yariv Cohen had assured him that he was reliable.

"I see that you are naturally being rather secretive about this," Abu Mussa went on. "However, let me assure you that it is of vital importance that wires should not become crossed."

David looked first at the Christian and then at Fatima before deciding that it made sense to reveal his cover. He told them how he had been orphaned in Kuneitra and that he had later fought in the Syrian army on the Golan Heights.

"That is good," beamed Abu Mussa. "It always helps if you are already well versed in the art of war, although I suspect it was not the Syrians for whom you fought."

The Maronite began slowly chiselling at his teeth with a toothpick. "Nevertheless," he said at length, "the fact that you are an orphan does not help matters if we have to impress Mehdi Laham of your suitability as a bridegroom for his niece. I have therefore taken the liberty of arranging for you an 'uncle', a Shi'ite spice merchant who lives not far from your apartment. His name is Selim Jaafar and he is an old acquaintance of

Laham's. He, too, originated from Syria and you will have been working for him since your arrival from Damascus where you acted as his agent. You have three days to become acquainted with your mother's long lost brother. Do not worry, he is being extremely well paid for his trouble."

Abu Mussa could see the puzzled frown on the Israeli's face. Maybe, he thought, there were some tenets of Islam the Jew had not learned. After all, he could hardly have expected to become a prospective bridegroom so soon after arriving in Beirut. "I shall explain, my friend," he said slowly. "You see, it would have been impossible for Fatima herself to have raised your name before her uncle. That would have suggested impropriety. Our friend Selim Jaafar has already had a number of meetings with Mehdi Laham. They have agreed on a match following your uncle's pledge of a bride-price. The mullah, of course, pledged the amount of Fatima's dowry although, needless to say, it was a fraction of the amount I gave Jaafar to put up."

David remained silent. It was obvious that the Maronite had thought his tactical ploy through. It remained to be seen whether the charade would be convincing enough to produce the required results.

Sensing his guest's scepticism, Abu Mussa hastened to explain, "You see, my friend, a Muslim marriage is not a sacrament but a contract. You will simply have to sign in the presence of an official authorized by religious and civil law. And that official, in this case, will be the man who gives the bride's consent. Uncle Mehdi."

"But the contract is binding," David said, aware that while all this was being explained Fatima Fadas had blinked not an eyelid.

The Maronite burst into hearty laughter. "Of course, my friend, but not consummated." He paused to enjoy the puzzlement in his guest's eyes.

"You see, it is simple. The religious wedding ceremony is booked for next June and, as far as both Laham and myself are concerned, you will not be allowed to see your new bride again until then."

Abu Mussa chuckled again, his heavy jowls dancing with amusement. "Of course," he added, "by that time I would sincerely hope that our mission would have been a success. You will be safely returned to your family and Fatima will join me here. Permanently."

David was forced to admire the Maronite's ingenuity. It was clear that this was the best way of gaining an introduction to the mullah and then it would be up to him to persuade the cleric of his passion for the Shi'ite cause.

"Oh, by the way," said Abu Mussa interrupting David's train of thought, "as you know, you were instructed by Monsieur Ben-Yaacov that all communication between you and the Mossad is to go through me. This was one of the stipulations I demanded in return for my assistance. If the worst should happen I want enough prior warning to enable us to leave the country."

The big Maronite suddenly clapped his hands three times and, as if from nowhere, a small man with a thick black moustache and beard entered the room. He wore a red check shirt and jeans and looked uncomfortably out of place in the sumptuous surroundings.

"This is Yussef," said Abu Mussa, "one of my most trusted men. He is a true Christian, although he looks, speaks and acts like a Shi'ite.

"Yussef Ibrahim here is your liaison with me," Abu Mussa went on. "He is known as a regular customer at Jaffar's spice store and so will not arouse suspicion. Do not hesitate to take advantage of his services. Study his face well and do not forget it."

David studied the features closely. The man's nostrils were

wide and his eyebrows thick. He reckoned him to be about twenty-five years of age, although the luxuriant beard made him look older. He could just about make out a mole above the hairline of his moustache.

Yussef stared sternly and David could see that he, too, was the subject of a thorough inspection. The man's piercing gaze made the Israeli feel uncomfortable. He was glad that they were supposed to be on the same side.

"Shukkran, Yussef," Abu Mussa said, his words a command. The mysterious Yussef wheeled and left the room. "He is a good man, Monsieur Hindawi, use him well."

The Maronite then produced a sheet of paper from his jacket pocket. "I have prepared a list of codewords for you to use in our communication. As you will see, each keyword relates to the business of spices. If anyone were by mischance to come into possession of one of our messages, they should not think anything amiss. Nevertheless, kindly destroy each one after you have read it."

David took the sheet. On it was a list of about thirty words, all of them connected with the spice trade. By the word 'terrorist' was 'sack', by the words 'terrorist headquarters', 'warehouse.' 'Bags of cinnamon' were 'Kalashnikovs' and other spices related to an assortment of weapons. The Israeli smiled thinly as he noted the word 'groundnuts' next to 'bomb'. The phrase 'groundnuts still in short supply' meant that he had been unable to discover the whereabouts of the weapon at any given time. He himself was 'tapioca'.

Abu Mussa's commanding voice interrupted David's study. "Come, my friend, you can peruse that more closely on the way to Beirut. Fatima must be home within the hour."

David started at the mention of her name. In all the time he had been the Maronite's guest she had been silent. It was if she was in such awe of the Christian that, like a child, she was expected to be seen and not heard. And yet David Katri felt sure that behind the eyes of this beautiful enigma lay an intelligence that matched his own.

The Israeli gave Fatima Fadas only a cursory glance as he arose from the table. He knew the Maronite was watching him closely for any sign of undue attention. It was clear that Abu Mussa was an extremely jealous man.

As the two men walked towards the blue Mercedes, David noticed that Fatima Fadas was not with them. As if reading his thoughts, the Maronite put his arm around the Israeli's shoulder. "Do not worry, my friend," he said slyly, "your bride-to-be is getting changed. The niece of a mullah cannot be seen in Shi'ite south Beirut dressed like Madame Pompadour."

A few minutes later David found himself transfixed by the transformation Fatima Fadas had undergone. In place of Parisien haute couture was the austere black garb of a daughter of Islam. Gone, too, were the other trappings of Western civilisation, lipstick and eye shadow. Despite this, it seemed to David that in her natural state she was even more beautiful, possessing an almost childlike innocence.

"She will wear the headdress of the chador as soon as we enter southern Beirut," said Abu Mussa, as if wishing to clear up any lingering doubt in his guest's mind that the metamorphosis could be so complete.

The three entered the Mercedes, the Maronite and his mistress in the front and David Katri, alone, in the rear. The Israeli was surprised by the big man's decision to drive. He was rich enough to have employed a hundred chauffeurs.

It soon became obvious that Abu Mussa derived great pleasure from hurling the tank-like Mercedes around the bleak contours of Mount Lebanon. It was as if, once behind the wheel, he could regress to his youth and display a virility that may have been lacking in his advanced years.

Whenever they came to a straight section, David could see the Maronite's eyes surveying him in the mirror. They bored through him as a skewer through kebab.

The blue Mercedes had been travelling about five minutes when it passed the first of many chapels perched precariously on almost sheer cliffs. Suddenly a white Peugeot 504 screeched out of its gates and began to follow them.

"Do not worry, my friend," the eyes said. "I own everything and everybody around here. They are my qabadayat. I like the term in English: musclemen. You do not think I would enter either western or southern Beirut alone, do you? I have too many enemies, sahbi."

Abu Mussa swung his attention back to the road as another curve loomed. He failed to notice the arm of the girl in black drop to the side of her seat.

David Katri's heart pounded as he saw her delicate and unblemished hand release a small piece of paper, neatly folded, into his footwell. He quickly covered it with his shoe and waited for the next sharp bend.

CHAPTER ELEVEN

Professor Abe Bernstein smiled as he showed his special pass to the young military policeman at the entrance to the Kirya. It was not the first time he had been called upon to visit the hub of his country's military defence. He always thought the massive complex, with its web of sensitive aerials and antennae, looked curiously out of place in what was essentially a residential area of north Tel Aviv.

"Boker tov," the scientist said, the drawl of his accent in Hebrew immediately conveying to the guard that the visitor was an immigrant from North America.

"Good morning, sir," the young conscript rejoined, delighted at the chance to practise his high school English. He broke into a popular jingle for a Japanese electronics firm which used an Albert Einstein look-alike in its press campaign.

Bernstein smiled at the soldier's chutzpah. He knew he resembled the man who portrayed Einstein in the advertisement and sometimes it proved embarrassing. Mostly though, he decided to make light of the matter.

"No, I don't think Sanyo electronics is the Einstein of Japan and I don't have any tape recorders for sale," he joked.

The guard laughed and returned the pass, unaware that the visitor was indeed a distant relative of the great man and that he was also Israel's foremost nuclear physicist.

"Have a nice day, sir," the guard called out as the man with the shock of white hair accelerated away.

Professor Abe Bernstein, formerly of Brooklyn but for the past twenty-five years a citizen of Israel and a resident of the nuclear village at Dimona, did not expect to have a good day.

194

On the seat beside him lay a box of slides, reems of computer statistics and a twenty-page summation of a particular scenario of nuclear attack against the Jewish State.

Bernstein drove to Mossad headquarters and was soon ushered into one of the smaller conference rooms. A slide projector and screen was already set up and the professor speedily prepared the groundwork for his lecture. After about five minutes, he was joined by two men, one of whom he knew well since his lecture to Mossad leaders several years earlier on Iraq's nuclear capacity.

"Good morning and welcome, Professor," Yariv Cohen said with outstretched hand. "This is my colleague Rahamim and he'll be taking a few notes. Did you bring the material?"

"Yes, it is all here."

Cohen bade the professor to be seated. He liked the old American. One thing was for sure: without him, Israel's nuclear deterrent would still have been in its formative stages.

"Abe, first of all protocol demands that I remind you that you have signed your compliance with your country's Official Secrets Act. Any leakage of the context of this meeting will subject you to prosecution."

"I understand, Yariv," the professor smiled. He knew the penalty for a loose tongue could be anything up to fifteen years.

Although high treason could be punishable by death theoretically, Cohen knew that as far as Professor Abe Bernstein was concerned indiscretion was as likely as rain in Eilat in August. Still, since Vanunu procedures had been tightened up.

"There's just one thing," the scientist added. "I'd like to conduct the lecture in English if you don't mind. There are many technicalities and they do not translate too well."

"That's fine by us," Cohen replied. "At this stage we only need a general picture in layman's terms."

That was easier said than done, thought Bernstein. Like most scientists, he was more at home with technical minutae than an overview.

"We might as well start at the beginning," he said switching on the projector and pointing to two diagrams on the screen. "There are two general methods for bringing about a nuclear explosion."

Yariv Cohen and Rahamim Ben-Yaacov peered intently at the screen. The diagrams were simple to understand. They hoped the explanation would be likewise.

"In the first method," the scientist went on, "two or more pieces of fissionable material, each less than a critical mass, are brought together very rapidly in order to form one piece that exceeds the critical mass. This may be achieved in a kind of gun-barrel device, in which explosives are used to blow one subcritical piece of fissionable material from the breech end of the gun into another subcritical piece firmly held in the muzzle end."

Yariv Cohen felt like the only racehorse left in the stalls after the rest had bolted. "Hold on, Professor," he said gently, "I'm afraid you're way ahead of us. We don't know what the critical mass means."

Bernstein blushed and pulled at his mane of white hair. "Er, let me see," he stammered. "The easiest way to describe it, I suppose, is to say that it is the point at which the whole chain reaction of the explosion can become self-sustaining."

"And what about the second method?" Ben-Yaacov asked.

"Ah," the scientist answered with relish, "that is when a subcritical quantity of an isotope of—in this case uranium—is strongly compressed by means of a spherical arrangement of specially fabricated shapes of ordinary high explosive. It's called implosion."

In his brief to the professor, Yariv Cohen had requested scenarios based on the surface detonations of bombs of varying power from ten to thirty kilotons placed at distances of one hundred, two hundred and three hundred kilometres east of Tel

Aviv and Haifa. He had also requested the scientist to imagine that an easterly wind was blowing at the time of the explosion. What he had not requested was an explanation of the methods of exploding the device.

"Abe," the head of the Mossad interrupted courteously, "does the method of exploding the bomb make any difference to the end result?"

"Why no."

"Then, if it is all right with you, perhaps we could skip this part."

If Bernstein was hurt he did not show it. He was wise enough to know that his hosts had good enough reason to have requested his help and that they were worried men. He was there to answer questions, not to ask them.

"In this slide," the professor continued, "you see the formation of the dirt cloud in a surface burst. If this takes place in a desert, then I think we can discount damage done by the ensuing fireball. It is likely to affect a few nomads, but that is all."

The scientist paused as the two intelligence men gazed at the awesome sight on the screen. "No, gentlemen," he went on, "I think the main danger will come from fall-out and, even though a bomb may be, shall we say, the same size as that which was dropped on Hiroshima, there would be a marked difference in its effects. Hiroshima was an air burst and therefore caused a vast amount of damage to buildings and property as well as killing eighty thousand people. However, injuries due to fall-out were absent."

The two Mossad men shifted uneasily in their seats as the scientist went on to explain that ground bursts sucked up huge quantities of earth and sand into the fireball; that this first vaporized, then collected fission products and cooled before forming large fall-out particles, some as big as marbles.

"Because of the relatively close proximity of our major towns and cities to ground zero and depending on the strength of the wind, some areas may be subject to this bombardment of large particles.''

The scientist paused to present the next slide. It showed a series of cigar-shaped contours, one inside the other. ''However, gentlemen,'' he continued, ''I think it more likely we may be subjected to lower doses of radiation over Tel Aviv and Haifa. Jerusalem, however would probably suffer most along with the Jordanian capital. As you can see from this diagram, the inner cigar represents the greatest concentration of radiation and the outer the least.''

Yariv Cohen was already beginning to feel queasy. ''What's the bottom line, Abe?'' he asked quietly.

''Well, our country is pretty small and most of the population is centred on the coastal plain. Although it's possible that the doses of radiation may not prove lethal immediately, there would be enough to cause long term illnesses, cancers and birth defects. Also the fall-out would affect the livestock and crops upon which we rely so heavily.''

''In other words?''

The professor looked Yariv Cohen squarely in the eyes before answering. ''In other words,'' he said slowly, ''Israel would become virtually uninhabitable.''

At that moment, the head of one of the world's finest intelligence services knew for sure that the fate of his people lay in his hands. He knew that although Israel's civil defence precautions were second to none, nothing could prevent the annihilation of the Jewish State should he fail.

''Shema Yisrael,'' croaked Cohen. The phrase calling on Israel to heed its God was used colloquially as an expression of horror. But they were also the first two words of Judaism's most revered prayer and they struck a concordant note in the hearts of his two companions.

Hear, O Israel. The Lord Our God, The Lord is One.

David Katri had read Fatima's note a thousand times. In neat Arabic was written her address and an invitation to visit her only after sunset. He knew that what he was about to do might prejudice his mission and that it was a betrayal of his love for Yael. Yet, try as he might, he could not wipe the vision of the beautiful Shi'ite from his mind, a vision made all the more powerful by her silence in the Maronite's mountain refuge. There were so many questions he needed to ask. The double life she led was at once so vitally important to his success and yet also a source of the greatest personal danger. It demanded not only great courage, but also the ability to switch from one mode of life to another with a change of dress. He, too, was performing a double act and suffered the mental strain that this placed upon the actor.

The moon was full as he approached the house where she lived. It was just as well, for most of the street lights were not working, a tribute to the run-down state of the city's services. Most of the houses did not have numbers. They looked as though they had been cobbled together from cardboard boxes, storey being heaped upon storey as families grew and expanded.

It reminded him of the Shabazi quarter of Tel Aviv where immigrants from Aden and the Yemen had made their homes.

By a method of deduction, David arrived at a part of the street that should have contained Fatima's house. Suddenly, he saw the number twenty-five in white on the outside of a two-storey building. He paused before knocking. The street was empty although he could hear the sound of a baby crying from a building some doors away.

As David lifted the wrought-iron knocker, the door opened slightly.

Sensing her presence although he could not see her, he prodded the door with his finger and entered.

"Come in and close the door," came a voice from a room to his right. It was soft and delicate like the woman herself. He smiled to himself that until now she had been only seen and not heard. He wondered whether this night he would succeed in unravelling the enigma of the Maronite's beautiful mistress. David started as he entered the room. There, sitting expressionless in a faded green dralon armchair, was a wizened old woman. Her eyes were glazed and her posture gave the impression that she was blind.

"Do not worry, my mother can neither understand nor communicate. She suffers from a progressive disease of the brain which is incurable."

David found himself staring at the source of the explanation. Fatima Fadas was dressed as he had last seen her, in a black chador. She looked so very young, although from deep within her almond eyes emanated a sense of wisdom and worldliness. She appeared to him more beautiful than ever.

"I'm sorry, Fatima," he said, lines of concern creasing his brow, "it must be very difficult for you."

Fatima Fadas did not answer but stared at her guest. How tall and handsome he was. His bearing was unlike any other man she had been allowed to meet. How ironic, she thought, that she should be attracted only to enemies of her people.

David could feel an involuntary stirring in his lions. He felt the sexual intensity of her gaze suffuse his body with yearning. Yet he knew that he must first learn more about Fatima Fadas. If he should make love to her without knowing her it would be like tasting an unlabelled bottle of wine. As if reading his thoughts, she led him towards the kitchen.

"Come," she said, "I will make tea and we shall talk."

As he sipped the hot sweet nectar, David's mind was so full of questions he did not know where to begin. Once again, it was this extraordinary woman who took the initiative.

"I know you must be wondering how, at such a young age, my life has become so entangled. How, you must ask, can a woman who has had such a strictly religious upbringing deny her faith in this way?"

Fatima Fadas poured herself some of the beverage and sat down in the chair opposite David. He could see tears welling in her eyes.

"I am a woman," she said emotionally, "but in the world of Islam I am little more than a possession to be hidden and veiled. There is no love, only 'ird, the man's honour.''

David felt the pain he knew she was suffering. It was clear that the level of her intelligence was so high that it had sought to question the very precepts her faith insisted were not open to question.

"The Koran itself is not unkind towards us," she went on, "but it is patronising. I agree with the female lawyer in Teheran who said the right only to breath is not enough today. For both of us, Islam is the Dark Ages."

David, dumbstruck, saw the anger flame in the dark pools of her eyes.

"You know," she said contemptuously, "there is a Shi'a saying that a man should have intercourse with a woman for a son, with a goat for relief and with a boy for pleasure."

"I know, Fatima," David said kindly, "I spent many months studying your religion and its ways. As is the way with most religions, the original precepts are forsworn by those who pretend to uphold them. Many of our religious leaders, too, are so hidebound by tradition that they became insensitive to the needs of their own people."

Fatima Fadas looked at David closely. She felt a sense of helplessness at being infatuated with a bitter enemy of her people.

"You know," she said wistfully, "I had almost forgotten.

Even as a little girl, after eighty-two I hated all Jews."

"If it will help, Fatima, I, too, was angry about many aspects of that war. But we are not all ogres."

She held up her hand and placed a forefinger to her lips. "Please, please," she said, "do not tell me anything about yourself. To me, you are and must remain Anwar Hindawi. If I knew too much about you, even your real name, a slip of the tongue could undo all our plans. Sedition is more grievous than killing."

David recognised the saying from the Koran. "Sura two, verse one-nine-one," he said, almost automatically.

Fatima Fadas smiled. "It is as well you know these things, Anwar, for our society is ruthless and pitiless. You must be strong for it worships strength and has no compassion for weakness."

David was amazed by her erudition. "You speak so well and so learnedly, although I am sure you have never been to university."

"Ah," and it was the first time he had heard her laugh, "but I have read many, many books and most of them my uncle would have burned if he had known."

David needed to know more about this strange man who had played such an important part in her life and was now to become part of his.

"What is he like?"

"Who, my uncle?" She paused before continuing. "He is typical of our clergy, a man whose word is law but whose compassion is limited by the edicts of the Koran. Only that which is written is permissible and he will allow only that which is permissible."

"Then he is stern and unbending?"

"Yes," she sighed, "simply a product of our society."

"How does he treat you?"

Fatima Fadas shrugged her shoulders. "He treats me as he

would any woman, as a chattel. He sends for me when he needs me. I believe I am the only female he has around him."

"Do you think he loves you?" David felt his questions might be becoming too personal but he had to learn more about the man.

Fatima stared hard and long at the cup in front of her. "I do not think he is capable of love in the Western sense. His feelings are guided by the precepts of the Koran. For instance, he provided just enough for me to care for his sister, my mother. He will do what is necessary but no more. He cares for her at a distance. He will not even allow us a telephone to maintain contact freely. The stigma of her senility must not be allowed to taint him in any way for it would reduce his standing as a cleric, even though he is obliged to protect the mustadh'afeen, the downtrodden."

"How do you think I should behave during my meeting with him?" David asked, aware that her knowledge of her uncle's character was vital to his success and that Abu Mussa's assessment was based only on his business dealings.

Fatima Fadas, her delicate brow creased in concentration, poured him some more tea. "I think you should impress him without being too eager," she said at length. "He will search for weakness. It will not be enough that we are betrothed. You must direct the conversation so that he will see military potential in you."

"Will he alone decide?"

"No, I believe his is greatly influenced by Rashid Sedawi."

The mention of Sedawi's name made David's hackles rise.

"I know little of Sedawi," she continued, as if in answer to his unspoken question, "only that he has an aura of evil and that you must beware of him. He frightens me."

The Israeli felt his heart go out towards this olive-skinned beauty who had not yet even come of age. His own courage was dwarfed by hers, She had risked her life many times in the quest for knowledge outside the confines of the Koran and its hadiths. She had mocked at those who sought to supress her individuality. She was simply extraordinary.

David was just about to speak when he heard a gurgling sound emanating from the salon.

"It is my mother," said Fatima, rising, "I will put her to bed. Stay here, I will be only a few minutes."

The interlude gave David time to gather his thoughts. It was true that he still possessed an unquenchable urge to make love to her, but his respect for Fatima Fadas had reached such magnitude that he decided he would not make a move unless she so desired. Lost in his own thoughts, he was startled when she re-entered the kitchen.

"She is at peace now," she said sadly, "at least until the dawn."

David wanted desperately to understand her relationship with Abu Mussa and her comment gave him his lead. "What will you do when you go to live with Abu Mussa?" he asked, hoping that she would not be upset by his question.

"My mother will come with me. Mehdi Laham will search high and low but he will never find us. The Maronite strongholds are impenetrable."

David decided the moment was appropriate to broach the subject of her relationship with the Christian. "Please forgive me, Fatima, but I would like to know how you met Abu Mussa and what attracted you to him?"

Fatima smiled. She had wondered when he would get around to the inevitable. She clasped her hands in front of her, the long fingernails unpainted yet sensuous nonetheless.

"I was serving coffee at a meeting between Abu Mussa and my uncle two years ago. I was fascinated by him. He was the first real dhimmi I had ever seen. My uncle cursed him loudly after he had left but I could not erase him from my mind. I knew that he was immensely wealthy and powerful and I suppose that is what attracted me to him. Also, my father was killed when I was very young and I suppose I looked upon him as a father figure, although that really only came later.''

"How did he make contact with you afterwards?''

"I don't know how he found out our address. Probably through a Shi'ite contact or somebody. Anyway, he sent me a letter asking me to meet him outside a well-known coffee house on Hamra.'' For a moment, a wondrous look came into her eyes. "Can you imagine,'' she said, "I had never even ventured into that area before. I could not sleep that night for excitement.''

Fatima poured him some more tea before continuing. "When we met, he immediately bought me some wonderful clothes, although we both knew I could never wear them at home. He wined and dined me and then took me to visit his palace. I was overcome.''

"But it was a Cinderella existence,'' said David gently.

"Yes,'' she smiled, "and it still is.''

"Are the risks worth it, Fatima?''

She sighed before answering. "Abu Mussa had taught me many things. Do you know that I have a library of French classics hidden in our cellar? Whenever I am not with him I read and read and read. Once freedom has been tasted it is impossible to give it up.''

"But why hasn't Abu Mussa taken you away until now?''

"He needed me to inform him of my uncle's plans.''

"Then, in a way, you are still a slave.'' David regretted the comment immediately. He knew it was grossly unfair of him. "I'm sorry, Fatima,'' he added before she could speak.

"Mon cher, I do it because I want to do it. And now I am the reason you are here in Lebanon and that you are sitting opposite me at this moment. It is because I want it so. I am the mistress of my own destiny.''

At that moment David Katri wanted to sweep her up in his

arms. How could he have doubted her? She may have been captive in body but her spirit was as free as the wildest sabra youth of his own country.

"Fatima," he said weakly, "I—"

"Shush, azzizi," she said placing her forefinger to his lips, "come with me."

As he followed her to her bedroom David Katri felt as if all his senses were being pounded by pneumatic drills. He forced himself to push away fleeting images of Yael and the children and replaced them with a love and tenderness born of the mutual danger that both he and Fatima faced.

He undressed her slowly and delicately and then slipped out of his own clothes. For a moment they stood naked opposite one another. In the moonlight he could see that she was in awe of the rigid fulcrum of his power. He pulled her to him and carefully lifted her towards the bed, the scent of her body's natural oils exciting him even further. Slowly he began caressing the contours of her body, reaching slowly down to the well of her desire.

"Be gentle, mon cheri," she murmured as waves of ecstasy engulfed her. "I am unbroken."

"But—"

"Shush, my darling, I shall explain later. Now love me as every woman should be loved."

For the next three days David Katri did as Fatima suggested and did not visit her after sunset. "We must not prejudice our mission, my darling," she had said. "Although they suspect nothing, it is best you do not visit me until after your meeting with my uncle."

But, try as he might, David could not erase the memory of their first night together. He had been so gentle with her and she had responded in kind. Despite the initial pain, she had taken to lovemaking without inhibition and with a fervour born of a deep desire to experience the ecstasy of womanhood. It pained him that they might enjoy one another's body and intellect only a few times over the coming months. She would then disappear into the inner reaches of Mount Lebanon, to a life of material riches but one devoid of the very sexual gratification she craved. He had found it almost impossible to believe. The Maronite, for all his wealth and power, was devoid of the very strength that made him truly a man. Whether or not his impotence stemmed from a physiological or a psychological source was immaterial. His mistress in name only was prepared to lead a life of celibacy in order to escape the strictures of her own culture.

David had tried to explain to her that she was substituting one kind of prison for another.

"Anwar, azzizi," she had replied, "for the first time in my life I can decide my own destiny. For me he is like a father and for him I am the daughter he never had. I shall always love you and cherish our time together but we both know there is no future for us. It is not a question of choosing the lesser of two evils. Just as I love you, I am genuinely fond of Abu Mussa and am prepared to marry him even though our marriage may never be consummated."

Her words rang in his ears as he walked through the crowded streets of the Shi'ite sector towards the Mosque of Hussein. Selim Jaafar had said to meet him there after noon prayers when he would introduce him to the mullah Mehdi Laham.

David entered the courtyard of the mosque and washed his hands and feet at the fountain. Along with the other worshippers, he recited the prayer for ablution. The cry of the muezzin reverberated through the crisp winter air as the Israeli placed his shoes carefully in line with the others at the entrance. The mosque was much the same as others in which he had worshipped. The dome and walls were covered in the ornate calligraphy that proclaimed the power of the Koran.

He joined the first line of supplicants facing the mihrab. In front of the semi-circular recess stood an elderly grey-haired Imam. After a few moments he held up his hands for silence and then, too, turned to face Mecca. The old man then opened his hands and touched the lobes of his ears with his thumbs. "Allahu Akhbar," he called and bowed. The congregation followed suit. The Imam then lowered his hands and folded them, the left within the right. He began reciting the Fatiha, the first chapter of the Koran.

"Praise belongs to God, Lord of the Worlds,

The compassionate, the Merciful,

King of the Day of Judgement,

'Tis thee we worship and Thee we ask for help.

Guide us on the straight path,

The path of those whom Thou has favoured,

Not the path of those who incur Thine anger nor of those who go astray."

The old man bowed again before continuing. "Say, God is One, the eternal God; begetting not and unbegotten; none is equal to Him."

The Imam waited for his congregants to finish before bowing from the hips with hands on knees. "I extol Thy perfection my Lord the Great." He then assumed an upright position with the words "Allahu Akhbar" before sinking gently to his knees. The cleric placed his hands on the ground followed by his nose and face. The congregation followed suit. Along with them, David rose to his knees and, sitting on his heels, performed a second prostration proclaiming the same words.

The Israeli followed the Imam closely until the last rak'a had been completed. Finally, the old man looked over his right shoulder and said, "Peace be on you and the mercy of God." He then looked over his left shoulder and repeated the blessing.

There was a feeling of excitement amongst the congregation and when David saw the Imam walk towards a podium to the right of the mihrab, he knew that they were about to be preached to. At the same time, he felt an uncomfortable presence behind him. It was Selim Jaafar. Alongside him was a man he had never seen but whom he knew well. He nodded to Jaafar, taking care not to intimate to Rashid Sedawi that he recognised him in any way.

The Israeli felt his hackles rise as the Imam instructed his congregation to be seated. David estimated that there were about one hundred people present and they all sat cross-legged on the floor in unison. The first words of the Imam's sermon struck fear into his very soul. He felt as if a knife was ripping through his vitals.

"Western philosophy is a web of intrigues concocted by the Jews," the cleric ranted. "Jews and their backers are opposed to the very foundations of Islam and want to establish an international Jewish government."

David had to force himself to express his concurrence with the Imam's views as the cleric continued his tirade against the Jews and their ally, the Great Satan America. He was thankful that Jaafar and Sedawi were behind him and could not see the pain and frustration in his eyes.

"The West talks empty words about human rights," the old man raged on, his wiry beard trapping globules of spittle, "but the peace they talk about is their peace, not ours. The culture is their culture, not ours. Welfare is their welfare, not ours. Security is their security, not ours. Human rights are for them, not us. They try to delude us. They try to deceive through their television, their radio and their newspapers so that they can turn the world against us as they desire."

The audience began chanting: "Allahu wahed, there is only one God, Victory to Islam, Death to Israel. Onward, onward, onward to victory; marching, marching, marching to

Jerusalem.''

The Imam wiped his brow with a white handkerchief and held up his hands for silence. He paused a few moments before uttering the words that David knew could signal the death knell for civilisation.

"Victory belongs to Allah," the old man screamed. "Our triumph is close.''

The congregation then began chanting for martyrdom.

"Is'tish'had! Is'tish'had! Is'tish'had!''

David Katri felt the last vestiges of self-control slipping away. His whole body felt as if it were being flagellated as at the festival of Ashura. He wanted to scream at them that theirs was the way of the fascists and the way of all the religious tyrants and bigots throughout history. He wanted to convince them that there was another way, that enmity between peoples was tragic, wasteful and unnecessary.

Then, as quickly as it had been whipped up, the frenzy died. The congregation began to move slowly towards the exits. Only David Katri stood as if transfixed.

"He is a great orator, don't you think?'' came a voice behind him.

David turned to be faced by Selim Jaafar and Rashid Sedawi. By the tone of the voice he knew that it was not Jaafar who had spoken.

"Er, yes, he is truly a leader of men,'' the Israeli said, uncomfortably aware of Sedawi's stare.

"This is my friend, Rashid Sedawi," said Selim. "He is a friend of Mehdi Laham.''

"It is my pleasure,'' said David, regaining his composure and stretching out his hand.

Sedawi shook his hand firmly. "I have a feeling I know you from somewhere,'' he said.

David was genuinely puzzled. "I'm afraid that cannot be so,'' he said. "I come from Damascus and have only been in Beirut some few weeks.''

"Yes, I know all about you.''

The Israeli felt the clammy hand of fear fleetingly grip his throat. The very presence of this strange man with the golden tooth was intimidating. He felt the need to change the subject. "I am looking forward to seeing Mehdi Laham.''

"You have already seen him,'' said Sedawi, his smile making David feel even more uncomfortable.

"I don't understand.''

"The Imam you were so enthusiastic about. That was he.''

For a moment David Katri felt bemused. It was as if secretly he wanted to believe that any relative of Fatima's could not be so repugnant.

The high-pitched voice of Selim Jaafar broke what had become a pregnant silence. "Come Anwar, let us go to his office so that you may meet him.''

The spice merchant led him through a small arch to the rear of the mihrab and knocked twice on a heavy oak door. A gruff voice from within bade them enter.

The mullah, his rheumy eyes aglow with suspicion, looked up from a pile of papers on the desk in front of him. One wall of the small room was lined with theological tomes while against another, almost incongruously, stood a nargillah. A wisp of smoke rose lazily towards the ceiling, indicating that it had been used recently. The mosque elders would not have been pleased. Smoking was forbidden unless, it seemed, you were the Imam.

"Tfadal,'' the old man said, "please be seated.''

Three chairs had already been arranged facing the table. David Katri sat in the middle, flanked by Jaafar to his left and Sedawi to his right. The cleric stroked his grey beard before speaking. He stared long and hard at the guest who until now had been known to him in name only.

"You know why you are here,'' he said at length. "A marriage contract has been arranged between Jaafar and myself for you to marry my niece. Is there any reason that would disqualify you from such a match?''

"No, sir," David answered firmly. "I am a true son of Hussein."

Unmoved, Mehdi Laham again stroked his long wiry beard. "What are your views on marriage?"

David hesitated as he sought for an appropriate reply. "As the Prophet said," he answered slowly, "marriage saves half of a man's faith." The Israeli thought to append the adage that bachelors were prey to Satan but decided not to. Sedawi was single and he might have taken offence.

"Do you have any friends among the infidels?" the mullah asked. The question was carefully planned to test the newcomer's faith

"Believers do not make friends with any men other than their own people," David replied, reciting the Koranic injunction. If the cleric was impressed he did not show it. The suitability of the man before him as a match for his niece was of little consequence. Selim Jaafar, however, had said the suitor was desperate to become a soldier of Islam and it was to this end he was now being tested.

"What do you think of those who oppose the leadership of the clerics?" Mehdi Laham asked, more interested in the style of the suitor's answer than its content.

David was surprised that the questioning had strayed completely away from his marital application, but he saw an opening looming that could give him the chance to convince those present of his worth as a fighter rather than as a husband. "Those who oppose the mullahs oppose Islam itself," he said with conviction, knowing that any trace of obsequiousness would not stand him in good stead. "It is only the mullahs who can bring the people into the streets and make them die for Islam, begging to have their blood shed for Islam."

"And would you be prepared to shed your blood for Islam?"

The question was uttered by the golden-tooth man to his right. David looked directly into the cruel eyes, knowing that his opportunity had arrived.

"I am prepared for martyrdom," he said slowly. "I will do anything to destroy our enemies."

"And who are our enemies?"

"The Zionists and Capitalists and all those who do not accept the true path."

"And what should we do against the Zionist Entity?"

David tried hard not to flinch at either the question or Sedawi's stale breath. He knew that when Arabs spoke to each other their faces could almost be touching. It was a trait he found both disconcerting and very difficult to perform.

"It is an abomination," he replied, "and should be wiped from the face of the earth."

Sedawi smiled cruelly and looked again towards the mullah.

"I think we have heard enough," the cleric growled. "I have signed this contract and now so shall you. I have set the wedding for the last day of the month of Sha'baan."

David rose and took the pen the mullah handed to him. He could make out the title 'marriage contract' at the top of the form but the contents were covered by another sheet of paper. He signed the appropriate place just above the mullah's signature. It seemed strange that he was not being allowed to read the contract although, strictly speaking, it was not necessary as the arrangements were between Laham and Selim Jaafar.

The mullah fixed the signature with some powder and then folded the document. He withdrew some sealing wax from a drawer and lit a taper. David watched in fascination as the cleric completed the marriage contract. He knew the wedding would never take place for by its date the first winds of Kedem would already have blown and the fate of himself and Israel decided.

The cleric placed the document in an ornate wooden box on

his desk. His hand then moved towards a small brass bell, which his long spindly fingers grasped and then shook three times.

David heard a door creak in an alcove to his right. His heart skipped a beat as the wraith-like figure glided to take its place beside the mullah. The woman in the black chador was fully veiled, her eyes being the sole visible part of her anatomy. The Israeli knew and loved those eyes. To the others present in the mullah's office they betrayed not a flicker of emotion, but to David Katri the black almonds exuded caring and affection.

After what seemed an interminable pause, the mullah looked up at his niece. "Remove your veil, girl," he said brusquely. Slowly, Fatima Fadas pulled away the layer of black cloth which effectively separated her from the rest of humanity. The face, exquisite in its austere frame, neither frowned nor smiled. It was simply statuesque.

"This is your bride, Anwar Hindawi," said Mehdi Laham. "Look at her well, for the next time you shall see her will be on your wedding day."

David thought he detected a trace of sarcasm in the mullah's voice. He could not think why and at that moment he did not care. Fatima Fadas filled his heart and his mind.

Suddenly, the cleric rose. He ordered his niece to replace the veil and leave the room the way she had come. He waited until she had gone before turning again to his male audience. "Would you and Selim please wait outside," he said to David, at the same time wiping some seepage from his rheumy eyes.

The mullah waited until the two men had left the room before retaking his seat. He began stroking his beard pensively. "What do you think, Rashid?" he said at length.

"I think we can use him," the younger man answered. "Jaafar said Hindawi told him he was a tank gunner in the Syrian army during the Ramadan War. Fortunately, I am in a position to help verify that."

"Yes, find out more about him. Perhaps we should set him

a task to prove himself. If he succeeds, he should be given the opportunity for martyrdom.''

''But he is to be married to your niece,'' Sedawi said, puzzled that the mullah should wish his new relative to become expendable.

''The contract is blank,'' the mullah said matter-of-factly.

''But I do not understand? How...''

''My niece will marry no-one,'' the mullah cut him short firmly. ''She carries the seed of idiocy and it must not be allowed to propagate.''

''As you wish,'' Rashid Sedawi shrugged, thinking how strange were the complexes of his spiritual leader, although there may have been something in what the old man said for he himself had never heard Fatima Fadas speak.

''Now, bring me my nargillah,'' the mullah ordered.

The Lebanese farmer's son helped light the bubble pipe and left Mehdi Laham smoking contentedly as he rejoined the two men outside the door.

''We shall meet again soon, Anwar,'' he said shaking David's hand. ''I shall come to Selim's spice shop either tomorrow or the day after.''

Rain began falling as David Katri left the mosque. Alongside him strode his new employer and erstwhile uncle.

''Come, Anwar, we must hurry,'' exhorted Selim Jaafar. ''The clouds are dark and some of my spice sacks are uncovered.''

David hurried after the merchant, his heart beating wildly. He knew he was on the verge of infiltrating the Cell.

The sun sets with haste in the Middle East, especially in the winter when its rays are most welcome. And by the time the street lights were beginning to flicker, David Katri had finished his work at the store and was weaving his way through the crowded streets of the Shi'ite sector towards the home of the woman he had seen in the mosque of Hussein a few hours earlier. He was excited and felt a desperate need to talk to her. As with his first visit, he utilized the skills taught him by his Mossad instructors. On several occasions he turned back on his tracks and carried out various ingrained manoeuvres in order to ascertain whether or not he was being followed. His route was even more painstaking this time, for while his first visit to a place was fairly safe, a second or third began smacking of routine. And routine was an agent's greatest enemy.

The distance between Selim Jaafar's shop and Fatima's home was little more than a kilometre, but darkness had already descended by the time David felt satisfied that there was no chance of his being followed.

Fatima must have been expecting him for she opened the door almost before he had finished knocking. She had turned off the lights in the entrance hall to thwart the prying eyes of neighbours. Her concern for his safety had prompted her to suggest that he dress as a woman and wear the chador and veil on his visits. "I am too tall, my darling," he had countered. "I would draw more attention to myself than if I were naked." They had laughed at the thought. But now David Katri was concerned that he might place his whole mission in jeopardy should he continue to see her. And yet, alone in his modest apartment, the vision of her beauty had tormented him.

"Enter quickly, azzizi!" she said, her voice breaking. "We have so little time."

As she switched on the light, David was shocked to see circles of red around her eyes. It was clear that she had been crying.

"What is wrong, my darling?" he asked, concern knotting his stomach.

She did not answer but, instead, led him past the empty armchair in the sparsely furnished lounge. He felt instinctively that something had happened to her mother.

"What is it Fatima?" he repeated as she led him to her bedroom. She closed the door and then collapsed into his arms, sobbing bitterly.

"Uma, Uma," she cried. "She is dead. Dead."

"There, there, my darling," he said, stroking her long ebony hair. "Tell me what happened."

She withdrew a handkerchief from the sleeve of her chador and wiped her eyes. "I-I came home from the meeting at the mosque," she stammered, "and an ambulance was parked outside. I knew but I did not want to believe. When I saw my mother's nurse and the sadness in her eyes it was clear. They let me see her for a few moments before they took her to the mortuary. She looked so serene. Her torment was finally over."

"How did it happen?"

"The ambulance man said it was a stroke. They had tried to resuscitate her but to no avail."

The tears again began trickling down her smooth olive cheeks and into the delicate recesses of her swollen lips. "She suffered, Anwar. She suffered all her life. When my father was killed, she brought me up alone and she was treated so shabbily by her only brother."

She looked into his eyes and he could see her pupils dilate as the anger within her arose. "I hate him," she said vehemently. "I hate him. I hate him."

David did not know what to say. No words ever seemed appropriate to comfort those who had suffered a grievous loss.

"You must not hate, my darling," he said finally, "it will not bring her back."

"I hate my uncle. I hate him. He is old and evil."

"Does he know about your mother?"

"Yes, the nurse told him. Apparently, he said he would make all the necessary arrangements."

"Then he will at least arrange a decent burial."

"Maybe."

"What do you mean?"

"I mean that it would not surprise me if he gave her a pauper's funeral. Oh, how I hate my religion!''

David was surprised at her vehemence. ''Fatima,'' he said clasping her hands, ''you must not hate your religion because of your uncle and his ways. There are millions of good Moslems, as there are millions of good Jews and Christians. It is the fanatics who do not tolerate others who are the cause of so much misery in the world.''

Fatima Fadas looked into the kindest eyes she had ever known. The time had come for her to reveal that they could never see one another again. The words stuck in her throat. ''Th-There is more, azzizi,'' she stammered.

''What do you mean?'' he asked, his stomach beginning to knot again.

''As you know,'' she said, the pain in her eyes leaping out at him, ''we are betrothed. And now that my mother is no longer alive, my uncle has ordered that I am to be chaperoned day and night until the wedding.''

David felt his senses begin to reel. Theirs was an impossible love but that it must end so soon devastated him. He could find no words to express his dejection.

''When?'' he asked simply, his voice cracking.

Fatima Fadas took her lover's head and placed it on her breast.''From tomorrow, my darling,'' she sighed. ''From tomorrow.''

David felt the warmth of her caress suffuse his whole body with a burning desire to make his last night with her a memory they would both cherish for as long as they lived. As he removed her clothes, it was if what she had said was immaterial; that their relationship was just beginning rather than ending.

As he entered her he could not help thinking of the occasions when he and Yael had tried for a baby. How extraordinarily exquisite and gentle had been their lovemaking up until the moment the morning temperature readings had confirmed that she was pregnant.

Fatima Fadas was already wet by the time her lover began moving slowly and gently within her. There was no pain, only joy as his lips sucked hard at her tender nipples. As his seed spurted within her she knew somehow that her affair with the Israeli had not only made her a woman but that it had been her destiny.

"Insh'a'Allah," she whispered as his body went limp upon hers. She was envisioning the birth of their child.

"What was that, my darling?" he moaned, the sun within his brain still enveloping him in its exquisite warmth.

"Nothing, azzizi, nothing."

David Katri and Fatima Fadas made love twice more during the night, the second time even longer and more gentler than the first. They fell asleep as wrapped vine leaves, Jew and Arab in perfect yet ephemeral repose.

The first light of dawn was already beginning to filter through the slats of the window shutters when Fatima awoke. "Anwar! Anwar!" she shook him roughly. "You must wake up. It is already dawn. Hurry! Hurry!"

Katri sprang up and began dressing quickly. There was little time for him to dwell on the fact that he might never see his beautiful Shi'ite again.

As he was about to open the front door, she hugged him tightly, her head just reaching the upper part of his chest. "Anwar, please get a message to Abu Mussa that I cannot come to him until your mission is over."

The Israeli looked into the sad almond eyes. "I understand," he said simply and kissed her sensuous lips for what he feared might be the last time.

In their haste neither Fatima Fadas nor David Katri noticed the man crouching by a nearby culvert in the half-light of the dawn. The man lingered for a few moments before he, too, disappeared into the early morning mist.

The following day David Katri worked hard in Selim Jaafar's spice store. He filled and stacked the sacks of cardamom and cumin with a vengeance, the aching in his muscles somehow overcoming the mental anguish of his parting from Fatima. In an hour night would fall and he would have to return to his apartment to face further loneliness and torment.

If Selim Jaafar thought his new assistant rather morose, he said nothing. The younger man was a hard worker and whatever scheme Abu Mussa was concocting was none of his business. The sum he had received more than compensated for the danger inherent in dealing with Laham and Sedawi. Earlier in the day, he had received a telephone call from the latter asking him what time his nephew would be finished for the day. He did not care for Sedawi. The man exuded evil and his very presence made him shudder.

"Anwar," he called out, "leave those sacks now and start cleaning up. I forgot to tell you that Rashid Sedawi called. He says he wants you to attend a meeting of some kind and he'll be picking you up soon."

David's heart skipped a beat. He had not expected to be given his chance so soon. He knew instinctively that he was about to face his greatest test since his return to Lebanon.

The Israeli had just finished drying his hands and face in the washroom at the rear of the shop when he heard Jaffar's voice calling him again. He hurriedly weaved his way between the spice sacks to the front counter. Rashid Sedawi appeared to be chatting idly with the spice merchant, at the same time running his right hand through a mound of rice in one of the open sacks. Selim Jaafar resembled a frightened rabbit, thought David as he approached the pair.

"Ah, Hindawi," Sedawi said, the sparkle in his eyes at once

friendly and suspicious, "kif halak, sahbi?"

"Al-hamdu li'llah, sayidi," David replied shaking his visitor's hand firmly.

"Minich, Minich," Sedawi enthused. "Good, good, perhaps you would care to join me. I believe Selim here informed you that I would like you to attend a meeting with me."

David knew what the subject would be but feigned ignorance. "What kind of meeting?" he asked.

"Well, my friend," Sedawi replied, "let us say that you may be able to help a cause in which you have already expressed some interest."

"I do not understand, sayidi," David lied.

The man with the golden tooth smiled. "Please, come with me and all shall be explained."

David shrugged and donned his coat. "If you insist."

Sedawi led the Israeli out of the store and into a white Peugeot 504. The driver and another man were sitting in the front and David sat between Sedawi and a fourth man in the rear. After about five minutes' drive during which no word passed between them, their leader at last spoke.

"Do not be alarmed, my friend," he said, his face close to David's, "Mohammed here will just place a blindfold over your eyes. For security reasons, you understand."

Katri felt as if he was about to gag on Sedawi's stale breath. He swallowed hard and allowed the man named Mohammed to slip the blindfold over his eyes. In the blackness he realised that the time he had spent memorising their route during the first five minutes was now completely wasted. He should have known that Sedawi would act cautiously.

David guessed that they had travelled for about half-an-hour by the time the car pulled to a final halt and his blindfold was removed. It was already dark and so the transition from blindness to vision did not bother him too much. He rubbed his eyes, nevertheless.

"Where are we?" he asked, not really expecting a precise answer.

"One of our safe houses," Sedawi replied. "Now, come with me."

David followed the smaller man up some stairs to the third floor of an ordinary apartment block. He guessed that they were still in the Shi'ite sector and that most of the journey was spent going round in circles. He had practised the situation often enough in Tel Aviv during his training.

Rashid Sedawi opened the front door of the apartment himself and led his prospective new recruit into the salon. He had told his driver and one of the men to stay in the car down below to guard the entrance. The other man who accompanied him was also new. To be surrounded by novices was a price he was prepared to pay now that the bomb was in place and he held all the cards. He had told Mehdi Laham that the men who accompanied him to plant it were staying in Amman and awaiting their orders.

The mullah had accepted his explanation without question, indicating that the old man was either senile or had grown tired of the exercise.

Rashid bade his guest be seated in an armchair and then sat down himself opposite. He examined Hindawi closely. The man certainly was a handsome specimen, enough to make him wish that he was of his own sexual persuasion. But then, he remembered, this same Hindawi was engaged to Fatima Fadas. A waste.

"Ahmed, make us some tea," he ordered the third man in the room.

"Naam, sayidi," the man said and turned towards the kitchen his jacket swinging open. The butt of a pistol could just be seen jutting from his shoulder holster.

Rashid looked back towards his guest and smiled. "I'd just like you to answer a few questions, my friend. It is just a matter of course with all our new recruits.''

"New recruits?'' asked David, feigning surprise. "I'm afraid I do not understand.''

"If you remember, my friend,'' said Sedawi, with a smile that could curdle milk, "you expressed, how shall we say, similar notions as ourselves in relation to the Zionist abomination. I take it you have not changed your views since yesterday.''

"Why no sir,'' David replied, trying to look puzzled.

"Good! Now, my friend, if you had a chance to participate in an action that would bring about an end to the Zionist entity would you not be eager to do so?''

David paused before replying. "If you mean by employing violent means,'' he said at length, "then I am prepared to become a martyr for the cause. Violence is no stranger to me.''

"Yes, Anwar, so I believe,'' Sedawi said, raising his eyebrows. "It appears that you were a tank gunner in the Syrian army during the Ramadan War.''

"I had that honour, sayidi.''

"By coincidence, Anwar, my friend, so was I, although I would not exactly call it an honour.''

David felt as if an armour-piercing shell had hit him from point-blank range. It was all he could do to maintain his composure. His briefing on the man had not included this information.

"Yes,'' David replied, his mind racing, "we had a chance then to destroy the enemy but we lost it.''

Sedawi sneered. "The Syrian army is a paper tiger. Why, one man could achieve more than they did.''

David gave the impression that he could not fathom the cryptic statement. "I'm afraid I do not understand,'' he said.

The man with the golden tooth smiled again. "Never mind,'' he said. "I may explain at a later date. Meanwhile, I would like to ask you some more questions about the war. You know, we may have been in the same brigade for I am sure I have seen you before.''

This was the second time Sedawi had made this statement and David was as perplexed as at the first. Only now was the added risk that he might be caught out by the man's questioning. He knew he must try to discover which brigade Sedawi was in and then choose another for himself.

"Why, which brigade were you in, sayidi?" he asked, trying to sound as naturally inquisitive as possible.

Sedawi smiled again and David knew he had failed to out-manoeuvre the Shi'ite. "I believe," the Lebanese said at length, "that you were at Kuneitra with the third armoured division. Who was your brigade commander?"

David knew that if both men had had the same commander, then the Shi'ite would make mincemeat of him. He could not hope to possess the same knowledge as the Lebanese. However, the odds still favoured him. He just had to keep his cool.

"I was with Shukeri's first. I was a gunner in a T-62 of the ninth battalion.''

For a few moments there was silence as Sedawi assimilated the information. For David Katri they were the longest moments of his life.

"I know of Shukeri," the Shi'ite said at last, "but I never met him. I was with Mohammed al-Husseini in the third.''

"Don't you mean Yasser al-Husseini?" countered David, recalling from his sessions at Sarafand the name of the brigade commander who was famed for his bravery and was the only leader in the field to escape unsullied from the debacle.

"Of course, of course, my friend. How silly of me.''

David knew it was a trap and he had sprung it successfully. He prayed Sedawi would now let up.

Indeed, apart from a few perfunctory questions on the attributes and disadvantages of the T-62, Rashid Sedawi concentrated the rest of the questioning on David's childhood, his being orphaned in the catastrophe of nineteen sixty-seven and his subsequent life in Damascus. Katri recited his cover story perfectly and knew it could not be checked.

"Good," Sedawi said at last, "I think there have been enough questions." The man with the golden tooth was impressed by his new recruit. The Cell needed men gifted with intelligence and the knowledge of war, at least until the first shurqiyas. There was still work to be finished in Europe and he could think of no-one in the group who might be more capable than Anwar Hindawi. Anyway, he himself felt the need for more adventure. There was nothing more he could do sitting around in Beirut waiting for the Spring. Some of his new men had carried out successful attacks against Israeli troops in the south and had helped prove to Hezbollah that the Cell, too, was a force to be reckoned with.

"Anwar, my friend, how is your rifle aim since your war days?"

"A little rusty," David replied apprehensively.

"We will soon fix that," the Shi'ite said. "I will arrange for you to get some practice at sniping."

"May I ask why, sayidi?"

"Tfadal. You see every new recruit has to accomplish some task before he is fully accepted into our organisation. I think you may be the right man for a quick hit operation in Europe, in Vienna actually. But I will inform you more of my plans later."

David's elation at being accepted was suddenly cut short by trepidation about what he might be asked to do. Nevertheless, he knew he had to sound enthusiastic. "I shall do whatever you command, sir."

"Good, good." Sedawi enthused. "It is decided then."

"There is just one thing, sayidi."

"Yes. What is it?"

"I still do not know the name of the group I am about to join."

"Ah, yes," laughed Sedawi, his mouth twisting cruelly, "we are called the Islamic Jihad Fundamentalist Cell. If you remember, we carried out the sabotage of the El Al airliner."

David feigned amazement. "Then I am proud to be part of your cause," he lied. "Allahu Akhbar!"

"Allahu Akhbar!" repeated Rashid Sedawi, the fire of fanaticism ablaze in his eyes.

The next day, David went to work as usual at Selim Jaafar's spice store. He wanted desperately to speak to Yariv Cohen personally but knew he was constrained to work through Abu Mussa. The Mossad chief had gone to great lengths to assure him that, in this case, primitive means of communication were best.

"You must understand," his boss had said, "that in the normal course of events we would have had you plant all manner of bugs and other surveillance devices. However, we believe Sedawi is an expert at ferreting these out and we cannot afford even the slightest suspicion to fall on you."

David at first thought that his weeks of studying the latest in technical gadgetry had gone to waste, but in the end he knew Cohen was right. Old-fashioned espionage was probably best under the circumstances. Should he in the end need to be equipped with some sophisticated piece of apparatus, then it would reach him somehow. Meanwhile, there were other things which occupied his mind. Foremost among these was the task which Sedawi intended setting him. When and why was he being sent to Europe? He did not know whether he was capable of detonating a bomb and killing innocent people, his own people, or murdering even one person by sniper fire. He recalled Yariv Cohen's chilling words: "The lives of even a hundred

Israelis are not worth the millions who will probably die painfully and slowly should you fail."

Cohen's missive was playing on his mind when he noticed Yussef Ibrahim enter the store. Abu Mussa's aide strode towards him purposefully. "Here is a list of things I need. Please get them for me, will you," said the small man with the bushy moustache and beard. "You're new here, aren't you?"

"Yes, I am," replied David. "And I shall be glad to be of assistance to you, sayidi." Instinctively, David felt the back pocket of his jeans.

The cryptic note he had prepared for Abu Mussa was still there. However, nowhere in his lexicon was anything that would help him relay the message from Fatima Fadas. He knew he had to speak to Ibrahim and that the best place was directly outside the store amid the roar of the traffic. However unlikely, it was just possible that Sedawi had planted an ultra-sensitive listening device in the store which could pick up conversations from the vibration of window panes or glass cabinets.

The Israeli began preparing Ibrahim's order. There were at least ten full sacks of rice, barley and other commodities to load onto his vehicle.

"I will use the trolley to help load your goods, sir," he said. "Is your car outside?"

"Naam, shukkran."

David helped Yussef Ibrahim load the sacks onto the Mitsubishi pick-up. He did not utter a further word until the last sack was aboard. "I will just get you your bill, sayidi. Shall I debit your account with us?"

Ibrahim nodded.

The Israeli hurried back into the store and rang up his customer's bill on an adding machine. He entered the amount on Yussef Ibrahim's card and then quickly withdrew the message from his jeans pocket. He slipped it inside the bill-slip and returned to the waiting vehicle.

"Here is your bill," David said loudly. As the bearded man took it, David grabbed his hand tightly, his voice dropping to a whisper.

"Tell Abu Mussa that Fatima's mother has died and that Mehdi Laham has ordered her to be chaperoned day and night until the wedding."

If he was surprised by David's revelation, Yussef Ibrahim did not show it. He knew his master would be hurt at first and then angry. As was his wont, the Za'im would also be suspicious. "I will inform him, sayidi," pledged the smaller man and climbed into his cab.

David stared after the Mitsubishi as it disappeared into the passing traffic. Just as he was about to return to the shop he felt a presence behind him. He wheeled round and his heart raced as he was confronted by the sinister smile of Rashid Sedawi.

"I see Selim gives you plenty of work to do, Anwar," the Shi'ite said. "I think I'll have to arrange that you get some time off."

"I am at your service, sir," David said, trying to disguise his surprise.

Sedawi smiled again. "You may call me Rashid, Anwar. I prefer it that way."

"As you wish," said David, wondering if he could ever get used to calling the fanatic by his first name. "I deem it an honour."

Sedawi nodded his approval of David's attitude. "After lunch a car will pick you up to take you to a firing range that we use in a derelict part of town. The buildings are half-destroyed but they give one the opportunity to practise, especially sniping. I shall explain to Selim that he should no longer require your services in the afternoons over the next month."

David stood and stared as the Shi'ite entered Jaafar's store. Everything had gone so smoothly that he wondered if Sedawi was playing a game and in fact suspected something. The Israeli felt his enemy was taking more than a casual interest in his progress. Also the look in Sedawi's eye was discomforting. He could swear it was almost one of lust.

Further north in the same country, but in a place which might just as well have been on a different planet, Abu Mussa sat in the long garden of his palace perusing Anwar Hindawi's note. The groundnuts still may have been in short supply, but Yariv Cohen would need to know that the tapioca had arrived at the warehouse and was awaiting shipment to Europe where it would be tested for flavour. He would also be informed that accompanying the tapioca would be a container of golden wheat. There was as yet no precise destination, and no date had been given for the shipment, although it was estimated that at least one month would elapse before its arrival.

The rays of the tepid wintry sun granted the Maronite only brief respite from the ice that was within his heart. Did the mullah really think he could wrap his niece in cotton wool? Did he not know that Abu Mussa was more powerful than he; that Abu Mussa could take his precious niece whenever he so desired?

The Maronite saw visions of himself whisking Fatima Fadas away from the stinking Moslem sector to his mountain refuge, of the consternation that would cause Mehdi Laham and his Shi'ite scum. However, Abu Mussa was nothing if not practical, and while there was still hope of Hindawi's success there was also a chance of his collecting from the Israelis. For one-and-a-half million dollars he would remain parted from the woman he desired but could never have.

"Georges!" the Maronite called out tetchily.

As if he had been hiding among the nearby bracts of magenta, the ascetic manservant appeared suddenly at Abu Mussa's side.

"You called, master?"

The Maronite godfather looked up at his faithful aide. Sometimes he wished the man would not be so thorough in every task he was allotted. There were some things a man really did not want to know even when he said he did.

"Georges," he sighed, "relay this message to our Israeli friends. Add that I would wish a further meeting with Cohen. You know what to do."

"Naam, Ra'is," the thin man replied and repeated his ceremony of obeisance before sidling away towards the beautifully symmetrical northern pavilion and its bizarre adornment of antennae.

CHAPTER TWELVE

As Arik Ben-Ami entered his office he felt more and more as if he were in a time warp. Vienna and its civilised behaviour and elegant streets were beginning to get to him. He missed the hurly-burly of other major cities but especially that of Tel Aviv. How he longed for its frenetic Levantine buzzing, its fumes and, above all, its sun and sea. He envied those Israelis who had never experienced a central European winter.

Besides, he had had another row with Inge the previous night. True, they had made up for it with a particularly energetic bout of lovemaking but he knew that nothing could paper over the cracks in their relationship. As a source of information, she had dried up and it was a question of time before he would be forced to ditch her. He hoped secretly that his cover job as Ephraim Epstein, head of a small import-export operation in the city, would soon come to an end. He would jump at the chance of a posting to a warmer country. A return to Tel Aviv would be nice but he was put off by the huge cut in salary that would accompany it. Arik shivered. His office was cold, despite the central heating. He swivelled round and peered through the window at the snow which was beginning to settle again following a few days' respite of clement weather. The Israeli spent more than five minutes staring at the whiteness; seeing it, yet not seeing it, his thoughts residing in warmer climes.

Suddenly, the low-pitched voice of his secretary, Rivka Fischer, interrupted his daydreaming. He did not know why it was that so many Israeli girls had such deep voices. Rivka was a true amazon. She had told him she had served with the paratroopers and had made fifty-three jumps. It was a pity, she could even have been pretty if she were not so masculine.

"There are five telexes for you, Ephraim," she said gruffly, "although one of them is just a bunch of numbers."

He took them from her outstretched hand, angry with himself that he had not checked the machine as he usually did. Like most good bosses, he was always first in the office every weekday. This was not, however, due to any over-zealous loyalty to his company, which was merely a front operation for the Mossad. It simply gave him the opportunity to check telexes that came in overnight. Most were about business, but sometimes he would receive a message of numbers with a callback sign relating to a small import-export office in Rothschild Boulevard, Tel Aviv. The message, once unscrambled, bore no relation to either imports or exports. Arik would spend the hour before the office opened deciphering it and, if necessary, constructing one of his own. Following transmission, he simply removed it from the telex's computerised memory and destroyed the paper read-out.

He waited for the amazon to enter her office adjoining his before withdrawing from a locked drawer in his desk his faithful blue book, a pad of about fifty pages. No two pages were alike and no two pads were the same except that they were produced in double sets for the use of encoder and decoder. Arik used a different sheet for every message, which he then tore off after sending the dispatch. Upon decoding the message, the signals operative in Tel Aviv tore the same page from his one-time pad. If everything was clear, he would telex a simple 'Recvd OK'. In the one-time pad system, each letter of the message was given a number arrived at by working backwards through the alphabet with A equal to twenty-six and Z to one. The numbers from a single sheet were taken one by one in a vertical or horizontal sequence agreed in advance and added to the number substituted for each letter. The number transmitted was the total of those two figures.

Each sheet of the pad contained a random key in the form of six-digit groups, and no key was ever repeated. The great advantage of the system was that similar letters did not produce similar final numbers. The only drawback came if it was stolen, although the thief would still have to guess whether the vertical or horizontal sequence was being used.

It took Arik a few minutes to work out the message. He read the decoded numbers on the blue pad.

TERRORIST ACTION EXPECTED SOON EUROPE. NO FURTHER DETAILS AVAILABLE YET. EXERCISE EXTRA CARE.

The Israeli scratched his head. The plain fact was that the PLO and its various factions had not been active in Vienna for a long time. He thought it strange that Central could not provide him with more information.

Arik screwed up the telex and threw it into the waste basket. By itself it was meaningless. He was just about to rip the top page from the blue pad when he heard a commotion in Rivka's room. "I'm afraid you can't go in their, Fraulein..." came Fischer's harsh voice.

Inge Muller, beautiful, blonde and distraught, swept into Arik's office.

The Israeli stood up angrily. "Inge, I thought I told you never to come to my office," he seethed.

"I just had to see you, Arik. It is so important."

Arik noticed Rivka Fischer's eyes glaring at him from the adjoining doorway.

"Zeh beseder, Rivka," Arik said firmly. "It's okay. Please leave us. I will handle this." His secretary looked ready to put her army training to good use.

By this time, Inge Muller had planted herself in the chair opposite his desk and was staring sullenly at the desktop. Suddenly bursting into tears, she withdrew a handkerchief from her foxfur coat. It slipped from her hand and she leaned forward to retrieve it.

"I thought I told you never to come here, Inge," the Israeli repeated.

The Austrian sat upright. Her eyes flickered as they met his. "I had to Ephraim liebling," she said tearfully. "You see, I have just come from my doctor. I have been feeling very sick in the mornings lately."

"Well, what's wrong?" Arik asked irritably.

"He thinks I am pregnant, liebling."

"You're what!" the Israeli exploded. "You can't be."

"But I am."

Arik could not decide whether her voice registered pleasure or distress. "Look, look," he said in a conciliatory manner, "we'll discuss it tonight. Come to my place about seven. Okay."

"Please don't be angry with me, Ephraim," she said rising from her chair. "I do not know what to do."

"Tonight at seven, Inge," repeated Arik, ushering his mistress to the door. "We'll discuss it then."

Arik gave his mistress a kiss on the cheek and turned in time to notice his secretary's door slightly ajar. It closed immediately. "Damned amazon," he muttered, returning to his desk. He picked up the blue pad and ripped off the top page. Clicking his lighter, he set fire to one corner of the paper. Within seconds it was reduced to smouldering ashes. He then flicked the lighter again and lit himself a Marlboro.

Pleased with herself, Frau Muller hailed a taxi and entered the Inner City. She had arranged to meet her host for lunch at the expensive Kervansaray Turkish restaurant in Mahlerstrasse, but there was still plenty of time to do some window shopping along the Karntnerstrasse.

She strolled past snow-capped St Stephen's Cathedral and turned right into Kartnerstrasse. Her excitement grew as she realised that soon she would be able to buy some of the things she had desired so much but could never afford. Staring at the items of exquisite jewellery in the shop window of Haben's she recalled how the Arab had approached her while she was sipping coffee in Demel's only a few shops away from where she now stood. At first she had recoiled from the bull-necked man with the ugly mole above his lip, but he had known her name and had insisted that he had an important business proposal to make to her. Intrigued, she had followed him to a smaller, more mundane, coffee house on Rauhenstrasse. There the Arab explained that he was involved in industrial espionage and that he needed information on her boyfriend, his office and his movements and that he was willing to pay handsomely. Her first reaction had been to say that she would never betray her lover.

It was then that the Arab had related some of the more intimate conversations she had had with Ephraim recently. "Your relationship is over, Frau Muller, we both know he wants to ditch you."

"But how could you know all this?" she had asked. The Arab had then produced a small metal listening device from his pocket.

"With one of these," he smirked.

It was then that the sallow-skinned man had made her the offer. It was true that Ephraim had been good to her in the early days of their relationship, but of late he had become mean in both love and money. If she had to admit the truth to herself, she did not really like him any more. Life could be tough for a widow with two young children to raise and twenty thousand American dollars would go a long way towards alleviating that burden. Anyway, the Israeli had expressed interest only in her body and in the information she supplied him. It was clear he did not desire a deep and more lasting relationship and was only using her.

"Two can play at that game, liebling," she muttered, the

steam of her breath misting the jeweller's window.

Two hours later, Frau Inge Muller turned into Mahlerstrasse and entered the Kervansaray. She ascended the stairs to the Hummer Bar fish restaurant. As one of the waiters took her coat, she could see the bull-necked Arab sitting at a table for two in the corner. "Guten Arbend, Frau Muller," he said as she sat down opposite him. "I have taken the liberty of ordering fresh lobster. It is flown in daily from the Bosphorous."

"That will be fine, danke," she said.

After exchanging a few pleasantries about the weather, the Arab's eyes narrowed. "Did you do as I ordered?"

"Ja, it is done. I planted it beneath his desk."

"Good. Now describe to me the entrance to the office, the office itself and the number of workers you saw."

Inge Muller spent the next few minutes describing what she had managed to observe of Epstein's office and of her conversation with the Israeli.

"Do you think he'll believe you?" the Arab asked.

"At least for the first ten weeks or so. Then he's bound to notice I am not swelling."

"That is all the time we need," the Arab said, scratching the large mole on his upper lip. "In the meantime, tell him you intend to keep the baby but that you will not demand anything from him. That will keep his mind occupied for a while. In a moment of weakness he may divulge something."

"If you have already bugged my home, you must know that he never talks about his work," the Austrian said.

Mustapha Bedawi smiled. The blonde whore was learning fast. "Is there anything else?" he asked.

"Ja, I think so. There was a blue pad on his desk with a series of numbers on it. Under each series he had scribbled a word, in Hebrew I think. Anyway, I could not understand it."

"Danke mein frau," the Arab said and withdrew a small brown packet from inside his jacket. "Here is the first five thousand as we agreed. You have done well.''

Frau Inge Muller took the parcel and placed it gingerly in her handbag.

"The lobster you ordered, mein herr," said the Turkish waiter, appearing suddenly at their table.

David Katri squinted as the blindfold was removed and the sudden burst of light dazzled him. At first, all he could see were ghostly figures darting to and fro. But as his eyes grew accustomed to the light, he saw that he was standing in a large courtyard surrounded by derelict and shell-pocked buildings.

"These are new recruits like yourself," a voice said to his left, "but most of them have had little or no military training."

As David's vision regained its clarity, he could see about twenty young men, most of them still in their teens, lining up before what appeared to be an obstacle training course. They were clutching fake wooden rifles.

Four older men stood either side of each row of walls, empty pickle barrels, tarpaulins, drains and trip-wires. In their hands were Soviet AK-47s, their barrels pointing towards the ground.

Suddenly, one of the instructors blew a whistle. As if a coiled spring had been released, the youths darted towards the first obstacle, a two metre-high wall. Almost at once the instructors began firing into the air in an effort to simulate battle conditions. David understood by the fear in the faces of the recruits that the armed men were not firing blanks.

Once over the wall, each recruit crawled through a barrel and then ran a further ten metres to a tarpaulin under which he wriggled. Almost immediately, the Kalashnikovs were directed earthwards and bullets began spewing out either side of the tarpaulins. Mound after mound tried to skit through the darkness as fast as possible.

"Brings back memories, doesn't it," shouted Rashid Sedawi above the din.

David looked calmly at the man to his left and smiled. "Yes, but in armour we only had to suffer this sort of stuff in basic training."

"Yes," the Shi'ite laughed, "that's why I, too, chose tanks."

Almost as soon as it had begun, the exercise was over. The new recruits, some looking terrified and others sheepish, stood bedraggled at the far end of the course.

"Mohammed!" Sedawi called out to one of his instructors. "Put them through that again until they can do it under thirty seconds."

"Naam, Ra'is," the man saluted.

"Come, my friend," said Sedawi turning back towards David, "I do not think you will need to go through all that. Instead, let me show you my little baby."

The Israeli realised by the Arab's tone that he was to be shown an item of weaponry. He returned and followed the smaller man over mounds of rubble to one of the shell-pocked apartment blocks. Sedawi, hurrying, was already several paces ahead of David when he suddenly disappeared below ground level.

"I'm here," he heard the Shi'ite call out. "Come on down."

David descended the twenty or so steps to be confronted by a huge steel door. Painted on it was a large skull and crossbones in red with the words 'Strictly No Smoking' in Arabic. In the reduced light, the Israeli could see Sedawi pressing buttons on some kind of locking mechanism to the right of the door. Suddenly, there was a click and the Shi'ite pushed it open. David gasped as Sedawi switched on the lights. In front of him was a vast underground cavern.

"Come, I want to show you something, Anwar."

Katri followed the Arab into a room to his right. The sight was astounding. There, piled up before him, were arms and ammunition of almost every description. Row upon row of

Kalashnikovs, machine guns and mortars stood in line as if on parade. Boxes of grenades and ammunition were stacked high to the ceiling.

"Elo- Ya Allah!" David exclaimed, correcting himself just in time. In a moment of excitement he had almost used the familiar Hebrew expression 'Elohim Gadol' instead of the Arabic. God was indeed great, but one more slip like that would be the end of him.

"Allahu Akhbar!" Sedawi enthused, apparently wrapped up in his own euphoria. "It is magnificent, is it not?"

"How did we get all this weaponry?" David asked, being careful to use the word 'we' to imply that he at least already saw himself as a fully committed member of the Cell.

"It's all thanks to the Palestinians," Sedawi said, slapping David on the back in a rare moment of bonhomie. "And the Israelis."

"I do not understand."

"Well, the Cell was formed during the Israeli invasion of nineteen eighty-two," Sedawi explained. "Some of our villages in the south had come under air attack and we simply decided that enough was enough. However, we did not want to be part and parcel of Hezbollah and be completely subject to the Iranians. So we needed separate finance and our own weapons."

"But where do the Palestinians come into this?" asked David, intrigued.

"The fools," Sedawi laughed. "They were so busy worrying about the Israelis, they did not realise that they were vulnerable from another quarter. Most of their men were further south. All we had to do was overcome a few guards and then shift the arms and ammunition to a safer place."

Sedawi laughed again, this time even more heartedly. "You know, my friend, we need not have bothered with all that hard work."

"What do you mean?"

"The Palestinians. They never came back. The Israelis ridded us of the Palestinians and now we shall rid ourselves of the Israelis."

It was the first time David had heard the Shi'ite allude to what he knew was a plan to destroy the Jewish State. The Israeli knew he had to be careful in what he said next.

"Insh'a'Allah!" he exclaimed. "But how shall we do that with such limited means?"

Realising he had spoken a little too freely, Sedawi tried to cover his mistake.

"Attrition, Anwar," he said. "Attrition. Eventually the power of Islam will drive the Israelis into the sea. By our willingness to become martyrs we shall succeed where the Palestinians have failed."

David knew he must not push too far, too soon. Another opportunity to press Sedawi would arise at a later date. He discreetly changed tack. "I should like to try some of these weapons," he said enthusiastically.

"And so you shall, my friend," the smaller man replied. "Although there is one weapon in particular that I want to show you."

Rashid Sedawi led David away from the racks of rifles and into a small alcove. Alone in a glass cabinet stood a rifle. It was unlike any he had seen before.

"Do you know what this is Anwar?" asked Sedawi, opening the cabinet with his own key.

"No, I'm afraid I do not recognise it," David replied truthfully.

The Shi'ite cradled the rifle in his arms as he would a baby. "This," he said stroking the barrel, "is, aptly enough, an Austrian Steyr-Mannlicher. It's the model MC Mannlicher Schoenauer with Monte Carlo type stock, the type Lee Harvey Oswald used. Here, catch!"

David's reactions were quick and he caught the rifle in mid-flight. Cradling it in his arms, he reckoned it weighed around three to three-and-a-half kilos. Upon inspection, he noted the Steyr used a bolt with multiple interrupted screw-type locking lugs which were rear mounted and locked into the receiver behind the receiver bridge. The Israeli saw that Sedawi was watching him intently as he pulled back the bolt and then released it. Most rifles were based on the same principle and he knew that anyone with a knowledge of arms should have little difficulty in figuring out how each piece came apart.

The bolt, in fact, comprised three principal pieces, one of which was the main body, a long cylindrical section carrying the extractor and bored out for the firing pin. The rear quarter of the bolt body was of reduced diameter so that the sleeve containing the locking lugs, handle and plug could be fitted on the body. The rifle had a single set-trigger and the sliding safety was mounted to the rear of the bolt handle root. The cocking piece unit fitted over the rear of the striker shaft and was held by a nut screwed onto the end of the striker.

David inspected the plastic magazine. It was of the rotary type with a charger clip.

"You can, of course, load with individual cartridges," Sedawi pointed out. "The magazine stop springs back as you insert each cartridge and so prevents any unwinding."

With this, the Shi'ite withdrew two cardboard boxes from the drawer at the bottom of the cabinet, one long and slender and the other cubed.

"Bullets and 'scope," Sedawi explained. "It takes five rounds of seven millimetre calibre. I hope you'll learn not to need that many. In Lebanon, a soldier who cannot shoot is a corpse. Now, follow me."

As David followed his leader to the exit, he noted that there were several rooms leading from the ammunition store. As he passed one, he saw it contained desks and chairs with a blackboard at the far end. Obviously it was an improvised classroom of some kind, although the setting seemed totally incongruous.

Once outside, the sudden stream of daylight made him blink hard. He heard the whirr of an electronic mechanism as the Arab closed the giant steel door.

"Only myself and a few trusted lieutenants know the combination to this place," the Shi'ite said. "If you succeed in your mission, you may be allowed to become one of them."

The Israeli felt a sudden rush of blood to his head, but said nothing.

The two men ascended the stairs. Instead of heading off towards the courtyard, they continued climbing until they had reached the top of the building. There were no doors or windows, just jagged holes through which David followed the Arab. Eventually they entered a large room and Sedawi crossed to an open balcony. Scattered on the floor were a number of shell casings. "Come and look," Sedawi beckoned as he stood by the shapeless gap which had once been the balcony of someone's home.

David, still carrying the Steyr, picked his way through the debris and joined the Lebanese. His jaw dropped as he gazed down on the street below. Instead of the view of war's destructiveness as seen from the other side of the building, the scene could almost have been one of a tranquil street in another country. There were wooden benches, street lights and shop fronts. On the far side was a battered old black Mercedes, its body full of holes with yellow rings painted around them. But what most surprised David were the lifelike characters in varying degrees of stance. Some were standing behind lamp-posts, others sitting on the benches, crossing the street or leaving shop doorways. He noticed that some of the figures were perched on wheeled platforms.

"Those dummies look really lifelike, do they not," said Sedawi. "Those masks cost ten American dollars each."

"It's fantastic," gasped David.

"Yes, and you know what. I am pleased when I have to keep replacing those masks. It means my snipers are hitting their targets."

"But why not just draw faces on the heads?"

"You will see, my friend. You will see."

With this, the Shi'ite withdrew the optical sight from its box and took the Steyr from David. He affixed the sight above the bolt and pointed the rifle at one of the dummies. He then adjusted the sight before handing the rifle back to David.

"Look at that character standing by the Mercedes."

David took the Steyr and did as he was ordered. "Allah!" he exclaimed. "It looks human."

"Precisely," smiled Sedawi. "The more you shoot at those heads the more you do not care whether they are human or not." David was forced to agree with the logic of the fanatic. When it came to the real thing, a living target became just another mask to the sniper. The only difference being that behind the mask lay no head of straw.

Sedawi began loading the magazine. He then took the Steyr from his student and removed the 'scope. "I want you to try to hit targets without this at first," he said. "Take it. It has an aperture sight, which should make the job easier for you."

It was a long time since David had used a rifle with an aperture sight. He studied the sight on the Steyr and twiddled with the range adjusting screw. The sight was removable and the outside of the barrel had been specially turned to accommodate a silencer.

"I want you to try from the kneeling position the first time," said Sedawi. "You can aim at that figure by the Mercedes again. Sometimes we use remote control to make it a moving target. But not this time."

It had been several months since David had received his weapons training with the Mossad. It had concentrated mainly on pistol firing. Training with rifles had been limited, although he had done some sniping with the Israeli Galil 7.62mm and the British L42 A1. He knew that whatever make of calibre Sedawi gave him, it was vital he create a good first impression.

The Israeli reckoned his target was about sixty metres away and that a hit of some kind should be quite easy.

As if reading his mind, Rashid Sedawi pointed to the masked dummy. "The right eye," he said laconically.

"Excuse me?"

"I want you to try hitting the dummy in the right eye."

David nodded and, kneeling down, noticed his instructor was using the telescopic sight himself to view the target. The Israeli tried to recall the instructions for firing from the kneeling position. He inclined his trunk slightly forwards and rested the full weight of his body on the three-point position - left foot, right knee, right foot - to support it evenly. He let his shoulders hang forward loosely and made sure his chest faced the target.

He then shifted his left foot so that it was directly underneath the weapon and at an angle of forty-five degrees to the direction of shooting. Being tall, he allowed his left calf to incline slightly forwards below the weapon. He knew that if he allowed his leg to tip sideways, it would stretch the muscles of his upper leg, arm and left shoulder resulting in unpredictable backward vibration of the muzzle.

Suddenly, David stood up. He knew he had forgotten something and the look in Sedawi's eyes confirmed it.

The Arab smiled at his student and removed his leather jacket to form a makeshift kneeling roll. David then knelt again, positioning the roll directly under the right instep. He went through his previous procedure before picking up the rifle at his side. He felt the bone of his right buttock ache as it rested on the heel of his right shoe. He then placed his left elbow in the hollow between the kneecap and the femur. The left forearm rested on the extension of the femur, thus transferring the weight of the weapon directly to the thigh.

David positioned the front part of the gunstock onto the ball of his left thumb. His fingers were relaxed and did not touch the stock. He then brought his right arm into play, lifting the stock gently but firmly into his right shoulder and, holding its neck with three fingers, he snuggled his cheek into the depression which made the Monte Carlo version of stock so comfortable. By chance, the range adjusting screw was set about right and the image of the upper right side of the dummy's mask came between aperture backsight and post foresight.

David curled his right forefinger around the trigger and pulled directly backwards. He felt the stock jar into his shoulder as the percussion cap exploded to send the deadly projectile on its way.

"Well, how did I do?" he asked, looking up at Sedawi, who was still peering intently through the 'scope.

"You missed his eye," the Arab said at length. He then lowered the 'scope and smiled. "But you hit him plum in the forehead."

David Katri did not know why, but at that moment he felt proud. It was if he had just won a giant teddy-bear at a fairground shooting range.

"We will try you out on a few more positions and targets tomorrow," Sedawi said, kneeling down and putting his arm around David's shoulder. Once again, the Israeli felt uncomfortable at his touch.

But if David Katri believed that over the next few weeks he would be given the opportunity to further impress Rashid Sedawi, he was greatly mistaken. Each afternoon a car arrived at Selim Jaafar's store to transport him blindfolded to the training compound. But the Shi'ite fanatic did not appear again. The Steyr, too, went missing and David was tutored instead by Mohammed Fawzi on a more mundane Belgian FN. It was only after persistent but careful prompting of his instructor that he learned that Rashid Sedawi was somewhere in Europe.

It did not take great powers of deduction for the Israeli to guess that his enemy was sizing up the Cell's next victim and that he, David Katri, would be the victimizer.

While Katri was learning the art of the assassin, Abu Mussa was once again driving south towards the border with Israel. He was glad that the Mossad chief had responded quickly to his call for a second meeting. Things were starting to move, but not necessarily to the big Maronite's liking. The Israelis had to be made to understand the risks he was taking and that his sacrifices were beyond that originally envisaged. Every trip south of Jounieh carried with it concomitant risk. Every roadblock set up by the Syrians or the various militias had to be negotiated. His wallet carried more barricade passes than credit cards. More often than not they had been obtained through the time-honoured proffering of bribes, although sometimes his working relationship with some of the sectarian commanders had been enough to ensure the continuation of his journey and his safety. Abu Mussa's back was aching by the time he drove the blue Mercedes into the Israeli army compound at the Good Fence. He saw Yariv Cohen and Rahamim Ben-Yaacov relaxing on a bench trying to trap the rays of warmth from the wintry sun. The temperature was probably around ten degrees but it seemed much colder. The two Israelis rose as he switched off his motor and opened the car door.

"Ahalan wa'sahalan, ya Abu Mussa," Cohen called out as he limped towards the Maronite. "Kif halak, sahbi?"

"Al-humdu-l'illah," the Christian smiled wanly, hoping that the meeting would be short and to his liking.

"Would you care for some refreshment after your long journey?" said the Israeli, leading his guest towards a Nissen hut. "There is already some fresh fruit juice on the table."

"Shukkran. That will do nicely."

While his guest drank a second glass of orange juice, Yariv Cohen observed him closely. It was true they were desperate for more extensive news of Katri's situation, but the Maronite was known for never giving without taking. The Mossad chief just hoped the price would not be too high. The loose folds of the Christian's throat undulated as he finished the last drop from his glass and smacked his lips. "Ah, that was very welcome, my friend," he enthused.

"Can we now get down to business, sir," Cohen said firmly. "We have received the transmissions from you using the trade code. Naturally, the air waves are alive with unobserved listeners and we have had to keep radio contact to a minimum. What more can you tell us?"

The Maronite cleared his throat before replying.

"As you know, my friend," he began slowly, "your agent has managed to infiltrate the Cell. If I may say so, this was due in no small measure to a brilliant idea of mine."

Abu Mussa chuckled as he observed the scepticism in the faces of the two Israelis. "You remember, of course, my impeccable source within the Cell," he went on. "Well, she is now betrothed to your Mr Hindawi."

"What?" cried Cohen in disbelief. He found it impossible to comprehend that a man as acquisitive as Abu Mussa would be prepared to give up somebody who was obviously his mistress.

"Relax, sahbi, relax," the Maronite rejoined. "I can now tell you that she is Mehdi Laham's niece and that the only way I could get your man an audience with the mullah was by arranging through a friend that he be betrothed to her. Clever, no?"

"Amazing!" enthused Ben-Yaacov, pandering to the Christian's ego.

"Although, as you probably know," the Maronite hurried on, "under Shi'ite law the bridegroom usually doesn't see his bride-to-be again until the wedding date."

"And when will that be?" Cohen asked.

"According to the Muslim calendar it works out to the middle of May."

"By which time we will already know our fate."

"If that is the will of God," the Christian smiled.

Although Yariv Cohen found the story of the Maronite's machinations intriguing, he knew the preamble had a purpose. "What is the problem, Abu Mussa?"

The Christian clasped his hands in front of him and looked at his Israeli hosts with baleful eyes. "My mistress," he shrugged, "her mother has died. She was very ill for a long time." Abu Mussa paused to enjoy the puzzled expressions on the faces of the Israelis.

"Well?" asked Cohen impatiently.

"Well," the Maronite continued morosely, "her uncle, in his wisdom, has decided that she be chaperoned day and night until her wedding."

"I don't understand," said Ben-Yaacov.

The Maronite looked even more sorrowful. "It means," he said, "that I can no longer see her as I used to. I fear for her safety and, as I told you before, I will allow nothing to harm her, even at the expense of the success of your mission."

"And what do you suggest we do about this matter?" asked Cohen, increasingly irritated.

"Nothing, nothing," the Maronite replied in mock surprise at the Israeli's attitude. "It is that for the sacrifices I am being asked to make, the rewards are so little."

"I don't call one and half million dollars little reward, Abu Mussa."

"Surely, surely, sahbi," the Maronite smiled, "and it is not that I do not trust you, but I have not seen one cent yet. And my expenses are so heavy.''

Yariv Cohen had wondered when the Christian would get around to the question of money. While it was true he had not been paid up front, it was also true that Katri had been unable to confirm that Sedawi had indeed stolen the bomb. Up till now they had relied on the testimony of Abu Mussa and his fancy woman and the report from their agent in Vienna.

''We are apparently still nowhere near finding out where this bomb is,'' the Israeli said, knowing in his heart that the Maronite had achieved all that could be expected of him.

''That is the problem of your agent, my friend,'' Abu Mussa replied. ''I can do no more for him except act as a go-between.''

''What do you want?'' Cohen asked bluntly.

Abu Mussa withdrew a slip of paper from one of the pockets of his parka and handed it to the Israeli. ''Here is the name and address of my bank in Switzerland. Below it you see an account number. Kindly get your government to make a deposit of one million dollars by this time next week.''

Cohen remained unmoved. ''I don't believe they will sanction that amount on the basis of our progress so far,'' he said. ''But I'll convince them that half is about right.''

Abu Mussa did not feel in the mood to fight a tactical battle over the matter. The Jews had a saying for it: 'tafasta merubeh, lo tafasta'. If one tried to catch everything, one ended up with nothing. ''So be it,'' he said succinctly and rose to go.

''Haven't you forgotten something, sahbi,'' Cohen said, grabbing the Maronite's sleeve.

''I am sorry, my friend, I do not understand.''

''So far we have talked mainly about your problems, not ours. I want to know everything about Katri's situation in depth. Don't miss out a single detail.''

''Of course, of course, how silly of me to forget,'' said Abu Mussa returning to his seat. ''Please accept my apologies.''

During the next hour, the Mossad leaders heard how Sedawi

had at first treated Katri as his protege and had then left their agent to tackle the terrorist training courses alone. They heard the big Maronite swear that no-one had any idea of the exact location of the terrorist base except the gold-toothed Shi'ite and a few of his henchmen. Even the other new recruits were transported there blindfolded.

By the time the Christian drove through the gates of the Good Fence on his way back to Jounieh, Yariv Cohen and Rahamim Ben-Yaacov were fully aware that time was against them.

"There is a high probability that we will never learn where the bomb is, Rahamim," said the head of the Maronite turning to his olive-skinned companion.

Ben-Yaacov sighed heavily. "What can we do, boss?"

Cohen stood pensively watching the blue Mercedes disappear into the distance. He did not speak for at least a minute. Finally, "Get me the Chief of Staff when we arrive back in Tel Aviv. He'll have to be brought in."

"May I ask why, Yariv?"

Cohen again appeared lost in thought. "I think in the end it'll be a job for the Sayeret Mat'kal," he said at length. The General Staff Reconnaissance Unit, the group responsible for the Entebbe rescue in nineteen-seventy-six and dozens of other successful missions against terrorists inside enemy territory, were the best Israel had to offer. He knew they would need to be.

"It's a gamble, Yariv."

"Everything is a gamble when one is facing what we are facing. It will require meticulous planning and someone in authority should be on the spot."

"Who do you mean?" Cohen looked at his comrade and best friend. There was a glint in the Ashkenazi Jew's eye as he said simply, "Me."

"Are you mad!"

"Why not?" said Cohen placing his arm around the little man's shoulders. "Arik Sharon did it in nineteen eighty-two.

He went to Beirut before the war.''

"But he was in disguise.''

Cohen burst into hearty laughter. "How can anyone hope to disguise that man,'' he guffawed.

It was one of the few times that Rahamim could remember his dour boss expressing levity. But he had to admit that the portly silver-haired former war hero and cabinet minister was a camouflage artist's nightmare.

"Anyway, Rahamim,'' the head of Israel's Secret Service said more sourly, "who will notice one more man with a limp in Beirut? That damned city is full of cripples, both mental and physical.''

"When, boss?'' asked Ben-Yaacov, his voice sharpened by apprehension.

"If Katri doesn't come up with anything before the end of February, we move in.''

"Isn't that cutting it a bit fine, Yariv?''

"Let's just pray the first Winds of Kedem will be late this year.''

CHAPTER THIRTEEN

It had been three weeks since her mother's funeral and Fatima Fadas was feeling the effects of her enforced separation from both the Israeli and Abu Mussa. From one she craved the touch and warmth of his naked body and from the other security and the materialistic things of life. She had cried for her mother as only daughters can. Despite her senility, the woman who had suffered so much in her life had given Fatima an opportunity to create for herself the chance of a better existence. It was as if the unintelligible wraith in the green baize armchair had willed her daughter to abandon her for hours every day. 'Go, my daughter,' she seemed to say, 'make for yourself a better life, far away from the poverty of our home and of our religion.'

"Did you say something, Fatima?"

The beautiful Shi'ite's eyes recovered their focus and turned towards the source of the question. Her chaperon, Jehan Husseini, seemed to hang like a wrinkled bat by the open window. A sudden gust of wind had caught her black chador and it seemed for a moment that she would become airborne in a paroxysm of flapping.

"No, nothing, Jehan," Fatima replied. "I was just thinking what a wonderfully sunny day it is outside." For three weeks she had been badgered by constant repetition of the obligations of a dutiful wife and how she should prepare herself for complete subjugation to her new husband. Fatima did not decry the old woman's single-mindedness. It was just that it felt more like being under house arrest than being chaperoned.

"Can't we just go out for a little walk, Jehan? I am desperate for some fresh air.''

"Your uncle said that you should be kept at home during the period of mourning,'' the bat replied.

"But enough time has passed,'' said Fatima desperately. "Please, perhaps we can go out for a walk together.''

Jehan Husseini, her sixty-five years etched cruelly into her wizened face, rubbed her hands nervously. She, too, was becoming tired of the unrelenting boredom of being cooped up in a small house with a young woman who refused to be moved by her ministrations.

"Very well,'' she sighed. "But only on one condition.''

"Yes, anything,'' Fatima replied excitedly.

"Like me, you must wear a veil at all times. No-one must recognise us.''

"Perhaps we could go for a walk along the spice market,'' Fatima suggested excitedly. During their conversations together, it had been apparent that the old woman knew nothing of the identity or whereabouts of her prospective bridegroom.

"Well, I don't know.''

"Arjuki, Jehan, Arjuki, please, I love the smells of the spices.'' The old woman hoisted her heavy black coat from the bamboo stand in the hall. "Minich,'' she said. "So be it. But only for an hour or two, mind.''

At that moment, Fatima Fadas wanted to hug and kiss her ugly old chaperon. She hoped against hope that she would have the opportunity of at least catching sight of her lover at Selim Jaafar's spice shop.

After only fifteen minutes' walk, they approached the Street of Spices. Fatima luxuriated in the hustle and bustle, the relentless traffic, both vehicular and pedestrian. It surprised her how much she had missed her freedom over the past few weeks.

The two Shi'a women progressed slowly down the street. A casual observer would have been hard put to differentiate between them, except maybe that one appeared more lighter of step than the other or that one had slightly hunched shoulders. Apart from this, an observer would have had to stand extremely close to inspect the only naked part of their anatomies. He may then have noticed that whilst one pair of eyes was bright and full of youth, the other was rheumy and lacked sparkle. But then, in the Shi'a quarter of Beirut, no man was likely to be attracted simply by a woman's eyes. The shapeless chador was designed to thwart a man's salacious desires, and to that end it was extremely effective.

Fatima's heart began to beat faster as she approached Selim Jaafar's store. "Come, Jehan, let us buy some helba and paprika," she suggested, "we are short of it at home and this store looks as good as any." She prayed the older woman would agree.

"As you wish, girl," said Jehan, "but we must not tarry."

Fatima could feel her palms begin to sweat as they walked through the store entrance. The heady aroma of the spices was overpowering. Almost at once, she saw the tall and handsome figure of the man who had de-flowered her. He was halfway up a ladder with what appeared to be a heavy sack on his shoulders.

"I'll just be a moment, ladies," he grunted, heaving the sack into a space alongside some others on the high shelf.

"Tfadalu, what can I do for you?" he asked, climbing down and clapping his hands to remove the dust. These women in their chadors always reminded him of Fatima.

The older woman spoke first as was her prerogative. "A kilo of paprika and a kilo of helba, sayidi," she said in a gagging voice.

"Oh, I'm sorry about all the dust in here, madam," David apologised, at the same time removing a scoop from his counter and digging first into a sack full of fenugreek.

Fatima could not remove her eyes from the man she loved. It was good that Jehan was a little in front of her, for if the chaperon had noticed her staring, she would surely have received a scolding. As a bride-to-be she knew she was not permitted to utter a single word to a male stranger lest her voice beguile him.

As David handed the spice packets to the squeaky-voiced woman, he felt a strange sensation that the taller one was surveying him with a perseverance unbecoming an ultra-religious female. It was only after the pair had moved towards the exit and the tall one had turned her head to cast him a parting glance that he understood.

"Fatima," he whispered hoarsely, his heart pounding within his breast.

For the next three days David Katri could not remove the encounter with Fatima Fadas from his mind. He knew the almond eyes were hers. No other religious Shi'a woman would have turned her head to look at him the way she did. It had to be her, he told himself. He wished that he had had at least one chance to speak to her, to hear the sweetness of her voice once more. There was so much and yet so little they knew about one another.

However, by the evening of the third day of their separation, a turn of events forced the memory of Fatima Fadas into the deeper recesses of his mind. David had just completed a particularly gruelling session of training with Mohammed Fawzi when his instructor took him to one side.

"I wanted to save the good news for last," the Arab said.

"I do not understand, ya Mohammed."

The Arab smiled and clenched his hands. He was obviously delighted. "You are being sent on a mission, sayidi,"

It was the first time the Arab had addressed him as 'sir', and for a moment David was stunned. Although the news was not unexpected, the realisation that his greatest test was imminent left his mouth parched.

"When?" he asked, barely able to disguise his trepidation.

"Tomorrow morning."

"Where will I be going?"

Fawzi smiled. "I personally do not know. My orders were to inform you to be at the airport by ten tomorrow morning. You are to wait by the Middle East Airlines check-in counter. A man named Ahmed Bashri will meet you there. He will have the tickets, money and everything else you will need. Just take a toothbrush. Apparently, you'll only be away for a day or two."

David breathed deeply. He made a mental note to contact the Mossad in Tel Aviv by whichever means possible once he knew his destination.

The safest bet would be to ring from a public call box from the European city itself. Some warning, however minimal, should be passed on to likely targets.

"There's just one thing," Fawzi cut short David's musings. "Bashri will be accompanying you to your rendezvous with the Leader. He's not the talkative type, either, so he'll probably be boring company. We all call him sour face."

The Israeli grimaced. Did Rashid Sedawi leave nothing to chance? He must try to learn more about this evil enigma before it was too late. Fawzi himself seemed in talkative mood although David knew he must take care not to arouse the Arab's suspicions.

"Shukkran, Mohammed," he enthused, slapping the moustacheoed instructor on the back. "It is no small measure due to you that I feel fit to set out on this great task for the glory of Allah." Fawzi grinned again, obviously delighted. His student was a likeable type and, besides, he knew the Ra'is was grooming Anwar Hindawi for greater things.

"I am good at what I do, Anwar, and I know my place is to serve our cause the best way that I can."

"So you have never been on a mission?"

"Tsk!" Mohammed clicked his teeth in the Arab custom of

expressing negation. "But over the past five years I have trained everyone who has."

"Including Rashid Sedawi?"

"Including the Ra'is."

Fawzi was obviously in awe of his leader and David decided it was about time to find out how much he knew about the man with the golden tooth. "I have not had long to get to know him. What is he like?"

"From the moment he succeeded on his first solo mission, I knew that he would eventually become our leader," replied Fawzi.

"When was that?" David prompted.

"Early last year. You know, the El Al plane bombing."

David whistled through his teeth. "That was a fantastic feat. No wonder he rose through the ranks so rapidly. But what of Mehdi Laham, is he not our true leader?"

"Our spiritual leader, yes. But he is old and unable to take an active part in our mission."

David knew he was rapidly approaching the moment of truth. It was obvious Fawzi was speaking openly and seriously. Yet by his sudden willingness to talk he was also expressing a naivete that made sense of why he had remained an underling in the Cell. "And what is our mission?" David asked, knowing that his question would have aroused incredulity in most intelligent men. However, he was sure by now that Mohammed Fawzi was simply a foot soldier.

"To destroy Israel and all enemies of Islam," Fawzi said, repeating the rhetoric that had been drummed into him. It did not occur to him that his questioner should be expected to know such a thing.

"But how can we hope to do that by such punitive attacks against lone targets?" David asked, hoping that Fawzi understood the question and that it might elicit the breakthrough for which he prayed.

"There are bigger things to come, my friend," Fawzi replied.

David's heart raced. Was this underling really party to the innermost secrets of the Cell?

"What do you mean, Mohammed?"

"I mean, ya Anwar, that most of our leaders have been sent abroad to prepare a major attack. Rumour has it that some are in Amman and others are somewhere in the Far East, although I can't think why."

Mohammed Fawzi's revelation was so lacking in guile that David believed him. And if what the instructor said was true, then those who might possibly possess knowledge of the bomb's whereabouts were spread far and wide over the continents of Europe and Asia. The Israeli knew with sinking heart that in the unlikely event Rashid Sedawi could be captured and made to talk, there were others who might be in a position to press the button. And, besides, time was running out fast.

"There is just one thing, sayidi," the Arab said, interrupting David's train of thought, "do not ask too many questions of the Ra'is."

"What do you mean?" asked David, fearing that Mohammed Fawzi was, after all, more clever than he appeared.

"Just do what he asks of you, sayidi. He will guide you this time, and the next time you will be on your own."

"Shukkran, my friend, shukkran," David said, gripping the smaller man's arm warmly. "I shall see you when I return, InshAllah." The Israeli used the more colloquial intonation of the appeal to God's will. It implied that His protection could be taken for granted.

"InshAllah," Fawzi repeated, taking David by the arm and leading him to a white Renault van. "I'm afraid I must blindfold you again, but I am sure this will be for the last time. Upon your return, you shall truly be one of us, and you will be invited to attend our special general meeting at the end of the month."

"What do you mean, Mohammed?"

"Apparently all the mystery of the previous months will be explained. There is a rumour that it will cause the power of Islam to be heard throughout the world. Our fighters are already very excited about the whole thing."

"Where will this meeting be held?" asked David, his mind racing.

"In one of the rooms underground. You've already seen part of our complex there, haven't you?"

"Yes, it is truly amazing. How many of us will be there?"

"Probably about one hundred. It is the first time I can remember a special general meeting being called since the early days.

"And when did you say this meeting will be, Mohammed?" asked David as a blindfold was slipped over his eyes.

"On the thirtieth day of Jumada Al-Ula at dusk."

The sudden blackness helped concentrate Katri's mind on converting the date on the Muslim calendar to the Gregorian. The date was February the twenty-seventh, less than a month hence and possibly a week or two prior to the start of the shurqiya season. The Israeli knew he would have no time to make contact with Abu Mussa's envoy prior to his departure. He would just have to take a chance and call the Maronite direct from a public telephone booth that evening. The details of his mission were scant but they were all he had.

On the morning that David Katri was flying to Europe, Yariv Cohen was once again ensconced in the Prime Minister's office. The difference this time was that besides the Premier and the Defence Minister, the Chief of Staff had also been invited. Since receiving the coded message from Abu Mussa the previous day, the head of the Mossad had wrestled with two major dilemmas. The first was whether or not to inform the Armed Forces' most senior man of the nuclear threat against Israel. The second was whether or not to inform all three men that, in order to safeguard his mission, one Israeli was being sanctioned to perpetrate an act of terrorism against another or others. Yariv Cohen knew that the decision was his and his alone; that should his duplicity ever be revealed, then it would mean not only the end of his career, but also that he would be hounded by his own people until his dying day.

"Nu, Yariv?" the Prime Minister asked tetchily. "We are waiting. What do you suggest?"

Cohen shuffled the papers in front of him nervously. "As I have told you, gentlemen," he said at length, "I believe that in the end we may have to choose our moment to wipe out these terrorists while attempting to catch their leaders alive. However, I believe the fewer people who know the real reason for the raid, the better. A wagging tongue can undo all our efforts, although this is in no way meant to reflect on Yehuda Bar-Ilan."

The Defence Minister coughed. The chief of staff was his man and he felt duly obliged to protect the general's integrity. "I think it only right that Yehuda should be made fully aware of the facts," he said firmly.

Cohen looked at the Prime Minister. He could sense that, like himself, the nation's leader was groaning under the heavy burden that had been forced upon him. But he trusted the man to make the correct decision.

"Moshe," the premier patted the hand of the man sitting alongside him, "I appreciate your concern, but I think Yariv is right. This is a special case. We cannot afford even the slightest leak. Even we can make mistakes and it takes only a single slip of the tongue."

Cohen looked at the younger man, expecting a response. There was none, just a shrug of the shoulders. He looked again at the Prime Minister. "Perhaps, with your permission, sir, we may now invite Yehuda to join us." The grey-haired man rubbed his eyes wearily and then pressed the intercom on his desk. "Ruth, kindly send in Yehuda."

Ruth Segal, the Prime Minister's personal secretary, was on firstname terms with every politician in the country and many more personalities besides. She had seen chiefs of staff come and go, but there was no doubting that Yehuda Bar-Ilan was the most handsome. He was blond and tanned and looked much younger than his fifty years.

"You heard that, Yehuda," she smiled, "you can go in now."

Bar-Ilan stretched his large frame and rubbed his posterior. "I can't feel my tuchus I've been waiting so long," he joked.

Ruth Segal laughed with him but not at him. His paratrooper's beret and the yellow ribbon of the Ot Ha'Gvura on his tunic indicated that the man was anything but frivolous. The recipient of his country's highest award for valour, Yehuda Bar-Ilan was a household name in Israel even before his promotion to general and appointment as Chief of Staff. In a country which boasted a citizen army, the head of the Israel Defence Forces was highly respected and in some cases even revered.

"Good morning, gentlemen," he beamed. A career officer and a sabra, the informality of his approach was accepted with equanimity by the politicians. They, too, had been soldiers once, and the army thrived on informal discipline it created in an ordinary soldier; a feeling that he was important and a willingness to accept responsibility, especially when the chips were down. Bar-Ilan judged by the glum faces that a serious matter was to be discussed. His attitude changed to suit the occasion.

"Sit down, Yehuda," the Prime Minister said. "You know that Yariv Cohen arranged this meeting, so you won't be surprised to see him here."

Bar-Ilan nodded to the boss of the Mossad, removed his red beret and sat down.

"If I may begin, adoni rosh ha'memshelah," said Cohen more formally. He was, after all, Polish-born and of the old school.

"Bevakashah," the Prime Minister nodded.

The man with the scarred lip tapped a pencil on the table before relating to Bar-Ilan the story of how the Mossad had infiltrated the terror group responsible for the El Al disaster and that it had been decided to send a task force of commandos into Beirut to wipe it out.

Yariv Cohen revealed the identity of his man in Beirut but did not mention the task Katri had been allotted by Rashid Sedawi. He did, however, inform the Chief of Staff of details which the two other men in the room already knew: that the Islamic Jihad Fundamentalist Cell was planning another terror raid and that the Mossad's head of European Section had informed its agents to exercise special care.

Yehuda Bar-Ilan listened intently, although at times his mind drifted back to the raid on Entebbe and other anti-terrorist operations in which he had participated. He envied the younger man who would be chosen to lead this current mission.

Israel's top soldier waited patiently for Yariv Cohen to finish his dissertation. There were two vital details the Mossad chief had left unmentioned.

"When and where?" asked Bar-Ilan.

"The answer to your first question, Yehuda, is at the end of February, and the answer to your second is that I don't yet know."

"You are joking, surely?"

"I'm afraid I'm not," replied Cohen, refusing to allow himself to be upset by the military man's outburst. He realised that Yehuda Bar-Ilan had every reason to be incredulous. "I expect to have the exact location of the terrorist headquarters very shortly. We know that it is in an underground complex beneath some derelict buildings in the Shi'ite sector of southern Beirut."

"But that could be anywhere," the general protested loudly. "And, anyway, just under four weeks to prepare is not long enough."

"You did it at Entebbe in less time," Cohen replied coldly.

"Beirut is a hornet's nest," Bar-Ilan countered. "We are not dealing with kushim there."

Cohen dismissed the soldier's derisory attitude towards negroes. "Nevertheless, Yehuda, the Ugandans were an unknown quantity. They might have surprised us."

The blond man's cheeks flushed with anger. "And why, may I ask, has there to be such a rush?"

Cohen knew the question would arise eventually. He had discussed various options with the Prime Minister. "Because, Yehuda, those bastards are planning a whole series of terror attacks beginning early in March. Hundreds may die in Israel and all over Europe if we do not act quickly." As he finished speaking, Cohen noticed the Defence Minister's raised eyebrows.

"Impossible," the general huffed.

The Prime Minister chose this moment to intervene. He knew that once everyone had let off a little steam, they could get down to the serious business of saving the nation.

"Yehuda," he said in a conciliatory tone, "you of all people know that this is the Land of Miracles. Is this one too much to ask for?"

Bar-Ilan was forced to smile. The old bastard certainly knew how to lay on the charm. No wonder he had succeeded in controlling the meddling religious parties in the government. "Beseder," the general replied, "let's get on with the umpteenth miracle."

"Good, Yehuda," said the Prime Minister, relieved, "we would like your suggestion as to which commando we should use."

"I think this is a job for Sayeret Mat'kal, sir."

Cohen nodded. He, too, believed the Reconnaissance Unit attached to the General Staff was probably the best for the main job, although in an operation of this kind there would have to be a joint effort.

"I agree with Yehuda, Prime Minister," he said quickly, "but by necessity this will have to be a combined services operation."

"What do you mean, Yariv?" asked the Defence Minister.

"Do you all remember our raid against the PLO on the ninth of April, nineteen seventy-three?"

The three men nodded. The event was etched into the annals of the elite forces that had begun with the British-sponsored Special Night Squads commanded by Orde Wingate prior to the Second World War and had continued with the Haganah and Palmach during the War of Independence and, later, Entebbe. Following the 1972 Munich Olympics massacre of Israeli athletes, both the Mossad and the Army became obsessed with revenge against the terrorists of Black September.

In the early hours of the morning of April the ninth, six dinghies loaded with equipment and more than thirty reconnaissance paratroopers landed at a secluded beach in Beirut. They were met by a team of Israeli naval commandos which had secured the beach landing area, and a group of Mossad agents who had prepared the way for the assault on the homes of three high-ranking officers in Black September.

The paratroop commandos, dressed in civilian clothes, were driven to their targets by the Mossad agents in specially rented cars. One group made towards a luxury apartment block where they eliminated the PLO sentries and also the three slumbering terrorist leaders in their beds. At the same time, a second group of paratroopers attacked the headquarters of the Democratic Front for the Liberation of Palestine and killed scores of terrorists. A third group proceeded to a 'bomb factory' used by Black September and blew it sky-high. Air Force helicopters hovered over the area to remove the Israeli wounded while those unhurt made their way back to the beach, where they climbed aboard the dinghies to return to navy missile boats waiting offshore.

Yariv Cohen paused to allow his colleagues time to recall the event. Again he rapped his pencil nervously on the table. "I think," he said, "the same sort of operation is called for again, although this time it's going to be much harder."

Cohen, noting the puzzled looks of his audience, ploughed straight on. "This time, gentlemen, we may have to carry out the raid just after dusk, when Beirut will still be awake."

"Isn't that suicidal, Yariv?" the Prime Minister asked, concern etched into his pallid face.

"A lot will depend on how fast we can evacuate the scene, sir. If we can manage to blow up their underground ammunition dump, it will keep the civil authorities busy for hours. However, our main task is to capture the leaders of the Cell alive and, of course, secure the safety of our agent inside the group."

"My God," Bar-Ilan exploded, "how on earth are we going to achieve that with all the mayhem going on?"

Cohen could understand the general's consternation. It was indeed a tall order.

"The Cell is due to hold a special meeting at its headquarters at the end of this month, February the twenty-seventh to be precise. Apparently, the leaders, a mullah by the name of Mehdi Laham and Rashid Sedawi, their most dangerous man, will outline their plans for the forthcoming orgy of terrorism."

"Are there any photographs?" asked Bar-Ilan, his voice still heavy with scepticism.

"No, not yet," relied Cohen. "But the mullah has a long white beard and, anyway, he'll be dressed as a cleric. Sedawi will present more of a problem."

The Mossad chief scratched his head with the pencil before continuing. "The best I can think of is that our man on the spot positions himself near Sedawi at the start of the raid. He'll try to tackle the Arab himself, at the same time sticking a green luminescent sticker on the Shi'ite's back. This way, should he fall, you'll be able to keep our target in sight." Cohen sighed. He could see the incredulity on their faces. It was comic-strip stuff.

"As at Entebbe and elsewhere," he went on quickly, "our men also wore luminous markings to lessen the chances of confusion." He then looked at the general and withdrew a colour portrait of David Katri from the file in front of him. "Yehuda, here is a photograph of our agent. Make sure all your men memorize his face. He'll also be supplied with the same identity markings you will use yourselves."

The uniformed man leaned forward across the table and took the photograph. "And who, may I ask, is going to deliver an identity sash to your man?"

"I will."

"But that's unheard of for the head of the Mossad to get involved personally."

"Are you sure it's necessary, Yariv," the Prime Minister asked softly.

"Yes, I'm afraid that given the time available, it will be much easier for me to organise things on the ground to prepare the way for the attack. I'd like to take six of my own men with me to help set everything up."

"We'll, if you're going, I'm going," said Bar-Ilan petulantly.

"I see no reason why you should not, although I think it would be best if you ran the military side of the operation from the missile boat. There aren't many tall blond men in Lebanon, maybe among the Maronites, but certainly not among the Shi'ites. And that leads me on to another point...."

"And what's that?" asked Bar-Ilan stiffly.

"I want you to choose your men carefully. I want only those members of the General Staff Commando whose parents are from Arab lands. To all intents and purposes, they must look like Arabs and speak Arabic. I am sorry, I must insist on this."

"But that cuts my selection possibilities by eighty percent."

"I'm sure you will choose the right people, Yehuda," the Defence Minister cut in.

Bar-Ilan, seeing that his own immediate superior concurred with the Pole, shrugged his shoulders. "I've no more objections. Let's go over what is known again."

David Katri felt the tension ripple through him as the Middle East Airlines Boeing 727 touched down at Wien Schwechat. The morning flight out of Beirut had already been delayed three hours due to a heavy fall of overnight snow in the Austrian capital.

The Israeli glanced at his watch and peered out at the ploughs busily plying their way to and fro along the perimeter of the runway. It was already nearly three in the afternoon local time and he prayed that the roads into town were clear. The man beside him had been like a limpet and had done nothing to belie Mohammed Fawzi's description of him. Ahmed Bashri might just as well have been a deaf mute. The sour face, restricting itself to monosyllables, had parried all David's attempts to instigate conversation. The man, short and squat, had approached him at the MEA check-in counter at Beirut airport. After a curt greeting, the Arab had handed him a brown packet. Among the contents were the flight ticket to his destination and another ticket, for a British Airways flight from the Austrian capital to London Heathrow booked for the following evening. Also included was a Spanish passport bearing a photograph David had provided when he had first jointed the Cell. The passport was made out to the name of Manuel Santilana.

Apart from the travel documents, there were five thousand Austrian schillings and three hundred pounds sterling, a map of Vienna and a tourist leaflet about the Danube Tower. The words 'Four p.m.' had been written on the front of the leaflet. In a rare moment of locquacity, Bashri had explained that they were expected to rendezvous with Sedawi at that time on the observation platform of the Donauturm.

Within a quarter of an hour the two men, neither of them carrying baggage, had passed through passport control. Bashri had allowed David to take the lead and it was clear to the Israeli that the man was observing him closely. Perspiring under his heavy clothing despite the bitterly cold wind outside the airport complex, Katri led his companion quickly towards the nearest taxi rank.

"We want to get to the Danube Tower" he shouted at the driver, who was sitting in his Mercedes with the window closed. He hoped the man spoke English.

"Bitte?" the man asked, at the same time lowering his window.

David gasped as a particularly icy blast of air took his breath away. "We want to get to the, er, Donauturm."

"It is okay, meine Herren, I speak well English. Please to get in."

Bashri opened the rear door and motioned David to enter. The Arab then climbed in and slammed the door hard.

"Eh, be careful, mein herr, I only last week bought her."

Bashri said nothing, but David noted the hatred in his eyes.

"Now, where is it you want to go, Der Donauturm?"

"Yes, and as quickly as possible."

"Ach, ja," the driver said, "you can see the whole of Vienna from there. Maybe you two have dates with our beautiful girls in the restaurant at the top."

David glared at the ruddy upper cheeks and the wrinkled eyes surveying him in the mirror. He wished the man would get a move on. "Yes, you are quite right." he replied. "Please hurry up. We do not want to keep the ladies waiting."

"Jawohl!" And with this, the Mercedes roared away. Within a few minutes they were already on the Ostautobahn and David noted with relief that the traffic appeared to be running smoothly.

"How long should it take us?" he asked the driver, at the same time glancing at his watch. It was already half past three. It was going to be a close run thing.

"On a normal day, I can do it in under fifteen minutes. But you never know with new snow. It is a question of luck."

David's anxiety grew as the taxi turned right at the Sudost-tangente Wien. The traffic was getting heavier even though they were driving away from the city centre. The Israeli looked at his map. They could either drive straight over the Danube and then turn left or cross the river higher up and make straight for the Donauturm.

As the Mercedes approached the Handelskai junction, the traffic was already proceeding at a snail's pace.

"Can't you do anything, driver?" shouted David, exasperated at having to compete with the taxi's radio.

"Maybe we'll try along the Handelskai," the blue eyes in the mirror replied. And with this the Mercedes veered off to the right before curving left along the west bank of the Danube. "You are lucky, meine Herren," the driver said suddenly, his voice booming as he switched off the radio.

"What do you mean?"

"They just announced that there has been an accident on the Praterbrucke crossing. If we had carried straight on, you two would not see your girl friends until tomorrow." With this, the Austrian burst into hearty laughter.

David forced himself to smile. The driver could make all the jokes he wanted as long as he got them to the Danube Tower before four. As he peered out of the window he could see that the snow had ceased and the setting sun was making a forlorn effort to remind the Viennese of its existence. It glinted from the windows of the collection of layer-cake buildings David knew to be the United Nations complex on the far side of the river. UNO-City was across the Donaupark from the Danube Tower. They should be there within minutes.

The Mercedes seemed to fly over the Brigittenauer Brucke and pulled up alongside the giant needle and its revolving restaurants at exactly five minutes to four. David paid the driver quickly and he and Bashri took one of the express elevators to the one hundred and fifty metre-high lookout terrace, which from the bottom had resembled the shape of a giant Wankel rotary engine.

The Israeli had little time to assemble his thoughts as the elevator raced up inside the central column. Within forty seconds they had reached the terrace. At first, David thought Bashri had got his instructions wrong. The observation platform appeared bereft of sightseers.

David shuddered as the wind cut through him mercilessly. Pulling his fur hat closer about his ears, he began to circle the giant central cylinder. Suddenly, he saw two men in fur coats gazing out over Vienna and its surroundings. He knew instinctively that one of them was Rashid Sedawi. The Lebanese turned as he approached.

"Ah, my good friend Anwar," the gold tooth gleamed. "Ahalan wa'sahalan. Vienna is such a beautiful city, don't you think?"

"Ahalan Tik, Ra'is," replied David. "I hope I have not kept you waiting long."

"Let us say that I like a man who is punctual," said Sedawi, glancing at his watch. It was exactly four. "And you are punctual, Anwar."

The Israeli was puzzled. Sedawi was addressing him in the

singular, as if he had arrived unaccompanied. Instinctively, the Israeli glanced over his shoulder. He was just in time to glimpse a short squat figure disappear around the concrete cylinder.

"Ahmed has other things to do,"said Sedawi curtly.

David averted his leader's steely gaze and looked at the other man present. Slightly taller than Sedawi, he was clean-shaven and had rather a large mole just above the right side of his lips.

"May I introduce Mustapha Bedawi,"said the Ra'is more courteously. "He has been our agent in Vienna for many months."

David stretched out his hand. Bedawi, obviously in awe of his leader, glanced at Sedawi before taking it.

"The view is beautiful, is it not,"Sedawi went on, turning once again to face the white panorama around them. "There,"he pointed, "you can see the foothills of the Alps and Hungarian lowlands. Only a short while ago you could not see anything due to the blizzards."

As David gazed at the milky expanse, he suddenly realised the reason for his being with the two Arabs. He had been so concerned at turning up on time that he had forgotten the task he was now to be set. For a moment he felt his knees weaken. "It is indeed magnificent, Ra'is," he said clapping his body with his arms to increase circulation.

"You are right, Anwar," said Sedawi, turning once again to face the taller man, "it is cold up here and there is work to be done down there. Come let us go."

Dusk was already settling in by the time the three men reached a grey Audi parked nearby. Sedawi got into the driver's seat and his two passengers sat in the rear. Within a minute, the car was already crossing the Brigittenauer Brucke on its way to Handelskai.

The three men were silent as the car turned right at Lasalle Strasse, veering left to circumvent the Praterstern. The Audi was just on the edges of the first and third districts when Sedawi pulled to a halt. Mustapha Bedawi alighted from the vehicle and bade them farewell.

"He has other important work to do," Sedawi said by way of explanation.

"He will meet up with us again in Beirut in a few days."

David felt the tension rise within him again. He had to know what was expected of him. The suspense all but consumed him. "May I ask, ya Rashid, what my mission is to be?" he ventured. The evil beady eyes surveyed him in the mirror.

"Anwar, my friend," the Shi'ite replied almost haughtily, "you have the honour of disposing of the Mossad's top agent in Central Europe."

Katri's stomach muscles tightened. So that was it. He was being asked to murder not only one of his own countrymen, but also a fellow agent. The supreme irony. The eyes in the mirror once again demanded a reaction.

"It shall indeed be an honour to strike such a blow for our faith," said David in a voice he tried to make sound as convincing as possible. His mind was in turmoil. How could he do this thing, he asked himself, only to be answered by Yariv Cohen's admonition that millions would die should he not do as Sedawi ordered. An old Hebrew saying flashed through his mind: 'Every man is a world in himself'. To take one life was just as heinous as slaughtering a thousand.

Lost in a bewildering kaleidoscope of emotion, David failed to notice that the Audi had drawn to a halt and that Sedawi had switched off the engine. It was almost dark.

"Anwar, we are here," Rashid Sedawi repeated. He could understand his ward's apprehension. He, too, had felt the same way on his first mission. "I shall enter the third building on the right. In that first street on the right over there. It is number twenty-one and you should proceed in the lift to the third floor. Knock three times on the door of apartment number twelve. Give me five minutes before you make your move. Put your briefcase in the boot and leave the car doors unlocked. Is that clear?''

"Yes, sir," David replied weakly, looking at his watch.

During the next few minutes the Israeli tried to drive from his mind all thought of what he was about to do. Instead, he surveyed the street with its collection of baroque apartment and office blocks. The snow was at least four inches deep. The night was clear and the street lighting barely adequate. It appeared he would be required to make the hit in relative darkness. In a way he was thankful. With any luck he would not have to suffer the agony of seeing the face of his fellow agent. The masks of Beirut flooded his mind.

David looked at his watch again. Five minutes had already elapsed. He donned his fur hat, raised the collar of his coat and climbed out of the Audi. Following Sedawi's instructions, he soon found himself on the third floor of a musty apartment building. Everything about the place was ancient, including the lift. There was just enough light for him to make out the number twelve in metal on the first door to his right. He knocked three times.

The door was opened by Sedawi. The whiteness of all but one of his teeth seemed to jump at David in the dark. By the window, the Israeli could barely make out the silhouette of tripod and rifle. The high-ceilinged room was completely bare.

"Follow me," Sedawi ordered. "We have rented the whole building, so you need not worry about disturbing anyone."

David followed the Arab to the window, which was closed. The room was freezing and Katri shivered despite his heavy clothing.

"Our man is usually last out of his office," said Sedawi crouching alongside the rifle. "He usually locks the door of the building himself. Here, look through this."

David took the image intensifying viewer and peered in the general direction in which Sedawi was pointing.

"There," the Arab said, "just before the third light along, across the street. Can you see the number ten on the door? It's even lit up for us."

The distance was only some sixty metres or so and the powerful Italian Officina Galileo viewer quickly brought the door into focus. David felt he could almost touch it.

"Now try lining it up with my baby," said Sedawi, touching David gently on the shoulder.

Katri handed the Arab the viewer, removed his coat and gloves and took up a kneeling position behind the Steyr. He adjusted the extended bipod to his own shoulder height and focused the telescopic sight. In normal light, the one point five unity magnification was easily enough to pick out a woodworm hole in the door. At this relatively short range the target would present no trouble at all, although there was some distortion caused by the still closed window.

"In about half an hour, some people will start leaving that office block," said Sedawi. "We will then open the window slightly and you will take up your position again. I will let you know when he appears."

David felt the question burn within him. He had not asked Sedawi the name of the man he was about to destroy and he did not intend to. Should the Arab volunteer the information, then so be it. It might be any of the men with whom he had trained. although he considered it more likely that the man was an experienced Mossad veteran who had been in Vienna many years. He had not been of sufficient rank within the organisation to be party to such information and for that he was now truly grateful. Anyway, he recalled Mohammed Fawzi's advice not to ask Sedawi too many questions and decided silence was the best policy.

"You will have at least five or six seconds to draw a bead on him while he locks up the premises," the Shi'ite went on. "Once we have completed our mission, we will change to another of our cars parked about half a kilometre away in the direction of the airport. Here is a British Airways ticket for the seven-fifteen flight to London. Stay at the Post House hotel overnight and book a return Middle East Airlines flight to Beirut for the following morning. I shall return via Paris.''

"What about the Steyr?" David asked, almost involuntarily.

"I shall leave it here, under the floorboards. It is as good a place as any to bury it."

"What do you mean?"

"I won't be needing it any more. It is old and has seen better days."

David thought the admission strange from the same man who had earlier extolled the Steyr's virtues and had labelled it his 'baby'. The phrase 'I won't be needing it any more' stuck in the Israeli's mind. Katri knew it had something to do with the bomb.

"See," said the Arab, deftly changing the subject, "people are just beginning to leave their offices. The traffic will build up, although within half an hour everything will be quiet again. The main rush will be over and our man will leave his place of work. He usually locks up at around half past five to a quarter to six."

"That does not leave us long to get to the airport, Ra'is."

"It should be long enough. The autobahns are pretty fast here."

David shivered. The Shi'ite was still dressed in his heavy fur coat, while he himself was protected from the cold only by a thick woollen sweater.

"Oh, I am sorry, sahbi," said Sedawi apologetically. "I forgot that Mustapha had got hold of a small electric heater for us to use. I think it is in the kitchen. I will get it."

The warm flow of the bar heater chased away the ice in David's muscles. Almost perversely, he felt an insidious cosiness. It seemed to make the heinous crime he was about

275

to commit more acceptable.

"Can't we be seen from here?" he asked the shadow beside him, his tone conspiratorial.

"You will notice, my friend, that the nearest street lamp to us is not working. It was put out of action a few hours ago. The Vienna City Council may be thorough, but it usually takes them a day or two to respond."

Did the man leave nothing to chance, David asked himself. He had the distinct feeling that Sedawi would always prove too clever for him, that the Shi'ite would never allow himself to be trapped into revealing anything of importance.

"There!" Sedawi exclaimed suddenly. "His secretary is leaving. She never works overtime. It won't be long now. Take up your position."

With that, the Arab opened the window just enough for the strange configuration of the barrel and its silencer to poke through.

David's heart pounded. The fine mist of his breathing quickened. He tried to believe that it was all part of a bad dream, but the lethal combination of wood and metal that felt so heavy in his hands told him otherwise.

"Zero in on the secretary's head but don't fire," ordered Sedawi. "Quickly!"

The girl obligingly stood still in the doorway for a few seconds before making her way further down the street. It proved just long enough for David to focus on her head. The poor light affected the sharpness of the image but not its magnitude. David wondered why he was not allowed to use the optronic night vision equipment also, although at a range of sixty metres he could hardly miss, even with an ordinary sight.

"Now you may relax a little," said Sedawi, still peering through his viewer, "But be ready to take up your position again quickly when I say the word."

After about five minutes David noticed that pedestrian and

vehicular traffic in the street had tapered off. His angle of trajectory was such that cars did not present any problem. However, there was always danger that a passerby could foul things up.

"Now!" Sedawi barked suddenly. "He's just opening the door."

By the time David had aligned his weapon once more, his target was facing away from him and was in the process of locking the door. The man wore a fur hat and a scarf was wrapped tightly around his neck. The centre of the cross hairs of the sight zeroed on a spot just above the top edge of the scarf and just below the rim of the hat.

David once again felt emotion welling inside him. This was crazy. He was about to murder one of his own people. "For God's sake don't turn around," he pleaded silently. "I never want to see your face."

"Fire!" shrieked Sedawi.

In another part of the city, the first district near the Alte Rathaus to be precise, a casual observer might have been impressed by the tall and beautiful blonde woman striding along the street. The woman possessed the aristocratic gait of one who had just purchased a new winter wardrobe and who knew she looked extremely good in it.

Frau Inge Muller glanced at her watch as she took the lift to the third floor. It was already six-thirty and Ephraim should be home by now. Her mother was looking after the children, as she did two or three evenings a week, thus giving her more time to spend with her lover. It had taken all her skill to convince the Israeli that she was still worthwhile to have around. They had argued bitterly over her revelation that she was pregnant, but she had fed him some false information from the

Atomic Energy Authority and his attitude towards her had softened. However, she knew it was only a matter of a few weeks before she would be constrained to break off their relationship. Pregnancy could not be faked for long.

As she approached his apartment, she noticed the door slightly ajar. It was strange because Ephraim had always had a thing about leaving doors open.

"Ephraim," she called out softly, at the same time prodding the door with her toe. She called out again and once more was met by total silence. She entered the hall and closed the door behind her.

"Ephraim, liebling, where are you?"

"Come in here, Frau Muller," a strange yet vaguely familiar voice ordered suddenly.

Her heart skipped a beat as she entered the salon. She gasped as she saw the Arab sitting in an armchair facing her.

"Mein Gott! What are you doing here?"

"Bitte," the Arab smiled, pointing to the armchair opposite him.

Frau Inge Muller sat down gingerly. "Where is Ephraim?" she asked, a first note of panic entering her voice.

"You no longer need concern yourself with him, Frau Muller."

"What do you mean?"

The bull-necked man smiled again. "Let us say that he has been transferred."

The blonde Austrian shuddered. She suddenly realised how naive she had been. She had become involved in more than simply industrial espionage. She was a participant in a game of death between bitter enemies. What were Jews and Arabs to her? They had done nothing but use her.

"What about the rest of my money?" she asked hesitantly, pushing from her mind the unthinkable but feeling the tell-tale dampness of fear between her legs. "I have served you well."

"Indeed, you have served us well, Frau Muller," the bull-necked man replied, at the same time sliding his right hand towards the bulge inside his coat. "And we always repay our debts."

It was already eight in the evening in the Tel Aviv suburb of Tzahala when one of its residents received an urgent call from Mossad headquarters. Yariv Cohen's grip tightened on the receiver. There had to be something wrong. David Katri might have been capable of executing a fellow Israeli, a stranger, but not his best friend. Of all the scores of Mossad agents throughout Europe, Arik Ben-Ami had had to be the target. It was either sheer coincidence or, worse still, the Cell had rumbled Katri. This still left unanswered the question of how he had pulled the trigger, if at all. The possible explanations were endless, and for the first time in his life Yariv Cohen felt helpless. At best he had caused a man to murder his best friend in order to safeguard his mission. At worst, Israel was now at the total mercy of one of its cleverest and most intractable foes.

"Are you still there, sir," asked a voice at the other end of the line.

"Mea culpa," Cohen mumbled.

"I'm sorry, sir. Could you repeat that?"

Cohen took a deep breath. He had to pull himself together quickly. He could not undo the events in Vienna.

"Shlomo, listen very carefully," he said firmly. "I want a meeting with the editors of all our news media within the hour at the Kirya. They know the form."

"What about those who will have to come from Jerusalem, sir?"

"We'll give them an extra half hour to get here. At this time of night the traffic is light and it should take them only forty minutes to reach Tel Aviv," replied Cohen, thankful that only the State-run television and radio services and the Jerusalem Post operated out of the nation's capital.

"And Shlomo—"

"Yes, sir."

"Arrange a meeting for tomorrow morning with all departmental heads, the Chief of Staff and the heads of the Navy and Air Force. Nine o'clock will do fine."

"Yes, sir."

Cohen replaced the receiver, thankful at least that his wife was attending a fashion show at the Hilton. Although she was used to his unorthodox hours, it always pained him to abandon her on the few evenings they managed to share together at home. However, Nehama was nothing if not resilient, although if she had known the location of her husband's next visit abroad it might have stretched her loyalty to the limits.

The chimes of the front door bell suddenly disturbed his train of thought. He guessed that it might be his next door neighbour and closest friend.

"Shalom, Rahamim," the Mossad chief said, opening the door. "I take it you've been informed."

Rahamim Ben-Yaacov looked drained. The Yemenite's olive skin had taken on the appearance of parchment, the pain etched into the contours of his face.

"You'd better come in," Cohen sighed, placing his arm gently around his friend's shoulders.

"We murdered Arik," the Yemenite croaked. "Why did it have to be him?"

"We honestly did not know what or whom the target would be, you know that," Cohen replied, at the same time crossing towards a drinks cabinet in the lounge. Like most Israelis, he kept it full but drank rarely. "Arak, Rahamim?"

The Yemenite took the glass of colourless anise and downed it in one gulp. He looked at his boss balefully. "I can't believe that Katri did it. He would never knowingly murder Ben-Ami, I don't care how many lives were at stake. Perhaps we should have pulled Arik out."

"And prejudice the whole mission before it could have a chance to succeed? Then Sedawi would definitely have smelled a rat."

The Yemenite sighed. "I suppose you're right. The target could have been anyone, anywhere. Nevertheless, it seems too much of a coincidence to me."

"We have no choice, Rahamim. Until we get confirmation to the contrary, we must assume that Katri is continuing to pursue his mission."

"You know, it wouldn't have been so bad if they hadn't been best friends. To all intents they were brothers," the Yemenite said, holding out his glass for a refill.

"I know. I saw the file. I seem to have been inextricably tied in with Katri's welfare ever since he arrived in this country."

Ben-Yaacov crossed to an armchair and sat down. "Did you know they fought in the same tank unit in seventy-three?"

"Yes, I did," Cohen replied, glancing at his watch.

"But did you know that Ben-Ami saved Katri's life?"

Visibly shaken, Cohen moved back to the drinks cabinet and poured himself a large whisky. "I didn't know that, Rahamim," he said quietly, "I don't recall it being in their files."

"Ben-Ami pulled Katri from a burning tank on the Golan," the Yemenite went on. "Ordinarily, Arik would have won a medal, but apparently there was no-one left alive to witness it and Katri himself was unconscious. Anyway, neither of them bothered to report the incident."

Cohen sighed. Suddenly he felt the sadness of Job. The life of every Israeli was in his hands and yet that responsibility seemed minimised by the sacrifice of two of the nation's bravest men. One was dead and the other, assuming he had somehow been responsible, might just as well be. The Mossad chief looked again at his watch. It was time he made tracks for the Kirya. "Come, Rahamim. We'll discuss matters further on the way to the Kirya. I've called a meeting with the media for nine o'clock."

But Yariv Cohen did not speak further until he turned his Volvo into Derekh Haifa.

"From the reports I've received, Arik's face was unidentifiable," he said suddenly, the revelation shocking his companion.

"In a way, that may prove to be a godsend if he kept strictly to our rules and did not keep photographs of himself or his family."

"What about his passport?"

"Again, I hope he followed the rules and stowed it in a safety deposit box somewhere, preferably at the airport."

"You're supposing an awful lot, Yariv."

"I know," said Cohen, lifting his left hand from the steering wheel and rubbing his chin pensively, "supposition is all we seem to have to go on at the moment."

Ben-Yaacov looked at his boss as the Volvo sped towards its destination. The man seemed to have aged considerably in the last hour. "Why the media, Yariv?" he said at length.

"We need them. If by chance they should get a picture of Ben-Ami from somewhere, we'll have to stop them from using it. I'll slap an Official Secrets order on them."

"But they'll have to use some kind of photograph or the public will smell something fishy."

Cohen smiled for the first time since he had received the telephone call.

"I'll arrange for them to be issued with a suitably blurred photograph of the deceased and an equally suitable biography."

"And they'll issue our denial that Epstein was one of our agents."

"Of course."

"Do you think they'll bite the bullet?"

Cohen paused before answering. "They have to Rahamim. And, it wouldn't be the first time they've cooperated."

Both men knew that Israel's media had always cooperated in matters of national security. There was Entebbe, the raid on the Iraqi nuclear reactor and many smaller anti-terrorist actions. But the other major occasion on which the media had deliberately published or broadcast lies was in the early stages of the Yom Kippur War. Things were going so badly at first that the then Chief of Staff, Moshe Dayan, had constrained them not to publish or broadcast the truth about the debacle lest it damage the nation's morale irreparably. Instead, the impression was given deliberately that Israel was coping well with the two-pronged Egyptian and Syrian attack.

"Couldn't we just apply censorship?" the Yemenite asked, recalling the myriad occasions on which white spaces had appeared in the press.

"No. That would imply that the dead man was indeed our agent. This time we have to get their cooperation to release a fictitious account of Ephraim Epstein. They'll be told it is a matter of national security. They have no choice."

"But what about Ben-Ami's family? How will they be told?"

"They won't."

"I don't understand."

Cohen again glanced at his watch before replying. "In two months' time they'll get a report that their son is dead, burned to death in a fire or lost overboard while on a Mediterranean cruise. It should not be hard to come up with something."

"You've thought of everything, haven't you."

It was the first time Yariv Cohen recalled his friend ever expressing cynicism. It was not the usual style of Israelis of Yemenite origin.

"Don't ever forget what is at stake here, Rahamim," the Ashkenazi Jew sighed.

CHAPTER FOURTEEN

David Katri mulled over the events of the previous few hours again and again. Fortunately, the British Airways flight to Heathrow was half empty and he could choose a window seat to himself. He stared out at the blackness, living and re-living the moment that he knew would haunt him for the rest of his life.

He recalled a television documentary he had seen in which cameramen described how photographing war through a lens invariably gave them a sense of being divorced from the danger around them. There was the classic scene of the television news cameraman in Chile who had filmed his own death. Lulled into a false sense of security by the apparatus through which he was peering the man had continued filming a truck-load of troops, unaware that one of them was pointing a rifle at him. The tell-tale pinprick of light of the rifle being fired remained an image David could not forget. Almost instantaneously, the scene being filmed began to meander crazily until there was blackness. And death. David gripped his temples and swallowed hard to fight back the nausea. The incessant hum of the aircraft seemed to reach a crescendo. Like that soldier, he, too, had not differentiated between good and evil. The target was big and the target was easy. And, as with the cameraman, the Steyr's telescopic lens had divorced David from time and place. The man in the centre of his sights might just as well have been posing for a glossy magazine. He thanked God he had not seen the face of his victim before pressing the trigger. He had envisaged one of Sedawi's masks instead.

How ecstatic had been the man at his side peering through his scope. "Ya Allah! You have blown his head right off. Hilou!

Hilou!'' the animal had roared. At least Rashid Sedawi had had hate for an excuse. "I would like to drink your blood, Zionist dog, as they did with Wasfi Tel's," Sedawi had seethed, the steam of his breath whistling through his teeth. The niceties of Black September's revenge against the Jordanian minister years earlier had obviously impressed the Shi'ite. Rashid Sedawi had secreted the Steyr and led David out of the room towards a landing at the rear of the building. In less than a minute they were driving away from the scene.

David had never seen Sedawi so happy. "Allahu Akhbar!"the Arab had screamed, slamming his palm on the steering wheel. "We may have missed him once before, but now that Zionist dog is dead."

David had felt too numb to press Sedawi on his statement, instead restricting his responses to bland monosyllables.

"You are so cool, my friend," Sedawi had enthused. "That is a fine asset to have in our profession."

It was not until he had bade Sedawi farewell at the airport that the full horror of what he had done struck home to David Katri. In some ways, Sedawi's presence had helped him to detach himself from the event. It was almost as if Sedawi had pulled the trigger and that he had been simply an innocent observer.

"Innocent," he mumbled. "I am innocent."

"Excuse me, sir. What was that you said?"

David looked up at the stewardess, his eyes glazed and unseeing.

"Er, I'm sorry. It's nothing. Nothing."

The stewardess smiled. Her passenger showed all the signs of one afraid of flying. "Please fasten your seatbelt, sir," she said kindly. "We shall be landing at Heathrow in approximately ten minutes."

"Thank you," he replied automatically. "Of course, of course."

By the time the Israeli had checked in at an airport hotel, it was already close to nine in the evening. Feeling completely drained, he flung himself onto the bed and tried in vain to relax. He was tormented by a further dilemma. At the flick of a switch, television or radio, he could learn the full horror of what he had done. He would be informed of a name, alias or otherwise, which would attach a label to a murdered man. A man he had murdered.

However, exhaustion took its toll before the dilemma could be resolved. It was already past nine the following morning when a knock on the door awoke him where he lay, fully clothed and bathed in sweat.

"Who is it?" he mumbled.

"Your breakfast, sir," said a voice from the other side. "You ordered it for eight but you must have been asleep when I knocked before."

"Oh, yes, just a moment, please."

David tried to smooth his hair and make himself more or less presentable. He had not remembered ordering breakfast in his room, but then most of the events following the shooting were now blurred.

"Leave it outside the door, please. I'll take it in a few minutes."

"Yes, sir," came the voice.

David heard the rattle of crockery. He was ravenous but needed to brush his teeth and wash first.

The Israeli showered quickly, the needles of hot water seeming at once to comfort him and to chide him. Once dressed, he opened the door of his room and looked down at the breakfast tray. Beside the fruit juice, coffee and croissants was a rolled-up newspaper. He recognised it immediately as the International Herald Tribune. For a few moments David Katri did not move. He placed his hands on his hips and took a deep breath before bending to pick up the tray. He closed the door and placed the tray gently on a table before sitting next to it. For a full minute the Israeli stared at the collection of edible and inedible objects in front of him. He then picked up the glass of fruit juice and drank it slowly. Placing the empty glass on the tray with his right hand, he picked up a croissant in his left and began eating, all the while his gaze fixed on the rolled newspaper.

By the time David had finished drinking his coffee he knew that he would be unable to resist the temptation to read it. Slowly and deliberately, he removed the elastic band and unfurled it. The headline at the top right of the front page blared its unequivocal message.

ISRAELI 'SPY' AND GIRL FRIEND
SLAIN IN VIENNA
Shi'ite Terror Group
Claims Responsibility

Vienna (Agencies) — An Israeli businessman, claimed by Arab terrorists to have been a spy, was found shot to death outside his office in Vienna's third district last night.

Police said Mr Ephraim Epstein was apparently the victim of a sniper. They later forced their way into his apartment and found a woman, Frau Inge Muller, also shot to death. Frau Muller, a divorcee and a secretary at the International Atomic Energy Authority here, was said by police to have been Mr Epstein's girl friend.

A Shi'ite terror group in Lebanon calling itself the Islamic Jihad Fundamentalist Cell telephoned Reuters' office in Beirut and claimed responsibility for the murders. A spokesman for the Cell alleged Mr Epstein was working as a spy for the Mossad, the Israeli Secret Service, and that their action was "a warning of things to come."

The Cell first rose to prominence last......

David Katri felt he had read enough. He threw the newspaper onto the floor, donned his jacket and coat, picked up his briefcase and left the room.

The newspaper story had been accompanied by a photograph of Frau Muller but not one of his victim. And for that he was grateful. The fact that the man he murdered now had a name was punishment enough. It was not that David Katri was naive enough to believe that Ephraim Epstein was his victim's real name. It was that a name, any name, conjured up visions of a bereaved family; parents, wife, children. He knew that somewhere in Israel a family was in mourning, a family which probably had no idea of the true occupation of the dead Israeli businessman in Vienna.

As Mohammed Fawzi had predicted, David Katri's next visit to the Cell's training base was undertaken without the necessity of the blindfold. And as the Israeli had guessed, the car that transported him this time took less than ten minutes to arrive. It proved that on previous occasions twenty minutes had been spent driving round in circles.

This time David had every opportunity to note the roads down which he travelled. Some were named and some were not, although one thing was for sure: they never once drove out of the teeming suburbs of south Beirut. Banners were everywhere exhorting the masses to follow the example of the Iranian revolution and rise up against the 'Great Satan', America, and its Zionist ally. He hardly saw a woman who was not wearing the chador. The hotchpotch of apartment blocks and their poverty-stricken inhabitants were the seedbed and the seeds from which Islamic fundamentalism flourished.

"We'll soon be there, sayidi," his companion said.

David had vaguely recalled the man from one of his training

exercises. His driver had greeted him at the airport effusively waving a reem of Lebanese newspapers, each headline screaming the news of the assassination. The man simply could not understand David's disdain to read them.

"You are a great hero, sayidi," the man went on. "You have been blessed by Allah."

David felt nauseous. He had no desire to be extolled, yet he knew that every successful act against the enemy was treated as if a great war had been won. The Arabs were desperate for every crumb that reminded them of the glory that was Islam nine hundred years earlier. They were such children.

"Allah blesses all who fight in His name," the Israeli replied, the sarcasm in his voice completely lost on his companion.

"Allahu Akhbar!" the man exclaimed as they entered the rubble-strewn compound with barely a nod to those guarding the entrance. Suddenly, before David had even managed to open his door, the white Peugeot was surrounded by excited youths firing wildly in the air. Such crass irresponsibility, he thought. The PLO had done the same during its withdrawal from Beirut in eighty-two. More than seventy innocent civilians had been killed or wounded by the bullets which, by Newtonian law, were obliged to return to earth somewhere.

"Ahalan, ya Anwar!" the crowd howled. "Allahu Akhbar!"

By the time David had managed to extricate himself from the Peugeot, there must have been at least sixty people trying to press his hand. Suddenly, a familiar figure pushed itself to the fore. Mohammed Fawzi hugged his pupil and kissed him on both cheeks.

"Ahalan wa'sahalan, rais awwal," he said warmly.

At first, Fawzi's use of the Arabic words for major had failed to register with David. It was only after the general hubbub had subsided that he realised he was now an officer in the Cell and therefore one step closer to entering its inner sanctum. "Where is our leader?" he asked Fawzi as the excited Shi'ite led him into the underground fortress where tea and baklava had been prepared in one of the classrooms.

"He sends you his best wishes, sayidi. He is too busy preparing for our general meeting to have welcomed you home personally. Now, take tea with us. We are all proud of you."

David felt cheated somehow. The effect that Sedawi's absence had on him was pernicious. It was incredible that he actually felt hurt. Did he crave the fanatic's praise so much or was it simply frustration that the man could not be drawn on the vital question?

Where was the damned bomb?

Over the next three days David Katri's curiosity as to Rashid Sedawi's whereabouts was not to be satisfied. No-one seemed to know for sure, although there were rumours. One had it that the man with the golden tooth had been seen in the private airplane compound at Beirut International Airport. Another that, of all things, he was undergoing emergency dental treatment.

The Israeli continued working at Selim Jaafar's spice store in the mornings, giving him an opportunity to pass a message about his progress to Abu Mussa through Yussef Ibrahim, the Maronite's emissary. In the afternoons, Katri was inveigled to lecture to the Cell's rookies on the art of warfare, ostensibly overt. None of his pupils had seemed to him remotely the sort of material which might be nurtured for covert operations. As a sign of his new standing within the group, Fawzi had presented him with a Beretta and hip holster. He knew that he could wear it freely within the confines of the southern suburbs. It was taken by all Shi'ites as a sign of rank within the various militias.

On the evening of the fourth day following his return from Europe, David returned to his apartment the owner of a white Renault nineteen presented to him by Fawzi. The car was his to use whenever he wished and the Israeli saw this as a further sign that his standing within the Cell had risen rapidly.

He climbed the stairs wearily. Most of his neighbours were

serving the evening meal and the clink of cutlery mixed with the excited voices of adults and children. Some of them knew him from the spice store, although he had succeeded in dissuading them from pursuing friendship. The Beretta at his hip would now signal to them that his business was not confined strictly to dealing in spices. He was a guardian of the faith and it was in their interests not to ask too many questions.

As David turned the Chubb key of his second floor apartment, he felt a wave of apprehension. The sound of the lock and movement of the door told him that the lock was released. Yet he had always made a point of turning the Chubb twice and that morning had been no exception. Slowly he withdrew the Chubb key before inserting his Yale into its mother cylinder with his left hand, at the same time withdrawing his Beretta with his right and holding it close to his right ear. David turned the Yale and immediately felt the door give. He allowed the door to swing open fully before leaping into the hall and adopting the classic pose of the small arms marksman: knees slightly bent and left hand gripping the wrist of the outstretched and rigid right arm.

The hall was empty and so, too, the kitchen to his right. Ahead lay the smoked glass door of the lounge. It was closed now, whereas he remembered having left it slightly ajar. Slowly he turned the doorknob.

"Kaness, David, al'tifahed."

David froze. For a moment the familiar Eastern European accented Hebrew failed to register. Somebody was ordering him to enter and not to be afraid.

If only because the voice had spoken in Hebrew, David Katri lowered his Beretta and opened the door. He gaped as he caught sight of the two men in white keffiyahs sitting on his settee. The man to his right slowly pulled away the cloth that was covering the lower half of his face.

"Yariv!" gasped David.

"Shalom, David, ma nishmah?"

David's reaction was instinctive. He pressed his right forefinger to his lip in a plea for silence.

"If you mean the place is bugged. It was," said Cohen laconically. He pointed to three small metal objects on the table in front of him. "We've put them out of commission temporarily. We'll replace them before we go."

Also on the table was a three-plug wall socket extension.

"I'm sure you recognise this," said Ben-Yaacov picking up the device.

David nodded. He had checked it out as soon as he had moved into the apartment. Similar to one of the devices he had studied during his spy course in Tel Aviv, the socket extension possessed a built in transmitter powered directly by the mains. This offered eavesdropping facilities without the need to change batteries. The device had a range of about three hundred metres.

"I just leave it plugged in and run the television from it," he said. "As you can see, I haven't got a telephone here and there's nothing they could possibly have learned from bugging this place. Until now, that is."

It was then that David Katri's second uninvited guest uncovered his face. Rahamim Ben-Yaacov smiled warmly at David, trying to overcome the fear that his agent was aware of the true identity of the man who had died in Vienna.

"I don't understand," the younger man said. "What are you both doing here? You are placing the whole mission in jeopardy. You are in a Shi'ite area dressed as Sunnis. You must never come here again. Never."

"Have you managed to learn where the bomb is, David?" asked Cohen firmly.

"No," Katri replied, still bemused by the fact that before him in southern Beirut sat the head of the Mossad. "But I have just achieved the exalted rank of major in the organisation and I feel I'm getting close, although Sedawi is a very clever operator.''

He did not know, thought Cohen. The man did not know who he had killed in Vienna. If he had known it was Ben-Ami there would already have been an outburst. Katri would have been at their throats. Or even worse, he would not even have returned to Beirut.

"Tell us about it, David," said Cohen softly.

"I don't want to talk about it," Katri sighed. "What is done is done."

"Then you did do it," said Ben-Yaacov, almost choking on the words.

"Of course I did it," replied David, puzzled by the Yemenite's doubt.

"We thought maybe Sedawi relieved you of the task and did it himself," Cohen interjected quickly.

"He was with me," the tall handsome man said with glazed eyes. "It was horrible. Horrible."

Katri sat down in the armchair opposite his visitors. It was so terribly dangerous yet, in a way, he was glad they were with him. He had felt so alone during the past months. Rubbing his eyes with his palms, he felt a desperate need to pour out his feelings.

"You know I never even caught sight of his face," he said. "He had his back to me when I pulled the trigger."

Cohen glanced at Ben-Yaacov. The relief in the Yemenite's face mirrored his own.

"If it makes you feel any better, David, you didn't know our man in Vienna personally," the head of the Mossad lied. "We'd only recently transferred him from Central America."

"I never want to know his real name," David said sternly. "To me he will always be Ephraim Epstein."

Yariv Cohen knew it was futile to try to lighten the burden for his operative. Katri had suffered enough, but the plain fact was that they were no nearer the truth.

"Why have you come?" David asked again. "It is too dangerous. For you and for me."

"Time is too short, David," said Cohen.

"But I'm nearly there. I think the next time I see him, he may confide in me."

"When's the last time you saw him?" asked Cohen coolly.

"In Vienna."

"When's the next time you'll see him?"

David paused. "I don't know," he sighed. The words themselves provided the answer as to why the boss of the Mossad had decided to move so dramatically.

"There are too many don't knows, David," said Ben-Yaacov. "We don't know how many people know where the bomb is; we don't know where it is and we don't know what Sedawi really plans to do with it, although it wouldn't be too hard to guess."

Yariv Cohen decided to inject some optimism into the situation. Israel had overcome all obstacles in the past. What was it that Golda Meir once said? Every Jew was an optimist by nature. It's the only way we could survive.

"Let us discuss what we do know," the intelligence chief interjected. "Correct me if I am wrong, David, but according to the information you've supplied, I believe it can safely be assumed that Sedawi intends to address the Cell on February the twenty-seventh at his headquarters."

"Yes," said David. "But he's as slippery as an eel and it wouldn't surprise me if he had made other plans."

"Nevertheless," Cohen went on, "this is the only semi-concrete information we have and it is on this we must act. The Winds of Kedem are almost upon us. There is simply no time left for dilly-dallying."

"What do you mean?" asked David, knowing there could only be one answer.

"We are going to attack," said Cohen curtly.

David stared at the two men before him. He knew they were

right. He knew also that he had failed and this made the burden of what he had done even harder to bear.

"I understand," the Syrian-born Jew said quietly. "But before we discuss what you want me to do, please just tell me about my wife and children."

"Of course," Cohen replied. "We keep an eye on them as much as we are able and I can assure you that they are well."

For a few seconds David Katri's mind flashed back to Tel Aviv and the loving arms of Yael. The happy faces of Boaz and Shoshana beamed at him and once again he suffered the familiar stab of fear that he would never see them again.

"Okay, what's the plan?"

"Firstly, we need to know everything that you know," said Cohen. "We need to know the exact location of the Cell's headquarters, every nook and cranny."

By the time their discussions had neared completion, the three men were fully aware of the task that lay before them. The risks were enormous, the chances of success no more than minimal. David had expressed his view that, of all the terrorists based in Beirut, only Sedawi and Laham were likely to possess knowledge of the bomb's whereabouts and that they would never allow themselves to be captured alive. Cohen had countered that David's role would be vital; that the younger man had to position himself next to Sedawi at the time of the attack and put the Lebanese out of commission himself.

"But how?" David had asked. The idea of pistol-whipping Sedawi with his Beretta seemed faintly ridiculous.

"With this," the head of the Mossad replied, withdrawing a syringe and phial from the briefcase at his side. "It'll knock him out within a few seconds. Then stick these luminous tapes on yourself and him. We don't want our men to shoot either of you by mistake."

"But what about Laham?"

"He's an old man. I doubt whether he'll be in a fit state to offer any resistance.''

"Let me get this right, Yariv. You are planning to attack during the meeting?''

"Yes,'' replied Cohen firmly, "there will then be a number of factors in our favour, surprise not the least of them.''

"But that underground complex is a time bomb. A stray bullet will blow it sky-high.''

"We hope there won't be too many of those since, according to you, Sedawi is the only one likely to be carrying arms on his person. We'll cut off the exit to the meeting hall. Once we've achieved our objectives, we'll blow it up.''

"With the rest of the terrorists inside?''

"Yes.''

"There's just one thing,'' countered David, trying hard to disguise his scepticism. "How will you know when the meeting is in full swing?''

Cohen smiled. "We've brought you a few presents. David,'' he replied, at the same time withdrawing a selection of objects from the attache case at his side and placing them on the table in front of him. "You've probably seen one of these hybrid room transmitters before. You can hide it easily in your clothing. It's got a range of about two hundred metres, but don't activate it until just before you enter the meeting as the battery only lasts for about five hours.''

"So you'll be listening in.''

"Yes,'' replied Cohen, handing Katri the next item from his box of tricks.

David turned the ordinary-looking brown belt over in his hands. "I take it this thing isn't only for keeping my trousers up.''

"It's the latest of its type,'' Ben-Yaacov cut in. "It has a beacon transmitter built into the buckle.''

"What's the range?''

"About five kilometres surface and twenty in the air.''

"Frequency?"

"It's set for three hundred and fifty-nine point five. The operating time is twenty-five to thirty hours so activate it before you enter the meeting. It'll enable us to keep track of you—"

"Should anything go wrong," cut in David, by now unable to disguise his scepticism.

The two visitors chose to ignore the barb. All they could do was try to cover every eventuality.

David Katri stared at the collection of surveillance equipment before him and then at his two superiors in their white keffiyahs. The whole thing seemed so absurd and yet he had to admit to himself that he could think of nothing better.

"Let's hope Sedawi shows his hand sooner," he said wistfully. "It would be much neater if we could isolate him and then pick him up."

"We can't rely on miracles any more, my friend," said Cohen sadly.

David Katri stood up. "You'd better go now," he said, his voice cracking with emotion. "I need to be alone for a while."

As Yariv Cohen left the apartment he prayed that the assassination had not shattered his agent's will. The price was too high for David Katri to crack up now.

The weather was warm for late February as Yehuda Takoah parked his grey Lancia outside Israel's Central Meteorological Institute at Beit Dagan. Situated a few kilometres south east of Tel Aviv, the institute was strategically situated on one of the country's main crossroads. To the east lay Jerusalem, to the south Ashdod and Beersheba and to the north Tel Aviv and Haifa. Instead of going to his office, he went straight to the forecast room. Ever since his meeting with the head of his country's intelligence services, he had been particularly on the lookout for a possible scenario which might presage the Kedem wind's presence over Israel. It was already February twenty-sixth and the first wind would soon be due. Most Israelis confused the shurqiya with the famous khamsin wind which was caused by depressions over the desolate wastelands of North Africa. But whether it was called khamsin, hamseen or scirocco, it was not the wind which he had been asked to forecast.

Takoah looked first at the synoptic charts hanging on the wall. He had had a sneaking suspicion for a couple of days that the large anticyclone which had started over Siberia and had moved southwards would eventually set up the conditions for the Kedem.

He looked at the chart for midnight. It showed a ridge of high pressure spreading south behind a cold front over the Caucuses and Turkey. On the 0600 GMT chart the cold front had moved down to Cyprus.

Yehuda Takoah did not know the reason why the Mossad was so interested in the easterly wind and it did not trouble him unduly. Nevertheless, the head of the meteorological institute felt the tingle of expectation as he moved over to the prognosis charts hanging on the wall. They were divided into groups according to millibars of air pressure, showing the pressure distributed in layers above the earth's surface up to twelve kilometres.

He first perused the chart which predicted events twenty-four hours ahead, then thirty-six and finally forty-eight. It was all there. Barring an act of God, the Winds of Kedem would sweep down across the sea of Galilee and the valleys of Beisan and Jezreel in two days' time.

Yehuda Takoah descended quickly to his office on the second floor and picked up his phone.

"Get me the the Kirya," he said tersely to the girl on the switchboard.

CHAPTER FIFTEEN

The Saar class fast attack missile boat Aliyah slashed through the black waters of the Mediterranean, its four Maybach diesel engines roaring their protest at being pushed to the limit. The 488-ton vessel, launched in nineteen eighty, carried the usual complement of four Gabriel surface-to-surface missiles forward and four harpoons amidships.

However, there were certain refinements which made the Aliyah different from any other vessel in its class. The 76mm gun had been removed from its aft deck to make way for a helicopter platform and hangar. In daylight the Hughes Defender could be seen resting on its perch like a giant locust. But this night was pitch black and the Aliyah displayed no lights with which to inform an enemy of its unusual payload.

The Hughes was not the only strange cargo aboard the Israeli vessel. An astute observer might have noticed a ramp protruding from the starboard side of the platform. Upon the ramp sat what to the untrained eye appeared to be a model airplane. In fact, it was a model airplane, but one with a vital difference. The ubiquitous mazlat, a little over four metres long and one of the heroes of Israel's war in Lebanon, was a spy in the sky par excellence. The Israel Aircraft Industries Mini Remotely Piloted Vehicle was simply the best in the world at doing its job. It was called the Scout and that is exactly what it did.

The Scout had won its own personal battle against other RPV's because the operator had merely to transmit flight demands to it, such as changes in altitude or new headings, rather than use a link between the plane and a ground station to convey signals for direct operation of its aerodynamic control surfaces. The demands transmitted to the vehicle were simply fed directly to an autopilot. There was no need for continuous transmission from ground to air via the command link, and this made the Scout less vulnerable to countermeasures.

The Scout could cruise at ninety-six kilometres an hour, reach a maximum altitude of three thousand metres and stay in the air for seven hours. Its precious payload was housed in a transparent dome on the underside of the fuselage. The gyro-stabilized television camera was equipped with a 1:15 ratio zoom lens and panoramic fracture and, in this instance, an image intensifier for night surveillance.

The RPV had exacted a heavy price from the Palestinian resistance to the Israeli invasion in nineteen eighty-two. In many engagements, its cameras had observed almost every enemy move. With air and armour superiority guaranteed, the Scouts had freedom of the skies, their built-in counter measures jamming, deceiving and manipulating both Syrian and Palestinian radar.

And so it was that Israel's Chief of Staff, General Yehuda Bar-Ilan, could call on a vast array of modern technology to destroy his enemy. Seated in the small operations room on board the boat, the general went over the known details with major Rami Yefet, who was to lead the Sayeret Mat'kal task force. Also listening in was Gilad Blum, the pilot of the Hughes Defender.

"That's about the gist of it, Rami," said Bar-Ilan. "You and your men have heard most of it before. Just be sure that when you give your boys the final briefing, each one will know what is expected of him."

Rami Yefet nodded, the ebony ringlets of his hair bouncing like springs. His features, large brown eyes and reddish olive skin were typical of Jews of the Yemen. His parents had fled Aden just before the birth of the Jewish State in nineteen forty-eight and he had been born a sabra eight years later, the second of the nine Yefet children to be native-born Israelis.

The third man in the room was also a sabra. Air Force captain Gilad Blum was born in the Tel Aviv suburb of Ramat Gan, the son of survivors of Auschwitz. Despite the fact that the soldier was dark and the airman fair, both shared a feature common to all sabras in their country's armed forces. They were usually more afraid of letting down their hevreh in battle than of the enemy, or even of death itself. It was not machismo. It was something much deeper: the knowledge that while for the enemy defeat in war was a setback, for Israel it would be a catastrophe.

"What about me?" asked Blum, eager not to miss out on the action.

Bar-Ilan looked steadily at the young pilot. He knew he would be disappointed. "At the moment, Gilad, you're just along for the ride. We've got three Bell Twin Two-Twelves standing by in southern Lebanon. They'll be flying in to pick up our boys at the allotted hour."

Blum tied hard not to show his disappointment. The Bells were search and rescue craft and some possessed emergency hospital facilities. He reckoned the Chief was expecting heavy casualties.

"Nevertheless," Bar-Ilan went on, "you'll be on permanent stand-by until the operation is over and it's just as well you know the attack plan."

The Chief of Staff stood up. "I believe that is all, gentlemen. Are your boys waiting for me on deck, Rami?"

"Yes, sir."

"Then I'd like to give them a final word," said Bar-Ilan. He turned and led the two younger men up the gangway.

Bar-Ilan was stunned by the blast of cold air which hit him as he reached the deck. Thanks to some cloud cover, the night itself was not too cold. It was the windchill factor produced by the craft's speed of thirty-one knots that caused the discomfort. He looked at the dark faces of the twenty-nine commandos huddled before him. He had not liked the idea of choosing only those of oriental origin for the operation. It smacked of discrimination, although all involved knew the true reason. All of them spoke Arabic after a fashion, although he hoped they would never have to use it before reaching their target.

"Hevreh," Bar-Ilan began slowly, "for some of you this will be your first operation of this kind, while others have already tasted anti-terrorist actions of one sort or another. Whatever your experience, you now know what Israel expects of you. Do your job well and do it thoroughly. Success is founded on your willingness to follow orders to the letter. Nevertheless, should you find that circumstances force you to take the initiative, then do not be afraid to act. The only asset that keeps us one step ahead of the enemy is our grey matter. Use it. Good luck and I'll see you when you get home."

With this, Israel's Chief of Staff went to each man and shook his hand firmly, repeating "be'hatzlaha," over and over. He knew they would need all the luck in the world. It was already 0300 hours on February the twenty-seventh when the engines of the Aliyah died and eight Zodiac rubber dinghies were lowered into the sea. Each was piloted by a sailor who would return it to the missile boat once he had discharged his cargo, both human and material. The distance to the shore was about one kilometre and the lights on the Lebanese coastline beckoned them with twinkling allure.

As soon as he was aboard the lead dinghy, Rami Yefet held the infra-red scope to his right eye. Immediately, he saw the intense, strobe lighting effect of a Firefly night tag winking at him in the darkness. He knew he was the only one who could see the pulses and he knew also that they would lead the task force to a secluded beach southwest of Beirut.

At about half a kilometre from the beach, he ordered the outboard motors cut. The commandos then paddled the dinghies through the murky waters until they felt them scrape the bottom of the shore. Silently, they disembarked. Yefet was met on the beach by the man he knew must be the head of his country's secret service.

"Bruchim haba'im," said Yariv Cohen in lowered tone, his teeth gleaming. They were the only part of his pale European face not covered in boot black. "Welcome to Beirut."

"I've been here before sir," countered the dark-skinned man, shaking Cohen's hand firmly. "In eighty-two. I presume it's just as big a hole now."

"Affirmative," Cohen replied, pointing to a group of dark shapes about thirty metres away. "Come, we've got eight four-wheel drive vehicles to transport you to the warehouse. Tell your men to load the two Toyotas at the rear with the arms and equipment."

"Can I borrow your Firefly for a while?"

"Why?" asked Cohen, surprised at the request.

"I have to signal the commander of the dinghies when he can make safely back to the boat. The warehouse is due north of here, a few minutes drive, right?"

"Yes."

"That's okay then," said the major. "He'll be training his scope in that direction to wait for my signal."

Cohen reluctantly parted with his strobe. He would need it back to guide in the rescue helicopters on completion of the mission. For a few seconds the head of the Mossad watched the young officer organise his men. Cohen then turned away and made for the first of the vehicles, a black Volkswagen Transporter. He would drive it while seven more of his men, including Rahamim Ben-Yaacov, would be at the wheels of the others.

Within two minutes Cohen, accompanied by Rami Yefet at his side and six commandos in the rear, was driving up the sandy road which led from the beach to a large deserted warehouse.

"This is it," said Cohen, pulling to a halt.

Rami Yefet saw two more of Cohen's men open a pair of giant doors. The place was almost as big as an aircraft hangar.

"There are gaping holes in the roof, but it was the best we could do under the circumstances," said Cohen, slamming into reverse and backing into the awning. Each of the other vehicles followed suit until they were all lined up ready for their next, and final, exit.

After all the commandos had alighted, Cohen pulled Yefet to one side. "Before you go to signal the sailors, look up there."

Rami Yefet looked up to see a canopy of stars framed by the edges of a huge hole in the warehouse roof.

"Beautiful, isn't it," said Cohen quietly. "It's almost like a painting." Yefet said nothing, but prayed silently that he would live to see those same stars over the Land of Israel within the next twenty-four hours.

As the boss of the Mossad limped away towards the waiting men, the major remembered the message he had for him.

"Er, sir-"

Cohen stopped and waited while the soldier made up the few paces between them. "What is it?"

"This was passed to me by the Chief of Staff. Apparently, it came from your office."

Cohen took the sealed white envelope from the major's outstretched hand and opened it. The boss of the Mossad felt the blood drain from his blackened face.

"What is it?" asked Yefet, noticing that Cohen appeared mesmerised by the contents of the letter.

"Nothing," Cohen replied, regaining his composure. "Just an updated weather report."

While the Mossad and the General Staff Reconnaissance Unit were spending the next five hours trying to gain some sleep, another Israeli, only ten minutes drive away, was tossing and turning in his bed, haunted by visions first of beauty and then of the devil.

David Katri had destroyed the letter he had received from Fatima the previous morning, but its contents tormented him. How stupid she had been to write to him. It could have been all their undoing had it been intercepted. And yet he knew also that her words were born of desperation in the knowledge that they might never see one another again. The words burned within him.

My darling Anwar

Please forgive me for writing to you. I know it is dangerous, but ever since I saw you in Selim Jaafar's spice shop, the vision of you has never left me. I saw your eyes and I knew that you had guessed who was behind the veil. It was unfair of me to taunt you in this way, but the need to see you again had engulfed me to such an extent that I felt I was possessed of the jinns. The spirits in this land are evil, my darling. They do not let us rest. We are all cursed whether we be Moslem, Christian or Jew. For the ways of our diverse cultures are seared into our souls and the occasional healing is like scar tissue, tender and raw. It ulcerates with the slightest friction. Allah, in His wisdom, has created a family of strangers, each wary of the others within His domain.

I despair of ever seeing you again and yet I long for it so, until the pain within my breast becomes intolerable and the tears run down my cheeks as at the fountain of Nirvanah. Only the tears are blood red and Paradise is Hell.

I shall return to the aged Christian and you will re-unite with the woman of your choosing. My darling, we have both sinned: you against the sacrament of marriage and I against the tenets of my faith. But what are our sins as compared to those around us who kill and maim in His name? I can write no more. It is too painful.

May Allah bless you and care for you on earth and in heaven, my life, my soul.

Ana b'hebak

F.

'Ana b'hebak'. I love you. The words echoed through his mind, and yet were replaced suddenly by others of a poem that he had learned by heart when he had first arrived in Eretz Yisrael. A poem written by Israel's Joan of Arc.

Blessed is the match consumed
    in kindling flame.
Blessed is the flame that burns
    in the secret fastness of the heart.
Blessed is the heart with strength to stop
    its beating for honour's sake.
Blessed is the match consumed
    in kindling flame.

The poems of Hannah Senesh were etched into his soul. She had parachuted behind Nazi lines to warn the Jews of Hungary of their impending fate, only to be captured, brutally tortured and finally executed by her stricken people's tormentors. David wondered whether Fatima was destined to share the same fate.

Suddenly, the faces of Hannah Senesh and Fatima Fadas were side by side, both young, both prepossessing of beauty at opposite ends of the semitic spectrum. Both serene. A riposte to the evil that dwelt in the heart of man.

In his dreams, David Katri felt suffused by a warmth generated by the vision of the two women, so different and yet so alike. ''Ana b'hebak,'' he mumbled. What language other than Arabic could better express the sentiment of love. And hate.

Suddenly a devil incarnate destroyed the tranquility of his dream. Out of his golden fang flowed the lava of hell. 'Arik behind you! Arik, behind you!'

David Katri, his legs aflame, awoke in a pool of sweat, his body rigid with sheer terror. After a few seconds he went limp as a great tiredness overcame him. He looked languidly at the clock by the side of the bed. It was eight o'clock and the bright Mediterranean sun was already streaming in through the window to dispel the lingering cold of the night.

After a few more seconds of torpor, David arose sharply. There was much to do. He had been assigned to help organise the meeting at which the fate of his nation might be decided. When Mohammed Fawzi had given him the message, he had asked to see Sedawi. Fawzi had replied that he had received his instructions through Mehdi Laham and that the mullah had made it clear that the man with the golden tooth would be unavailable until the hour of the meeting.

Sedawi. The enigma. Would it ever be possible to capture him alive? David showered quickly and dressed in flannel check shirt and jeans. After snatching a hasty breakfast of leben and bread and jam, he donned his green parka. Hidden in the lining was the microphone, no bigger than a calculator battery. In the left pocket were some luminescent green identification stickers.

The Israeli then went to the top drawer of his dresser and withdrew a plastic packet. Inside was a disposable syringe. Next he entered the kitchen, and from the refrigerator withdrew a small bottle. He pushed the needle carefully through the top of the bottle and into the colourless liquid within. He made sure to expel any air before replacing it in its receptacle. He prodded the plastic case into the breast pocket of his parka. Opening the second drawer from the top, he withdrew his Beretta, hip holster and belt. Securing the belt around his waist, he gave a friendly tap to the buckle which contained the miniature transmitter.

David Katri, murderer and saviour, was as ready as he would ever be.

CHAPTER SIXTEEN

The late evening was overcast, although no rain had fallen by the time the first of the eight Mossad-hired vehicles left the seashore base for its final destination, a few blocks from the terrorist headquarters. The second would follow two minutes later and so forth until each vehicle was parked in a different side street in the area where the Ouzai district bordered on Borj el-Barajneh. The commander of each unit would lead his men to a pre-arranged site less than two hundred metres from target zero.

Yariv Cohen looked skywards at the threatening clouds. The sun set quickly in the Mediterranean and it would be only a matter of minutes before darkness would emphasise their isolation. Radio silence had to be maintained until the mission neared completion. The Mossad chief's only comfort was the knowledge that high above them flew the RPV. The cyclops in the sky would warn them of the need to abort, the only possible reason for infraction of the airwaves.

Cohen had watched Rami Yefet go over the attack plan time and again with his men. Dressed in civilian clothes, they did not look like a group of hardened commandos, Israel's best. Yet he was sure each man knew what was expected of him and had prepared himself mentally for the task. Much would depend on those selected to dispatch the guards, two of whom, he knew, would be placed at the top of the stairs leading to the bunker. Six others were due to be stationed at strategic sites on the first floors of bombed-out buildings surrounding the cavern.

Cohen thought of David Katri. After their first meeting, it

had been decided that it was far too dangerous for him to visit Katri again. Instead, a drop had been arranged in the Hamra area and the updated details had proven invaluable to the task of preparation. The information had been so thorough and precise that it was as if the Syrian Jew had been responsible himself for all security at the base.

Everything had gone so smoothly that Cohen could not help wondering when and where the catch would come. It was true that Entebbe and the attack on Black September had gone almost according to the book, but anti-terrorist actions were no respecters of past glory. Each presented its own particular challenge and each, inevitably, required a certain amount of improvisation.

"Penny for your thoughts."

It was Rami Yefet, the confidence in his voice calming the older man.

"It seems the older we get the more scared we get, Rami," said Cohen. He could afford to be open with the major. They were about to share an experience that one or both might not survive.

"It is good to be a little afraid, sir," said the olive-skinned soldier. "It keeps the adrenelin flowing and protects us from making rash mistakes."

How Cohen admired the Jews of the Yemen. People said they were true descendants of the tribes of the ancient Hebrews and in modern Israel they commanded the utmost respect. Everyone made jokes about each successive wave of immigrants. It was either the crude and backward Moroccans, the miserly Persians, and cheating Romanians or, lately, the light-fingered Georgians from the Soviet Union. There were no derogatory jokes about Yemenites, or at least none that he could remember.

"What's your secret, Rami?"

Yefet looked into the older man's eyes, the whites made all the more conspicuous by the shoe black surrounding them. "It's called the Wisdom of Life, sir," he replied without a trace of vanity. "My mother could not read or write, yet she had it. And she passed it on to us. That is why we love and respect her so much and that is why we will never allow her to be alone in her old age."

"You're a lucky man, Rami. And your mother's a lucky woman."

"Thank you, sir."

Just then a voice called them from the line of parked vehicles.

"Rami, tor'kha!"

Yefet held out his hand. "It's my turn, sir. I look forward to seeing you aboard the Bell after the show's over."

"Be'hatzlaha, Rami."

"Thank you, sir. You too."

Cohen watched the Toyota disappear through the awning at the front of the warehouse and into the darkness. Soon he too would be driving once more through the teeming streets of Shi'ite Beirut, with its banners extolling Khomeiniism and death to the twin Satans of America and Israel. This time he was to be a bit player, observing from the wings while the main drama between the forces of two opposing cultures played itself out on stage both above and below ground.

In the Middle East there were no winners, he mused. Only losers.

David Katri paced up and down at the top of the stairs leading to the entrance to the cavern as members of the Cell, some on foot and others in cars, began arriving for the general meeting arranged by the Higher Council.

Incredible as it had seemed to him, upon his arrival earlier in the day he had been given the responsibility of organising final security. It was now dark and he had posted the guards around the perimeter. Or, rather, he had given Fawzi and others that impression. In effect, the only men guarding the meeting would be the two at the main entrance.

David glanced at his watch. Cohen and his commandos would now be in place and he had to relay the new facts to them. He stepped away from the mass of bodies lining up to enter the underground chamber and found some open space. Keeping his back to them he spoke freely. "This is David. There has been a change in the security plan. I repeat. There has been a change in the security plan. There are now no men guarding the perimeter. I repeat. There are now no men guarding the perimeter. You will just have to deal with the two at the front entrance. There is still no sign of Sedawi."

Katri moved back towards the throng of men, at the same time switching on the beacon transmitter in his belt. He was worried about Sedawi. He had greeted Mehdi Laham on his arrival but the main target appeared to be missing.

As David approached the line of waiting men, those at the rear made way for him. It was a sign of deference to his new rank in the Cell. The Israeli was about half-way down the stairs when one of the men swung round. The butt of the rifle he was carrying hit David in the chest.

"Samikhni, sayidi, samikhni!"

David looked at the man sternly and waved aside his suffusive apologies. The blow didn't hurt and he was more concerned with the fact that the man was carrying a weapon.

"You know you should have checked that rifle in days ago. Make sure you give it to the quartermaster when you get below."

"Naam, sayidi. Samikhni. Samikhni."

The man spoke Arabic with a Persian accent. It was the first time David had heard the accent among Sedawi's men. He had always had the impression that all of them were Lebanese Shi'ites, although the Iranian influence was bound to express itself in some form or other. The shadow of Khomeini would cast itself over the Middle East for years to come, regardless of whether Israel disappeared or not.

David brushed past the Iranian and continued his descent. At the foot of the stairs he was greeted by a smiling Mohammed Fawzi.

"Come, sayidi. Come. The Ra'is would like to see you personally."

The Israeli was taken aback. How could Sedawi already have been inside? He had turned his back for only a few seconds, hardly long enough for the leader to have made his entrance. Also, the waiting throng would have undoubtedly raised a cheer.

"Follow me," said Fawzi.

David followed the sergeant through the meeting hall, where some of the men were already seated. The hall was chilly. They meandered towards an alcove. Deep within was a small door, which he had not noticed before. Fawzi knocked three times.

"Enter!" came the familiar voice from within.

Both men had to stoop to enter the tiny office.

"Ah, come in, Anwar," said Sedawi. "Thank you, Mohammed, you may go."

Fawzi bowed and left the room. It was sparsely furnished with three chairs, a desk and a chest of drawers.

"Take a seat, my friend," said Sedawi, his voice warm and friendly. "There is much to discuss."

David lifted the hip holster as he sat down. He opened the zip of the parka slightly. The knowledge that it contained, among other things, a microphone was highly reassuring.

"I should like to thank you firstly for the excellent job you have done so far in organising this meeting," beamed the man with the golden tooth.

"Thank you, Ra'is. It was a great honour that you chose me to assist you in such a task, but-"

"But what?"

David knew that Sedawi respected humility. It was unwise for any man to act too brashly in his presence.

"But Ra'is, to be honest, I have found my meteoric rise within the Cell quite baffling. I simply did my duty, like anyone else."

"Not like anyone else, Anwar. We have almost one hundred members in our group. Fifty will probably be here tonight. Most of them I could not trust to boil a cup of coffee."

"I do not understand, Ra'is."

Sedawi clasped his hands and placed them on the desk in front of him. "I hate the Israelis with every part of my being, but one thing that fighting them has taught me is that quality is more important than quantity."

For one horrifying moment David believed that the Shi'ite was on to him. The Israeli felt the blood rush to his head. Dumb-struck, he felt Sedawi's eyes pierce him. Once again they contained that strange leer that had bothered him on previous occasions.

"No-one knows where I live, not even Laham. But you shall come to my home after the meeting and we shall discuss the finer details." Sedawi smiled, the lust in his voice and eyes now clearly discernible.

"I'm afraid I do not understand, Ra'is," said David, stalling in order to re-assemble his emotions.

"It is quite simple, really," the Shi'ite went on. "I have achieved something that all the Arab armies together could not. I have assured the total destruction of the Zionist entity."

"I am afraid I still do not understand," said David, the adrenelin pumping once again.

Sedawi smiled, realising that for the ignorant it would indeed be a profound shock.

"I have stolen the so-called Islamic Bomb from Pakistan," he said matter-of-factly.

"What!" gasped David in mock horror.

"Come now, you must have heard the rumours about what

this meeting was being called for.''

"Only that it would cause the power of Islam to be heard throughout the world."

"That it will," the Shi'ite laughed, the gold tooth gleaming in the light of the single bulb above his head.

"How did you do it?" David asked, hoping that it was a logical question under the circumstances.

"It is past history," Sedawi replied smugly. "Let us just say that Laham will announce tonight that we have the bomb and that it is in such a place that will cause the maximum destruction to Israel. Later, he will telephone one of the wire services and threaten the Zionists with annihilation if they do not pack their bags."

"It is fantastic, ya Ra'is."

"It would be fantastic, ya Anwar. But you and I know the Israelis."

Yet again David felt the panic rising within him. What did he mean that they both knew the Israelis?

"Sorry, Ra'is-"

"We both fought against them. It is a waste of energy threatening them. They are like us. They would rather die than surrender."

The sense of relief that David felt was tinged with foreboding. The man was obviously mad.

"Laham is old and is not ruthless enough," Sedawi went on, cutting David short. "I shall tell you where the bomb is when you come to my home tonight."

"Why me, Ra'is?"

The Shi'ite had been expecting the question.

"If anything should happen to me, I want someone young and intelligent enough to complete the task given to me by Allah. You have impressed me with your dedication. I have chosen you."

"It is a great honour for me, ya Ra'is. But what could possibly

315

happen to you?''

"Lebanon is a hotbed of intrigue, my friend,'' Sedawi sighed, shaking his head. "I would rather trust a stranger than my brother.''

"But if Laham believes you have deceived him, he may enlist the help of others. What if they were to overcome you?''

Sedawi smiled. He was forced to admire the handsome man before him. Tonight he would seduce his deputy and tomorrow he would invite Hindawi to join him in the final act of faith.

"I have been to the dentist,'' he said laconically, and then laughed at the quizzical expression on the face of his companion. "It was an old trick of the Nazis, my friend. Some of them had cyanide capsules inserted into their molars in case they were captured by the advancing Russians. Death without dishonour, a sentiment I share.''

David Katri realised at that moment that Cohen must abort the attack. Sedawi would end his life before he could plunge home the needle. Even then, the sedative would take a few seconds to act. The Israeli knew he was within a few hours of discovering the location of the bomb. His comrades had heard every word. They must abort.

"Anwar, Anwar-''

"Yes, what is it?'' the Israeli started, realising he must have been daydreaming.

"Come, my friend. The season of the Shurqiya is upon us. It will soon be time for us to glorify His name.''

With intense trepidation, Katri followed the Shi'ite into the meeting room, which was already buzzing with high expectation.

Rami Yefet was in a quandary. On the one hand he had been fed information which made penetrating the terrorist head-quarters infinitely easier, while on the other, that information had suddenly dried up. He had heard a general hubbub of voices over the receiver, a banging sound and then silence. The microphone had malfunctioned just when they needed it most. The communications man next to him was still picking up signals on his direction finder from the transmitter in Katri's belt. But the Mossad man could be dead and the belt would continue transmitting, at least for the next five hours until the battery ran out.

Despite being overcast, the city lights from the surrounding streets still gave off enough power for his image-intensifying night binoculars to be effective. Yefet looked firstly at the two guards outside the entrance and then turned one hundred and eighty degrees to focus on a spot about one hundred metres to his rear. He knew Yariv Cohen possessed the same equipment as himself and that the head of the Mossad was fully aware of the situation. They had decided that should there be any malfunc-tion of surveillance equipment, then the attack would go ahead approximately twenty minutes after the last terrorist had been seen entering the cavern. Ultimate discretion was left to the com-mander in the field, although it had been mutually agreed that Cohen would use his Firefly if he believed the mission should be aborted. Yefet knew he would still have that final discre-tion, but at least he could have the luxury of a second opinion.

The major looked at his watch. It was nearly time. He peered through his infra-red scope towards the deserted buildings to his rear. There was no tell-tale flashing. The time had come for action. Yefet gave the signal to two of his men and watched through the night binoculars as they began their circuitous route towards the entrance to the bunker less than eighty metres away. A full five minutes had elapsed before he again saw his men. It had seemed like an eternity.

A split second later he watched spellbound as the commandos sneaked up to pounce on their unsuspecting victims. He sighed with relief as his men gave the thumbs-up sign. The major signalled to the remainder of the men to follow him and they began walking stealthily across the rubble towards their target. Yefet gripped his Uzi sub-machine gun tightly, every nerve in his body as taut as cat-gut.

Meanwhile, in the bunker, the fanatical chants of the audience made David Katri shudder.

"Allahu Akhbar! Allahu Akhbar!"

The throng had greeted the mullah's pronouncements with characteristic fervour, paying scant heed to common sense. He thought it doubtful that any of them knew the real effects of nuclear weapons. He recalled Lawrence of Arabia's famous words that the Arabs could be swung as if on a chord. Anyone who stood up and shouted loud enough could gain a following.

David had been chosen to sit at the main table in front of the Cell's ecstatic rank and file. Sitting cross-legged on the floor, most of them were barely out of their teens. To his left sat Sedawi and further to his left was Mehdi Laham, standing at the podium with arms aloft. David had never seen the mullah looking so happy. The long grey beard glistened with the spray of oratory. David kept one eye on the mullah and the other on the door at the back of the room. The commotion had barely died down than his worst fears were realised. Seemingly unobserved by the audience, who were by this time jumping up and down in religious fervour, a number of figures had entered the chamber. Through the flurry of waving arms, David recognised his own kind. He could not see below their shoulders but he was sure that they had their weapons trained on the throng. It was too late for him to do anything. All was lost.

"Death to the Zionists! Death to America!" the crowd screamed.

Suddenly, automatic weapons fire began pumping into the seething mass. Through the screams and the mayhem, David heard the mullah exhort his soldiers to fight the invaders with their bare hands. A split second later the Israeli agent, still rooted to the spot, felt a dull thud in his head. His senses began to reel although he remained conscious. He sank to his knees, the pain growing more intense as his vision became blurred. He felt the silky softness of his own blood seep into his eyes. David heard a terrible curse in Arabic and then felt himself being hauled to his feet. Half-stumbling and groping blindly, he found he could offer no resistance to the force which was dragging him through the blackness and away from the screams of dying men and the stench of cordite.

After what seemed an eternity of stooping and stumbling, a blast of cold air stung his cheeks. Unseeing, he was bundled onto something soft yet firm. Then he felt his hands being secured firmly behind his back. Through a mist of pain he heard the urgent staccato of a starter motor. Then came a blackness as welcome as it was consuming.

Major Rami Yefet first realised something had gone drastically wrong by the time he had reached the podium and table at the front of the room. Although there were not as many of the Shi'ites present as expected, their resistance had been fierce. They had used their bare hands to attack his men. The Uzi of one of his commandos had jammed and the man had been overwhelmed immediately by four or five shrieking Shi'ites.

Precious seconds had been wasted while the Arabs were hauled off and shot. Also, his men had been constrained by the limitation on their direction of fire. Each was acutely aware that in a room only fifteen metres away stood the Cell's ammunition dump.

Yefet found the mullah lying in a crumpled heap on the floor, the white shroud around his knees revealing painfully thin and pale legs. The man was obviously dead, although there were no immediate signs of physical injury. Mehdi Laham had probably died of a heart attack.

The cordite almost choked the major as he searched around and under the top table for Katri and Sedawi. With sinking heart, he realised the cleric was the only one of his targets in the immediate vicinity. And he could no longer tell them anything. Yefet decided to make his way back to the rear of the room.

Suddenly, the lights failed. In the pitch darkness the screams and wails of dying men seemed to reach a crescendo. He found himself stumbling over a number of bodies until some of his men switched on their torches.

"Who's that?" the major shouted, temporarily blinded by a light shone in his face.

"It's me, sir. Yigal," said a voice beyond the light.

"Give me the torch, Yigal, and get the men out as fast as you can. Shit! This whole thing's a mess."

"Yes, sir, but what about Pinni."

Yefet had forgotten about the sapper. "Where is he?"

"I'm here, sir," came a voice behind another torch.

"Come with me, Pinni. Are the explosives set?"

"Yes, sir. Timed to go off in twenty minutes, when we're clear."

"Good. Let's go."

Yefet pushed past some of the men who were already moving towards the exit stairs and in a few bounds reached the ordnance room. Noticing that the door was slightly ajar, he thrust it open with a sharp kick.

The major played his torch in a wide arc over the interior. The beam picked up something white in the far left corner. He could make out a man sitting propped up against some ammunition boxes. His shirt was bloodstained and it was not immediately clear whether he was dead or alive. As Major Ram Yefet of the Chief of Staff Reconnaissance Unit advanced he noticed that the man was clutching something in his right hand. And that he was smiling.

Mohammed Fawzi basked in the sudden glare. It was as if the Garden of Paradise was beckoning him. "Allahu Akhbar!" he cried weakly, at the same time releasing a pineapple-shaped object from his grasp.

CHAPTER SEVENTEEN

Abu Mussa rocked gently in the rocking chair on the veranda of his mountain retreat. He had watched the sun go down over the Mediterranean, the last vestiges of its warmth replaced quickly by a gnawing chill that matched the ice in his heart. For weeks he had not ventured from his palace. He had declined all telephone calls and had told Georges to inform all inquirers that he was abroad on business.

The Maronite, a thick grey-white stubble covering his face, looked haggard and drawn. He had not shaven since his enforced separation from Fatima. His Shi'ite mistress had consumed his every thought, day and night. Just as the Christian rose wearily from his chair he heard a dull crump to his left. Previous experience told him that an explosion had gone off in Beirut, although the capital had been relatively quiet for months. He shuffled to the southern rampart. In the distance he could see a ball of flame rising into the sky. Explosion was followed by explosion, with tracers arcing into the blackness. It was the sort of fireworks display at which Beirut excelled. "Damned Arabs," he cursed under his breath. "Let them kill each other until there's no-one left."

Abu Mussa stood transfixed by the pyrotechnics and moved only after his house telephone had rung for the second time. He shuffled back to the veranda and lifted the receiver.

"Yes, what is it?"

"Master, master! Come quickly!" squeaked the voice of Georges. "I am in the northern pavilion. I was fiddling with the receiver and suddenly picked up sounds of explosions overlaid by urgent voices. I think they are speaking

Hebrew.''

Abu Mussa felt his whole body tingle.

"Georges, get my car ready," he croaked. "We are going to Beirut."

Yariv Cohen fell forward instinctively as the earth shuddered beneath his feet. Even from a distance of almost one hundred metres the sounds of the exploding arsenal shattered his senses.

"Rahamim! Rahamim!" he screamed as chunks of masonry began falling from the sky.

"I'm here boss. I'm here," came the muffled reply.

Cohen peered through a rain of fine particles of earth and sand. He could just about make out a figure lying prone a few metres away. The man was lying with his hands protecting the back of his head and he was covered in debris.

"Are you all right there?" Cohen bellowed.

"Yes, Yariv. It's me, Rahamim. I'm okay. What about you?" the Yemenite called back as he struggled to his feet.

"Thank God," cried a relieved Cohen. "Where the hell is the radio ma—." Cohen's question was cut short by another huge explosion. For the next few moments neither man dared make a move as bullets screamed past them followed by a kaleidoscope of tracers. In those thirty seconds both men realised fully the horror of what had happened. Yefet and his men should have rendezvoused with them at least ten minutes before the dump was to have been blown up. Israel had lost its finest. No-one could have lived through that inferno.

As the air cleared, Cohen rose gingerly to his feet, ignoring the bullets still whizzing crazily past him. He looked first one way and then the other but could not see his radioman.

"He's over here, Yariv!" came Ben-Yaacov's urgent voice.

Cohen stumbled towards his colleague, his gammy leg seeming to drag more than usual.

"He's dead, Yariv," said the Yemenite, kneeling by the body.

By the light of the huge fire to his right, Cohen could make out the hole in the man's temple. "Is the radio all right?" he asked, his voice shaking.

"I think so. I'll just take it off and see."

"I didn't know you could use it."

"I did a brief course on avionics last year," the Yemenite grunted as he fought to relieve the dead man of his equipment. "I thought I told you about it."

Cohen watched intently as Ben-Yaacov began to re-dial the frequency which had been lost when the radioman had hit the ground.

"....is happening? Are you receiving me? Over." The voice on the radio was panic itself. "Green One, this is Red Leader. What is happening? Are you receiving me? Over."

Cohen snatched the telephone from his colleague. "Red Leader, this is Green One. Abort. I repeat. Abort. Over."

There was silence for at least ten seconds before he heard another voice on the line. It was that of Yehuda Bar-Ilan.

"Green One. This is Red Leader. What the fuck do you mean abort? The Bells will be there within three minutes. What has happened. Relate your casualties. Over."

"I don't know what happened, Yehuda," Cohen screamed as further explosions rent the night air. "Their ammunition dump blew prematurely. All our men were inside. Over."

"Shit! What about you? Over."

"Don't waste a helicopter on us. I'm with Ben-Yaacov. We'll be all right. Over."

"We'll stay around for thirty more minutes. Let us know when you are clear. Over and out."

Despite the quality of reception, Cohen could make out the disappointment in Bar-Ilan's voice. The Chief of Staff had lost his own boys. It would devastate him.

"Let's get back to the van, Rahamim. Quickly."

The two made towards the alley where the Volkswagen was parked. For the first time they could hear the wail of sirens. In seconds the whole area would be cordoned off. Ben-Yaacov hoisted the radio into the rear of the Transporter and climbed in next to it. Cohen switched on the engine and slammed it into gear. Still trying to assemble his thoughts, he had decided they could just possibly make it out of the area in time if they made straight for the warehouse. His other operatives would be there already, having returned once they had off-loaded the commandos and equipment.

As he drove through the streets of the suburb, people were already out in the streets. Some were running towards the bright light to his rear. Cars, too, were driving crazily towards him, their horns blaring. As Cohen turned a corner into a road which he knew would lead him to the sea shore, his knee bumped against something hard positioned just below the dashboard. He had forgotten all about the direction finder console.

The head of the Mossad did not know what prompted him to switch it on. There was, after all, no doubt that David Katri and his belt transmitter were buried beneath tons of masonry and earth. They had probably been vaporized in the explosion.

"Beep, beep. Beep, beep."

Cohen gasped. "It can't be," he croaked. "It can't be."

"What is it, Yariv?" came a voice from the rear.

"I can't believe it. I'm picking up a signal from Katri's belt transmitter."

"Maybe it's still working even though he's dead."

For a second Cohen thought his friend may have been right but then he realised that they were travelling south-west. The signal was strong and the needle was directly in the centre of the dial. Wherever Katri was, he was in front of them. The giant fire in the sky was behind them. Katri was alive. Katri was alive.

"He's straight ahead of us, Rahamim," he mumbled incredulously.

"I don't understand, boss."

"What's dead ahead of us besides the warehouse?"

Rahamim Ben-Yaacov paused while he tried to figure out what Cohen was getting at. Suddenly, it struck him. "The airport!" he exploded.

"Precisely," said Cohen, stepping harder on the accelerator. "I never told Katri about the warehouse. We never expected he'd have to use it. He was due to be airlifted out along with us. It must be the airport."

"But surely, he's not just going to hop on a plane out of here. It doesn't make sense."

Cohen was just about to answer when he noticed the signal growing weaker. The dial showed the directional path had changed to LEFT. Left, in this case, was due south east. The head of the Mossad suddenly pulled of the highway and onto a slip road.

"Hey, this is the way to the warehouse, not to the airport," shouted Ben-Yaacov.

For a few seconds Cohen remained silent. His worst fears were being realised. Everything pointed to the fact that Katri was airborne. To escape he would have to fly west, yet he was travelling due southeast. To the southeast lay Damascus and Amman, the Syrian Desert and the An Nafud. The Winds of Kedem were about to strike. Either David Katri was having a brainstorm or he was being held against his will aboard an aircraft headed not only for its own destruction but for the annihilation of a people.

"There's no point in driving to the airport," Cohen said, his voice taut with apprehension. "Get me Bar-Ilan again."

By the time the Chief of Staff had answered, the Volkswagen had already pulled up outside the doors of the warehouse. Several of Cohen's men came out to meet him, their faces grim.

They, too, had been tuned in to his earlier conversation with Bar-Ilan.

"...Red Leader. This is Green One. Listen very carefully. We have reason to believe that Katri has been kidnapped and is headed due southeast or south southeast aboard an aircraft. Judging by the gradual decrease in signal strength from his belt it might be a helicopter. The transmitter has signal range of only about twenty kilometres airborne. Imperative you intercept. I repeat, imperative you intercept. Do you read me? Over."

Yehuda Bar-Ilan had not left the radio room of the missile boat since the RPV had relayed the scene of the debacle. He had lost the cream of his men and all Cohen seemed to be concerned about was his damned agent. Why the hell was it so important any more?

"By intercept, do you mean destroy?" he asked, his voice heavy with sarcasm.

Cohen paused, the gibe striking hard and true. He was about to become the first head of his country's intelligence services to sanction the murder of not one, but two of his own men. There was simply no time to prevaricate and no real choice.

"Affirmative. For God's sake get the fucking Hughes into the air or we'll be searching for a needle in a haystack. He's heading due southeast. The frequency is three-four-nine-point-five. I repeat, three-four-nine-point-five. Over."

There was a pause before Bar-Ilan answered. "I read you three-four-nine-point-five. Order given. You bastard, Cohen. Now explain. Over."

Yariv Cohen sighed with a mixture of relief and foreboding. He knew that another man was listening in on their conversation. A man who had burned the night oil in the communications room at the Kirya and who must be feeling as drained as he.

"I leave that to you, Mister Prime Minister," said Cohen gravely. "Over and out."

Within less than thirty seconds of being given the order to take off, Gilad Blum had donned his helmet, utility vest and mae west and was climbing into the cockpit of the Hughes Defender, codenamed Haystack. Climbing in the other side was his co-pilot, Avi Miller. Nervously, the two men watched the mechanic plug in the electric starter circuit, untie the blades and release the footclamps.

As Blum strapped himself in, he saw the mechanic move round in front of him. The clouds had cleared and the man was merely a silhouette against a starlit backdrop, the only things clearly visible being his red luminescent jacket and the fire extinguisher in his right hand. With every engine start there was a danger of flare-up and the more rushed the take-off, the more dangerous it was. The last thing Blum wanted was to open the throttle too fast during ignition and have a ball of flame exit out of the tailpipe to bring a premature end to his mission. Nevertheless, he knew he would have to take risks. Bar-Ilan had screamed at him to take off as quickly as possible, not even sparing the time to give him his instructions. "For God's sake get airborne first, Haystack," the Chief of Staff had ranted.

As the mechanic gave the thumbs-up, Blum slammed all the fuses in the overhead panel, pushed the engine start button and opened the throttle. The Allison turboshaft burst into life. While watching the rev counter and listening for the familiar tone of the engine to tell him all was well, he told Miller to switch on the radio and get their instructions.

"Fly due southeast," came Bar-Ilan's voice over the intercom. "From our position it runs diagonally across Beirut airport. Your target is a slow-moving aircraft, probably a helicopter, although type unknown. My guess is it will be flying low to avoid radar detection. Search and destroy using your direction finder to pick up beacon transmitting on three-four-nine point-five megaHertz. Repeat three-four-nine point-five. Confirm. Over."

"Message received and understood," replied Miller. "Three-four-nine point-five. This is Haystack over and out."

As his mechanic gave the final all-clear, Blum looked first to his left and then to his right. The boat was rocking and normally he would wait for the moment when it was almost level to time his lift-off from the pad. In the past he may have waited up to a minute for the right conditions to prevail. But this time there was no time.

Gilad Blum saw the rev pointer reach the green. "It's going to be dangerous, Avi," he shouted over the intercom. "Release!"

Miller released the catch on the grid clamp. "Releasing, two, three, off."

Blum pulled up hard on the collective pitch lever and waited for the torque meter to reach red. At the same time he kept his eye on the front edge of the disc described by the whirling blades in relation to the distant Beirut skyline. The gas turbine roared as the Hughes lifted off the deck in a jerking sideways movement. Immediately he began to straighten up and gain altitude.

"Three hundred feet," Miller called out.

Blum heaved a sigh of relief. He'd cheated the 'graph of death' inherent in the sort of high speed take-off he'd attempted. He moved the cyclic-pitch stick forward and the helicopter started to gain rapid forward motion. Suddenly, the beacon transmitter's signal appeared on the direction finder. The dial showed it came from the general direction of the airport or beyond.

"What's the highest point between here and the airport?" Blum asked his co-pilot. Miller unwrapped his map and re-folded it to highlight the small area between his present position and the airport. Already underlined were all the high altitude points.

"Five hundred feet."

Blum climbed immediately to five hundred and fifty feet. Knowing that the signal from a beacon transmitter could be distorted by the topography of the area, he decided to ignore it and make straight for the airport.

The pilot donned his night vision goggles, which intensified the light to such a degree that he was forced to switch off all the instrument lights inside the cockpit. Once clear of the coastline he decided to shallow dive in order to get up as much speed as possible. Gilad Blum was pushing the Defender to the limit and its engine screamed in protest.

Suddenly, he started to feel the dreaded one-on-one vibration of a tip stall. The tips were starting to rotate faster than the main body of the blades. Breaking into a cold sweat, he eased back on the throttle and the cyclic pitch stick. His heart was in his mouth as the indignant Allison first bucked and then responded. The air speed began to drop.

"That was close, Avi," he gasped through the intercom. "What's with the direction finder."

The co-pilot peered at the darkened instrument panel. "Dead ahead," he cried. "Dead ahead."

Blum remained at one hundred feet as the Hughes roared over first one hangar and then another. He paid scant attention to the parked airliners of various nations. He was looking for much smaller fry.

"Three degrees right," Miller called again.

The Hughes responded.

"Two degrees right."

Again the helicopter answered as Blum eased the stick to starboard.

"Hard right now!" screamed Miller as the needle went off the dial.

Blum, realising he had passed over the line of the homing

device, went into a quick-stop manoeuvre. He reduced his speed to forty knots and pulled hard right before once again tilting the rotor down to increase speed.

"Dead ahead, Gilad! Dead ahead!"

Blum gingerly removed his image intensifiers, which had limited his vision because of their narrow field of scope. He was now over open country and his target was still ahead of him, possibly by as much as twenty kilometres. He reckoned the target was flying fast and low to avoid Syrian radar in the Bekaa valley. The Israeli realised he would have to do likewise. The last thing he wanted was Syrian anti-aircraft involvement. The pilot switched on the lights on his instrument panel and glanced at the direction finder. It showed dead centre. But for how long? Should the target be travelling at a greater speed than he, it would eventually be out of range. Gilad Blum knew that every few seconds he would have to make slight alterations in course as his prey weaved its way along the contours of southeastern Lebanon, skirting the missile-infested Bekaa. Speed was crucial. Height was crucial.

"I'm going to jettison the TOWs, Avi," said Blum. "They're causing too much drag."

Miller leaned forward and lifted the lever to jettison. They were essentially anti-tank missiles anyway. "TOWs away!" he cried.

Blum felt the Defender shoot forward as it shed its load. The only armament he had left was the 7.62mm chain gun. One thing was for sure. It was going to be one hell of a chase.

Oblivious of the pursuit in the skies above him, Abu Mussa drove down the coast road of southwestern Beirut, keeping well away from the area which he knew would be choked with traffic following the Israeli attack. To his left flames were still leaping high into the sky and the sirens of ambulances and fire engines wailed constantly.

He had exchanged hardly a word with his companion, seated ashen-faced alongside him. Georges knew what to do and would carry out his instructions to the letter. The Maronite pulled the Mercedes to a halt outside the home of the woman he cherished above all other of his many possessions. Wearily, he hoisted his large frame from the front seat, his faithful manservant quickly at his side to assist him. Together, the two men walked up the path to the front door. The big man paused for a few seconds before ringing the doorbell. The faithful Georges removed the silenced automatic from the shoulder holster beneath his blue parka.

''Mi'in?'' came a scratchy voice from within. ''Who's there?''

''An emissary from Mehdi Laham,'' replied Georges, muffling his voice with a handkerchief. After a few seconds they heard the sound of a bolt being drawn back and the door opened slightly, allowing only a chink of light to escape. The thin man wedged his left toe into the gap and pushed hard. However slight was his frame, the woman on the other side of the door was no match for it. Jehan Husseini collapsed onto the floor in mute surprise. The two men entered swiftly and closed the door behind them.

The chaperon, lying spreadeagled on the floor like a grounded bat, gasped as she saw the pistol pointed at her head. The wizened features framed by the black chador froze. Then came the plop-plop of the silenced automatic as it carried out its deadly task.

''Who's there, Jehan?'' came a familiar voice from the kitchen. It was much younger and much sweeter. Fatima Fadas put down the knife she was using to slice some tomatoes and entered the hall.

''Allah!'' she gasped as she caught sight of the two men standing over the lifeless body of her chaperon. A pool of blood lay about Jehan Husseini's barely recognizable features.

"Allah, what have you done," Fatima moaned, burying her face in her hands.

"It is the will of God," replied Abu Mussa almost matter-of-factly.

For the first time Fatima Fadas noticed how much her patron had changed. How wan and aged he looked, how unkempt his appearance and how dishevelled his clothes. The richest man in Lebanon resembled a tramp.

"The Israelis have attacked," he said listlessly. "You probably heard the explosions."

"Yes. We thought it was another car bomb or something."

Fatima walked slowly towards the old man, at the same time averting her eyes from the horror at his feet. Abu Mussa retreated from her until he was clear of the body.

"You did not have to kill her, my darling," she said sadly, still unaware of the true purpose of the Maronite's visit.

The Christian said nothing as she put her arms around his waist and buried her head in his chest. He ran his fingers through her ebony hair and luxuriated once more in the delicate fragrance of her silky skin. For a fleeting moment it was as it had always been. His fingers then descended to the contours of her neck and began to exert a subtle yet intense pressure.

"Why did you betray me?" he rasped.

Fatima felt her head jerk back and found herself gazing directly into the rheumy, sleep-starved eyes.

There was so much she wanted to say that the vice around her throat would not allow. She wanted to say that she loved him. She wanted to say that her affair with Anwar Hindawi was but a logical outcome of her desire to become a woman, that she had made her choice and that he, Abu Mussa, was to be her future. But the words would not come. Instead, she gazed helplessly into the eyes of her murderer and saw only those of another man, a man who also possessed a great capacity for hate and revenge. As the envelope of final darkness closed around her, Fatima Fadas saw only the face of her uncle. He was admonishing her for her betrayal.

CHAPTER EIGHTEEN

The first sensation David Katri felt upon regaining consciousness was a tremendous throbbing in his ears. The sound was familiar and yet he could not place it immediately, no doubt because he could not ally the sense of sight with that of hearing. His eyelids seemed to be caked together with adhesive He would have forced them open with his fingers but those, too, seemed rigid and incapable of movement.

"Afo ani?" he groaned in Hebrew, the words forcing their way out of his parched throat. He then repeated his plea, this time in Arabic.

"Aha, the Jew is conscious," came a familiar voice. "Good. Good. You are with me, my friend, and now you shall witness the moment of destruction of your accursed nation."

The realisation that it was Sedawi who was speaking was followed by intense pain as David felt the ropes around his wrists cut into his flesh. He was trussed up like a chicken, a blind chicken at that.

"Cus em'ak!" David screamed. It was the vilest of Arab curses.

"You are the cunt of your mother, Jew!" came the hysterical reply.

The swishing sound told David that he was aboard a helicopter but how he came to be there was a mystery. The last thing he recalled were the exhortations of Mehdi Laham. The rest was a blur.

The Israeli fought to clear the confusion in his mind. How he had arrived in his present state was immaterial. The fact was that Rashid Sedawi had won. The Shi'ite was about to give vent to his fanaticism and murder millions, both Jew and Arab.

"You are mad, Sedawi. Completely mad."

There was no reply other than the thrumming of the helicopter as it ploughed through the dark skies. Perhaps because David could not see or perhaps because it made more sense, he imagined it was night and that the firmament was clear and bright. If his situation were not so desperate it might even have been romantic. Suddenly, he felt fingers prodding his eyes. He could smell stale breath on his cheeks as his lids, caked in his own blood, were forced apart. He could make out a dark figure leaning over him. He knew it was Sedawi.

"I would prefer you to see your death, Zionist dog," the Shi'ite spat. "The blood which cakes your eyes is but an hors d'oeuvre for the main course. Our blood may mix in death, but it is the blood of your people which will make the rivers of the Middle East run red."

David struggled to straighten himself. It was only then that he realised that his legs, as well as his hands, were tied together firmly. His hands were secured behind him to a stanchion in the helicopter's fuselage. Each change in direction caused him excruciating pain. In its perverse way, it helped concentrate his mind.

Katri looked past the dark shape and could see another silhouetted against the aircraft's instrument lights.

Sedawi spoke again, this time with less belligerence. "You have the honour of being piloted by Abdullah Sanjani, whose services have been granted me by Hezbollah as a special concession. Like most of his fellow Iranians, he is prepared to sacrifice his life to Allah in order to avenge Hussein."

The shape at the front of the craft did not stir. David guessed that the pilot was about six feet away and that the helicopter must therefore be of medium size, a six- or seven-seater.

As David's eyes grew more accustomed to the darkness inside the cabin, he also became more aware of the configuration of the passenger quarters. Sedawi was sitting opposite him, with his back to the pilot, although it was still difficult to make out his features. The Israeli could see the shape of an arm held aloft as Sedawi began to speak again.

"This little black box in my right hand is the key to Paradise, sahbi," the Shi'ite gloated. "You, of course, shall be residing with Satan."

David began to clench and unclench his fists in order to restore circulation. His only hope was to try to fray the rope against the stanchion to which his hands were secured. For the first time he noticed his Beretta was missing from its holster. "Why did you save me?" he asked, figuring Sedawi's mind was better concentrated on his own rhetoric than on any untoward movements by his captive.

"It was my intention all along that you should die with me. There were others who were as clever as you, but they died under different circumstances. I could allow no-one to thwart my aims. I alone had been chosen to carry out the will of Allah."

"Then the cyanide tooth was bluff."

"Of course."

"Then you told only me about it."

"You were the only one left in the organisation capable of presenting a threat to me, although I never wanted to believe that."

"What about Laham?"

Sedawi laughed. "He thinks the bomb is somewhere in the An Nafud of Arabia. As I told you before, he was an old man surrounded by imbeciles. I could not leave such a vital task in the hands of such men."

"Then you suspected me all along."

"I am a suspicious type, Anwar, or whatever your real name is. But I suspected you no more than anyone else although, as I said, I recognised that you had a superior mental capacity to the others. They are mainly children pretending to be fighters

337

for Islam. Terrorism is a serious business."

David's mind raced. He had to keep the Shi'ite talking while he himself continued scraping the rope around his wrists against the sharp edge of the stanchion.

"You still haven't told me why you bothered to save me."

"As I said, I wanted you to die with me. I was genuinely fond of you. When I received the weather report that a Shurqiya was expected this morning, I decided that it was time to act, regardless of what Laham had planned."

"Then our attack was just coincidence."

"Yes."

"Then you did not know that I was a spy in your midst?"

"No," the shadow replied, "not until I saw you slump at my feet, blood running down your face."

Although the thrum of the engine suddenly seemed extraordinarily loud, David imagined the scraping sounds he was making were dwarfing it. He stopped abruptly, breathing a sigh of relief as the Shi'ite continued his explanation.

"I always had a feeling that I had seen you before. And in that split second I recognised the bloodied face of a wounded Israeli tankist on the Golan Heights."

David felt himself go cold. The vision that so often haunted him in the hours of slumber returned. The golden fanged monster of his nightmares had been none other than Sedawi. *Arik, behind you! Arik, behind you!* No, it could not be. It was too fantastic.

"It was written that our paths should have crossed again," the Shi'ite went on. "It is the will of Allah."

Katri fought to control his emotions. "B-but I still cannot understand," he stammered. "Why did you save me?"

"I do not know. sahbi. I heard a voice of God calling me above the sounds of the guns and the screams. He demanded that I save you. That you should die with me in subjugation to His will."

The helicopter banked suddenly and David winced in pain as his buttocks began to chafe against the floor. His arms were stretched out behind him almost at right angles to his shoulder blades. As the aircraft straightened, he inched his way back along the floor until he felt his spine rest against the stanchion.

While the effort exhausted him totally, the voice of his tormentor droned on.

"There was a secret exit from the bunker which was known only to Laham and myself. It was the way I had arrived. I had parked my car at the other end. I heard the explosions as I drove to the airport. I pray to Allah that my children overcame the aggressors."

Suddenly, the Arab turned away and called out to his Iranian comrade. "Abdullah, where are we?"

"We are coursing through the valley of the Yarmuk, Ra'is. We will follow the line of the Syrian-Jordanian border."

"How long?"

"About fifteen minutes, Ra'is. Maybe a little less."

David Katri knew he had less than a quarter of an hour in which to free himself from his shackles and attempt to avert a catastrophe. Should he by extraordinarily good fortune be able to overcome his attackers, then there was still the matter of landing the helicopter.

David Katri imagined all sorts of scenarios, the only common denominator being his own demise.

"Red Leader. This is Haystack. Target has entered the Yarmuk. I don't seem to be making up much ground. It could be another six or seven minutes before I might get close enough to shoot him down. Please instruct. Over."

Yehuda Bar-Ilan listened with dismay to Gilad Blum's plaint. There was no choice. He would have to scramble a couple of

F-15s. The McDonnell-Douglas fighter was the best of its type in the world, but it was designed to shoot down other supersonic warplanes. The best instrument to shoot down a helicopter was another helicopter.

"Haystack. This is Red Leader. I'm scrambling a couple of Eagles to help you out. Keep on your present course. They'll be with you almost immediately."

The Chief of Staff, now fully aware of the implications of failure, turned to his orderly. "Get me Ramat David, quickly!"

Within a minute of receiving his orders, Captain Dov Grunner was strapped into the seat of his F-15 Eagle on the runway at Ramat David airbase in the Valley of Jezreel.

Grunner's leg muscles tightened as he held the brakes and eased the throttles up to military power. The giant Pratt and Whitney F100 turbofan engine roared its response. Checking the gauges, he released the brakes and selected the afterburner. The airspeed climbed rapidly. At one hundred and twenty knots he raised the nose ten degrees above the horizon and broke ground in about three hundred metres.

Gear and flaps up, Grunner pulled back quickly on the stick and climbed in a thirty-five degree pitch altitude while accelerating to two hundred and fifty knots. At ten thousand feet, he pulled the throttles out of afterburner. He knew that Lieutenant Yossi Ze'evi was following suit in the second Eagle. Within seconds the two F-15s had already left northern Israel and were banking high over southern Lebanon to prepare their run-in.

"Eagle one calling Haystack. We're over the south of Lebanon. Twenty thousand feet and climbing. Heading zero-one-zero. What is your position?"

A second later came the reply. "Eagle one. This is Haystack. I'm following the Yarmuk. Treetop level, heading southeast. Over."

"Haystack. This is Eagle one. Squawk on your IFF."

Grunner peered at his radar scope on the left side of his instrument panel. Almost immediately, he saw the triple banana blips of the Identification Friend or Foe signal repeater appear on the screen and radioed confirmation back to the helicopter. The fighter pilot knew that the target helicopter was also flying low and that it might not be picked up on his radar easily without squawking. And squawking was something it was unlikely to do.

The two F-15s roared out across the Mediterranean coastline, then banked steeply before beginning their run-in. Suddenly another voice broke into the frequency. It was Air Force Chief Matti Vishubsky.

"Eagle One and Eagle Two. This is Command Leader. Be advised, the Syrian missile defences are waking up. Get out of Lebanese territory immediately."

Grunner and Ze'evi immediately sucked their planes into a sharp right five-G turn and, once over Israeli territory, throttled back. They then eased into an attack mode along the northern border and due southeast towards the Yarmuk.

Within seconds Grunner had picked up the squawk again on his radar. He realised the helicopters might be too close together for him to take action against the pursued without prejudicing the safety of the pursuer.

"Shit! I've overshot," he screamed as his plane flew six thousand feet over the target at Mach One. However good the F-15 was, it was not designed to hit anything flying slowly at treetop level.

"What's the matter with you guys? Can't you slow down?" The voice of Gilad Blum echoed Grunner's own frustration. Then Blum broke into the airwaves again. "Hey! I can see the glare from his exhaust on night vision." He paused before adding a rider. "He's heading one-one-zero straight for Mafraq."

"Haystack. This is Eagle One. Do you think you can get his range. He has to be shot down immediately."

"Negative, Eagle One. At this rate it might take another five or six minutes."

Another voice, more urgent and more harsh, snapped over the air. "This is Red Leader. Get the bastard, Eagle One. Now!"

Grunner winced. His pride was at stake. He would have to try the unorthodox.

"Haystack. This is Eagle One. Read me his heading and then drop back. Repeat. Read me his heading and drop back. Over."

Grunner banked again and this time flew low over the Syrian desert, reducing his speed to only one hundred knots. The Pratt and Whitney snorted its disgust at being throttled down to such a ridiculously low speed. The Hughes was already behind him as he closed in on approximate position of the target. If only he could have seen it on his radar screen, he would have blasted it out of the sky with cannon.

Grunner looked to his left. Ze'evi was already alongside him in the second F-15. "Arm missiles," the captain ordered. "Instigate search mode for target."

"Missiles armed. Search mode instigated," came the reply.

Almost immediately a flag appeared on the head-up display as the Sparrow missiles locked on.

"Are you locked on, Eagle Two?"

"Affirmative."

Dov Grunner was now certain of a kill. All he had to do was press the button. "Wait for my signal to fire, Eagle Two," he said confidently.

Oblivious of the danger above and behind them, the two Shi'ites and their Israeli captive continued the journey to what each knew was certain death.

David Katri had continued to encourage Rashid Sedawi to talk. He reckoned they had been in the air for more than an hour since he had regained consciousness and the Shi'ite had seemingly chosen the occasion to relate the story of his life. It was almost a confessional. A tale of how a man had become victim and then victimizer. The Israeli learned the whole truth of the Shi'ite's merciless disposal of both allies and opponents. It had been an orgy of blood-letting.

As the shadow droned on, David felt the ropes begin to fray. He was already oblivious to the pain racking his body in general and his wrists in particular.

"We are nearly there, Ra'is."

The pilot's harsh Persian accent interrupted Sedawi in full flow. The Lebanese rose and, half stooping, stepped gingerly towards the passenger seat alongside the Iranian. Laughing nervously, he withdrew the small black box from his right pocket and a small image intensifying scope from his left. Peering through the scope for a sign of the well's luminous rim, he continued to talk.

"You know what pleases me most, Jew? It is that you, too, are guilty of murdering your own people. You killed one of your fellow agents back there in Vienna. How sickening that must have been for you. But you did it, didn't you. It is the supreme irony."

David felt nauseous. It was true. Everything Sedawi said was true. And the truth hurt the Israeli more than the ropes that were shredding his wrists.

The Arab's words continued to pierce him.

"You proved just how much you were a loyal servant to our cause by disposing of a man we had been trying to eliminate for more than a year. He may have called himself Epstein, but that blond bastard Ben-Ami was one of the Mossad's best agents."

For a moment, the Arab's words failed to register. Then came the pounding in the heart and the head concomitant with the torture of a guilty conscience. It had to be another Ben-Ami. And yet he knew it could not be so.

THEN YOU DID DO IT.

Ben-Yaacov's words in Beirut came flooding back to him. Now he understood why he and Cohen had been so surprised. The bastards.

"I can see it!" screamed Sedawi. "I can see the well!"

David Katri took a deep breath, the pain and anger in his heart sending the adrenelin shooting into his aching muscles. In one tremendous burst of energy he broke free from his shackles and launched himself headlong at the Shi'ite. Grabbing Sedawi around the neck, he pulled the Arab backwards out of his seat. Neither man had time to heed the small black box which had dropped into the footwell of the front passenger seat.

Katri tried to grip Sedawi's throat as the two men rolled over in the aisle between the front and rear compartments, but the fingers would not work. The initial burst of adrenelin having exhausted an already spent body, David knew that however much he possessed the will, his muscles would refuse to comply. Suddenly, he felt the full weight of the Arab upon him. Sedawi's hands began gripping his throat, the vice becoming tighter and tighter.

A kaleidoscope of faces flashed before David's eyes, reminding him of a childhood game he used to play with cigarette cards. Firstly, there were his parents, his father looking up at him benignly as he burnished a copper dish in the little workshop attached to their home. Then came the small courtyard with its aromas of jasmine, coffee and cardamom.

Then came Rachel and Naftali. Funny, he could only recall them as they were when he had fled Damascus so many years before. Asleep. Innocent of the knowledge that they would never see their brother again. His life was a history of betrayal.

The pictures were becoming misty. No! Please don't let them go. Just one last look. He must flick the cards again. There now, Yael. Darling Yael. My little nurse. And Shoshana. And Boaz. I betrayed you all. Forgive me.

Arik! Dear Arik. Save me again as you did on the Golan. Forgive my perfidy, my brother. Had I but known. Arik! Don't leave me!

A two-headed gargoyle: Abu Mussa and Fatima Fadas. As incompatible as they were inseparable. Finally, as always, his Nemesis. The Devil Incarnate. Rashid Sedawi.

David felt himself floating high in the roof of the throbbing vessel. Was that himself lying beneath the hunched form in the craft's belly? How strange. The dark figure appeared to be pleading desperately.

"No, Abdullah! Give it to me. It is I who has been chosen by God to do this deed. It is I who must press the button. Only I..."

EPILOGUE

Hamed shivered as the cold east wind began to make brittle his bones. The Shurqiya would soon attain its full ferocity and he was already feeling the last vestiges of his life slipping away. But God was great, and soon he would be joining uncle Ahmed in the Garden of Paradise. The old man was sure to have saved for him the most succulent of dates and figs.

The bedouin could hear the jinns roaring their protest at being subjected to the merciless bluster. Upon the setting of the sun, he had crawled around to the leeside of the well. And yet he was forced to shield his eyes from the swirling sand, each grain whipping him cruelly. The evil jinns were hovering overhead. Why had they decided to vent their anger on him? Was he not already nine-tenths dead?

Suddenly, through the maelstrom, he saw streaks of brilliant white and gold. He was sure they were the good jinns, come to save him from his torment.